The Count of Monte Cristo

Monica Corwin *and* Alexandre Dumas

CRIMSON ROMANCE
F+W Media, Inc.

This edition published by
Crimson Romance
an imprint of F+W Media, Inc.
10151 Carver Road, Suite 200
Blue Ash, Ohio 45242
www.crimsonromance.com

ISBN 10: 1-4405-6883-9
ISBN 13: 978-1-4405-6883-1
eISBN 10: 1-4405-6884-7
eISBN 13: 978-1-4405-6884-8

Dearest Readers

There are tales of adventure and then there are stories of love and devotion and occasionally, in a very rare set of circumstances, the two become one, and an adventure can feature the truth and meaning of love in all its forms. Occasionally, on the way to love a character might have to experience loss, pain, and an acute reckoning with himself to achieve it. This is the story of Edmond Dantes and his journey to love through betrayal, redemption, and revenge. A journey as unique as the man himself.

Chapter 1. Marseilles—The Arrival.

On the 24th of February, 1815, the look-out at Notre-Dame de la Garde signaled the three-master, the *Pharaon* from Smyrna, Trieste, and Naples.

As usual, a pilot put off immediately, and rounding the Chateau d'If, got on board the vessel between Cape Morgion and Rion Island.

Immediately, and according to custom, the ramparts of Fort Saint-Jean were covered with spectators; it is always an event at Marseilles for a ship to come into port, especially when this ship, like the *Pharaon*, has been built, rigged, and laden at the old Phocee docks, and belongs to an owner of the city.

The ship drew on and had safely passed the strait and approached the harbor under topsails, jib, and spanker, but so slowly and sedately that the idlers, with that instinct which is the forerunner of evil, asked one another what misfortune could have happened on board. However, those experienced in navigation saw plainly that if any accident had occurred, it was not to the vessel herself, for the pilot, who was steering the *Pharaon* towards the narrow entrance of the inner port, was a young man, who, with activity and vigilant eye, watched every motion of the ship, and repeated each direction of the pilot.

The vague disquietude which prevailed among the spectators had so much affected one of the crowd that he did not await the arrival of the vessel in harbor, but jumping into a small skiff, desired to be pulled alongside the *Pharaon*, which he reached as she rounded into La Reserve basin.

When the young man on board saw this person approach, he left his station by the pilot, and, hat in hand, leaned over the ship's bulwarks.

He was a fine, tall, slim young fellow of eighteen or twenty, with black eyes, and hair as dark as a raven's wing; and his whole appearance bespoke that calmness and resolution peculiar to men accustomed from their cradle to contend with danger.

"Ah, is it you, Dantes?" cried the man in the skiff. "What's the matter? And why have you such an air of sadness aboard?"

"A great misfortune, M. Morrel," replied the young man,—"a great misfortune, for me especially! Off Civita Vecchia we lost our brave Captain Leclere."

"And the cargo?" inquired the owner, eagerly.

"Is all safe, M. Morrel; and I think you will be satisfied on that head. But poor Captain Leclere—"

"What happened to him?" asked the owner, with an air of considerable resignation. "What happened to the worthy captain?"

"He died."

"Fell into the sea?"

"No, sir, he died of brain-fever in dreadful agony." Then turning to the crew, he said, "Bear a hand there, to take in sail!"

All hands obeyed, and at once the eight or ten seamen who composed the crew, sprang to their respective stations. The young sailor gave a look to see that his orders were promptly and accurately obeyed, and then turned again to the owner.

"And how did this misfortune occur?" inquired the latter, resuming the interrupted conversation.

"Alas, sir, in the most unexpected manner. After a long talk with the harbor-master, Captain Leclere left Naples greatly disturbed in the mind. In twenty-four hours he was attacked by a fever, and died three days afterwards. We performed the usual burial service, and he is at his rest, sewn up in his hammock with a thirty-six pound shot at his head and his heels, off El Giglio Island. We bring to his widow his sword and cross of honor. It was worthwhile, truly," added the young man with a melancholy smile, "to make war against the English for ten years, and to die in his bed at last, like everybody else."

"Why, you see, Edmond," replied the owner, who appeared more comforted at every moment, "we are all mortal, and the old must make way for the young. If not, why, there would be no promotion; and since you assure me that the cargo—"

"Is all safe and sound, M. Morrel, take my word for it; and I advise you not to take 25,000 francs for the profits of the voyage."

Then, as they were just passing the Round Tower, the young man shouted: "Stand by there to lower the topsails and jib; brail up the spanker!"

The order was executed as promptly as it would have been on board a man-of-war.

"Let go—and clue up!" At this last command all the sails were lowered, and the vessel moved almost imperceptibly onwards.

"Now, if you will come on board, M. Morrel," said Dantes, observing the owner's impatience, "here is your supercargo, M. Danglars, coming out of his cabin, who will furnish you with every particular. As for me, I must look after the anchoring, and dress the ship in mourning."

The owner did not wait for a second invitation. He seized a rope which Dantes flung to him, and with an activity that would have done credit to a sailor, climbed up the side of the ship, while the young man, going to his task, left the conversation to Danglars, who now came towards the owner. He was a man of twenty-five or twenty-six years of age, of unprepossessing countenance, obsequious to his superiors, insolent to his subordinates; and this, in addition to his position as responsible agent on board, which is always obnoxious to the sailors, made him as much disliked by the crew as Edmond Dantes was beloved by them.

"Well, M. Morrel," said Danglars, "you have heard of the misfortune that has befallen us?"

"Yes—yes: poor Captain Leclere! He was a brave and an honest man."

"And a first-rate seaman, one who had seen long and honorable service, as became a man charged with the interests of a house so important as that of Morrel & Son," replied Danglars.

"But," replied the owner, glancing after Dantes, who was watching the anchoring of his vessel, "it seems to me that a sailor needs not be so old as you say, Danglars, to understand his business, for our friend Edmond seems to understand it thoroughly, and not to require instruction from any one."

"Yes," said Danglars, darting at Edmond a look gleaming with hate. "Yes, he is young, and youth is invariably self-confident. Scarcely was the captain's breath out of his body when he assumed the command without consulting any one, and he caused us to lose a day and a half at the Island of Elba, instead of making for Marseilles direct."

"As to taking command of the vessel," replied Morrel, "that was his duty as captain's mate; as to losing a day and a half off the Island of Elba, he was wrong, unless the vessel needed repairs."

"The vessel was in as good condition as I am, and as, I hope you are, M. Morrel, and this day and a half was lost from pure whim, for the pleasure of going ashore, and nothing else."

"Dantes," said the ship-owner, turning towards the young man, "come this way!"

"In a moment, sir," answered Dantes, "and I'm with you." Then calling to the crew, he said—"Let go!"

The anchor was instantly dropped, and the chain ran rattling through the port-hole. Dantes continued at his post in spite of the presence of the pilot, until this maneuver was completed, and then he added, "Half-mast the colors, and square the yards!"

"You see," said Danglars, "he fancies himself captain already, upon my word."

"And so, in fact, he is," said the owner.

"Except your signature and your partner's, M. Morrel."

"And why should he not have this?" asked the owner; "he is young, it is true, but he seems to me a thorough seaman, and of full experience."

A cloud passed over Danglars' brow. "Your pardon, M. Morrel," said Dantes, approaching, "the vessel now rides at anchor, and I am at your service. You hailed me, I think?"

Danglars retreated a step or two. "I wished to inquire why you stopped at the Island of Elba?"

"I do not know, sir; it was to fulfill the last instructions of Captain Leclere, who, when dying, gave me a packet for Marshal Bertrand."

"Then did you see him, Edmond?"

"Who?"

"The marshal."

"Yes."

Morrel looked around him, and then, drawing Dantes on one side, he said suddenly—"And how is the emperor?"

"Very well, as far as I could judge from the sight of him."

"You saw the emperor, then?"

"He entered the marshal's apartment while I was there."

"And you spoke to him?"

"Why, it was he who spoke to me, sir," said Dantes, with a smile.

"And what did he say to you?"

"Asked me questions about the vessel, the time she left Marseilles, the course she had taken, and what her cargo was. I believe, if she had not been laden, and I had been her master, he would have bought her. But I told him I was only mate, and that she belonged to the firm of Morrel & Son. 'Ah, yes,' he said, 'I know them. The Morrels have been ship-owners from father to son; and there was a Morrel who served in the same regiment with me when I was in garrison at Valence.'"

"Pardieu, and that is true!" cried the owner, greatly delighted. "And that was Policar Morrel, my uncle, who was afterwards a captain. Dantes, you must tell my uncle that the emperor remembered him, and you will see it will bring tears into the old soldier's eyes. Come, come," continued he, patting Edmond's shoulder kindly, "you did very right, Dantes, to follow Captain Leclere's instructions, and touch at Elba, although if it were known that you had conveyed a packet to the marshal, and had conversed with the emperor, it might bring you into trouble."

"How could that bring me into trouble, sir?" asked Dantes; "for I did not even know of what I was the bearer; and the emperor merely made such inquiries as he would of the first comer. But, pardon me; here are the health officers and the customs inspectors coming alongside." And the young man went to the gangway. As he departed, Danglars approached, and said,—

"Well, it appears that he has given you satisfactory reasons for his landing at Porto-Ferrajo?"

"Yes, most satisfactory, my dear Danglars."

"Well, so much the better," said the supercargo; "for it is not pleasant to think that a comrade has not done his duty."

"Dantes has done his," replied the owner, "and that is not saying much. It was Captain Leclere who gave orders for this delay."

"Talking of Captain Leclere, has not Dantes given you a letter from him?"

"To me?—no—was there one?"

"I believe that, besides the packet, Captain Leclere confided a letter to his care."

"Of what packet are you speaking, Danglars?"

"Why, that which Dantes left at Porto-Ferrajo."

"How do you know he had a packet to leave at Porto-Ferrajo?"

Danglars turned very red.

"I was passing close to the door of the captain's cabin, which was half open, and I saw him give the packet and letter to Dantes."

"He did not speak to me of it," replied the ship-owner; "but if there be any letter he will give it to me."

Danglars reflected for a moment. "Then, M. Morrel, I beg of you," said he, "not to say a word to Dantes on the subject. I may have been mistaken."

At this moment the young man returned; Danglars withdrew.

"Well, my dear Dantes, are you now free?" inquired the owner.

"Yes, sir."

"You have not been long detained."

"No. I gave the custom-house officers a copy of our bill of lading; and as to the other papers, they sent a man off with the pilot, to whom I gave them."

"Then you have nothing more to do here?"

"No—everything is all right now."

"Then you can come and dine with me?"

"I really must ask you to excuse me, M. Morrel. My first visit is due to my father; though I am not the less grateful for the honor you have done me."

"Right, Dantes, quite right. I always knew you were a good son."

"And," inquired Dantes, with some hesitation, "do you know how my father is?"

"Well, I believe, my dear Edmond, though I have not seen him lately."

"Yes, he likes to keep himself shut up in his little room."

"That proves, at least, that he has wanted for nothing during your absence."

Dantes smiled. "My father is proud, sir, and if he had not a meal left, I doubt if he would have asked anything from anyone, except from Heaven."

"Well, then, after this first visit has been made we shall count on you."

"I must again excuse myself, M. Morrel, for after this first visit has been paid I have another which I am most anxious to pay."

"True, Dantes, I forgot that there was at the Catalans someone who expects you no less impatiently than your father—the lovely Mercedes."

Dantes blushed.

"Ah, ha," said the ship-owner, "I am not in the least surprised, for she has been to me three times, inquiring if there were any news of the *Pharaon*. Peste, Edmond, you have a very handsome mistress!"

"She is not my mistress," replied the young sailor, gravely; "she is my betrothed."

"Sometimes one and the same thing," said Morrel, with a smile.

"Not with us, sir," replied Dantes.

"Well, well, my dear Edmond," continued the owner, "don't let me detain you. You have managed my affairs so well that I ought to allow you all the time you require for your own. Do you want any money?"

"No, sir; I have all my pay to take—nearly three months' wages."

"You are a careful fellow, Edmond."

"Say I have a poor father, sir."

"Yes, yes, I know how good a son you are, so now hasten away to see your father. I have a son too, and I should be very wroth with those who detained him from me after a three months' voyage."

"Then I have your leave, sir?"

"Yes, if you have nothing more to say to me."

"Nothing."

"Captain Leclere did not, before he died, give you a letter for me?"

"He was unable to write, sir. But that reminds me that I must ask your leave of absence for some days."

"To get married?"

"Yes, first, and then to go to Paris."

"Very good; have what time you require, Dantes. It will take quite six weeks to unload the cargo, and we cannot get you ready for sea until three months after that; only be back again in three months, for the *Pharaon*," added the owner, patting the young sailor on the back, "cannot sail without her captain."

"Without her captain!" cried Dantes, his eyes sparkling with animation; "pray mind what you say, for you are touching on the most secret wishes of my heart. Is it really your intention to make me captain of the *Pharaon*?"

"If I were sole owner we'd shake hands on it now, my dear Dantes, and call it settled; but I have a partner, and you know the Italian proverb—*Chi ha compagno ha padrone*—'He who has a partner has a master.' But the thing is at least half done, as you have one out of two votes. Rely on me to procure you the other; I will do my best."

"Ah, M. Morrel," exclaimed the young seaman, with tears in his eyes, and grasping the owner's hand, "M. Morrel, I thank you in the name of my father and of Mercedes."

"That's all right, Edmond. There's a providence that watches over the deserving. Go to your father: go and see Mercedes, and afterwards come to me."

"Shall I row you ashore?"

"No, thank you; I shall remain and look over the accounts with Danglars. Have you been satisfied with him this voyage?"

"That is according to the sense you attach to the question, sir. Do you mean is he a good comrade? No, for I think he never liked me since the day when I was silly enough, after a little quarrel we had, to propose to him to stop for ten minutes at the island of Monte Cristo to settle the dispute—a proposition which I was wrong to suggest, and he quite right to refuse. If you mean as responsible agent when you ask me the question, I believe there is nothing to say against him, and that you will be content with the way in which he has performed his duty."

"But tell me, Dantes, if you had command of the *Pharaon* should you be glad to see Danglars remain?"

"Captain or mate, M. Morrel, I shall always have the greatest respect for those who possess the owners' confidence."

"That's right, that's right, Dantes! I see you are a thoroughly good fellow, and will detain you no longer. Go, for I see how impatient you are."

"Then I have leave?"

"Go, I tell you."

"May I have the use of your skiff?"

"Certainly."

"Then, for the present, M. Morrel, farewell, and a thousand thanks!"

"I hope soon to see you again, my dear Edmond. Good luck to you."

The young sailor jumped into the skiff, and sat down in the stern sheets, with the order that he be put ashore at La Canebiere. The two oarsmen bent to their work, and the little boat glided away as rapidly as possible in the midst of the thousand vessels which choke up the narrow way which leads between the two rows of ships from the mouth of the harbor to the Quai d'Orleans.

The ship-owner, smiling, followed him with his eyes until he saw him spring out on the quay and disappear in the midst of the throng, which from five o'clock in the morning until nine o'clock at night, swarms in the famous street of La Canebiere,—a street of which the modern Phocaeans are so proud that they say with all the gravity in the world, and with that accent which gives so much character to what is said, "If Paris had La Canebiere, Paris would be a second Marseilles." On turning round the owner saw Danglars behind him, apparently awaiting orders, but in reality also watching the young sailor,—but there was a great difference in the expression of the two men who thus followed the movements of Edmond Dantes.

Chapter 2. Father and Son.

We will leave Danglars struggling with the demon of hatred, and endeavoring to insinuate in the ear of the ship-owner some evil suspicions against his comrade, and follow Dantes, who, after having traversed La Canebiere, took the Rue de Noailles, and entering a small house, on the left of the Allees de Meillan, rapidly ascended four flights of a dark staircase, holding the baluster with one hand, while with the other he repressed the beatings of his heart, and paused before a half-open door, from which he could see the whole of a small room.

This room was occupied by Dantes' father. The news of the arrival of the *Pharaon* had not yet reached the old man, who, mounted on a chair, was amusing himself by training with trembling hand the nasturtiums and sprays of clematis that clambered over the trellis at his window. Suddenly, he felt an arm thrown around his body, and a well-known voice behind him exclaimed, "Father—dear father!"

The old man uttered a cry, and turned round; then, seeing his son, he fell into his arms, pale and trembling.

"What ails you, my dearest father? Are you ill?" inquired the young man, much alarmed.

"No, no, my dear Edmond—my boy—my son!—no; but I did not expect you; and joy, the surprise of seeing you so suddenly— Ah, I feel as if I were going to die."

"Come, come, cheer up, my dear father! 'Tis I—really I! They say joy never hurts, and so I came to you without any warning. Come now, do smile, instead of looking at me so solemnly. Here I am back again, and we are going to be happy."

"Yes, yes, my boy, so we will—so we will," replied the old man; "but how shall we be happy? Shall you never leave me again? Come, tell me all the good fortune that has befallen you."

"God forgive me," said the young man, "for rejoicing at happiness derived from the misery of others, but, Heaven knows, I did not seek this good fortune; it has happened, and I really cannot pretend to lament it. The good Captain Leclere is dead, father, and it is probable that, with the aid of M. Morrel, I shall have his place. Do you understand, Father? Only imagine me a captain at twenty, with a hundred louis pay, and a share in the profits! Is this not more than a poor sailor like me could have hoped for?"

"Yes, my dear boy," replied the old man, "it is very fortunate."

"Well, then, with the first money I touch, I mean you to have a small house, with a garden in which to plant clematis, nasturtiums, and honeysuckle. But what ails you, Father? Are you not well?"

"'Tis nothing, nothing; it will soon pass away"—and as he said so the old man's strength failed him, and he fell backwards.

"Come, come," said the young man, "a glass of wine, Father, will revive you. Where do you keep your wine?"

"No, no; thanks. You need not look for it; I do not want it," said the old man.

"Yes, yes, Father, tell me where it is," and he opened two or three cupboards.

"It is no use," said the old man, "there is no wine."

"What, no wine?" said Dantes, turning pale, and looking alternately at the hollow cheeks of the old man and the empty cupboards. "What, no wine? Have you wanted money, Father?"

"I want nothing now that I have you," said the old man.

"Yet," stammered Dantes, wiping the perspiration from his brow,—"yet I gave you two hundred francs when I left, three months ago."

"Yes, yes, Edmond, that is true, but you forgot at that time a little debt to our neighbor, Caderousse. He reminded me of it, telling me if I did not pay for you, he would be paid by M. Morrel; and so, you see, lest he might do you an injury"—

"Well?"

"Why, I paid him."

"But," cried Dantes, "it was a hundred and forty francs I owed Caderousse."

"Yes," stammered the old man.

"And you paid him out of the two hundred francs I left you?"

The old man nodded.

"So that you have lived for three months on sixty francs," muttered Edmond.

"You know how little I require," said the old man.

"Heaven pardon me," cried Edmond, falling on his knees before his father.

"What are you doing?"

"You have wounded me to the heart."

"Never mind it, for I see you once more," said the old man; "and now it's all over—everything is all right again."

"Yes, here I am," said the young man, "with a promising future and a little money. Here, Father, here!" he said, "take this—take it, and send for something immediately." And he emptied his pockets on the table, the contents consisting of a dozen gold pieces, five or six five-franc pieces, and some smaller coin. The countenance of old Dantes brightened.

"Whom does this belong to?" he inquired.

"To me, to you, to us! Take it; buy some provisions; be happy, and to-morrow we shall have more."

"Gently, gently," said the old man, with a smile; "and by your leave I will use your purse moderately, for they would say, if they saw me buy too many things at a time, that I had been obliged to await your return, in order to be able to purchase them."

"Do as you please; but, first of all, pray have a servant, Father. I will not have you left alone so long. I have some smuggled coffee and most capital tobacco, in a small chest in the hold, which you shall have to-morrow. But, hush, here comes somebody."

"'Tis Caderousse, who has heard of your arrival and no doubt, comes to congratulate you on your fortunate return."

"Ah, lips that say one thing, while the heart thinks another," murmured Edmond. "But, never mind, he is a neighbor who has done us a service on a time, so he's welcome."

As Edmond paused, the black and bearded head of Caderousse appeared at the door. He was a man of twenty-five or -six, and held a piece of cloth, which, being a tailor, he was about to make into a coat-lining.

"What, is it you, Edmond, back again?" said he, with a broad Marseillaise accent, and a grin that displayed his ivory-white teeth.

"Yes, as you see, neighbor Caderousse; and ready to be agreeable to you in any and every way," replied Dantes, but ill-concealing his coldness under this cloak of civility.

"Thanks—thanks; but, fortunately, I do not want for anything; and it chances that at times there are others who have need of me." Dantes made a gesture. "I do not allude to you, my boy. No!—no! I lent you money, and you returned it; that's like good neighbors, and we are quits."

"We are never quits with those who oblige us," was Dantes' reply; "for when we do not owe them money, we owe them gratitude."

"What's the use of mentioning that? What is done is done. Let us talk of your happy return, my boy. I had gone on the quay to match a piece of mulberry cloth, when I met friend Danglars. 'You at Marseilles?'—'Yes,' says he.

"'I thought you were at Smyrna.'—'I was; but am now back again.'

"'And where is the dear boy, our little Edmond?'

"'Why, with his father, no doubt,' replied Danglars. And so I came," added Caderousse, "as fast as I could to have the pleasure of shaking hands with a friend."

"Worthy Caderousse!" said the old man, "he is so much attached to us."

"Yes, to be sure I am. I love and esteem you, because honest folks are so rare. But it seems you have come back rich, my boy," continued the tailor, looking askance at the handful of gold and silver which Dantes had thrown on the table.

The young man remarked the greedy glance which shone in the dark eyes of his neighbor. "Eh," he said, negligently, "this money is not mine. I was expressing to my father my fears that he had wanted many things in my absence, and to convince me he emptied his purse on the table. Come, Father," added Dantes, "put this money back in your box—unless neighbor Caderousse wants anything, and in that case it is at his service."

"No, my boy, no," said Caderousse. "I am not in any want, thank God, my living is suited to my means. Keep your money— keep it, I say;—one never has too much;—but, at the same time, my boy, I am as much obliged by your offer as if I took advantage of it."

"It was offered with good will," said Dantes.

"No doubt, my boy; no doubt. Well, you stand well with M. Morrel I hear,—you insinuating dog, you!"

"M. Morrel has always been exceedingly kind to me," replied Dantes.

"Then you were wrong to refuse to dine with him."

"What, did you refuse to dine with him?" said old Dantes; "and did he invite you to dine?"

"Yes, my dear father," replied Edmond, smiling at his father's astonishment at the excessive honor paid to his son.

"And why did you refuse, my son?" inquired the old man.

"That I might the sooner see you again, my dear father," replied the young man. "I was most anxious to see you."

"But it must have vexed M. Morrel, good, worthy man," said Caderousse.

"And when you are looking forward to be captain, it was wrong to annoy the owner."

"But I explained to him the cause of my refusal," replied Dantes, "and I hope he fully understood it."

"Yes, but to be captain one must do a little flattery to one's patrons."

"I hope to be captain without that," said Dantes.

"So much the better—so much the better! Nothing will give greater pleasure to all your old friends; and I know one down there behind the Saint Nicolas citadel who will not be sorry to hear it."

"Mercedes?" said the old man.

"Yes, my dear father, and with your permission, now I have seen you, and know you are well and have all you require, I will ask your consent to go and pay a visit to the Catalans."

"Go, my dear boy," said old Dantes: "and heaven bless you in your wife, as it has blessed me in my son!"

"His wife!" said Caderousse; "why, how fast you go on, father Dantes; she is not his wife yet, as it seems to me."

"So, but according to all probability she soon will be," replied Edmond.

"Yes—yes," said Caderousse; "but you were right to return as soon as possible, my boy."

"And why?"

"Because Mercedes is a very fine girl, and fine girls never lack followers; she particularly has them by dozens."

"Really?" answered Edmond, with a smile which had in it traces of slight uneasiness.

"Ah, yes," continued Caderousse, "and capital offers, too; but you know, you will be captain, and who could refuse you then?"

"Meaning to say," replied Dantes, with a smile which but ill-concealed his trouble, "that if I were not a captain"—

"Eh—eh!" said Caderousse, shaking his head.

"Come, come," said the sailor, "I have a better opinion than you of women in general, and of Mercedes in particular; and I am certain that, captain or not, she will remain ever faithful to me."

"So much the better—so much the better," said Caderousse. "When one is going to be married, there is nothing like implicit confidence; but never mind that, my boy,—go and announce your arrival, and let her know all your hopes and prospects."

"I will go directly," was Edmond's reply; and, embracing his father, and nodding to Caderousse, he left the apartment.

Caderousse lingered for a moment, then taking leave of old Dantes, he went downstairs to rejoin Danglars, who awaited him at the corner of the Rue Senac.

"Well," said Danglars, "did you see him?"

"I have just left him," answered Caderousse.

"Did he allude to his hope of being captain?"

"He spoke of it as a thing already decided."

"Indeed!" said Danglars, "he is in too much hurry, it appears to me."

"Why, it seems M. Morrel has promised him the thing."

"So that he is quite elated about it?"

"Why, yes, he is actually insolent over the matter—has already offered me his patronage, as if he were a grand personage, and proffered me a loan of money, as though he were a banker."

"Which you refused?"

"Most assuredly; although I might easily have accepted it, for it was I who put into his hands the first silver he ever earned; but now M. Dantes has no longer any occasion for assistance—he is about to become a captain."

"Pooh!" said Danglars, "he is not one yet."

"Ma foi, it will be as well if he is not," answered Caderousse; "for if he should be, there will be really no speaking to him."

"If we choose," replied Danglars, "he will remain what he is; and perhaps become even less than he is."

"What do you mean?"

"Nothing—I was speaking to myself. And is he still in love with the Catalane?"

"Over head and ears; but, unless I am much mistaken, there will be a storm in that quarter."

"Explain yourself."

"Why should I?"

"It is more important than you think, perhaps. You do not like Dantes?"

"I never like upstarts."

"Then tell me all you know about the Catalane."

"I know nothing for certain; only I have seen things which induce me to believe, as I told you, that the future captain will find some annoyance in the vicinity of the Vieilles Infirmeries."

"What have you seen?—come, tell me!"

"Well, every time I have seen Mercedes come into the city she has been accompanied by a tall, strapping, black-eyed Catalan, with a red complexion, brown skin, and fierce air, whom she calls cousin."

"Really; and you think this cousin pays her attentions?"

"I only suppose so. What else can a strapping chap of twenty-one mean with a fine wench of seventeen?"

"And you say that Dantes has gone to the Catalans?"

"He went before I came down."

"Let us go the same way; we will stop at La Reserve, and we can drink a glass of La Malgue, whilst we wait for news."

"Come along," said Caderousse; "but you pay the score."

"Of course," replied Danglars; and going quickly to the designated place, they called for a bottle of wine, and two glasses.

Pere Pamphile had seen Dantes pass not ten minutes before; and assured that he was at the Catalans, they sat down under the budding foliage of the planes and sycamores, in the branches of which the birds were singing their welcome to one of the first days of spring.

Chapter 3. The Catalans.

Beyond a bare, weather-worn wall, about a hundred paces from the spot where the two friends sat looking and listening as they drank their wine, was the village of the Catalans. Long ago this mysterious colony quitted Spain, and settled on the tongue of land on which it is to this day. Whence it came no one knew, and it spoke an unknown tongue. One of its chiefs, who understood Provençal, begged the commune of Marseilles to give them this bare and barren promontory, where, like the sailors of old, they had run their boats ashore. The request was granted; and three months afterwards, around the twelve or fifteen small vessels which had brought these gypsies of the sea, a small village sprang up. This village, constructed in a singular and picturesque manner, half Moorish, half Spanish, still remains, and is inhabited by descendants of the first comers, who speak the language of their fathers. For three or four centuries they have remained upon this small promontory, on which they had settled like a flight of sea-birds, without mixing with the Marseillaise population, intermarrying, and preserving their original customs and the costume of their mother-country as they have preserved its language.

Our readers will follow us along the only street of this little village, and enter with us one of the houses, which is sunburned to the beautiful dead-leaf color peculiar to the buildings of the country, and within coated with whitewash, like a Spanish posada. A young and beautiful girl, with hair as black as jet, her eyes as velvety as the gazelle's, was leaning with her back against the wainscot, rubbing in her slender delicately moulded fingers a bunch of heath blossoms, the flowers of which she was picking off and strewing on the floor; her arms, bare to the elbow, brown, and modeled after those of the Arlesian Venus, moved with a kind of restless impatience, and she tapped the earth with her arched and supple foot, so as to display the pure and full shape of her well-turned leg, in its red cotton, gray and blue clocked, stocking. At three paces from her, seated in a chair which he balanced on two legs, leaning his elbow on an old worm-eaten table, was a tall young man of twenty, or two-and-twenty, who was looking at her with an air in which vexation and uneasiness were mingled. He questioned her with his eyes, but the firm and steady gaze of the young girl controlled his look.

"You see, Mercedes," said the young man, "here is Easter come round again; tell me, is this the moment for a wedding?"

"I have answered you a hundred times, Fernand, and really you must be very stupid to ask me again."

"Well, repeat it,—repeat it, I beg of you, that I may at last believe it! Tell me for the hundredth time that you refuse my love, which had your mother's sanction. Make me understand once for all that you are trifling with my happiness, that my life or death is nothing to you. Ah, to have dreamed for ten years of being your husband, Mercedes, and to lose that hope, which was the only stay of my existence!"

"At least it was not I who ever encouraged you in that hope, Fernand," replied Mercedes; "you cannot reproach me with the slightest coquetry. I have always said to you, 'I love you as a brother; but do not ask from me more than sisterly affection, for my heart is another's.' Is not this true, Fernand?"

"Yes, that is very true, Mercedes," replied the young man, "Yes, you have been cruelly frank with me; but do you forget that it is among the Catalans a sacred law to intermarry?"

"You mistake, Fernand; it is not a law, but merely a custom, and, I pray of you, do not cite this custom in your favor. You are included in the conscription, Fernand, and are only at liberty on sufferance, liable at any moment to be called upon to take up arms. Once a soldier, what would you do with me, a poor orphan, forlorn, without fortune, with nothing but a half-ruined hut and a few ragged nets, the miserable inheritance left by my father to my mother, and by my mother to me? She has been dead a year, and you know, Fernand, I have subsisted almost entirely on public charity. Sometimes you pretend I am useful to you, and that is an excuse to share with me the produce of your fishing, and I accept it, Fernand, because you are the son of my father's brother, because we were brought up together, and still more because it would give you so much pain if I refuse. But I feel very deeply that this fish which I go and sell, and with the produce of which I buy the flax I spin,—I feel very keenly, Fernand, that this is charity."

"And if it were, Mercedes, poor and lone as you are, you suit me as well as the daughter of the first ship-owner or the richest banker of Marseilles! What do such as we desire but a good wife and careful housekeeper, and where can I look for these better than in you?"

"Fernand," answered Mercedes, shaking her head, "a woman becomes a bad manager, and who shall say she will remain an honest woman, when she loves another man better than her husband? Rest content with my friendship, for I say once more that is all I can promise, and I will promise no more than I can bestow."

"I understand," replied Fernand, "you can endure your own wretchedness patiently, but you are afraid to share mine. Well, Mercedes, beloved by you, I would tempt fortune; you would bring me good luck, and I should become rich. I could extend my occupation as a fisherman, might get a place as clerk in a warehouse, and become in time a dealer myself."

"You could do no such thing, Fernand; you are a soldier, and if you remain at the Catalans it is because there is no war; so remain a fisherman, and contented with my friendship, as I cannot give you more."

"Well, I will do better, Mercedes. I will be a sailor; instead of the costume of our fathers, which you despise, I will wear a varnished hat, a striped shirt, and a blue jacket, with an anchor on the buttons. Would not that dress please you?"

"What do you mean?" asked Mercedes, with an angry glance,—"what do you mean? I do not understand you?"

"I mean, Mercedes, that you are thus harsh and cruel with me, because you are expecting someone who is thus attired; but perhaps he whom you await is inconstant, or if he is not, the sea is so to him."

"Fernand," cried Mercedes, "I believed you were good-hearted, and I was mistaken! Fernand, you are wicked to call to your aid jealousy and the anger of God! Yes, I will not deny it, I do await, and I do love him of whom you speak; and, if he does not return, instead of accusing him of the inconstancy which you insinuate, I will tell you that he died loving me and me only." The young girl made a gesture of rage. "I understand you, Fernand; you would be revenged on him because I do not love you; you would cross your Catalan knife with his dirk. What end would that answer? To lose you my friendship if he were conquered, and see that friendship changed into hate if you were victor. Believe me, to seek a quarrel with a man is a bad method of pleasing the woman who loves that man. No, Fernand, you will not thus give way to evil thoughts. Unable to have me for your wife, you will content yourself with having me for your friend and sister; and besides," she added, her eyes troubled and moistened with tears, "wait, wait, Fernand; you said just now that the sea was treacherous, and he has been gone four months, and during these four months there have been some terrible storms."

Fernand made no reply, nor did he attempt to check the tears which flowed down the cheeks of Mercedes, although for each of these tears he would have shed his heart's blood; but these tears flowed for another. He arose, paced a while up and down the hut, and then, suddenly stopping before Mercedes, with his eyes glowing and his hands clinched,—"Say, Mercedes," he said, "once for all, is this your final determination?"

"I love Edmond Dantes," the young girl calmly replied, "and none but Edmond shall ever be my husband."

"And you will always love him?"

"As long as I live."

Fernand let fall his head like a defeated man, heaved a sigh that was like a groan, and then suddenly looking her full in the face, with clinched teeth and expanded nostrils, said,—"But if he is dead"—

"If he is dead, I shall die too."

"If he has forgotten you"—

"Mercedes!" called a joyous voice from without,—"Mercedes!"

"Ah," exclaimed the young girl, blushing with delight, and fairly leaping in excess of love, "you see he has not forgotten me, for here he is!" And rushing towards the door, she opened it, saying, "Here, Edmond, here I am!"

Fernand, pale and trembling, drew back, like a traveler at the sight of a serpent, and fell into a chair beside him. Edmond and Mercedes were clasped in each other's arms. The burning Marseilles sun, which shot into the room through the open door, covered them with a flood of light. At first they saw nothing around them. Their intense happiness isolated them from all the rest of the world, and they only spoke in broken words, which are the tokens of a joy so extreme that they seem rather the expression of sorrow. Suddenly Edmond saw the gloomy, pale, and threatening countenance of Fernand, as it was defined in the shadow. By a movement for which he could scarcely account to himself, the young Catalan placed his hand on the knife at his belt.

"Ah, your pardon," said Dantes, frowning in his turn; "I did not perceive that there were three of us." Then, turning to Mercedes, he inquired, "Who is this gentleman?"

"One who will be your best friend, Dantes, for he is my friend, my cousin, my brother; it is Fernand—the man whom, after you, Edmond, I love the best in the world. Do you not remember him?"

"Yes!" said Dantes, and without relinquishing Mercedes' hand clasped in one of his own, he extended the other to the Catalan with a cordial air. But Fernand, instead of responding to this amiable gesture, remained mute and trembling. Edmond then cast his eyes scrutinizing at the agitated and embarrassed Mercedes, and then again on the gloomy and menacing Fernand. This look told him all, and his anger waxed hot.

"I did not know, when I came with such haste to you, that I was to meet an enemy here."

"An enemy!" cried Mercedes, with an angry look at her cousin. "An enemy in my house, do you say, Edmond! If I believed that, I would place my arm under yours and go with you to Marseilles, leaving the house to return to it no more."

Fernand's eye darted lightning. "And should any misfortune occur to you, dear Edmond," she continued with the same calmness which proved to Fernand that the young girl had read the very innermost depths of his sinister thought, "if misfortune should occur to you, I would ascend the highest point of the Cape de Morgion and cast myself headlong from it."

Fernand became deadly pale. "But you are deceived, Edmond," she continued. "You have no enemy here—there is no one but Fernand, my brother, who will grasp your hand as a devoted friend."

And at these words the young girl fixed her imperious look on the Catalan, who, as if fascinated by it, came slowly towards Edmond, and offered him his hand. His hatred, like a powerless though furious wave, was broken against the strong ascendancy which Mercedes exercised over him. Scarcely, however, had he touched Edmond's hand than he felt he had done all he could do, and rushed hastily out of the house.

Dantes watched the fellow run from the premises and, turning to Mercedes, gave her an enquiring look.

"Are you quite certain Fernand is a friend and not my enemy?"

"My love, I am. He has been a friend, a brother, and my cousin. Nothing more has passed between us."

"Then I will say no more of it." Edmond lifted Mercedes, twirling her in a circle; her feminine giggles brought joy to his heart. Being apart this three months had been nothing short of living hell. Once her feet touched the ground again no words need be spoken. Pulling Mercedes into the circle of his arms, he kissed the lips only dreams had shown him and took pleasure in the way her hand burrowed into the hair at the nape of his neck.

"Edmond," Mercedes whispered. "I don't want to wait. We will marry soon and I want to be yours, completely, right now." They both stared into each other's eyes; the depth of emotion each felt for the other was all consuming like a sandstorm that sweeps across the desert.

"Mercedes, nothing would make me happier than to have you right this minute; are you certain of your decision?"

"I have never been more positive of anything in life before now."

Edmond had known one woman before Mercedes, his occupation giving him cause to see many beautiful women but none compared to the ethereal quality of Mercedes' luminance.

He pressed his lips down to hers another time, attempting to rein in his ardor, to be a gentleman, but even with warnings dinging like bells in his mind, Mercedes' soft gentle curves along his body suspended those thoughts.

"Edmond, please."

He didn't respond to her cry, only lifted her slight weight easily and carried her to the small palette she kept off in a corner of her modest home.

"Make love to me, Edmond. I burn with need for you."

Laying her down on the fresh sun-bleached linen was so simple. She started to remove her dress and Edmond reached behind, helping with the stays. Even with the warm air, gooseflesh branched across her skin in small rounds as her breasts became exposed. Edmond exhaled at the first sight of the dusky pink nipples. Stunned at her enchanting beauty, he met her eyes once more.

"Mercedes. Once we do this, there is no going back; you will be my wife and bear my children. This is what I want and have always wanted. I need to be assuaged that it is absolutely what you want."

"I have wanted nothing more since the moment we met." She cupped his face in her delicate fingers, drawing him down along her body as she lay back on the palette. Edmond moved in haste, removing his clothing so his skin could finally lie alongside hers.

When she started to tremble he became quickly disconcerted. "My love, why do you tremble?"

"It is nothing. I am simply a bit anxious I suppose." She smoothed a hand down an errant strand of his hair.

"If you want to stop, simply say the words."

"Nothing in the world could induce me to use them. Please, Edmond."

Her body was like the air of the open ocean in the middle of summer, hot and sweet as he melded their bodies together. She clutched his shoulders in a tight grip, and he felt her maidenhead part as he entered her. Allowing her time to adjust to him, he waited until the whites of her fingers eased.

"I can still stop this," Edmond whispered.

"No; the pain has passed, please, continue."

Edmond wanted nothing more than for Mercedes to remember this time between them sweetly. He did as the young women he met before had shown him and reached between them, circling the tiny bud at the top of her sex. Her eyes flashed wide, and he understood for the first time what it meant to love and be loved completely. His person reflected in her eyes, the sweet passion building between them as he slid himself in and out of her wet flesh.

"Edmond." She sighed his name. A flush crept up her neck and into her cheeks; with each stroke he moved inside of her she held on to him tighter, trying to maintain composure in a situation devoid of it.

"Let go my love; I will catch you," Edmond told her, his hand gripping hers, allowing her an anchor to hold on to. The sound she emitted upon reaching her completion was the most glorious Edmond had ever heard, and he reveled in it as he found his own release inside her body. "My love, my beautiful betrothed. I could not imagine a life without you and hope never to have to."

A glistening sweat shone across her brow from their exertions but she seemed not concerned. "Never will you have to," Mercedes told him as she stroked her hand down his sun-tanned cheek.

He dropped his head on her shoulder and stayed there as the sun cast shadows around Mercedes' home. When it was time to dress, the whole world tumbled back to them both, reminding them of its existence.

"We must go visit my father; he is as anxious to see you as he was to see me." Edmond helped her dress and retied the stays in the back with trembling fingers. Even with the glorious glow of their lovemaking around them, he could not help but feel a sense of foreboding, an ominous cloud even he could not shake.

"Are you well, Edmond?" Mercedes inquired as they exited her home into the afternoon air.

"Of course. You will soon be my bride; a man could want for nothing else."

They strolled hand in hand through the streets en route to visit Edmond's father, stopping only to share a few brief kisses in the shadow of an alleyway off a pub. No one was afoot, and those small kisses bolstered their spirits, reminding them of the intimate moment they had shared previously.

• • •

"Oh," Fernand exclaimed, running furiously and tearing his hair—"Oh, who will deliver me from this man? Wretched—wretched that I am!"

"Hallo, Catalan! Hallo, Fernand! where are you running to?" exclaimed a voice.

The young man stopped suddenly, looked around him, and perceived Caderousse sitting at table with Danglars, under an arbor.

"Well," said Caderousse, "why don't you come? Are you really in such a hurry that you have no time to pass the time of day with your friends?"

"Particularly when they have still a full bottle before them," added Danglars. Fernand looked at them both with a stupefied air, but did not say a word.

"He seems besotted," said Danglars, pushing Caderousse with his knee. "Are we mistaken, and is Dantes triumphant in spite of all we have believed?"

"Why, we must inquire into that," was Caderousse's reply; and turning towards the young man, said, "Well, Catalan, can't you make up your mind?"

Fernand wiped away the perspiration steaming from his brow, and slowly entered the arbor, whose shade seemed to restore somewhat of calmness to his senses, and whose coolness somewhat of refreshment to his exhausted body.

"Good-day," said he. "You called me, didn't you?" And he fell, rather than sat down, on one of the seats which surrounded the table.

"I called you because you were running like a madman, and I was afraid you would throw yourself into the sea," said Caderousse, laughing. "Why, when a man has friends, they are not only to offer him a glass of wine, but, moreover, to prevent his swallowing three or four pints of water unnecessarily!"

Fernand gave a groan, which resembled a sob, and dropped his head into his hands, his elbows leaning on the table.

"Well, Fernand, I must say," said Caderousse, beginning the conversation, with that brutality of the common people in which curiosity destroys all diplomacy, "you look uncommonly like a rejected lover;" and he burst into a hoarse laugh.

"Bah!" said Danglars, "a lad of his make was not born to be unhappy in love. You are laughing at him, Caderousse."

"No," he replied, "only hark how he sighs! Come, come, Fernand," said Caderousse, "hold up your head, and answer us. It's not polite not to reply to friends who ask news of your health."

"My health is well enough," said Fernand, clinching his hands without raising his head.

"Ah, you see, Danglars," said Caderousse, winking at his friend, "this is how it is; Fernand, whom you see here, is a good and brave Catalan, one of the best fishermen in Marseilles, and he is in love with a very fine girl, named Mercedes; but it appears, unfortunately, that the fine girl is in love with the mate of the *Pharaon*; and as the *Pharaon* arrived to-day—why, you understand!"

"No; I do not understand," said Danglars.

"Poor Fernand has been dismissed," continued Caderousse.

"Well, and what then?" said Fernand, lifting up his head, and looking at Caderousse like a man who looks for someone on whom to vent his anger; "Mercedes is not accountable to any person, is she? Is she not free to love whomsoever she will?"

"Oh, if you take it in that sense," said Caderousse, "it is another thing. But I thought you were a Catalan, and they told me the Catalans were not men to allow themselves to be supplanted by a rival. It was even told me that Fernand, especially, was terrible in his vengeance."

Fernand smiled piteously. "A lover is never terrible," he said.

"Poor fellow!" remarked Danglars, affecting to pity the young man from the bottom of his heart. "Why, you see, he did not expect to see Dantes return so suddenly—he thought he was dead, perhaps; or perchance faithless! These things always come on us more severely when they come suddenly."

"Ah, ma foi, under any circumstances," said Caderousse, who drank as he spoke, and on whom the fumes of the wine began to take effect,—"under any circumstances Fernand is not the only person put out by the fortunate arrival of Dantes; is he, Danglars?"

"No, you are right—and I should say that would bring him ill-luck."

"Well, never mind," answered Caderousse, pouring out a glass of wine for Fernand, and filling his own for the eighth or ninth time, while Danglars had merely sipped his. "Never mind—in the meantime he marries Mercedes—the lovely Mercedes—at least he returns to do that."

During this time Danglars fixed his piercing glance on the young man, on whose heart Caderousse's words fell like molten lead.

"And when is the wedding to be?" he asked.

"Oh, it is not yet fixed!" murmured Fernand.

"No, but it will be," said Caderousse, "as surely as Dantes will be captain of the *Pharaon*—eh, Danglars?"

Danglars shuddered at this unexpected attack, and turned to Caderousse, whose countenance he scrutinized, to try and detect whether the blow was premeditated; but he read nothing but envy in a countenance already rendered brutal and stupid by drunkenness.

"Well," said he, filling the glasses, "let us drink to Captain Edmond Dantes, husband of the beautiful Catalane!"

Caderousse raised his glass to his mouth with unsteady hand, and swallowed the contents at a gulp. Fernand dashed his on the ground.

"Eh, eh, eh!" stammered Caderousse. "What do I see down there by the wall, in the direction of the Catalans? Look, Fernand, your eyes are better than mine. I believe I see double. You know wine is a deceiver; but I should say it was two lovers walking side by side, and hand in hand. Heaven forgive me, they do not know that we can see them, and they are actually embracing!"

Danglars did not lose one pang that Fernand endured.

"Do you know them, Fernand?" he said.

"Yes," was the reply, in a low voice. "It is Edmond and Mercedes!"

"Ah, see there, now!" said Caderousse; "and I did not recognize them! Hallo, Dantes! hello, lovely damsel! Come this way, and let us know when the wedding is to be, for Fernand here is so obstinate he will not tell us."

"Hold your tongue, will you?" said Danglars, pretending to restrain Caderousse, who, with the tenacity of drunkards, leaned out of the arbor. "Try to stand upright, and let the lovers make love without interruption. See, look at Fernand, and follow his example; he is well-behaved!"

Fernand, probably excited beyond bearing, pricked by Danglars, as the bull is by the bandilleros, was about to rush out; for he had risen from his seat, and seemed to be collecting himself to dash headlong upon his rival, when Mercedes, smiling and graceful, lifted up her lovely head, and looked at them with her clear and bright eyes. At this Fernand recollected her threat of dying if Edmond died, and dropped again heavily on his seat. Danglars looked at the two men, one after the other, the one brutalized by liquor, the other overwhelmed with love.

"I shall get nothing from these fools," he muttered; "and I am very much afraid of being here between a drunkard and a coward.

Here's an envious fellow making himself boozy on wine when he ought to be nursing his wrath, and here is a fool who sees the woman he loves stolen from under his nose and takes on like a big baby. Yet this Catalan has eyes that glisten like those of the vengeful Spaniards, Sicilians, and Calabrians, and the other has fists big enough to crush an ox at one blow. Unquestionably, Edmond's star is in the ascendant, and he will marry the splendid girl—he will be captain, too, and laugh at us all, unless"—a sinister smile passed over Danglars' lips—"unless I take a hand in the affair," he added.

"Hallo!" continued Caderousse, half-rising, and with his fist on the table, "hallo, Edmond! Do you not see your friends, or are you too proud to speak to them?"

"No, my dear fellow!" replied Dantes, "I am not proud, but I am happy, and happiness blinds, I think, more than pride."

"Ah, very well, that's an explanation!" said Caderousse. "How do you do, Madame Dantes?"

Mercedes curtsied gravely, and said—"That is not my name, and in my country it bodes ill fortune, they say, to call a young girl by the name of her betrothed before he becomes her husband. So call me Mercedes, if you please."

"We must excuse our worthy neighbor, Caderousse," said Dantes, "he is so easily mistaken."

"So, then, the wedding is to take place immediately, M. Dantes," said Danglars, bowing to the young couple.

"As soon as possible, M. Danglars; to-day all preliminaries will be arranged at my father's, and to-morrow, or next day at latest, the wedding festival here at La Reserve. My friends will be there, I hope; that is to say, you are invited, M. Danglars, and you, Caderousse."

"And Fernand," said Caderousse with a chuckle; "Fernand, too, is invited!"

"My wife's brother is my brother," said Edmond; "and we, Mercedes and I, should be very sorry if he were absent at such a time."

Fernand opened his mouth to reply, but his voice died on his lips, and he could not utter a word.

"To-day the preliminaries, to-morrow or next day the ceremony! You are in a hurry, Captain!"

"Danglars," said Edmond, smiling, "I will say to you as Mercedes said just now to Caderousse, 'Do not give me a title which does not belong to me'; that may bring me bad luck."

"Your pardon," replied Danglars, "I merely said you seemed in a hurry, and we have lots of time; the *Pharaon* cannot be under weigh again in less than three months."

"We are always in a hurry to be happy, M. Danglars; for when we have suffered a long time, we have great difficulty in believing in good fortune. But it is not selfishness alone that makes me thus in haste; I must go to Paris."

"Ah, really?—to Paris! And will it be the first time you have ever been there, Dantes?"

"Yes."

"Have you business there?"

"Not of my own; the last commission of poor Captain Leclere; you know to what I allude, Danglars—it is sacred. Besides, I shall only take the time to go and return."

"Yes, yes, I understand," said Danglars, and then in a low tone, he added, "To Paris, no doubt to deliver the letter which the grand marshal gave him. Ah, this letter gives me an idea—a capital idea! Ah; Dantes, my friend, you are not yet registered number one on board the good ship *Pharaon*;" then turning towards Edmond, who was walking away, "A pleasant journey," he cried.

"Thank you," said Edmond with a friendly nod, and the two lovers continued on their way, as calm and joyous as if they were the very elect of heaven.

Chapter 4. Conspiracy.

Danglars followed Edmond and Mercedes with his eyes until the two lovers disappeared behind one of the angles of Fort Saint Nicolas, then turning round, he perceived Fernand, who had fallen, pale and trembling, into his chair, while Caderousse stammered out the words of a drinking-song.

"Well, my dear sir," said Danglars to Fernand, "here is a marriage which does not appear to make everybody happy."

"It drives me to despair," said Fernand.

"Do you, then, love Mercedes?"

"I adore her!"

"For long?"

"As long as I have known her—always."

"And you sit there, tearing your hair, instead of seeking to remedy your condition; I did not think that was the way of your people."

"What would you have me do?" said Fernand.

"How do I know? Is it my affair? I am not in love with Mademoiselle Mercedes; but for you—in the words of the gospel, seek, and you shall find."

"I have found already."

"What?"

"I would stab the man, but the woman told me that if any misfortune happened to her betrothed, she would kill herself."

"Pooh! Women say those things, but never do them."

"You do not know Mercedes; what she threatens she will do."

"Idiot!" muttered Danglars; "whether she kill herself or not, what matter, provided Dantes is not captain?"

"Before Mercedes should die," replied Fernand, with the accents of unshaken resolution, "I would die myself!"

"That's what I call love!" said Caderousse with a voice more tipsy than ever. "That's love, or I don't know what love is."

"Come," said Danglars, "you appear to me a good sort of fellow, and hang me, I should like to help you, but"—

"Yes," said Caderousse, "but how?"

"My dear fellow," replied Danglars, "you are three parts drunk; finish the bottle, and you will be completely so. Drink then, and do not meddle with what we are discussing, for that requires all one's wit and cool judgment."

"I—drunk!" said Caderousse; "well that's a good one! I could drink four more such bottles; they are no bigger than cologne flasks. Pere Pamphile, more wine!" and Caderousse rattled his glass upon the table.

"You were saying, sir"—said Fernand, awaiting with great anxiety the end of this interrupted remark.

"What was I saying? I forget. This drunken Caderousse has made me lose the thread of my sentence."

"Drunk, if you like; so much the worse for those who fear wine, for it is because they have bad thoughts which they are afraid the liquor will extract from their hearts;" and Caderousse began to sing the two last lines of a song very popular at the time,—

*'Tous les mechants sont beuveurs d'eau; C'est bien prouve par le deluge.**

(*"The wicked are great drinkers of water; As the flood proved once for all.")

"You said, sir, you would like to help me, but"—

"Yes; but I added, to help you it would be sufficient that Dantes did not marry her you love; and the marriage may easily be thwarted, methinks, and yet Dantes need not die."

"Death alone can separate them," remarked Fernand.

"You talk like a noodle, my friend," said Caderousse; "and here is Danglars, who is a wide-awake, clever, deep fellow, who will prove to you that you are wrong. Prove it, Danglars. I have answered for you. Say there is no need why Dantes should die; it would, indeed, be a pity he should. Dantes is a good fellow; I like Dantes. Dantes, your health."

Fernand rose impatiently. "Let him run on," said Danglars, restraining the young man; "drunk as he is, he is not much out in what he says. Absence severs as well as death, and if the walls of a prison were between Edmond and Mercedes they would be as effectually separated as if he lay under a tombstone."

"Yes; but one gets out of prison," said Caderousse, who, with what sense was left him, listened eagerly to the conversation, "and when one gets out and one's name is Edmond Dantes, one seeks revenge"—

"What matters that?" muttered Fernand.

"And why, I should like to know," persisted Caderousse, "should they put Dantes in prison? He has not robbed or killed or murdered."

"Hold your tongue!" said Danglars.

"I won't hold my tongue!" replied Caderousse; "I say I want to know why they should put Dantes in prison; I like Dantes; Dantes, your health!" and he swallowed another glass of wine.

Danglars saw in the muddled look of the tailor the progress of his intoxication, and turning towards Fernand, said, "Well, you understand there is no need to kill him."

"Certainly not, if, as you said just now, you have the means of having Dantes arrested. Have you that means?"

"It is to be found for the searching. But why should I meddle in the matter? It is no affair of mine."

"I know not why you meddle," said Fernand, seizing his arm; "but this I know, you have some motive of personal hatred against Dantes, for he who himself hates is never mistaken in the sentiments of others."

"I!—motives of hatred against Dantes? None, on my word! I saw you were unhappy, and your unhappiness interested me; that's all; but since you believe I act for my own account, adieu, my dear friend, get out of the affair as best you may;" and Danglars rose as if he meant to depart.

"No, no," said Fernand, restraining him, "stay! It is of very little consequence to me at the end of the matter whether you have any angry feeling or not against Dantes. I hate him! I confess it openly. Do you find the means, I will execute it, provided it is not to kill the man, for Mercedes has declared she will kill herself if Dantes is killed."

Caderousse, who had let his head drop on the table, now raised it, and looking at Fernand with his dull and fishy eyes, he said,—"Kill Dantes! Who talks of killing Dantes? I won't have him killed—I won't! He's my friend, and this morning offered to share his money with me, as I shared mine with him. I won't have Dantes killed—I won't!"

"And who has said a word about killing him, muddle head?" replied Danglars. "We were merely joking; drink to his health," he added, filling Caderousse's glass, "and do not interfere with us."

"Yes, yes, Dantes' good health!" said Caderousse, emptying his glass, "here's to his health! his health—hurrah!"

"But the means—the means?" said Fernand.

"Have you not hit upon any?" asked Danglars.

"No!—you undertook to do so."

"True," replied Danglars; "the French have the superiority over the Spaniards, that the Spaniards ruminate, while the French invent."

"Do you invent, then," said Fernand impatiently.

"Waiter," said Danglars, "pen, ink, and paper."

"Pen, ink, and paper," muttered Fernand.

"Yes; I am a supercargo; pen, ink, and paper are my tools, and without my tools I am fit for nothing."

"Pen, ink, and paper, then," called Fernand loudly.

"There's what you want on that table," said the waiter.

"Bring them here." The waiter did as he was desired.

"When one thinks," said Caderousse, letting his hand drop on the paper, "there is here wherewithal to kill a man more sure than if we waited at the corner of a wood to assassinate him! I have always had more dread of a pen, a bottle of ink, and a sheet of paper, than of a sword or pistol."

"The fellow is not so drunk as he appears to be," said Danglars. "Give him some more wine, Fernand." Fernand filled Caderousse's glass, who, like the confirmed toper he was, lifted his hand from the paper and seized the glass.

The Catalan watched him until Caderousse, almost overcome by this fresh assault on his senses, rested, or rather dropped, his glass upon the table.

"Well!" resumed the Catalan, as he saw the final glimmer of Caderousse's reason vanishing before the last glass of wine.

"Well, then, I should say, for instance," resumed Danglars, "that if after a voyage such as Dantes has just made, in which he touched at the Island of Elba, someone were to denounce him to the king's procureur as a Bonapartist agent"—

"I will denounce him!" exclaimed the young man hastily.

"Yes, but they will make you then sign your declaration, and confront you with him you have denounced; I will supply you with the means of supporting your accusation, for I know the fact well. But Dantes cannot remain forever in prison, and one day or other he will leave it, and the day when he comes out, woe betide him who was the cause of his incarceration!"

"Oh, I should wish nothing better than that he would come and seek a quarrel with me."

"Yes, and Mercedes! Mercedes, who will detest you if you have only the misfortune to scratch the skin of her dearly beloved Edmond!"

"True!" said Fernand.

"No, no," continued Danglars; "if we resolve on such a step, it would be much better to take, as I now do, this pen, dip it into this ink, and write with the left hand (that the writing may not be recognized) the denunciation we propose." And Danglars, uniting practice with theory, wrote with his left hand, and in a writing reversed from his usual style, and totally unlike it, the following lines, which he handed to Fernand, and which Fernand read in an undertone:—

"The honorable, the king's attorney, is informed by a friend of the throne and religion, that one Edmond Dantes, mate of the ship Pharaon, arrived this morning from Smyrna, after having touched at Naples and Porto-Ferrajo, has been entrusted by Murat with a letter for the usurper, and by the usurper with a letter for the Bonapartist committee in Paris. Proof of this crime will be found on arresting him, for the letter will be found upon him, or at his father's, or in his cabin on board the Pharaon."

"Very good," resumed Danglars; "now your revenge looks like common-sense, for in no way can it revert to yourself, and the matter will thus work its own way; there is nothing to do now but fold the letter as I am doing, and write upon it, 'To the king's attorney,' and that's all settled." And Danglars wrote the address as he spoke.

"Yes, and that's all settled!" exclaimed Caderousse, who, by a last effort of intellect, had followed the reading of the letter, and instinctively comprehended all the misery which such a denunciation must entail. "Yes, and that's all settled; only it will be an infamous shame;" and he stretched out his hand to reach the letter.

"Yes," said Danglars, taking it from beyond his reach; "and as what I say and do is merely in jest, and I, amongst the first and foremost, should be sorry if anything happened to Dantes—the worthy Dantes—look here!" And taking the letter, he squeezed it up in his hands and threw it into a corner of the arbor.

"All right!" said Caderousse. "Dantes is my friend, and I won't have him ill-used."

"And who thinks of using him ill? Certainly neither I nor Fernand," said Danglars, rising and looking at the young man, who still remained seated, but whose eye was fixed on the denunciatory sheet of paper flung into the corner.

"In this case," replied Caderousse, "let's have some more wine. I wish to drink to the health of Edmond and the lovely Mercedes."

"You have had too much already, drunkard," said Danglars; "and if you continue, you will be compelled to sleep here, because unable to stand on your legs."

"I?" said Caderousse, rising with all the offended dignity of a drunken man, "I can't keep on my legs? Why, I'll wager I can go up into the belfry of the Accoules, and without staggering, too!"

"Done!" said Danglars, "I'll take your bet; but to-morrow—to-day it is time to return. Give me your arm, and let us go."

"Very well, let us go," said Caderousse; "but I don't want your arm at all. Come, Fernand, won't you return to Marseilles with us?"

"No," said Fernand; "I shall return to the Catalans."

"You're wrong. Come with us to Marseilles—come along."

"I will not."

"What do you mean? You will not? Well, just as you like, my prince; there's liberty for all the world. Come along, Danglars, and let the young gentleman return to the Catalans if he chooses."

Danglars took advantage of Caderousse's temper at the moment, to take him off towards Marseilles by the Porte Saint-Victor, staggering as he went.

When they had advanced about twenty yards, Danglars looked back and saw Fernand stoop, pick up the crumpled paper, and putting it into his pocket then rush out of the arbor towards Pillon.

"Well," said Caderousse, "why, what a lie he told! He said he was going to the Catalans, and he is going to the city. Hallo, Fernand!"

"Oh, you don't see straight," said Danglars; "he's gone right enough."

"Well," said Caderousse, "I should have said not—how treacherous wine is!"

"Come, come," said Danglars to himself, "now the thing is at work and it will affect its purpose unassisted."

Chapter 5. The Marriage-Feast.

The morning's sun rose clear and resplendent, touching the foamy waves into a network of ruby-tinted light.

The feast had been made ready on the second floor at La Reserve, with whose arbor the reader is already familiar. The apartment destined for the purpose was spacious and lighted by a number of windows, over each of which was written in golden letters for some inexplicable reason the name of one of the principal cities of France; beneath these windows a wooden balcony extended the entire length of the house. And although the entertainment was fixed for twelve o'clock, an hour previous to that time the balcony was filled with impatient and expectant guests, consisting of the favored part of the crew of the *Pharaon*, and other personal friends of the bride-groom, the whole of whom had arrayed themselves in their choicest costumes, in order to do greater honor to the occasion.

Various rumors were afloat to the effect that the owners of the *Pharaon* had promised to attend the nuptial feast; but all seemed unanimous in doubting that an act of such rare and exceeding condescension could possibly be intended.

Danglars, however, who now made his appearance, accompanied by Caderousse, effectually confirmed the report, stating that he had recently conversed with M. Morrel, who had himself assured him of his intention to dine at La Reserve.

In fact, a moment later M. Morrel appeared and was saluted with an enthusiastic burst of applause from the crew of the *Pharaon*, who hailed the visit of the shipowner as a sure indication that the man whose wedding feast he thus delighted to honor would ere long be first in command of the ship; and as Dantes was universally beloved on board his vessel, the sailors put no restraint on their tumultuous joy at finding that the opinion and choice of their superiors so exactly coincided with their own.

With the entrance of M. Morrel, Danglars and Caderousse were dispatched in search of the bride-groom to convey to him the intelligence of the arrival of the important personage whose coming had created such a lively sensation, and to beseech him to make haste.

Danglars and Caderousse set off upon their errand at full speed; but ere they had gone many steps they perceived a group advancing towards them, composed of the betrothed pair, a party of young girls in attendance on the bride, by whose side walked Dantes' father; the whole brought up by Fernand, whose lips wore their usual sinister smile.

Neither Mercedes nor Edmond observed the strange expression of his countenance; they were so happy that they were conscious only of the sunshine and the presence of each other.

Having acquitted themselves of their errand, and exchanged a hearty shake of the hand with Edmond, Danglars and Caderousse took their places beside Fernand and old Dantes,—the latter of whom attracted universal notice. The old man was attired in a suit of glistening watered silk, trimmed with steel buttons, beautifully cut and polished. His thin but wiry legs were arrayed in a pair of richly embroidered clocked stockings, evidently of English manufacture, while from his three-cornered hat depended a long streaming knot of white and blue ribbons. Thus he came along, supporting himself on a curiously carved stick, his aged countenance lit up with happiness, looking for all the world like one of the aged dandies of 1796, parading the newly opened gardens of the Tuileries and Luxembourg. Beside him glided Caderousse, whose desire to partake of the good things provided for the wedding-party had induced him to become reconciled to the Dantes, father and son, although there still lingered in his mind a faint and unperfected recollection of the events of the preceding night; just as the brain retains on waking in the morning the dim and misty outline of a dream.

As Danglars approached the disappointed lover, he cast on him a look of deep meaning, while Fernand, as he slowly paced behind the happy pair, who seemed, in their own unmixed content, to have entirely forgotten that such a being as himself existed, was pale and abstracted; occasionally, however, a deep flush would overspread his countenance, and a nervous contraction distort his features, while, with an agitated and restless gaze, he would glance in the direction of Marseilles, like one who either anticipated or foresaw some great and important event.

Dantes himself was simply, but becomingly, clad in the dress peculiar to the merchant service—a costume somewhat between a military and a civil garb; and with his fine countenance, radiant with joy and happiness, a more perfect specimen of manly beauty could scarcely be imagined.

Lovely as the Greek girls of Cyprus or Chios, Mercedes boasted the same bright flashing eyes of jet, and ripe, round, coral lips. She moved with the light, free step of an Arlesienne or an Andalusian. One more practiced in the arts of great cities would have hid her blushes beneath a veil, or, at least, have cast down her thickly fringed lashes, so as to have concealed the liquid lustre of her animated eyes; but, on the contrary, the delighted girl looked around her with a smile that seemed to say: "If you are my friends, rejoice with me, for I am very happy."

As soon as the bridal party came in sight of La Reserve, M. Morrel descended and came forth to meet it, followed by the soldiers and sailors there assembled, to whom he had repeated the promise already given, that Dantes should be the successor to the late Captain Leclere. Edmond, at the approach of his patron, respectfully placed the arm of his affianced bride within that of M. Morrel, who, forthwith conducting her up the flight of wooden steps leading to the chamber in which the feast was prepared, was gayly followed by the guests, beneath whose heavy tread the slight structure creaked and groaned for the space of several minutes.

"Father," said Mercedes, stopping when she had reached the centre of the table, "sit, I pray you, on my right hand; on my left I will place him who has ever been as a brother to me," pointing with a soft and gentle smile to Fernand; but her words and look seemed to inflict the direst torture on him, for his lips became ghastly pale, and even beneath the dark hue of his complexion the blood might be seen retreating as though some sudden pang drove it back to the heart.

During this time, Dantes, at the opposite side of the table, had been occupied in similarly placing his most honored guests. M. Morrel was seated at his right hand, Danglars at his left; while, at a sign from Edmond, the rest of the company ranged themselves as they found it most agreeable.

Then they began to pass around the dusky, piquant, Arlesian sausages, and lobsters in their dazzling red cuirasses, prawns of large size and brilliant color, the echinus with its prickly outside and dainty morsel within, the clovis, esteemed by the epicures of the South as more than rivaling the exquisite flavor of the oyster,—all the delicacies, in fact, that are cast up by the wash of waters on the sandy beach, and styled by the grateful fishermen "fruits of the sea."

"A pretty silence truly!" said the old father of the bride-groom, as he carried to his lips a glass of wine of the hue and brightness of the topaz, and which had just been placed before Mercedes herself.

"Now, would anybody think that this room contained a happy, merry party, who desire nothing better than to laugh and dance the hours away?"

"Ah," sighed Caderousse, "a man cannot always feel happy because he is about to be married."

"The truth is," replied Dantes, "that I am too happy for noisy mirth; if that is what you meant by your observation, my worthy friend, you are right; joy takes a strange effect at times, it seems to oppress us almost the same as sorrow."

Danglars looked towards Fernand, whose excitable nature received and betrayed each fresh impression.

"Why, what ails you?" asked he of Edmond. "Do you fear any approaching evil? I should say that you were the happiest man alive at this instant."

"And that is the very thing that alarms me," returned Dantes. "Man does not appear to me to be intended to enjoy felicity so unmixed; happiness is like the enchanted palaces we read of in our childhood, where fierce, fiery dragons defend the entrance and approach; and monsters of all shapes and kinds, requiring to be overcome ere victory is ours. I own that I am lost in wonder to find myself promoted to an honor of which I feel myself unworthy—that of being the husband of Mercedes."

"Nay, nay!" cried Caderousse, smiling, "you have not attained that honor yet. Mercedes is not yet your wife. Just assume the tone and manner of a husband, and see how she will remind you that your hour is not yet come!"

The bride blushed, while Fernand, restless and uneasy, seemed to start at every fresh sound, and from time to time wiped away the large drops of perspiration that gathered on his brow.

"Well, never mind that, neighbor Caderousse; it is not worthwhile to contradict me for such a trifle as that. 'Tis true that Mercedes is not actually my wife; but," added he, drawing out his watch, "in an hour and a half she will be."

A general exclamation of surprise ran round the table, with the exception of the elder Dantes, whose laugh displayed the still perfect beauty of his large white teeth. Mercedes looked pleased and gratified, while Fernand grasped the handle of his knife with a convulsive clutch.

"In an hour?" inquired Danglars, turning pale. "How is that, my friend?"

"Why, thus it is," replied Dantes. "Thanks to the influence of M. Morrel, to whom, next to my father, I owe every blessing I enjoy, every difficulty his been removed. We have purchased permission to waive the usual delay; and at half-past two o'clock the mayor of Marseilles will be waiting for us at the city hall. Now, as a quarter-past one has already struck, I do not consider I have asserted too much in saying that, in another hour and thirty minutes Mercedes will have become Madame Dantes."

Fernand closed his eyes, a burning sensation passed across his brow, and he was compelled to support himself by the table to prevent his falling from his chair; but in spite of all his efforts, he could not refrain from uttering a deep groan, which, however, was lost amid the noisy felicitations of the company.

"Upon my word," cried the old man, "you make short work of this kind of affair. Arrived here only yesterday morning, and married to-day at three o'clock! Commend me to a sailor for going the quick way to work!"

"But," asked Danglars, in a timid tone, "how did you manage about the other formalities—the contract—the settlement?"

"The contract," answered Dantes, laughingly, "it didn't take long to fix that. Mercedes has no fortune; I have none to settle on her. So, you see, our papers were quickly written out, and certainly do not come very expensive." This joke elicited a fresh burst of applause.

"So that what we presumed to be merely the betrothal feast turns out to be the actual wedding dinner!" said Danglars.

"No, no," answered Dantes; "don't imagine I am going to put you off in that shabby manner. To-morrow morning I start for Paris; four days to go, and the same to return, with one day to discharge the commission entrusted to me, is all the time I shall be absent. I shall be back here by the first of March, and on the second I give my real marriage feast."

This prospect of fresh festivity redoubled the hilarity of the guests to such a degree, that the elder Dantes, who, at the commencement of the repast, had commented upon the silence that prevailed, now found it difficult, amid the general din of voices, to obtain a moment's tranquility in which to drink to the health and prosperity of the bride and bride-groom.

Dantes, perceiving the affectionate eagerness of his father, responded by a look of grateful pleasure; while Mercedes glanced at the clock and made an expressive gesture to Edmond.

Around the table reined that noisy hilarity which usually prevails at such a time among people sufficiently free from the demands of social position not to feel the trammels of etiquette. Such as at the commencement of the repast had not been able to seat themselves according to their inclination rose unceremoniously, and sought out more agreeable companions. Everybody talked at once, without waiting for a reply and each one seemed to be contented with expressing his or her own thoughts.

Fernand's paleness appeared to have communicated itself to Danglars. As for Fernand himself, he seemed to be enduring the tortures of the damned; unable to rest, he was among the first to quit the table, and, as though seeking to avoid the hilarious mirth that rose in such deafening sounds, he continued, in utter silence, to pace the farther end of the salon.

Caderousse approached him just as Danglars, whom Fernand seemed most anxious to avoid, had joined him in a corner of the room.

"Upon my word," said Caderousse, from whose mind the friendly treatment of Dantes, united with the effect of the excellent wine he had partaken of, had effaced every feeling of envy or jealousy at Dantes' good fortune,—"upon my word, Dantes is a downright good fellow, and when I see him sitting there beside his pretty wife that is so soon to be, I cannot help thinking it would have been a great pity to have served him that trick you were planning yesterday."

"Oh, there was no harm meant," answered Danglars; "at first I certainly did feel somewhat uneasy as to what Fernand might be tempted to do; but when I saw how completely he had mastered his feelings, even so far as to become one of his rival's attendants, I knew there was no further cause for apprehension." Caderousse looked full at Fernand—he was ghastly pale.

"Certainly," continued Danglars, "the sacrifice was no trifling one, when the beauty of the bride is concerned. Upon my soul, that future captain of mine is a lucky dog! Gad, I only wish he would let me take his place."

"Shall we not set forth?" asked the sweet, silvery voice of Mercedes; "two o'clock has just struck, and you know we are expected in a quarter of an hour."

"To be sure!—to be sure!" cried Dantes, eagerly quitting the table; "let us go directly!"

His words were re-echoed by the whole party, with vociferous cheers.

At this moment Danglars, who had been incessantly observing every change in Fernand's look and manner, saw him stagger and fall back, with an almost convulsive spasm, against a seat placed near one of the open windows. At the same instant his ear caught a sort of indistinct sound on the stairs, followed by the measured tread of soldiery, with the clanking of swords and military accoutrements; then came a hum and buzz as of many voices, so as to deaden even the noisy mirth of the bridal party, among whom a vague feeling of curiosity and apprehension quelled every disposition to talk, and almost instantaneously the most deathlike stillness prevailed.

The sounds drew nearer. Three blows were struck upon the panel of the door. The company looked at each other in consternation.

"I demand admittance," said a loud voice outside the room, "in the name of the law!" As no attempt was made to prevent it, the door was opened, and a magistrate, wearing his official scarf, presented himself, followed by four soldiers and a corporal. Uneasiness now yielded to the most extreme dread on the part of those present.

"May I venture to inquire the reason of this unexpected visit?" said M. Morrel, addressing the magistrate, whom he evidently knew; "there is doubtless some mistake easily explained."

"If it be so," replied the magistrate, "rely upon every reparation being made; meanwhile, I am the bearer of an order of arrest, and although I most reluctantly perform the task assigned me, it must, nevertheless, be fulfilled. Who among the persons here assembled answers to the name of Edmond Dantes?" Every eye was turned towards the young man who, spite of the agitation he could not but feel, advanced with dignity, and said, in a firm voice, "I am he; what is your pleasure with me?"

"Edmond Dantes," replied the magistrate, "I arrest you in the name of the law!"

"Me!" repeated Edmond, slightly changing color, "and wherefore, I pray?"

"I cannot inform you, but you will be duly acquainted with the reasons that have rendered such a step necessary at the preliminary examination."

M. Morrel felt that further resistance or remonstrance was useless. He saw before him an officer delegated to enforce the law, and perfectly well knew that it would be as unavailing to seek pity from a magistrate decked with his official scarf, as to address a petition to some cold marble effigy. Old Dantes, however, sprang forward. There are situations which the heart of a father or a mother cannot be made to understand. He prayed and supplicated in terms so moving, that even the officer was touched, and, although firm in his duty, he kindly said, "My worthy friend, let me beg of you to calm your apprehensions. Your son has probably neglected some prescribed form or attention in registering his cargo, and it is more than probable he will be set at liberty directly he has given the information required, whether touching the health of his crew, or the value of his freight."

"What is the meaning of all this?" inquired Caderousse, frowningly, of Danglars, who had assumed an air of utter surprise.

"How can I tell you?" replied he; "I am, like yourself, utterly bewildered at all that is going on, and cannot in the least make out what it is about." Caderousse then looked around for Fernand, but he had disappeared.

The scene of the previous night now came back to his mind with startling clearness. The painful catastrophe he had just witnessed appeared effectually to have rent away the veil which the intoxication of the evening before had raised between himself and his memory.

"So, so," said he, in a hoarse and choking voice, to Danglars, "this, then, I suppose, is a part of the trick you were concerting yesterday? All I can say is, that if it be so, 'tis an ill turn, and well deserves to bring double evil on those who have projected it."

"Nonsense," returned Danglars, "I tell you again I have nothing whatever to do with it; besides, you know very well that I tore the paper to pieces."

"No, you did not!" answered Caderousse, "you merely threw it by—I saw it lying in a corner."

"Hold your tongue, you fool!—what should you know about it?—why, you were drunk!"

"Where is Fernand?" inquired Caderousse.

"How do I know?" replied Danglars; "gone, as every prudent man ought to be, to look after his own affairs, most likely. Never mind where he is, let you and I go and see what is to be done for our poor friends."

During this conversation, Dantes, after having exchanged a cheerful shake of the hand with all his sympathizing friends, had surrendered himself to the officer sent to arrest him, merely saying, "Make yourselves quite easy, my good fellows, there is some little mistake to clear up, that's all, depend upon it; and very likely I may not have to go so far as the prison to effect that."

"Oh, to be sure!" responded Danglars, who had now approached the group, "nothing more than a mistake, I feel quite certain."

Dantes descended the staircase, preceded by the magistrate, and followed by the soldiers. A carriage awaited him at the door; he got in, followed by two soldiers and the magistrate, and the vehicle drove off towards Marseilles.

"Adieu, adieu, dearest Edmond!" cried Mercedes, stretching out her arms to him from the balcony.

The prisoner heard the cry, which sounded like the sob of a brokenheart, and leaning from the coach he called out, "Good-by, Mercedes—we shall soon meet again!" Then the vehicle disappeared round one of the turnings of Fort Saint Nicholas.

"Wait for me here, all of you!" cried M. Morrel; "I will take the first conveyance I find, and hurry to Marseilles, whence I will bring you word how all is going on."

"That's right!" exclaimed a multitude of voices, "go, and return as quickly as you can!"

This second departure was followed by a long and fearful state of terrified silence on the part of those who were left behind. The old father and Mercedes remained for some time apart, each absorbed in grief; but at length the two poor victims of the same blow raised their eyes, and with a simultaneous burst of feeling rushed into each other's arms.

Meanwhile Fernand made his appearance, poured out for himself a glass of water with a trembling hand; then hastily swallowing it, went to sit down at the first vacant place, and this was, by mere chance, placed next to the seat on which poor

Mercedes had fallen half fainting, when released from the warm and affectionate embrace of old Dantes. Instinctively Fernand drew back his chair.

"He is the cause of all this misery—I am quite sure of it," whispered Caderousse, who had never taken his eyes off Fernand, to Danglars.

"I don't think so," answered the other; "he's too stupid to imagine such a scheme. I only hope the mischief will fall upon the head of whoever wrought it."

"You don't mention those who aided and abetted the deed," said Caderousse.

"Surely," answered Danglars, "one cannot be held responsible for every chance arrow shot into the air."

"You can, indeed, when the arrow lights point downward on somebody's head."

Meantime the subject of the arrest was being canvassed in every different form.

"What think you, Danglars," said one of the party, turning towards him, "of this event?"

"Why," replied he, "I think it just possible Dantes may have been detected with some trifling article on board ship considered here as contraband."

"But how could he have done so without your knowledge, Danglars, since you are the ship's supercargo?"

"Why, as for that, I could only know what I was told respecting the merchandise with which the vessel was laden. I know she was loaded with cotton, and that she took in her freight at Alexandria from Pastret's warehouse, and at Smyrna from Pascal's; that is all I was obliged to know, and I beg I may not be asked for any further particulars."

"Now I recollect," said the afflicted old father; "my poor boy told me yesterday he had got a small case of coffee, and another of tobacco for me!"

"There, you see," exclaimed Danglars. "Now the mischief is out; depend upon it the custom-house people went rummaging about the ship in our absence, and discovered poor Dantes' hidden treasures."

Mercedes, however, paid no heed to this explanation of her lover's arrest. Her grief, which she had hitherto tried to restrain, now burst out in a violent fit of hysterical sobbing.

"Come, come," said the old man, "be comforted, my poor child; there is still hope!"

"Hope!" repeated Danglars.

"Hope!" faintly murmured Fernand, but the word seemed to die away on his pale agitated lips, and a convulsive spasm passed over his countenance.

"Good news! good news!" shouted forth one of the party stationed in the balcony on the lookout. "Here comes M. Morrel back. No doubt, now, we shall hear that our friend is released!"

Mercedes and the old man rushed to meet the shipowner and greeted him at the door. He was very pale.

"What news?" exclaimed a general burst of voices.

"Alas, my friends," replied M. Morrel, with a mournful shake of his head, "the thing has assumed a more serious aspect than I expected."

"Oh, indeed—indeed, sir, he is innocent!" sobbed forth Mercedes.

"That I believe!" answered M. Morrel; "but still he is charged—"

"With what?" inquired the elder Dantes.

"With being an agent of the Bonapartist faction!" Many of our readers may be able to recollect how formidable such an accusation became in the period at which our story is dated.

A despairing cry escaped the pale lips of Mercedes; the old man sank into a chair.

"Ah, Danglars!" whispered Caderousse, "you have deceived me—the trick you spoke of last night has been played; but I cannot suffer a poor old man or an innocent girl to die of grief through your fault. I am determined to tell them all about it."

"Be silent, you simpleton!" cried Danglars, grasping him by the arm, "or I will not answer even for your own safety. Who can tell whether Dantes be innocent or guilty? The vessel did touch at Elba, where he quitted it, and passed a whole day in the island. Now, should any letters or other documents of a compromising character be found upon him, will it not be taken for granted that all who uphold him are his accomplices?"

With the rapid instinct of selfishness, Caderousse readily perceived the solidity of this mode of reasoning; he gazed, doubtfully, wistfully, on Danglars, and then caution supplanted generosity.

"Suppose we wait a while, and see what comes of it," said he, casting a bewildered look on his companion.

"To be sure!" answered Danglars. "Let us wait, by all means. If he be innocent, of course he will be set at liberty; if guilty, why, it is no use involving ourselves in a conspiracy."

"Let us go, then. I cannot stay here any longer."

"With all my heart!" replied Danglars, pleased to find the other so tractable. "Let us take ourselves out of the way, and leave things for the present to take their course."

After their departure, Fernand, who had now again become the friend and protector of Mercedes, led the girl to her home, while the friends of Dantes conducted the now half-fainting man back to his abode.

The rumor of Edmond's arrest as a Bonapartist agent was not slow in circulating throughout the city.

"Could you ever have credited such a thing, my dear Danglars?" asked M. Morrel, as, on his return to the port for the purpose of gleaning fresh tidings of Dantes, from M. de Villefort, the assistant procureur, he overtook his supercargo and Caderousse. "Could you have believed such a thing possible?"

"Why, you know I told you," replied Danglars, "that I considered the circumstance of his having anchored at the Island of Elba as a very suspicious circumstance."

"And did you mention these suspicions to any person beside myself?"

"Certainly not!" returned Danglars. Then added in a low whisper, "You understand that, on account of your uncle, M. Policar Morrel, who served under the other government, and who does not altogether conceal what he thinks on the subject, you are strongly suspected of regretting the abdication of Napoleon. I should have feared to injure both Edmond and yourself, had I divulged my own apprehensions to a soul. I am too well aware that though a subordinate, like myself, is bound to acquaint the ship-owner with everything that occurs, there are many things he ought most carefully to conceal from all else."

"'Tis well, Danglars—'tis well!" replied M. Morrel. "You are a worthy fellow; and I had already thought of your interests in the event of poor Edmond having become captain of the *Pharaon*."

"Is it possible you were so kind?"

"Yes, indeed; I had previously inquired of Dantes what was his opinion of you, and if he should have any reluctance to continue you in your post, for somehow I have perceived a sort of coolness between you."

"And what was his reply?"

"That he certainly did think he had given you offence in an affair which he merely referred to without entering into particulars, but that whoever possessed the good opinion and confidence of the ship's owner would have his preference also."

"The hypocrite!" murmured Danglars.

"Poor Dantes!" said Caderousse. "No one can deny his being a noble-hearted young fellow."

"But meanwhile," continued M. Morrel, "here is the *Pharaon* without a captain."

"Oh," replied Danglars, "since we cannot leave this port for the next three months, let us hope that ere the expiration of that period Dantes will be set at liberty."

"No doubt; but in the meantime?"

"I am entirely at your service, M. Morrel," answered Danglars. "You know that I am as capable of managing a ship as the most experienced captain in the service; and it will be so far advantageous to you to accept my services, that upon Edmond's release from prison no further change will be requisite on board the *Pharaon* than for Dantes and myself each to resume our respective posts."

"Thanks, Danglars—that will smooth over all difficulties. I fully authorize you at once to assume the command of the *Pharaon*, and look carefully to the unloading of her freight. Private misfortunes must never be allowed to interfere with business."

"Be easy on that score, M. Morrel; but do you think we shall be permitted to see our poor Edmond?"

"I will let you know that directly I have seen M. de Villefort, whom I shall endeavor to interest in Edmond's favor. I am aware he is a furious royalist; but, in spite of that, and of his being king's attorney, he is a man like ourselves, and I fancy not a bad sort of one."

"Perhaps not," replied Danglars; "but I hear that he is ambitious, and that's rather against him."

"Well, well," returned M. Morrel, "we shall see. But now hasten on board, I will join you there ere long." So saying, the worthy ship-owner quitted the two allies, and proceeded in the direction of the Palais de Justice.

"You see," said Danglars, addressing Caderousse, "the turn things have taken. Do you still feel any desire to stand up in his defense?"

"Not the slightest, but yet it seems to me a shocking thing that a mere joke should lead to such consequences."

"But who perpetrated that joke, let me ask? neither you nor myself, but Fernand; you knew very well that I threw the paper into a corner of the room—indeed, I fancied I had destroyed it."

"Oh, no," replied Caderousse, "that I can answer for, you did not. I only wish I could see it now as plainly as I saw it lying all crushed and crumpled in a corner of the arbor."

"Well, then, if you did, depend upon it, Fernand picked it up, and either copied it or caused it to be copied; perhaps, even, he did not take the trouble of recopying it. And now I think of it, by Heavens, he may have sent the letter itself! Fortunately, for me, the handwriting was disguised."

"Then you were aware of Dantes being engaged in a conspiracy?"

"Not I. As I before said, I thought the whole thing was a joke, nothing more. It seems, however, that I have unconsciously stumbled upon the truth."

"Still," argued Caderousse, "I would give a great deal if nothing of the kind had happened; or, at least, that I had had no hand in it. You will see, Danglars, that it will turn out an unlucky job for both of us."

"Nonsense! If any harm come of it, it should fall on the guilty person; and that, you know, is Fernand. How can we be implicated in any way? All we have got to do is, to keep our own counsel, and remain perfectly quiet; not breathing a word to any living soul; and you will see that the storm will pass away without in the least affecting us."

"Amen!" responded Caderousse, waving his hand in token of adieu to Danglars, and bending his steps towards the Allees de Meillan, moving his head to and fro, and muttering as he went, after the manner of one whose mind was overcharged with one absorbing idea.

"So far, then," said Danglars, mentally, "all has gone as I would have it. I am, temporarily, commander of the *Pharaon*, with the certainty of being permanently so, if that fool of a Caderousse can be persuaded to hold his tongue. My only fear is the chance of Dantes being released. But, there, he is in the hands of Justice; and," added he with a smile, "she will take her own." So saying, he leaped into a boat, desiring to be rowed on board the *Pharaon*, where M. Morrel had agreed to meet him.

Chapter 6. The Deputy Procureur du Roi.

In one of the aristocratic mansions built by Puget in the Rue du Grand Cours opposite the Medusa fountain, a second marriage feast was being celebrated, almost at the same hour with the nuptial repast given by Dantes. In this case, however, although the occasion of the entertainment was similar, the company was strikingly dissimilar. Instead of a rude mixture of sailors, soldiers, and those belonging to the humblest grade of life, the present assembly was composed of the very flower of Marseilles society,—magistrates who had resigned their office during the usurper's reign; officers who had deserted from the imperial army and joined forces with Conde; and younger members of families, brought up to hate and execrate the man whom five years of exile would convert into a martyr, and fifteen of restoration elevate to the rank of a god.

The guests were still at table, and the heated and energetic conversation that prevailed betrayed the violent and vindictive passions that then agitated each dweller of the South, where unhappily, for five centuries religious strife had long given increased bitterness to the violence of party feeling.

The emperor, now king of the petty Island of Elba, after having held sovereign sway over one-half of the world, counting as his subjects a small population of five or six thousand souls,—after having been accustomed to hear the "Vive Napoleons" of a hundred and twenty millions of human beings, uttered in ten different languages,—was looked upon here as a ruined man, separated forever from any fresh connection with France or claim to her throne.

The magistrates freely discussed their political views; the military part of the company talked unreservedly of Moscow and Leipsic, while the women commented on the divorce of Josephine.

It was not over the downfall of the man, but over the defeat of the Napoleonic idea, that they rejoiced, and in this they foresaw for themselves the bright and cheering prospect of a revivified political existence.

An old man, decorated with the cross of Saint Louis, now rose and proposed the health of King Louis XVIII. It was the Marquis de Saint-Meran. This toast, recalling at once the patient exile of Hartwell and the peace-loving King of France, excited universal enthusiasm; glasses were elevated in the air a l'Anglais, and the ladies, snatching their bouquets from their fair bosoms, strewed the table with their floral treasures. In a word, an almost poetical fervor prevailed.

"Ah," said the Marquise de Saint-Meran, a woman with a stern, forbidding eye, though still noble and distinguished in appearance, despite her fifty years—"ah, these revolutionists, who have driven us from those very possessions they afterwards purchased for a mere trifle during the Reign of Terror, would be compelled to own, were they here, that all true devotion was on our side, since we were content to follow the fortunes of a falling monarch, while they, on the contrary, made their fortune by worshipping the rising sun; yes, yes, they could not help admitting that the king, for whom we sacrificed rank, wealth, and station was truly our 'Louis the well-beloved,' while their wretched usurper his been, and ever will be, to them their evil genius, their 'Napoleon the accursed.' Am I not right, Villefort?"

Villefort had no ear for the evening's conversation, his attention attuned to his betrothed and her hand beneath the crisp tablecloth. Her smooth white fingers undid his breeches and nothing on Earth could have drawn his attention away from her movements. The conversation continued around them as she took his flaccid member in hand while he stifled an inhale, almost giving the game away. She worked him slow and steady, allowing him time to grow rigid, the blood pounding in his ears as slid her hand in sharp vertical motions. The dinner party swirled around them, and this was the perfect way to celebrate his betrothal to one of the most beautiful and innocent maids at the height of social standing.

"Are you enjoying the celebration?" Renee whispered for him alone, careful to keep the deep timbre of her voice low; a breathy tingle perfused each word she spoke against his neck.

"My lady, I do believe it is one of the best soirees I have had the pleasure of attending." He smirked at her, allowing her to see the jest, but she punished him, dragging her hand back up and down the length of him again. A hiss escaped his closed lips but glancing around proved no one noticed what the young Renee did beneath the table. He reached down and gently untangled her clutch.

Villefort refastened his pants and Renee re-donned her dinner glove under the cover of the tablecloth.

"Mademoiselle, might I have the pleasure of speaking to you alone?" Villefort asked, somewhat loud, drawing the table's attention.

"Of course, Monsieur." Renee bowed her head in acquiescence, then smiled and nodded assurances at her mother and father before quietly following Villefort out the nearest door. He seized her just as the clock ticked like a cannon blast in complete silence. His hands lifted her skirts and found her seeping center in only moments. This was how it had always been between them, since the first time her quiet grin ensnared him and then the first night she snuck to an alcove to lie in his arms.

"Why, Mademoiselle, I do believe I might help you with your little problem." Villefort rubbed his thumb across her pearl, her skirts wrinkling, crushed between him and the door.

"Monsieur, please, I beg you, ease me."

"Oh, my love, I will, once you prove to me how much you want it." With those words, Villefort released Renee and pushed her hard to her knees. As she bent down she made quick work of the elbow length gloves encasing her slender arms. Under usual circumstances she might have removed her gloves in an almost sensual fashion and Villefort would have enjoyed watching her careful movements. Having been in this position many times before, Renee knew exactly what he enjoyed. She gripped him hard, a painful grip most men might crumple under, but he did not. Her lips closed around him, and he delved his hand into the bottom of her chignon, even then careful not to undo something they could not repair in haste.

"Does the taste of me please you, Renee?"

She made an unintelligible noise and continued the ministrations of her mouth as he guided her head with his hand.

"I have yet to understand how you can play such an innocent in public yet outside the parlors and ballrooms you are wanton and completely unapologetic about it. I am honestly more concerned with the fact that no one speaks of it—none of the men in court, that is."

Renee lifted her head. "What leads you to the conclusion I have had many men? Perhaps I read too many novels?" Her raised eyebrow and the way her eyes suggested more than she spoke, was his undoing. He lifted her bodily by the arms and pushed her back against the door. They had made love quite a few times but never fucked, never experienced this raw, sensual passion that ignited his blood and turned her knees to gelatin. Each finger bit into the tender flesh of her hip as he pushed inside her already wet, hot center.

She writhed in his hands, small and slight, which never failed to surprise him, her costume making up the bulk of her figure to anyone who had not the pleasure of getting beneath them.

"Renee." Villefort exhaled her name as he bent his knees and pumped up into her with more force. Each thrust brought on new sensations, a tingling awareness that the end was near. At this moment, no part of their bodies could be close enough, touching quiet enough, and as much skin was upon skin as possible in the rushed circumstances. The clutching and groping only increased until Villefort felt Renee's body spasm around him; this proved the catalyst that sent him over the edge and into oblivion. In the moments after completion there always seemed to be a heavy silence, filled only with the sound of a couple's mingled breaths and heavy heartbeats. Villefort and Renee shared a moment such as this, joined together through mashed clothes and silent panting. Even now they both knew that their relationship could grow to love from the infinite spark of their lustful natures.

As quickly as possible while maintaining dignity, they untangled their limbs and arranged their clothes according to decorum. Villefore even checked the pins underneath her hair, ensuring not a strand was out of place. In the dim lighting of the antechamber, Renee's skin glowed and Villefort did not resist the urge to trace a finger down the side of her face. Touching in public was not something a well born couple did and he could hardly control himself when she was near. Her coquettish smile only made him ready to take her against the door again but if they were gone too long it might be remarked upon and Villefort would not have his bride besmirched. The dinner party was as they left it, joyous and filled with revelry at their impending nuptials. Villefort helped Renee into her chair and took his own, turning to address the marquise.

"I beg your pardon, Madame. I really must pray you to excuse me, but—in truth—I was not attending to the conversation."

"Marquise, marquise!" interposed the old nobleman who had proposed the toast, "let the young people alone; let me tell you, on one's wedding day there are more agreeable subjects of conversation than dry politics."

"Never mind, dearest mother," said a young and lovely girl, with a profusion of light brown hair, and eyes that seemed to float in liquid crystal, "'tis all my fault for seizing upon M. de Villefort, so as to prevent his listening to what you said. But there—now take him—he is your own for as long as you like. M. Villefort, I beg to remind you my mother speaks to you."

"If the marquise will deign to repeat the words I but imperfectly caught, I shall be delighted to answer," said M. de Villefort.

"Never mind, Renee," replied the marquise, with a look of tenderness that seemed out of keeping with her harsh dry features; but, however all other feelings may be withered in a woman's nature, there is always one bright smiling spot in the desert of her heart, and that is the shrine of maternal love. "I forgive you. What I was saying, Villefort, was, that the Bonapartists had not our sincerity, enthusiasm, or devotion."

"They had, however, what supplied the place of those fine qualities," replied the young man, "and that was fanaticism. Napoleon is the Mahomet of the West, and is worshipped by his commonplace but ambitions followers, not only as a leader and lawgiver, but also as the personification of equality."

"He!" cried the marquise: "Napoleon the type of equality! For mercy's sake, then, what would you call Robespierre? Come, come, do not strip the latter of his just rights to bestow them on the Corsican, who, to my mind, has usurped quite enough."

"Nay, Madame; I would place each of these heroes on his right pedestal—that of Robespierre on his scaffold in the Place Louis Quinze; that of Napoleon on the column of the Place Vendome. The only difference consists in the opposite character of the equality advocated by these two men; one is the equality that elevates, the other is the equality that degrades; one brings a king within reach of the guillotine, the other elevates the people to a level with the throne. Observe," said Villefort, smiling, "I do not mean to deny that both these men were revolutionary scoundrels, and that the 9th Thermidor and the 4th of April, in the year 1814, were lucky days for France, worthy of being gratefully remembered by every friend to monarchy and civil order; and that explains how it comes to pass that, fallen, as I trust he is forever, Napoleon has still retained a train of parasitical satellites. Still, Marquise, it has been so with other usurpers—Cromwell, for instance, who was not half so bad as Napoleon, had his partisans and advocates."

"Do you know, Villefort, that you are talking in a most dreadfully revolutionary strain? But I excuse it, it is impossible to expect the son of a Girondin to be free from a small spice of the old leaven." A deep crimson suffused the countenance of Villefort.

"'Tis true, Madame," answered he, "that my father was a Girondin, but he was not among the number of those who voted for the king's death; he was an equal sufferer with yourself during the Reign of Terror, and had well-nigh lost his head on the same scaffold on which your father perished."

"True," replied the marquise, without wincing in the slightest degree at the tragic remembrance thus called up; "but bear in mind, if you please, that our respective parents underwent persecution and proscription from diametrically opposite principles; in proof of which I may remark, that while my family remained among the staunchest adherents of the exiled princes, your father lost no time in joining the new government; and that while the Citizen Noirtier was a Girondin, the Count Noirtier became a senator."

"Dear Mother," interposed Renee, "you know very well it was agreed that all these disagreeable reminiscences should forever be laid aside."

"Suffer me, also, Madame," replied Villefort, "to add my earnest request to Mademoiselle de Saint-Meran's, that you will kindly allow the veil of oblivion to cover and conceal the past. What avails recrimination over matters wholly past recall? For my own part, I have laid aside even the name of my father, and altogether disown his political principles. He was—nay, probably may still be—a Bonapartist, and is called Noirtier; I, on the contrary, am a staunch royalist, and style myself de Villefort. Let what may remain of revolutionary sap exhaust itself and die away with the old trunk, and condescend only to regard the young shoot which has started up at a distance from the parent tree, without having the power, any more than the wish, to separate entirely from the stock from which it sprung."

"Bravo, Villefort!" cried the marquis; "excellently well said! Come, now, I have hopes of obtaining what I have been for years endeavoring to persuade the marquise to promise; namely, a perfect amnesty and forgetfulness of the past."

"With all my heart," replied the marquise; "let the past be forever forgotten. I promise you it affords me as little pleasure to revive it as it does you. All I ask is, that Villefort will be firm and inflexible for the future in his political principles. Remember, also, Villefort, that we have pledged ourselves to his majesty for your fealty and strict loyalty, and that at our recommendation the king consented to forget the past, as I do" (and here she extended to him her hand)—"as I now do at your entreaty. But bear in mind, that should there fall in your way anyone guilty of conspiring against the government, you will be so much the more bound to visit the offence with rigorous punishment, as it is known you belong to a suspected family."

"Alas, Madame," returned Villefort, "my profession, as well as the times in which we live, compels me to be severe. I have already successfully conducted several public prosecutions, and brought the offenders to merited punishment. But we have not done with the thing yet."

"Do you, indeed, think so?" inquired the marquise.

"I am, at least, fearful of it. Napoleon, in the Island of Elba, is too near France, and his proximity keeps up the hopes of his partisans. Marseilles is filled with half-pay officers, who are daily, under one frivolous pretext or other, getting up quarrels with the royalists; from hence arise continual and fatal duels among the higher classes of persons, and assassinations in the lower."

"You have heard, perhaps," said the Comte de Salvieux, one of M. de Saint-Meran's oldest friends, and chamberlain to the

Comte d'Artois, "that the Holy Alliance purpose removing him from thence?"

"Yes; they were talking about it when we left Paris," said M. de Saint-Meran; "and where is it decided to transfer him?"

"To Saint Helena."

"For heaven's sake, where is that?" asked the marquise.

"An island situated on the other side of the equator, at least two thousand leagues from here," replied the count.

"So much the better. As Villefort observes, it is a great act of folly to have left such a man between Corsica, where he was born, and Naples, of which his brother-in-law is king, and face to face with Italy, the sovereignty of which he coveted for his son."

"Unfortunately," said Villefort, "there are the treaties of 1814, and we cannot molest Napoleon without breaking those compacts."

"Oh, well, we shall find some way out of it," responded M. de Salvieux.

"There wasn't any trouble over treaties when it was a question of shooting the poor Duc d'Enghien."

"Well," said the marquise, "it seems probable that, by the aid of the Holy Alliance, we shall be rid of Napoleon; and we must trust to the vigilance of M. de Villefort to purify Marseilles of his partisans. The king is either a king or no king; if he be acknowledged as sovereign of France, he should be upheld in peace and tranquility; and this can best be effected by employing the most inflexible agents to put down every attempt at conspiracy—'tis the best and surest means of preventing mischief."

"Unfortunately, Madame," answered Villefort, "the strong arm of the law is not called upon to interfere until the evil has taken place."

"Then all he has got to do is to endeavor to repair it."

"Nay, Madame, the law is frequently powerless to effect this; all it can do is to avenge the wrong done."

"Oh, M. de Villefort," cried a beautiful young creature, daughter to the Comte de Salvieux, and the cherished friend of Mademoiselle de Saint-Meran, "do try and get up some famous trial while we are at Marseilles. I never was in a law-court; I am told it is so very amusing!"

"Amusing, certainly," replied the young man, "inasmuch as, instead of shedding tears as at the fictitious tale of woe produced at a theatre, you behold in a law-court a case of real and genuine distress—a drama of life. The prisoner whom you there see pale, agitated, and alarmed, instead of—as is the case when a curtain falls on a tragedy—going home to sup peacefully with his family, and then retiring to rest, that he may recommence his mimic woes on the morrow,—is removed from your sight merely to be reconducted to his prison and delivered up to the executioner. I leave you to judge how far your nerves are calculated to bear you through such a scene. Of this, however, be assured, that should any favorable opportunity present itself, I will not fail to offer you the choice of being present."

"For shame, M. de Villefort!" said Renee, becoming quite pale; "don't you see how you are frightening us?—and yet you laugh."

"What would you have? 'Tis like a duel. I have already recorded sentence of death, five or six times, against the movers of political conspiracies, and who can say how many daggers may be ready sharpened, and only waiting a favorable opportunity to be buried in my heart?"

"Gracious heavens, M. de Villefort," said Renee, becoming more and more terrified; "you surely are not in earnest."

"Indeed I am," replied the young magistrate with a smile; "and in the interesting trial that young lady is anxious to witness, the case would only be still more aggravated. Suppose, for instance, the prisoner, as is more than probable, to have served under Napoleon—well, can you expect for an instant, that one accustomed, at the word of his commander, to rush fearlessly on the very bayonets of his foe, will scruple more to drive a stiletto into the heart of one he knows to be his personal enemy, than to slaughter his fellow-creatures, merely because bidden to do so by one he is bound to obey? Besides, one requires the excitement of being hateful in the eyes of the accused, in order to lash one's self into a state of sufficient vehemence and power. I would not choose to see the man against whom I pleaded smile, as though in mockery of my words. No; my pride is to see the accused pale, agitated, and as though beaten out of all composure by the fire of my eloquence." Renee uttered a smothered exclamation.

"Bravo!" cried one of the guests; "that is what I call talking to some purpose."

"Just the person we require at a time like the present," said a second.

"What a splendid business that last case of yours was, my dear Villefort!" remarked a third; "I mean the trial of the man for murdering his father. Upon my word, you killed him ere the executioner had laid his hand upon him."

"Oh, as for parricides, and such dreadful people as that," interposed Renee, "it matters very little what is done to them; but as regards poor unfortunate creatures whose only crime consists in having mixed themselves up in political intrigues"—

"Why, that is the very worst offence they could possibly commit; for, don't you see, Renee, the king is the father of his people, and he who shall plot or contrive aught against the life and safety of the parent of thirty-two millions of souls, is a parricide upon a fearfully great scale?"

"I don't know anything about that," replied Renee; "but, M. de Villefort, you have promised me—have you not?—always to show mercy to those I plead for."

"Make yourself quite easy on that point," answered Villefort, with one of his sweetest smiles; "you and I will always consult upon our verdicts."

"My love," said the marquise, "attend to your doves, your lap-dogs, and embroidery, but do not meddle with what you do not understand. Nowadays the military profession is in abeyance and the magisterial robe is the badge of honor. There is a wise Latin proverb that is very much in point."

"*Cedant arma togae*," said Villefort with a bow.

"I cannot speak Latin," responded the marquise.

"Well," said Renee, "I cannot help regretting you had not chosen some other profession than your own—a physician, for instance. Do you know I always felt a shudder at the idea of even a destroying angel?"

"Dear, good Renee," whispered Villefort, as he gazed with unutterable tenderness on the lovely speaker.

"Let us hope, my child," cried the marquis, "that M. de Villefort may prove the moral and political physician of this province; if so, he will have achieved a noble work."

"And one which will go far to efface the recollection of his father's conduct," added the incorrigible marquise.

"Madame," replied Villefort, with a mournful smile, "I have already had the honor to observe that my father has—at least, I hope so—abjured his past errors, and that he is, at the present moment, a firm and zealous friend to religion and order—a better royalist, possibly, than his son; for he has to atone for past dereliction, while I have no other impulse than warm, decided preference and conviction." Having made this well-turned speech, Villefort looked carefully around to mark the effect of his oratory, much as he would have done had he been addressing the bench in open court.

"Do you know, my dear Villefort," cried the Comte de Salvieux, "that is exactly what I myself said the other day at the Tuileries, when questioned by his majesty's principal chamberlain touching the singularity of an alliance between the son of a Girondin and the daughter of an officer of the Duc de Conde; and I assure you he seemed fully to comprehend that this mode of reconciling political differences was based upon sound and excellent principles. Then the king, who, without our suspecting it, had overheard our conversation, interrupted us by saying, 'Villefort'—observe that the king did not pronounce the word Noirtier, but, on the contrary, placed considerable emphasis on that of Villefort—'Villefort,' said his majesty, 'is a young man of great judgment and discretion, who will be sure to make a figure in his profession; I like him much, and it gave me great pleasure to hear that he was about to become the son-in-law of the Marquis and Marquise de Saint-Meran. I should myself have recommended the match, had not the noble marquis anticipated my wishes by requesting my consent to it.'"

"Is it possible the king could have condescended so far as to express himself so favorably of me?" asked the enraptured Villefort.

"I give you his very words; and if the marquis chooses to be candid, he will confess that they perfectly agree with what his majesty said to him, when he went six months ago to consult him upon the subject of your espousing his daughter."

"That is true," answered the marquis.

"How much do I owe this gracious prince! What is there I would not do to evince my earnest gratitude!"

"That is right," cried the marquise. "I love to see you thus. Now, then, were a conspirator to fall into your hands, he would be most welcome."

"For my part, dear mother," interposed Renee, "I trust your wishes will not prosper, and that Providence will only permit petty offenders, poor debtors, and miserable cheats to fall into M. de Villefort's hands,—then I shall be contented."

"Just the same as though you prayed that a physician might only be called upon to prescribe for headaches, measles, and the stings of wasps, or any other slight affection of the epidermis. If you wish to see me the king's attorney, you must desire for me some of those violent and dangerous diseases from the cure of which so much honor redounds to the physician."

At this moment, and as though the utterance of Villefort's wish had sufficed to effect its accomplishment, a servant entered the room, and whispered a few words in his ear. Villefort immediately rose from table and quitted the room upon the plea of urgent business; he soon, however, returned, his whole face beaming with delight. Renee regarded him with fond affection; and certainly his handsome features, lit up as they then were with more than usual fire and animation, seemed formed to excite the innocent admiration with which she gazed on her graceful and intelligent lover.

"You were wishing just now," said Villefort, addressing her, "that I were a doctor instead of a lawyer. Well, I at least resemble the disciples of Esculapius in one thing—that of not being able to call a day my own, not even that of my betrothal."

"And wherefore were you called away just now?" asked Mademoiselle de Saint-Meran, with an air of deep interest.

"For a very serious matter, which bids fair to make work for the executioner."

"How dreadful!" exclaimed Renee, turning pale.

"Is it possible?" burst simultaneously from all who were near enough to the magistrate to hear his words.

"Why, if my information prove correct, a sort of Bonaparte conspiracy has just been discovered."

"Can I believe my ears?" cried the marquise.

"I will read you the letter containing the accusation, at least," said Villefort:—

"'The king's attorney is informed by a friend to the throne and the religions institutions of his country, that one named Edmond Dantes, mate of the ship *Pharaon*, this day arrived from Smyrna, after having touched at Naples and Porto-Ferrajo, has been the bearer of a letter from Murat to the usurper, and again taken charge of another letter from the usurper to the Bonapartist club in Paris. Ample corroboration of this statement may be obtained by arresting the above-mentioned Edmond Dantes, who either carries the letter for Paris about with him, or has it at his father's abode. Should it not be found in the possession of father or son, then it will assuredly be discovered in the cabin belonging to the said Dantes on board the *Pharaon*.'"

"But," said Renee, "this letter, which, after all, is but an anonymous scrawl, is not even addressed to you, but to the king's attorney."

"True; but that gentleman being absent, his secretary, by his orders, opened his letters; thinking this one of importance, he sent for me, but not finding me, took upon himself to give the necessary orders for arresting the accused party."

"Then the guilty person is absolutely in custody?" said the marquise.

"Nay, dear mother, say the accused person. You know we cannot yet pronounce him guilty."

"He is in safe custody," answered Villefort; "and rely upon it, if the letter is found, he will not be likely to be trusted abroad again, unless he goes forth under the especial protection of the headsman."

"And where is the unfortunate being?" asked Renee.

"He is at my house."

"Come, come, my friend," interrupted the marquise, "do not neglect your duty to linger with us. You are the king's servant, and must go wherever that service calls you."

"O Villefort!" cried Renee, clasping her hands, and looking towards her lover with piteous earnestness, "be merciful on this the day of our betrothal."

The young man passed round to the side of the table where the fair pleader sat, and leaning over her chair said tenderly,—

"To give you pleasure, my sweet Renee, I promise to show all the lenity in my power; but if the charges brought against this Bonapartist hero prove correct, why, then, you really must give me leave to order his head to be cut off." Renee shuddered.

"Never mind that foolish girl, Villefort," said the marquise. "She will soon get over these things." So saying, Madame de Saint-Meran extended her dry bony hand to Villefort, who, while imprinting a son-in-law's respectful salute on it, looked at Renee, as much as to say, "I must try and fancy 'tis your dear hand I kiss, as it should have been."

"These are mournful auspices to accompany a betrothal," sighed poor Renee.

"Upon my word, child!" exclaimed the angry marquise, "your folly exceeds all bounds. I should be glad to know what connection there can possibly be between your sickly sentimentality and the affairs of the state!"

"O mother!" murmured Renee.

"Nay, Madame, I pray you pardon this little traitor. I promise you that to make up for her want of loyalty, I will be most inflexibly severe;" then casting an expressive glance at his betrothed, which seemed to say,

"Fear not, for your dear sake my justice shall be tempered with mercy," and receiving a sweet and approving smile in return, Villefort quitted the room.

Chapter 7. The Examination.

No sooner had Villefort left the salon, than he assumed the grave air of a man who holds the balance of life and death in his hands. Now, in spite of the nobility of his countenance, the command of which, like a finished actor, he had carefully studied before the glass, it was by no means easy for him to assume an air of judicial severity. Except the recollection of the line of politics his father had adopted, and which might interfere, unless he acted with the greatest prudence, with his own career, Gerard de Villefort was as happy as a man could be. Already rich, he held a high official situation, though only twenty-seven. He was about to marry a young and charming woman, whom he loved, not passionately, but reasonably, as became a deputy attorney of the king; and besides her personal attractions, which were very great, Mademoiselle de Saint-Meran's family possessed considerable political influence, which they would, of course, exert in his favor. The dowry of his wife amounted to fifty thousand crowns, and he had, besides, the prospect of seeing her fortune increased to half a million at her father's death. These considerations naturally gave Villefort a feeling of such complete felicity that his mind was fairly dazzled in its contemplation.

At the door he met the commissary of police, who was waiting for him. The sight of this officer recalled Villefort from the third heaven to earth; he composed his face, as we have before described, and said, "I have read the letter, sir, and you have acted rightly in arresting this man; now inform me what you have discovered concerning him and the conspiracy."

"We know nothing as yet of the conspiracy, monsieur; all the papers found have been sealed up and placed on your desk. The prisoner himself is named Edmond Dantes, mate on board the three-master the *Pharaon*, trading in cotton with Alexandria and Smyrna, and belonging to Morrel & Son, of Marseilles."

"Before he entered the merchant service, had he ever served in the marines?"

"Oh, no, monsieur, he is very young."

"How old?"

"Nineteen or twenty at the most."

At this moment, and as Villefort had arrived at the corner of the Rue des Conseils, a man, who seemed to have been waiting for him, approached; it was M. Morrel.

"Ah, M. de Villefort," cried he, "I am delighted to see you. Some of your people have committed the strangest mistake—they have just arrested Edmond Dantes, mate of my vessel."

"I know it, monsieur," replied Villefort, "and I am now going to examine him."

"Oh," said Morrel, carried away by his friendship, "you do not know him, and I do. He is the most estimable, the most trustworthy creature in the world, and I will venture to say, there is not a better seaman in all the merchant service. Oh, M. de Villefort, I beseech your indulgence for him."

Villefort, as we have seen, belonged to the aristocratic party at Marseilles, Morrel to the plebeian; the first was a royalist, the other suspected of Bonapartism. Villefort looked disdainfully at Morrel, and replied,—

"You are aware, monsieur, that a man may be estimable and trustworthy in private life, and the best seaman in the merchant service, and yet be, politically speaking, a great criminal. Is it not true?"

The magistrate laid emphasis on these words, as if he wished to apply them to the owner himself, while his eyes seemed to plunge into the heart of one who, interceding for another, had himself need of indulgence. Morrel reddened, for his own conscience was not quite clear on politics; besides, what Dantes had told him of his interview with the grand-marshal, and what the emperor had said to him, embarrassed him. He replied, however,—

"I entreat you, M. de Villefort, be, as you always are, kind and equitable, and give him back to us soon." This give us sounded revolutionary in the deputy's ears.

"Ah, ah," murmured he, "is Dantes then a member of some Carbonari society, that his protector thus employs the collective form? He was, if I recollect, arrested in a tavern, in company with a great many others." Then he added, "Monsieur, you may rest assured I shall perform my duty impartially, and that if he be innocent you shall not have appealed to me in vain; should he, however, be guilty, in this present epoch, impunity would furnish a dangerous example, and I must do my duty."

As he had now arrived at the door of his own house, which adjoined the Palais de Justice, he entered, after having coldly saluted the ship-owner, who stood, as if petrified, on the spot where Villefort had left him. The ante-chamber was full of police agents and gendarmes, in the midst of whom, carefully watched, but calm and smiling, stood the prisoner. Villefort traversed the ante-chamber, cast a side glance at Dantes, and taking a packet which a gendarme offered him, disappeared, saying, "Bring in the prisoner."

Rapid as had been Villefort's glance, it had served to give him an idea of the man he was about to interrogate. He had recognized intelligence in the high forehead, courage in the dark eye and bent brow, and frankness in the thick lips that showed a set of pearly teeth. Villefort's first impression was favorable; but he had been so often warned to mistrust first impulses, that he applied the maxim to the impression, forgetting the difference between the two words. He stifled, therefore, the feelings of compassion that were rising, composed his features, and sat down, grim and somber, at his desk. An instant after Dantes entered. He was pale, but calm and collected, and saluting his judge with easy politeness, looked round for a seat, as if he had been in M. Morrel's salon. It was then that he encountered for the first time Villefort's look,—that look peculiar to the magistrate, who, while seeming to read the thoughts of others, betrays nothing of his own.

"Who and what are you?" demanded Villefort, turning over a pile of papers, containing information relative to the prisoner, that a police agent had given to him on his entry, and that, already, in an hour's time, had swelled to voluminous proportions, thanks to the corrupt espionage of which "the accused" is always made the victim.

"My name is Edmond Dantes," replied the young man calmly; "I am mate of the *Pharaon*, belonging to Messrs. Morrel & Son."

"Your age?" continued Villefort.

"Nineteen," returned Dantes.

"What were you doing at the moment you were arrested?"

"I was at the festival of my marriage, monsieur," said the young man, his voice slightly tremulous, so great was the contrast between that happy moment and the painful ceremony he was now undergoing; so great was the contrast between the somber aspect of M. de Villefort and the radiant face of Mercedes.

"You were at the festival of your marriage?" said the deputy, shuddering in spite of himself.

"Yes, monsieur; I am on the point of marrying a young girl I have been attached to for three years." Villefort, impassive as he was, was struck with this coincidence; and the tremulous voice of Dantes, surprised in the midst of his happiness, struck a sympathetic chord in his own bosom—he also was on the point of being married, and he was summoned from his own happiness to destroy that of another. "This philosophic reflection," thought he, "will make a great sensation at M. de Saint-Meran's;" and he arranged mentally, while Dantes awaited further questions, the antithesis by which orators often create a reputation for eloquence. When this speech was arranged, Villefort turned to Dantes.

"Go on, sir," said he.

"What would you have me say?"

"Give all the information in your power."

"Tell me on which point you desire information, and I will tell all I know; only," added he, with a smile, "I warn you I know very little."

"Have you served under the usurper?"

"I was about to be mustered into the Royal Marines when he fell."

"It is reported your political opinions are extreme," said Villefort, who had never heard anything of the kind, but was not sorry to make this inquiry, as if it were an accusation.

"My political opinions!" replied Dantes. "Alas, sir, I never had any opinions. I am hardly nineteen; I know nothing; I have no part to play. If I obtain the situation I desire, I shall owe it to M. Morrel. Thus all my opinions—I will not say public, but private—are confined to these three sentiments,—I love my father, I respect M. Morrel, and I adore Mercedes. This, sir, is all I can tell you, and you see how uninteresting it is." As Dantes spoke, Villefort gazed at his ingenuous and open countenance, and recollected the words of Renee, who, without knowing who the culprit was, had besought his indulgence for him. With the deputy's knowledge of crime and criminals, every word the young man uttered convinced him more and more of his innocence. This lad, for he was scarcely a man,—simple, natural, eloquent with that eloquence of the heart never found when sought for; full of affection for everybody, because he was happy, and because happiness renders even the wicked good—extended his affection even to his judge, spite of Villefort's severe look and stern accent. Dantes seemed full of kindness.

"Pardieu," said Villefort, "he is a noble fellow. I hope I shall gain Renee's favor easily by obeying the first command she ever imposed on me. I shall have at least a pressure of the hand in public, and a sweet kiss in private." Full of this idea, Villefort's face became so joyous, that when he turned to Dantes, the latter, who had watched the change on his physiognomy, was smiling also.

"Sir," said Villefort, "have you any enemies, at least, that you know."

"I have enemies?" replied Dantes; "my position is not sufficiently elevated for that. As for my disposition, that is, perhaps, somewhat too hasty; but I have striven to repress it. I have had ten or twelve sailors under me, and if you question them, they will tell you that they love and respect me, not as a father, for I am too young, but as an elder brother."

"But you may have excited jealousy. You are about to become captain at nineteen—an elevated post; you are about to marry a pretty girl, who loves you; and these two pieces of good fortune may have excited the envy of someone."

"You are right; you know men better than I do, and what you say may possibly be the case, I confess; but if such persons are among my acquaintances I prefer not to know it, because then I should be forced to hate them."

"You are wrong; you should always strive to see clearly around you. You seem a worthy young man; I will depart from the strict line of my duty to aid you in discovering the author of this accusation. Here is the paper; do you know the writing?" As he spoke, Villefort drew the letter from his pocket, and presented it to Dantes. Dantes read it. A cloud passed over his brow as he said,—

"No, monsieur, I do not know the writing, and yet it is tolerably plain. Whoever did it writes well. I am very fortunate," added he, looking gratefully at Villefort, "to be examined by such a man as you; for this envious person is a real enemy." And by the rapid glance that the young man's eyes shot forth, Villefort saw how much energy lay hid beneath this mildness.

"Now," said the deputy, "answer me frankly, not as a prisoner to a judge, but as one man to another who takes an interest in him, what truth is there in the accusation contained in this anonymous letter?" And Villefort threw disdainfully on his desk the letter Dantes had just given back to him.

"None at all. I will tell you the real facts. I swear by my honor as a sailor, by my love for Mercedes, by the life of my father"—

"Speak, monsieur," said Villefort. Then, internally, "If Renee could see me, I hope she would be satisfied, and would no longer call me a decapitator."

"Well, when we quitted Naples, Captain Leclere was attacked with a brain fever. As we had no doctor on board, and he was so anxious to arrive at Elba, that he would not touch at any other port, his disorder rose to such a height, that at the end of the third day, feeling he was dying, he called me to him. 'My dear Dantes,' said he, 'swear to perform what I am going to tell you, for it is a matter of the deepest importance.'

"'I swear, Captain,' replied I.

"'Well, as after my death the command devolves on you as mate, assume the command, and bear up for the Island of Elba, disembark at Porto-Ferrajo, ask for the grand-marshal, give him this letter—perhaps they will give you another letter, and charge you with a commission. You will accomplish what I was to have done, and derive all the honor and profit from it.'

"'I will do it, Captain; but perhaps I shall not be admitted to the grand marshal's presence as easily as you expect?'

"'Here is a ring that will obtain audience of him, and remove every difficulty,' said the captain. At these words he gave me a ring. It was time—two hours after he was delirious; the next day he died."

"And what did you do then?"

"What I ought to have done, and what everyone would have done in my place. Everywhere the last requests of a dying man are sacred; but with a sailor the last requests of his superior are commands. I sailed for the Island of Elba, where I arrived the next day; I ordered everybody to remain on board, and went on shore alone. As I had expected, I found some difficulty in obtaining access to the grand marshal; but I sent the ring I had received from the captain to him, and was instantly admitted. He questioned me concerning Captain Leclere's death; and, as the latter had told me, gave me a letter to carry on to a person in Paris. I undertook it because it was what my captain had bade me do. I landed here, regulated the affairs of the vessel, and hastened to visit my affianced bride, whom I found more lovely than ever. Thanks to M. Morrel, all the forms were got over; in a word I was, as I told you, at my marriage-feast; and I should have been married in an hour, and to-morrow I intended to start for Paris, had I not been arrested on this charge which you as well as I now see to be unjust."

"Ah," said Villefort, "this seems to me the truth. If you have been culpable, it was imprudence, and this imprudence was in obedience to the orders of your captain. Give up this letter you have brought from Elba, and pass your word you will appear should you be required, and go and rejoin your friends."

"I am free, then, sir?" cried Dantes joyfully.

"Yes; but first give me this letter."

"You have it already, for it was taken from me with some others which I see in that packet."

"Stop a moment," said the deputy, as Dantes took his hat and gloves. "To whom is it addressed?"

"To Monsieur Noirtier, Rue Coq-Heron, Paris." Had a thunderbolt fallen into the room, Villefort could not have been more stupefied. He sank into his seat, and hastily turning over the packet, drew forth the fatal letter, at which he glanced with an expression of terror.

"M. Noirtier, Rue Coq-Heron, No. 13," murmured he, growing still paler.

"Yes," said Dantes; "do you know him?"

"No," replied Villefort; "a faithful servant of the king does not know conspirators."

"It is a conspiracy, then?" asked Dantes, who after believing himself free, now began to feel a tenfold alarm. "I have, however, already told you, sir, I was entirely ignorant of the contents of the letter."

"Yes; but you knew the name of the person to whom it was addressed," said Villefort.

"I was forced to read the address to know to whom to give it."

"Have you shown this letter to any one?" asked Villefort, becoming still more pale.

"To no one, on my honor."

"Everybody is ignorant that you are the bearer of a letter from the Island of Elba, and addressed to M. Noirtier?"

"Everybody, except the person who gave it to me."

"And that was too much, far too much," murmured Villefort. Villefort's brow darkened more and more, his white lips and clinched teeth filled Dantes with apprehension. After reading the letter, Villefort covered his face with his hands.

"Oh," said Dantes timidly, "what is the matter?" Villefort made no answer, but raised his head at the expiration of a few seconds, and again perused the letter.

"And you say that you are ignorant of the contents of this letter?"

"I give you my word of honor, sir," said Dantes; "but what is the matter? You are ill—shall I ring for assistance?—shall I call?"

"No," said Villefort, rising hastily; "stay where you are. It is for me to give orders here, and not you."

"Monsieur," replied Dantes proudly, "it was only to summon assistance for you."

"I want none; it was a temporary indisposition. Attend to yourself; answer me." Dantes waited, expecting a question, but in vain. Villefort fell back on his chair, passed his hand over his brow, moist with perspiration, and, for the third time, read the letter.

"Oh, if he knows the contents of this!" murmured he, "and that Noirtier is the father of Villefort, I am lost!" And he fixed his eyes upon Edmond as if he would have penetrated his thoughts.

"Oh, it is impossible to doubt it," cried he, suddenly.

"In heaven's name!" cried the unhappy young man, "if you doubt me, question me; I will answer you." Villefort made a violent effort, and in a tone he strove to render firm,—

"Sir," said he, "I am no longer able, as I had hoped, to restore you immediately to liberty; before doing so, I must consult the trial justice; what my own feeling is you already know."

"Oh, monsieur," cried Dantes, "you have been rather a friend than a judge."

"Well, I must detain you some time longer, but I will strive to make it as short as possible. The principal charge against you is this letter, and you see"—Villefort approached the fire, cast it in, and waited until it was entirely consumed.

"You see, I destroy it?"

"Oh," exclaimed Dantes, "you are goodness itself."

"Listen," continued Villefort; "you can now have confidence in me after what I have done."

"Oh, command, and I will obey."

"Listen; this is not a command, but advice I give you."

"Speak, and I will follow your advice."

"I shall detain you until this evening in the Palais de Justice. Should anyone else interrogate you, say to him what you have said to me, but do not breathe a word of this letter."

"I promise." It was Villefort who seemed to entreat, and the prisoner who reassured him.

"You see," continued he, glancing toward the grate, where fragments of burnt paper fluttered in the flames, "the letter is destroyed; you and I alone know of its existence; should you, therefore, be questioned, deny all knowledge of it—deny it boldly, and you are saved."

"Be satisfied; I will deny it."

"It was the only letter you had?"

"It was."

"Swear it."

"I swear it."

Villefort rang. A police agent entered. Villefort whispered some words in his ear, to which the officer replied by a motion of his head.

"Follow him," said Villefort to Dantes. Dantes saluted Villefort and retired. Hardly had the door closed when Villefort threw himself half-fainting into a chair.

"Alas, alas," murmured he, "if the procureur himself had been at Marseilles I should have been ruined. This accursed letter would have destroyed all my hopes. Oh, my father, must your past career always interfere with my successes?" Suddenly a light passed over his face, a smile played round his set mouth, and his haggard eyes were fixed in thought.

"This will do," said he, "and from this letter, which might have ruined me, I will make my fortune. Now to the work I have in hand." And after having assured himself that the prisoner was gone, the deputy procureur hastened to the house of his betrothed.

Chapter 8. The Chateau D'If.

The commissary of police, as he traversed the ante-chamber, made a sign to two gendarmes, who placed themselves one on Dantes' right and the other on his left. A door that communicated with the Palais de Justice was opened, and they went through a long range of gloomy corridors, whose appearance might have made even the boldest shudder. The Palais de Justice communicated with the prison,—a sombre edifice, that from its grated windows looks on the clock-tower of the Accoules. After numberless windings, Dantes saw a door with an iron wicket. The commissary took up an iron mallet and knocked thrice, every blow seeming to Dantes as if struck on his heart. The door opened, the two gendarmes gently pushed him forward, and the door closed with a loud sound behind him. The air he inhaled was no longer pure, but thick and mephitic,—he was in prison. He was conducted to a tolerably neat chamber, but grated and barred, and its appearance, therefore, did not greatly alarm him; besides, the words of Villefort, who seemed to interest himself so much, resounded still in his ears like a promise of freedom. It was four o'clock when Dantes was placed in this chamber. It was, as we have said, the 1st of March, and the prisoner was soon buried in darkness. The obscurity augmented the acuteness of his hearing; at the slightest sound he rose and hastened to the door, convinced they were about to liberate him, but the sound died away, and Dantes sank again into his seat. At last, about ten o'clock, and just as Dantes began to despair, steps were heard in the corridor, a key turned in the lock, the bolts creaked, the massy oaken door flew open, and a flood of light from two torches pervaded the apartment. By the torchlight Dantes saw the glittering sabres and carbines of four gendarmes. He had advanced at first, but stopped at the sight of this display of force.

"Are you come to fetch me?" asked he.

"Yes," replied a gendarme.

"By the orders of the deputy procureur?"

"I believe so." The conviction that they came from M. de Villefort relieved all Dantes' apprehensions; he advanced calmly, and placed himself in the centre of the escort. A carriage waited at the door, the coachman was on the box, and a police officer sat beside him.

"Is this carriage for me?" said Dantes.

"It is for you," replied a gendarme.

Dantes was about to speak; but feeling himself urged forward, and having neither the power nor the intention to resist, he mounted the steps, and was in an instant seated inside between two gendarmes; the two others took their places opposite, and the carriage rolled heavily over the stones.

The prisoner glanced at the windows—they were grated; he had changed his prison for another that was conveying him he knew not whither. Through the grating, however, Dantes saw they were passing through the Rue Caisserie, and by the Rue Saint-Laurent and the Rue Taramis, to the port. Soon he saw the lights of La Consigne.

The carriage stopped, the officer descended, approached the guardhouse, a dozen soldiers came out and formed themselves in order; Dantes saw the reflection of their muskets by the light of the lamps on the quay.

"Can all this force be summoned on my account?" thought he.

The officer opened the door, which was locked, and, without speaking a word, answered Dantes' question; for he saw between the ranks of the soldiers a passage formed from the carriage to the port. The two gendarmes who were opposite to him descended first, then he was ordered to alight and the gendarmes on each side of him followed his example. They advanced towards a boat, which a custom-house officer held by a chain, near the quay.

The soldiers looked at Dantes with an air of stupid curiosity. In an instant he was placed in the stern-sheets of the boat, between the gendarmes, while the officer stationed himself at the bow; a shove sent the boat adrift, and four sturdy oarsmen impelled it rapidly towards the Pilon. At a shout from the boat, the chain that closes the mouth of the port was lowered and in a second they were, as Dantes knew, in the Frioul and outside the inner harbor.

The prisoner's first feeling was of joy at again breathing the pure air—for air is freedom; but he soon sighed, for he passed before La Reserve, where he had that morning been so happy, and now through the open windows came the laughter and revelry of a ball. Dantes folded his hands, raised his eyes to heaven, and prayed fervently.

The boat continued her voyage. They had passed the Tete de Morte, were now off the Anse du Pharo, and about to double the battery. This maneuver was incomprehensible to Dantes.

"Whither are you taking me?" asked he.

"You will soon know."

"But still"—

"We are forbidden to give you any explanation." Dantes, trained in discipline, knew that nothing would be more absurd than to question subordinates, who were forbidden to reply; and so he remained silent.

The most vague and wild thoughts passed through his mind. The boat they were in could not make a long voyage; there was no vessel at anchor outside the harbor; he thought, perhaps, they were going to leave him on some distant point. He was not bound, nor had they made any attempt to handcuff him; this seemed a good augury. Besides, had not the deputy, who had been so kind to him, told him that provided he did not pronounce the dreaded name of Noirtier, he had nothing to apprehend? Had not Villefort in his presence destroyed the fatal letter, the only proof against him?

He waited silently, striving to pierce through the darkness.

They had left the Ile Ratonneau, where the lighthouse stood, on the right, and were now opposite the Point des Catalans. It seemed to the prisoner that he could distinguish a feminine form on the beach, for it was there Mercedes dwelt. How was it that a presentiment did not warn Mercedes that her lover was within three hundred yards of her?

One light alone was visible; and Dantes saw that it came from Mercedes' chamber. Mercedes was the only one awake in the whole settlement. A loud cry could be heard by her. But pride restrained him and he did not utter it. What would his guards think if they heard him shout like a madman?

He remained silent, his eyes fixed upon the light; the boat went on, but the prisoner thought only of Mercedes. An intervening elevation of land hid the light. Dantes turned and perceived that they had got out to sea. While he had been absorbed in thought, they had shipped their oars and hoisted sail; the boat was now moving with the wind.

In spite of his repugnance to address the guards, Dantes turned to the nearest gendarme, and taking his hand,—

"Comrade," said he, "I adjure you, as a Christian and a soldier, to tell me where we are going. I am Captain Dantes, a loyal Frenchman, thought accused of treason; tell me where you are conducting me, and I promise you on my honor I will submit to my fate."

The gendarme looked irresolutely at his companion, who returned for answer a sign that said, "I see no great harm in telling him now," and the gendarme replied,—

"You are a native of Marseilles, and a sailor, and yet you do not know where you are going?"

"On my honor, I have no idea."

"Have you no idea whatever?"

"None at all."

"That is impossible."

"I swear to you it is true. Tell me, I entreat."

"But my orders."

"Your orders do not forbid your telling me what I must know in ten minutes, in half an hour, or an hour. You see I cannot escape, even if I intended."

"Unless you are blind, or have never been outside the harbor, you must know."

"I do not."

"Look round you then." Dantes rose and looked forward, when he saw rise within a hundred yards of him the black and frowning rock on which stands the Chateau d'If. This gloomy fortress, which has for more than three hundred years furnished food for so many wild legends, seemed to Dantes like a scaffold to a malefactor.

"The Chateau d'If?" cried he, "what are we going there for?" The gendarme smiled.

"I am not going there to be imprisoned," said Dantes; "it is only used for political prisoners. I have committed no crime. Are there any magistrates or judges at the Chateau d'If?"

"There are only," said the gendarme, "a governor, a garrison, turnkeys, and good thick walls. Come, come, do not look so astonished, or you will make me think you are laughing at me in return for my good nature." Dantes pressed the gendarme's hand as though he would crush it.

"You think, then," said he, "that I am taken to the Chateau d'If to be imprisoned there?"

"It is probable; but there is no occasion to squeeze so hard."

"Without any inquiry, without any formality?"

"All the formalities have been gone through; the inquiry is already made."

"And so, in spite of M. de Villefort's promises?"

"I do not know what M. de Villefort promised you," said the gendarme, "but I know we are taking you to the Chateau d'If. But what are you doing? Help, comrades, help!"

By a rapid movement, which the gendarme's practiced eye had perceived, Dantes sprang forward to precipitate himself into the sea; but four vigorous arms seized him as his feet quitted the bottom of the boat. He fell back cursing with rage.

"Good!" said the gendarme, placing his knee on his chest; "believe oft-spoken gentlemen again! Harkye, my friend, I have disobeyed my first order, but I will not disobey the second; and if you move, I will blow your brains out." And he levelled his carbine at Dantes, who felt the muzzle against his temple.

For a moment the idea of struggling crossed his mind, and of so ending the unexpected evil that had overtaken him. But he bethought him of M. de Villefort's promise; and, besides, death in a boat from the hand of a gendarme seemed too terrible. He remained motionless, but gnashing his teeth and wringing his hands with fury.

At this moment the boat came to a landing with a violent shock. One of the sailors leaped on shore, a cord creaked as it ran through a pulley, and Dantes guessed they were at the end of the voyage, and that they were mooring the boat.

His guards, taking him by the arms and coat-collar, forced him to rise, and dragged him towards the steps that lead to the gate of the fortress, while the police officer carrying a musket with fixed bayonet followed behind.

Dantes made no resistance; he was like a man in a dream: he saw soldiers drawn up on the embankment; he knew vaguely that he was ascending a flight of steps; he was conscious that he passed through a door, and that the door closed behind him; but all this indistinctly as through a mist. He did not even see the ocean, that terrible barrier against freedom, which the prisoners look upon with utter despair.

They halted for a minute, during which he strove to collect his thoughts. He looked around; he was in a court surrounded by high walls; he heard the measured tread of sentinels, and as they passed before the light he saw the barrels of their muskets shine.

They waited upwards of ten minutes. Certain Dantes could not escape, the gendarmes released him. They seemed awaiting orders. The orders came.

"Where is the prisoner?" said a voice.

"Here," replied the gendarmes.

"Let him follow me; I will take him to his cell."

"Go!" said the gendarmes, thrusting Dantes forward.

The prisoner followed his guide, who led him into a room almost underground, whose bare and reeking walls seemed as though impregnated with tears; a lamp placed on a stool illumined the apartment faintly, and showed Dantes the features of his conductor, an under-jailer, ill-clothed, and of sullen appearance.

"Here is your chamber for tonight," said he. "It is late, and the governor is asleep. To-morrow, perhaps, he may change you. In the meantime there is bread, water, and fresh straw; and that is all a prisoner can wish for. Goodnight." And before Dantes could open his mouth—before he had noticed where the jailer placed his bread or the water—before he had glanced towards the corner where the straw was, the jailer disappeared, taking with him the lamp and closing the door, leaving stamped upon the prisoner's mind the dim reflection of the dripping walls of his dungeon.

Dantes was alone in darkness and in silence—cold as the shadows that he felt breathe on his burning forehead. With the first dawn of day the jailer returned, with orders to leave Dantes where he was. He found the prisoner in the same position, as if fixed there, his eyes swollen with weeping. He had passed the night standing, and without sleep. The jailer advanced; Dantes appeared not to perceive him. He touched him on the shoulder. Edmond started.

"Have you not slept?" said the jailer.

"I do not know," replied Dantes. The jailer stared.

"Are you hungry?" continued he.

"I do not know."

"Do you wish for anything?"

"I wish to see the governor." The jailer shrugged his shoulders and left the chamber.

Dantes followed him with his eyes, and stretched forth his hands towards the open door; but the door closed. All his emotion then burst forth; he cast himself on the ground, weeping bitterly, and asking himself what crime he had committed that he was thus punished.

The day passed thus; he scarcely tasted food, but walked round and round the cell like a wild beast in its cage. One thought in particular tormented him: namely, that during his journey hither he had sat so still, whereas he might, a dozen times, have plunged into the sea, and, thanks to his powers of swimming, for which he was famous, have gained the shore, concealed himself until the arrival of a Genoese or Spanish vessel, escaped to Spain or Italy, where Mercedes and his father could have joined him. He had no fears as to how he should live—good seamen are welcome everywhere. He spoke Italian like a Tuscan, and Spanish like a Castilian; he would have been free, and happy with Mercedes and his father, whereas he was now confined in the Chateau d'If, that impregnable fortress, ignorant of the future destiny of his father and Mercedes; and all this because he had trusted to Villefort's promise. The thought was maddening, and Dantes threw himself furiously down on his straw. The next morning at the same hour, the jailer came again.

"Well," said the jailer, "are you more reasonable to-day?" Dantes made no reply.

"Come, cheer up; is there anything that I can do for you?"

"I wish to see the governor."

"I have already told you it was impossible."

"Why so?"

"Because it is against prison rules, and prisoners must not even ask for it."

"What is allowed, then?"

"Better fare, if you pay for it, books, and leave to walk about."

"I do not want books, I am satisfied with my food, and do not care to walk about; but I wish to see the governor."

"If you worry me by repeating the same thing, I will not bring you any more to eat."

"Well, then," said Edmond, "if you do not, I shall die of hunger—that is all."

The jailer saw by his tone he would be happy to die; and as every prisoner is worth ten sous a day to his jailer, he replied in a more subdued tone.

"What you ask is impossible; but if you are very well behaved you will be allowed to walk about, and some day you will meet the governor, and if he chooses to reply, that is his affair."

"But," asked Dantes, "how long shall I have to wait?"

"Ah, a month—six months—a year."

"It is too long a time. I wish to see him at once."

"Ah," said the jailer, "do not always brood over what is impossible, or you will be mad in a fortnight."

"You think so?"

"Yes; we have an instance here; it was by always offering a million of francs to the governor for his liberty that an abbe became mad, who was in this chamber before you."

"How long has he left it?"

"Two years."

"Was he liberated, then?"

"No; he was put in a dungeon."

"Listen!" said Dantes. "I am not an abbe, I am not mad; perhaps I shall be, but at present, unfortunately, I am not. I will make you another offer."

"What is that?"

"I do not offer you a million, because I have it not; but I will give you a hundred crowns if, the first time you go to Marseilles, you will seek out a young girl named Mercedes, at the Catalans, and give her two lines from me."

"If I took them, and were detected, I should lose my place, which is worth two thousand francs a year; so that I should be a great fool to run such a risk for three hundred."

"Well," said Dantes, "mark this; if you refuse at least to tell Mercedes I am here, I will someday hide myself behind the door, and when you enter I will dash out your brains with this stool."

"Threats!" cried the jailer, retreating and putting himself on the defensive; "you are certainly going mad. The abbe began like you, and in three days you will be like him, mad enough to tie up; but, fortunately, there are dungeons here." Dantes whirled the stool round his head.

"All right, all right," said the jailer; "all right, since you will have it so. I will send word to the governor."

"Very well," returned Dantes, dropping the stool and sitting on it as if he were in reality mad. The jailer went out, and returned in an instant with a corporal and four soldiers.

"By the governor's orders," said he, "conduct the prisoner to the tier beneath."

"To the dungeon, then," said the corporal.

"Yes; we must put the madman with the madmen." The soldiers seized Dantes, who followed passively.

He descended fifteen steps, and the door of a dungeon was opened, and he was thrust in. The door closed, and Dantes advanced with outstretched hands until he touched the wall; he then sat down in the corner until his eyes became accustomed to the darkness. The jailer was right; Dantes wanted but little of being utterly mad.

Chapter 9. The Evening of the Betrothal.

Villefort had, as we have said, hastened back to Madame de Saint-Meran's in the Place du Grand Cours, and on entering the house found that the guests whom he had left at table were taking coffee in the salon. Renee was, with all the rest of the company, anxiously awaiting him, and his entrance was followed by a general exclamation.

"Well, Decapitator, Guardian of the State, Royalist, Brutus, what is the matter?" said one. "Speak out."

"Are we threatened with a fresh Reign of Terror?" asked another.

"Has the Corsican ogre broken loose?" cried a third.

"Marquise," said Villefort, approaching his future mother-in-law, "I request your pardon for thus leaving you. Will the marquis honor me by a few moments' private conversation?"

"Ah, it is really a serious matter, then?" asked the marquis, remarking the cloud on Villefort's brow.

"So serious that I must take leave of you for a few days; so," added he, turning to Renee, "judge for yourself if it be not important."

"You are going to leave us?" cried Renee, unable to hide her emotion at this unexpected announcement.

"Alas," returned Villefort, "I must!"

"Where, then, are you going?" asked the marquise.

"That, madame, is an official secret; but if you have any commissions for Paris, a friend of mine is going there to-night, and will with pleasure undertake them." The guests looked at each other.

"You wish to speak to me alone?" said the marquis.

"Yes, let us go to the library, please." The marquis took his arm, and they left the salon.

"Well," asked he, as soon as they were by themselves, "tell me what it is?"

"An affair of the greatest importance, that demands my immediate presence in Paris. Now, excuse the indiscretion, marquis, but have you any landed property?"

"All my fortune is in the funds; seven or eight hundred thousand francs."

"Then sell out—sell out, marquis, or you will lose it all."

"But how can I sell out here?"

"You have a broker, have you not?"

"Yes."

"Then give me a letter to him, and tell him to sell out without an instant's delay, perhaps even now I shall arrive too late."

"The deuce you say!" replied the marquis, "let us lose no time, then!"

And, sitting down, he wrote a letter to his broker, ordering him to sell out at the market price.

"Now, then," said Villefort, placing the letter in his pocketbook, "I must have another!"

"To whom?"

"To the king."

"To the king?"

"Yes."

"I dare not write to his majesty."

"I do not ask you to write to his majesty, but ask M. de Salvieux to do so. I want a letter that will enable me to reach the king's presence without all the formalities of demanding an audience; that would occasion a loss of precious time."

"But address yourself to the keeper of the seals; he has the right of entry at the Tuileries, and can procure you audience at any hour of the day or night."

"Doubtless; but there is no occasion to divide the honors of my discovery with him. The keeper would leave me in the background, and take all the glory to himself. I tell you, Marquis, my fortune is made if I only reach the Tuileries first, for the king will not forget the service I do him."

"In that case go and get ready. I will call Salvieux and make him write the letter."

"Be as quick as possible, I must be on the road in a quarter of an hour."

"Tell your coachman to stop at the door."

"You will present my excuses to the marquise and Mademoiselle Renee, whom I leave on such a day with great regret."

"You will find them both here, and can make your farewells in person."

"A thousand thanks—and now for the letter."

The marquis rang, a servant entered.

"Say to the Comte de Salvieux that I would like to see him."

"Now, then, go," said the marquis.

"I shall be gone only a few moments."

Villefort hastily quitted the apartment, but reflecting that the sight of the deputy procureur running through the streets would be enough to throw the whole city into confusion, he resumed his ordinary pace. At his door he perceived a figure in the shadow that seemed to wait for him. It was Mercedes, who, hearing no news of her lover, had come unobserved to inquire after him.

As Villefort drew near, she advanced and stood before him. Dantes had spoken of Mercedes, and Villefort instantly recognized her. Her beauty and high bearing surprised him, and when she inquired what had become of her lover, it seemed to him that she was the judge, and he the accused.

"The young man you speak of," said Villefort abruptly, "is a great criminal, and I can do nothing for him, mademoiselle." Mercedes burst into tears, and, as Villefort strove to pass her, again addressed him.

"But, at least, tell me where he is, that I may know whether he is alive or dead," said she.

"I do not know; he is no longer in my hands," replied Villefort.

And desirous of putting an end to the interview, he pushed by her, and closed the door, as if to exclude the pain he felt. But remorse is not thus banished; like Virgil's wounded hero, he carried the arrow in his wound, and, arrived at the salon, Villefort uttered a sigh that was almost a sob, and sank into a chair.

Then the first pangs of an unending torture seized upon his heart. The man he sacrificed to his ambition, that innocent victim immolated on the altar of his father's faults, appeared to him pale and threatening, leading his affianced bride by the hand, and bringing with him remorse, not such as the ancients figured, furious and terrible, but that slow and consuming agony whose pangs are intensified from hour to hour up to the very moment of death. Then he had a moment's hesitation. He had frequently called for capital punishment on criminals, and owing to his irresistible eloquence they had been condemned, and yet the slightest shadow of remorse had never clouded Villefort's brow, because they were guilty; at least, he believed so; but here was an innocent man whose happiness he had destroyed: in this case he was not the judge, but the executioner.

As he thus reflected, he felt the sensation we have described, and which had hitherto been unknown to him, arise in his bosom, and fill him with vague apprehensions. It is thus that a wounded man trembles instinctively at the approach of the finger to his wound until it be healed, but Villefort's was one of those that never close, or if they do, only close to reopen more agonizing than ever. If at this moment the sweet voice of Renee had sounded in his ears pleading for mercy, or the air Mercedes had entered and said, "In the name of God, I conjure you to restore me my affianced husband," his cold and trembling hands would have signed his release; but no voice broke the stillness of the chamber, and the door was opened only by Villefort's valet, who came to tell him that the travelling carriage was in readiness.

Villefort rose, or rather sprang, from his chair, hastily opened one of the drawers of his desk, emptied all the gold it contained into his pocket, stood motionless an instant, his hand pressed to his head, muttered a few inarticulate sounds, and then, perceiving that his servant had placed his cloak on his shoulders, he sprang into the carriage, ordering the postilions to drive to M. de Saint-Meran's. The hapless Dantes was doomed.

As the marquis had promised, Villefort found the marquise and Renee in waiting. He started when he saw Renee, for he fancied she was again about to plead for Dantes. Alas, her emotions were wholly personal: she was thinking only of Villefort's departure.

She loved Villefort, and he left her at the moment he was about to become her husband. Villefort knew not when he should return, and Renee, far from pleading for Dantes, hated the man whose crime separated her from her lover.

Villefort escorted Renee into the next room to steal away a moment without the marquis looking on. He led her to a chaise off to the side of the room, wide enough for their use. They sat, facing each other, the room dark as the curtains and shutters were drawn tight.

"You do not plead mercy then?"

Renee met his eyes, "I no longer feel merciful toward the man that causes your absence."

"My love, I will return with haste. I have no wish to be parted from you for longer than necessary"

"Will you stay with me for a moment, allow for a proper goodbye?"

His smile turned increasingly seductive.

"What sort of goodbye do you have in mind?"

"A goodbye that is not rushed behind a parlor door."

"Either way, my love, we will still need to make haste, I journey to Paris, remember."

"There is no need to tell me." Renee entrenched in the task of removing some of the easily accessible pieces of clothing she wore. A woman's clothing took entirely more work than a man's but Renee and Villefort adapted by leaving laces untied and hidden or folds gently rumpled. Sometimes people didn't notice things because they didn't care to look.

Villefore watched his lover undress as fast as she was able and he endeavored to help when she needed it. When every pale expanse of her skin was present Villefort could no longer hold back his ardor. He would take his fiancé, ignite her passions, and leave her needing for the next time they met, so she did not forget him during his journey, short as it may be.

Even while rushed, Villefort was capable of great pleasure. He stroked Renee to a slow burn, a frenzy, inciting panting moans with every breath. She clung to him like a leaf on a tree in autumn, with every part of her. Only once she was ready to receive him, did he lay himself between her spread thighs and make her his all over again.

This night showed him a new side of Renee, usually her heart remained guarded while opening her affections to him. Tonight she was open, he could feel her emotions in her touch, even though time ran short the words they needed to say held aloft on the tips of their tongues.

"Please." It was only a whisper, an entreaty into the darkness of the room. Villefort gave her what she needed, what she yearned for. Once he was seated fully inside her, he lay wrapped in her arms, her legs encircling his own. There were only minutes left but he allowed this one small pleasure, to cherish this moment before everything changed. The whole country would be ripped apart should Napoleon land and if his efforts proved fruitful the life of him and his bride would also be forever altered.

He pulled his mind back into the present and began to move inside Renee, slow and gentle, a far cry for their usual lovemaking. The cherished feeling he acquired in her arms was wondrous and he wanted to impart that to her as well. Slow and gentle did not last long, with her sex clenching his every thrust and her sharp nails digging into his back. He entered her in long shallow thrusts, trying to bring her to a completion unlike any she had previously. Even though he would soon be her husband, he wanted to be sure no other man eclipsed him in her mind.

Her breathing quickly became ragged and he could not help but match the pace she tried to set with her hips tilting this way and that. Only minutes passed before he lost all thought of anything other than her sex surrounding his. She arched her back drawing him further into herself, allowing him better angles for which to pleasure her.

"Gerard," she said, nothing more than a breath into his neck. It was enough to have him increasing the pace as she never uttered his given name. The sound of it on her lips was intoxicating and exhilarating.

"Renee," he answered in kind, pushing into her faster and with more force. Upon his return from Paris they would have more time, he draw things out with his lover, have her at his will for as long as either of them could stand it. For now, this was all they each had and he would take joy in it.

They reached the climax of their lovemaking together, both stifling a shout into the curves of one another's shoulder and neck. It crashed over them both like a wave at high tide, strong and insistent, drawing the last vestiges of pleasure from their bodies.

Villefore lay motionless, slumped, on top of his fiancé, and she bore his weight easily. A comfort spread through them both as they enjoyed the small quiet moment together. It ended quickly and finally Villefort rose to dress. Renee also rose as she would need to rejoin the marquise to properly see her lover away.

"Return quickly, my love. We shall marry soon and I may already bear your child."

His eyes flashes as his gaze pinned her.

"Truly?"

"It is too soon to tell but seeing as you are voracious in your appetites, it might be possible."

He clutches his pants in one hand and reached out to kiss Renee with his other.

"I would love nothing more than to return, marry you, and learn that you carry my son."

Having a son so soon after they marry would look very well for his lineage, and his efforts to secure a future without the stink of treason marring his name.

He helped Renee right her own attire after he finished his and they exited together, hand in hand. They had become adept at ensuring no one knew they had made love and tonight was no exception. The color on Renee's cheeks could be attributed to tears shed for her departing fiancé and no one would dare suggest otherwise.

• • •

Meanwhile what of Mercedes? She had met Fernand at the corner of the Rue de la Loge; she had returned to the Catalans, and had despairingly cast herself on her couch. Fernand, kneeling by her side, took her hand, and covered it with kisses that Mercedes did not even feel. She passed the night thus. The lamp went out for want of oil, but she paid no heed to the darkness, and dawn came, but she knew not that it was day. Grief had made her blind to all but one object—that was Edmond.

"Ah, you are there," said she, at length, turning towards Fernand.

"I have not quitted you since yesterday," returned Fernand sorrowfully.

M. Morrel had not readily given up the fight. He had learned that Dantes had been taken to prison, and he had gone to all his friends, and the influential persons of the city; but the report was already in circulation that Dantes was arrested as a Bonapartist agent; and as the most sanguine looked upon any attempt of Napoleon to remount the throne as impossible, he met with nothing but refusal, and had returned home in despair, declaring that the matter was serious and that nothing more could be done.

Caderousse was equally restless and uneasy, but instead of seeking, like M. Morrel, to aid Dantes, he had shut himself up with two bottles of black currant brandy, in the hope of drowning reflection. But he did not succeed, and became too intoxicated to fetch any more drink, and yet not so intoxicated as to forget what had happened. With his elbows on the table he sat between the two empty bottles, while spectres danced in the light of the unsnuffed candle—spectres such as Hoffmann strews over his punch-drenched pages, like black, fantastic dust.

Danglars alone was content and joyous—he had got rid of an enemy and made his own situation on the *Pharaon* secure. Danglars was one of those men born with a pen behind the ear, and an inkstand in place of a heart. Everything with him was multiplication or subtraction. The life of a man was to him of far less value than a numeral, especially when, by taking it away, he could increase the sum total of his own desires. He went to bed at his usual hour, and slept in peace.

Villefort, after having received M. de Salvieux' letter, embraced Renee, kissed the marquise's hand, and shaken that of the marquis, started for Paris along the Aix road.

Old Dantes was dying with anxiety to know what had become of Edmond. But we know very well what had become of Edmond.

Chapter 10. The King's Closet at the Tuileries.

We will leave Villefort on the road to Paris, travelling—thanks to trebled fees—with all speed, and passing through two or three apartments, enter at the Tuileriesthe little room with the arched window, so well known as having been the favorite closet of Napoleon and Louis XVIII., and now of Louis Philippe.

There, seated before a walnut table he had brought with him from Hartwell, and to which, from one of those fancies not uncommon to great people, he was particularly attached, the king, Louis XVIII., was carelessly listening to a man of fifty or fifty-two years of age, with gray hair, aristocratic bearing, and exceedingly gentlemanly attire, and meanwhile making a marginal note in a volume of Gryphius's rather inaccurate, but much sought-after, edition of Horace—a work which was much indebted to the sagacious observations of the philosophical monarch.

"You say, sir"—said the king.

"That I am exceedingly disquieted, sire."

"Really, have you had a vision of the seven fat kine and the seven lean kine?"

"No, sire, for that would only betoken for us seven years of plenty and seven years of scarcity; and with a king as full of foresight as your majesty, scarcity is not a thing to be feared."

"Then of what other scourge are you afraid, my dear Blacas?"

"Sire, I have every reason to believe that a storm is brewing in the south."

"Well, my dear duke," replied Louis XVIII., "I think you are wrongly informed, and know positively that, on the contrary, it is very fine weather in that direction." Man of ability as he was, Louis XVIII. liked a pleasant jest.

"Sire," continued M. de Blacas, "if it only be to reassure a faithful servant, will your majesty send into Languedoc, Provence, and Dauphine, trusty men, who will bring you back a faithful report as to the feeling in these three provinces?"

"*Caninus surdis*," replied the king, continuing the annotations in his Horace.

"Sire," replied the courtier, laughing, in order that he might seem to comprehend the quotation, "your majesty may be perfectly right in relying on the good feeling of France, but I fear I am not altogether wrong in dreading some desperate attempt."

"By whom?"

"By Bonaparte, or, at least, by his adherents."

"My dear Blacas," said the king, "you with your alarms prevent me from working."

"And you, sire, prevent me from sleeping with your security."

"Wait, my dear sir, wait a moment; for I have such a delightful note on the *Pastor quum traheret*—wait, and I will listen to you afterwards."

There was a brief pause, during which Louis XVIII. wrote, in a hand as small as possible, another note on the margin of his Horace, and then looking at the duke with the air of a man who thinks he has an idea of his own, while he is only commenting upon the idea of another, said,—

"Go on, my dear duke, go on—I listen."

"Sire," said Blacas, who had for a moment the hope of sacrificing Villefort to his own profit, "I am compelled to tell you that these are not mere rumors destitute of foundation which thus disquiet me; but a serious-minded man, deserving all my confidence, and charged by me to watch over the south" (the duke hesitated as he pronounced these words), "has arrived by post to tell me that a great peril threatens the king, and so I hastened to you, sire."

"*Mala ducis avi domum*," continued Louis XVIII., still annotating.

"Does your majesty wish me to drop the subject?"

"By no means, my dear duke; but just stretch out your hand."

"Which?"

"Whichever you please—there to the left."

"Here, sire?"

"I tell you to the left, and you are looking to the right; I mean on my left—yes, there. You will find yesterday's report of the minister of police. But here is M. Dandre himself;" and M. Dandre, announced by the chamberlain-in-waiting, entered.

"Come in," said Louis XVIII., with repressed smile, "come in, Baron, and tell the duke all you know—the latest news of M. de Bonaparte; do not conceal anything, however serious,—let us see, the Island of Elba is a volcano, and we may expect to have issuing thence flaming and bristling war—*bella, horrida bella.*" M. Dandre leaned very respectfully on the back of a chair with his two hands, and said,—

"Has your majesty perused yesterday's report?"

"Yes, yes; but tell the duke himself, who cannot find anything, what the report contains—give him the particulars of what the usurper is doing in his islet."

"Monsieur," said the baron to the duke, "all the servants of his majesty must approve of the latest intelligence which we have from the Island of Elba. Bonaparte"—M. Dandre looked at Louis XVIII., who, employed in writing a note, did not even raise his head. "Bonaparte," continued the baron, "is mortally wearied, and passes whole days in watching his miners at work at Porto-Longone."

"And scratches himself for amusement," added the king.

"Scratches himself?" inquired the duke, "what does your majesty mean?"

"Yes, indeed, my dear duke. Did you forget that this great man, this hero, this demigod, is attacked with a malady of the skin which worries him to death, prurigo?"

"And, moreover, my dear duke," continued the minister of police, "we are almost assured that, in a very short time, the usurper will be insane."

"Insane?"

"Raving mad; his head becomes weaker. Sometimes he weeps bitterly, sometimes laughs boisterously, at other time he passes hours on the seashore, flinging stones in the water and when the flint makes 'duck-and-drake' five or six times, he appears as delighted as if he had gained another Marengo or Austerlitz. Now, you must agree that these are indubitable symptoms of insanity."

"Or of wisdom, my dear baron—or of wisdom," said Louis XVIII., laughing; "the greatest captains of antiquity amused themselves by casting pebbles into the ocean—see Plutarch's life of Scipio Africanus."

M. de Blacas pondered deeply between the confident monarch and the truthful minister. Villefort, who did not choose to reveal the whole secret, lest another should reap all the benefit of the disclosure, had yet communicated enough to cause him the greatest uneasiness.

"Well, well, Dandre," said Louis XVIII., "Blacas is not yet convinced; let us proceed, therefore, to the usurper's conversion." The minister of police bowed.

"The usurper's conversion!" murmured the duke, looking at the king and Dandre, who spoke alternately, like Virgil's shepherds. "The usurper converted!"

"Decidedly, my dear duke."

"In what way converted?"

"To good principles. Tell him all about it, Baron."

"Why, this is the way of it," said the minister, with the gravest air in the world: "Napoleon lately had a review, and as two or three of his old veterans expressed a desire to return to France, he gave them their dismissal, and exhorted them to 'serve the good king.' These were his own words, of that I am certain."

"Well, Blacas, what think you of this?" inquired the king triumphantly, and pausing for a moment from the voluminous scholiast before him.

"I say, sire, that the minister of police is greatly deceived or I am; and as it is impossible it can be the minister of police as he has the guardianship of the safety and honor of your majesty, it is probable that I am in error. However, sire, if I might advise, your majesty will interrogate the person of whom I spoke to you, and I will urge your majesty to do him this honor."

"Most willingly, Duke; under your auspices I will receive any person you please, but you must not expect me to be too confiding. Baron, have you any report more recent than this dated the 20th February.—this is the 4th of March?"

"No, sire, but I am hourly expecting one; it may have arrived since I left my office."

"Go thither, and if there be none—well, well," continued Louis XVIII., "make one; that is the usual way, is it not?" and the king laughed facetiously.

"Oh, sire," replied the minister, "we have no occasion to invent any; every day our desks are loaded with most circumstantial denunciations, coming from hosts of people who hope for some return for services which they seek to render, but cannot; they trust to fortune, and rely upon some unexpected event in some way to justify their predictions."

"Well, sir, go;" said Louis XVIII., "and remember that I am waiting for you."

"I will but go and return, sire; I shall be back in ten minutes."

"And I, sire," said M. de Blacas, "will go and find my messenger."

"Wait, sir, wait," said Louis XVIII. "Really, M. de Blacas, I must change your armorial bearings; I will give you an eagle with outstretched wings, holding in its claws a prey which tries in vain to escape, and bearing this device—Tenax."

"Sire, I listen," said De Blacas, biting his nails with impatience.

"I wish to consult you on this passage, '*Molli fugiens anhelitu*,' you know it refers to a stag flying from a wolf. Are you not a sportsman and a great wolf-hunter? Well, then, what do you think of the *molli anhelitu*?"

"Admirable, sire; but my messenger is like the stag you refer to, for he has posted two hundred and twenty leagues in scarcely three days."

"Which is undergoing great fatigue and anxiety, my dear duke, when we have a telegraph which transmits messages in three or four hours, and that without getting in the least out of breath."

"Ah, sire, you recompense but badly this poor young man, who has come so far, and with so much ardor, to give your majesty useful information. If only for the sake of M. de Salvieux, who recommends him to me, I entreat your majesty to receive him graciously."

"M. de Salvieux, my brother's chamberlain?"

"Yes, sire."

"He is at Marseilles."

"And writes me thence."

"Does he speak to you of this conspiracy?"

"No; but strongly recommends M. de Villefort, and begs me to present him to your majesty."

"M. de Villefort!" cried the king, "is the messenger's name M. de Villefort?"

"Yes, sire."

"And he comes from Marseilles?"

"In person."

"Why did you not mention his name at once?" replied the king, betraying some uneasiness.

"Sire, I thought his name was unknown to your majesty."

"No, no, Blacas; he is a man of strong and elevated understanding, ambitious, too, and, *pardieu*, you know his father's name!"

"His father?"

"Yes, Noirtier."

"Noirtier the Girondin?—Noirtier the senator?"

"He himself."

"And your majesty has employed the son of such a man?"

"Blacas, my friend, you have but limited comprehension. I told you Villefort was ambitious, and to attain this ambition Villefort would sacrifice everything, even his father."

"Then, sire, may I present him?"

"This instant, Duke! Where is he?"

"Waiting below, in my carriage."

"Seek him at once."

"I hasten to do so." The duke left the royal presence with the speed of a young man; his really sincere royalism made him youthful again. Louis XVIII. remained alone, and turning his eyes on his half-opened Horace, muttered,—

"*Justum et tenacem propositi virum.*"

M. de Blacas returned as speedily as he had departed, but in the ante-chamber he was forced to appeal to the king's authority. Villefort's dusty garb, his costume, which was not of courtly cut, excited the susceptibility of M. de Breze, who was all astonishment at finding that this young man had the audacity to enter before the king in such attire. The duke, however, overcame all difficulties with a word—his majesty's order; and, in spite of the protestations which the master of ceremonies made for the honor of his office and principles, Villefort was introduced.

The king was seated in the same place where the duke had left him. On opening the door, Villefort found himself facing him, and the young magistrate's first impulse was to pause.

"Come in, M. de Villefort," said the king, "come in." Villefort bowed, and advancing a few steps, waited until the king should interrogate him.

"M. de Villefort," said Louis XVIII., "the Duc de Blacas assures me you have some interesting information to communicate."

"Sire, the duke is right, and I believe your majesty will think it equally important."

"In the first place, and before everything else, sir, is the news as bad in your opinion as I am asked to believe?"

"Sire, I believe it to be most urgent, but I hope, by the speed I have used, that it is not irreparable."

"Speak as fully as you please, sir," said the king, who began to give way to the emotion which had showed itself in Blacas's face and affected Villefort's voice. "Speak, sir, and pray begin at the beginning; I like order in everything."

"Sire," said Villefort, "I will render a faithful report to your majesty, but I must entreat your forgiveness if my anxiety leads to some obscurity in my language." A glance at the king after this discreet and subtle exordium, assured Villefort of the benignity of his august auditor, and he went on:—

"Sire, I have come as rapidly to Paris as possible, to inform your majesty that I have discovered, in the exercise of my duties, not a commonplace and insignificant plot, such as is every day got up in the lower ranks of the people and in the army, but an actual conspiracy—a storm which menaces no less than your majesty's throne. Sire, the usurper is arming three ships, he meditates some project, which, however mad, is yet, perhaps, terrible. At this moment he will have left Elba, to go whither I know not, but assuredly to attempt a landing either at Naples, or on the coast of Tuscany, or perhaps on the shores of France. Your majesty is well aware that the sovereign of the Island of Elba has maintained his relations with Italy and France?"

"I am, sir," said the king, much agitated; "and recently we have had information that the Bonapartist clubs have had meetings in the Rue Saint-Jacques. But proceed, I beg of you. How did you obtain these details?"

"Sire, they are the results of an examination which I have made of a man of Marseilles, whom I have watched for some time, and arrested on the day of my departure. This person, a sailor, of turbulent character, and whom I suspected of Bonapartism, has been secretly to the Island of Elba. There he saw the grand marshal, who charged him with an oral message to a Bonapartist in Paris, whose name I could not extract from him; but this mission was to prepare men's minds for a return (it is the man who says this, sire)—a return which will soon occur."

"And where is this man?"

"In prison, sire."

"And the matter seems serious to you?"

"So serious, sire, that when the circumstance surprised me in the midst of a family festival, on the very day of my betrothal, I left my bride and friends, postponing everything, that I might hasten to lay at your majesty's feet the fears which impressed me, and the assurance of my devotion."

"True," said Louis XVIII., "was there not a marriage engagement between you and Mademoiselle de Saint-Meran?"

"Daughter of one of your majesty's most faithful servants."

"Yes, yes; but let us talk of this plot, M. de Villefort."

"Sire, I fear it is more than a plot; I fear it is a conspiracy."

"A conspiracy in these times," said Louis XVIII., smiling, "is a thing very easy to meditate, but more difficult to conduct to an end, inasmuch as, re-established so recently on the throne of our ancestors, we have our eyes open at once upon the past, the present, and the future. For the last ten months my ministers have redoubled their vigilance, in order to watch the shore of the Mediterranean. If Bonaparte landed at Naples, the whole coalition would be on foot before he could even reach Piomoino; if he land in Tuscany, he will be in an unfriendly territory; if he land in France, it must be with a handful of men, and the result of that is easily foretold, execrated as he is by the population. Take courage, sir; but at the same time rely on our royal gratitude."

"Ah, here is M. Dandre!" cried de Blacas. At this instant the minister of police appeared at the door, pale, trembling, and as if ready to faint. Villefort was about to retire, but M. de Blacas, taking his hand, restrained him.

Chapter 11. The Corsican Ogre.

At the sight of this agitation Louis XVIII. pushed from him violently the table at which he was sitting.

"What ails you, Baron?" he exclaimed. "You appear quite aghast. Has your uneasiness anything to do with what M. de Blacas has told me, and M. de Villefort has just confirmed?" M. de Blacas moved suddenly towards the baron, but the fright of the courtier pleaded for the forbearance of the statesman; and besides, as matters were, it was much more to his advantage that the prefect of police should triumph over him than that he should humiliate the prefect.

"Sire"—stammered the baron.

"Well, what is it?" asked Louis XVIII. The minister of police, giving way to an impulse of despair, was about to throw himself at the feet of Louis XVIII., who retreated a step and frowned.

"Will you speak?" he said.

"Oh, sire, what a dreadful misfortune! I am, indeed, to be pitied. I can never forgive myself!"

"Monsieur," said Louis XVIII., "I command you to speak."

"Well, sire, the usurper left Elba on the 26th February, and landed on the 1st of March."

"And where? In Italy?" asked the king eagerly.

"In France, sire,—at a small port, near Antibes, in the Gulf of Juan."

"The usurper landed in France, near Antibes, in the Gulf of Juan, two hundred and fifty leagues from Paris, on the 1st of March, and you only acquired this information to-day, the 4th of March! Well, sir, what you tell me is impossible. You must have received a false report, or you have gone mad."

"Alas, sire, it is but too true!" Louis made a gesture of indescribable anger and alarm, and then drew himself up as if this sudden blow had struck him at the same moment in heart and countenance.

"In France!" he cried, "the usurper in France! Then they did not watch over this man. Who knows? they were, perhaps, in league with him."

"Oh, sire," exclaimed the Duc de Blacas, "M. Dandre is not a man to be accused of treason! Sire, we have all been blind, and the minister of police has shared the general blindness, that is all."

"But"—said Villefort, and then suddenly checking himself, he was silent; then he continued, "Your pardon, sire," he said, bowing, "my zeal carried me away. Will your majesty deign to excuse me?"

"Speak, sir, speak boldly," replied Louis. "You alone forewarned us of the evil; now try and aid us with the remedy."

"Sire," said Villefort, "the usurper is detested in the south; and it seems to me that if he ventured into the south, it would be easy to raise Languedoc and Provence against him."

"Yes, assuredly," replied the minister; "but he is advancing by Gap and Sisteron."

"Advancing—he is advancing!" said Louis XVIII. "Is he then advancing on Paris?" The minister of police maintained a silence which was equivalent to a complete avowal.

"And Dauphine, sir?" inquired the king, of Villefort. "Do you think it possible to rouse that as well as Provence?"

"Sire, I am sorry to tell your majesty a cruel fact; but the feeling in Dauphine is quite the reverse of that in Provence or Languedoc. The mountaineers are Bonapartists, sire."

"Then," murmured Louis, "he was well informed. And how many men had he with him?"

"I do not know, sire," answered the minister of police.

"What, you do not know! Have you neglected to obtain information on that point? Of course it is of no consequence," he added, with a withering smile.

"Sire, it was impossible to learn; the dispatch simply stated the fact of the landing and the route taken by the usurper."

"And how did this despatch reach you?" inquired the king. The minister bowed his head, and while a deep color overspread his cheeks, he stammered out,—

"By the telegraph, sire."—Louis XVIII. advanced a step, and folded his arms over his chest as Napoleon would have done.

"So then," he exclaimed, turning pale with anger, "seven conjoined and allied armies overthrew that man. A miracle of heaven replaced me on the throne of my fathers after five-and-twenty years of exile. I have, during those five-and-twenty years, spared no pains to understand the people of France and the interests which were confided to me; and now, when I see the fruition of my wishes almost within reach, the power I hold in my hands bursts, and shatters me to atoms!"

"Sire, it is fatality!" murmured the minister, feeling that the pressure of circumstances, however light a thing to destiny, was too much for any human strength to endure.

"What our enemies say of us is then true. We have learnt nothing, forgotten nothing! If I were betrayed as he was, I would console myself; but to be in the midst of persons elevated by myself to places of honor, who ought to watch over me more carefully than over themselves,—for my fortune is theirs—before me they were nothing—after me they will be nothing, and perish miserably from incapacity—ineptitude! Oh, yes, sir, you are right—it is fatality!"

The minister quailed before this outburst of sarcasm. M. de Blacas wiped the moisture from his brow. Villefort smiled within himself, for he felt his increased importance.

"To fall," continued King Louis, who at the first glance had sounded the abyss on which the monarchy hung suspended,—"to fall, and learn of that fall by telegraph! Oh, I would rather mount the scaffold of my brother, Louis XVI., than thus descend the staircase at the Tuileries driven away by ridicule. Ridicule, sir—why, you know not its power in France, and yet you ought to know it!"

"Sire, sire," murmured the minister, "for pity's"—

"Approach, M. de Villefort," resumed the king, addressing the young man, who, motionless and breathless, was listening to a conversation on which depended the destiny of a kingdom. "Approach, and tell monsieur that it is possible to know beforehand all that he has not known."

"Sire, it was really impossible to learn secrets which that man concealed from all the world."

"Really impossible! Yes—that is a great word, sir. Unfortunately, there are great words, as there are great men; I have measured them. Really impossible for a minister who has an office, agents, spies, and fifteen hundred thousand francs for secret service money, to know what is going on at sixty leagues from the coast of France! Well, then, see, here is a gentleman who had none of these resources at his disposal—a gentleman, only a simple magistrate, who learned more than you with all your police, and who would have saved my crown, if, like you, he had the power of directing a telegraph." The look of the minister of police was turned with concentrated spite on Villefort, who bent his head in modest triumph.

"I do not mean that for you, Blacas," continued Louis XVIII.; "for if you have discovered nothing, at least you have had the good sense to persevere in your suspicions. Any other than yourself would have considered the disclosure of M. de Villefort insignificant, or else dictated by venal ambition." These words were an allusion to the sentiments which the minister of police had uttered with so much confidence an hour before.

Villefort understood the king's intent. Any other person would, perhaps, have been overcome by such an intoxicating draught of praise; but he feared to make for himself a mortal enemy of the police minister, although he saw that Dandre was irrevocably lost. In fact, the minister, who, in the plenitude of his power, had been unable to unearth Napoleon's secret, might in despair at his own downfall interrogate Dantes and so lay bare the motives of Villefort's plot. Realizing this, Villefort came to the rescue of the crest-fallen minister, instead of aiding to crush him.

"Sire," said Villefort, "the suddenness of this event must prove to your majesty that the issue is in the hands of Providence; what your majesty is pleased to attribute to me as profound perspicacity is simply owing to chance, and I have profited by that chance, like a good and devoted servant—that's all. Do not attribute to me more than I deserve, sire, that your majesty may never have occasion to recall the first opinion you have been pleased to form of me." The minister of police thanked the young man by an eloquent look, and Villefort understood that he had succeeded in his design; that is to say, that without forfeiting the gratitude of the king, he had made a friend of one on whom, in case of necessity, he might rely.

"'Tis well," resumed the king. "And now, gentlemen," he continued, turning towards M. de Blacas and the minister of police, "I have no further occasion for you, and you may retire; what now remains to do is in the department of the minister of war."

"Fortunately, sire," said M. de Blacas, "we can rely on the army; your majesty knows how every report confirms their loyalty and attachment."

"Do not mention reports, Duke, to me, for I know now what confidence to place in them. Yet, speaking of reports, Baron, what have you learned with regard to the affair in the Rue Saint-Jacques?"

"The affair in the Rue Saint-Jacques!" exclaimed Villefort, unable to repress an exclamation. Then, suddenly pausing, he added, "Your pardon, sire, but my devotion to your majesty has made me forget, not the respect I have, for that is too deeply engraved in my heart, but the rules of etiquette."

"Go on, go on, sir," replied the king; "you have to-day earned the right to make inquiries here."

"Sire," interposed the minister of police, "I came a moment ago to give your majesty fresh information which I had obtained on this head, when your majesty's attention was attracted by the terrible event that has occurred in the gulf, and now these facts will cease to interest your majesty."

"On the contrary, sir,—on the contrary," said Louis XVIII., "this affair seems to me to have a decided connection with that which occupies our attention, and the death of General Quesnel will, perhaps, put us on the direct track of a great internal conspiracy." At the name of General Quesnel, Villefort trembled.

"Everything points to the conclusion, sire," said the minister of police, "that death was not the result of suicide, as we first believed, but of assassination. General Quesnel, it appears, had just left a Bonapartist club when he disappeared. An unknown person had been with him that morning, and made an appointment with him in the Rue Saint-Jacques; unfortunately, the general's valet, who was dressing his hair at the moment when the stranger entered, heard the street mentioned, but did not catch the number." As the police minister related this to the king, Villefort, who looked as if his very life hung on the speaker's lips, turned alternately red and pale. The king looked towards him.

"Do you not think with me, M. de Villefort, that General Quesnel, whom they believed attached to the usurper, but who was really entirely devoted to me, has perished the victim of a Bonapartist ambush?"

"It is probable, sire," replied Villefort. "But is this all that is known?"

"They are on the track of the man who appointed the meeting with him."

"On his track?" said Villefort.

"Yes, the servant has given his description. He is a man of from fifty to fifty-two years of age, dark, with black eyes covered with shaggy eyebrows, and a thick mustache. He was dressed in a blue frock-coat, buttoned up to the chin, and wore at his button-hole the rosette of an officer of the Legion of Honor. Yesterday a person exactly corresponding with this description was followed, but he was lost sight of at the corner of the Rue de la Jussienne and the Rue Coq-Heron." Villefort leaned on the back of an arm-chair, for as the minister of police went on speaking he felt his legs bend under him; but when he learned that the unknown had escaped the vigilance of the agent who followed him, he breathed again.

"Continue to seek for this man, sir," said the king to the minister of police; "for if, as I am all but convinced, General Quesnel, who would have been so useful to us at this moment, has been murdered, his assassins, Bonapartists or not, shall be cruelly punished." It required all Villefort's coolness not to betray the terror with which this declaration of the king inspired him.

"How strange," continued the king, with some asperity; "the police think that they have disposed of the whole matter when they say, 'A murder has been committed,' and especially so when they can add, 'And we are on the track of the guilty persons.'"

"Sire, your majesty will, I trust, be amply satisfied on this point at least."

"We shall see. I will no longer detain you, M. de Villefort, for you must be fatigued after so long a journey; go and rest. Of course you stopped at your father's?" A feeling of faintness came over Villefort.

"No, sire," he replied, "I alighted at the Hotel de Madrid, in the Rue de Tournon."

"But you have seen him?"

"Sire, I went straight to the Duc de Blacas."

"But you will see him, then?"

"I think not, sire."

"Ah, I forgot," said Louis, smiling in a manner which proved that all these questions were not made without a motive; "I forgot you and M. Noirtier are not on the best terms possible, and that is another sacrifice made to the royal cause, and for which you should be recompensed."

"Sire, the kindness your majesty deigns to evince towards me is a recompense which so far surpasses my utmost ambition that I have nothing more to ask for."

"Never mind, sir, we will not forget you; make your mind easy. In the meanwhile" (the king here detached the cross of the Legion of Honor which he usually wore over his blue coat, near the cross of St. Louis, above the order of Notre-Dame-du-Mont-Carmel and St. Lazare, and gave it to Villefort)—"in the meanwhile take this cross."

"Sire," said Villefort, "your majesty mistakes; this is an officer's cross."

"*Ma foi*," said Louis XVIII., "take it, such as it is, for I have not the time to procure you another. Blacas, let it be your care to see that the brevet is made out and sent to M. de Villefort." Villefort's eyes were filled with tears of joy and pride; he took the cross and kissed it.

"And now," he said, "may I inquire what are the orders with which your majesty deigns to honor me?"

"Take what rest you require, and remember that if you are not able to serve me here in Paris, you may be of the greatest service to me at Marseilles."

"Sire," replied Villefort, bowing, "in an hour I shall have quitted Paris."

"Go, sir," said the king; "and should I forget you (kings' memories are short), do not be afraid to bring yourself to my recollection. Baron, send for the minister of war. Blacas, remain."

"Ah, sir," said the minister of police to Villefort, as they left the Tuileries, "you entered by luck's door—your fortune is made."

"Will it be long first?" muttered Villefort, saluting the minister, whose career was ended, and looking about him for a hackney-coach. One passed at the moment, which he hailed; he gave his address to the driver, and springing in, threw himself on the seat, and gave loose to dreams of ambition.

Ten minutes afterwards Villefort reached his hotel, ordered horses to be ready in two hours, and asked to have his breakfast brought to him. He was about to begin his repast when the sound of the bell rang sharp and loud. The valet opened the door, and Villefort heard someone speak his name.

"Who could know that I was here already?" said the young man. The valet entered.

"Well," said Villefort, "what is it?—Who rang?—Who asked for me?"

"A stranger who will not send in his name."

"A stranger who will not send in his name! What can he want with me?"

"He wishes to speak to you."

"To me?"

"Yes."

"Did he mention my name?"

"Yes."

"What sort of person is he?"

"Why, sir, a man of about fifty."

"Short or tall?"

"About your own height, sir."

"Dark or fair?"

"Dark,—very dark; with black eyes, black hair, black eyebrows."

"And how dressed?" asked Villefort quickly.

"In a blue frock-coat, buttoned up close, decorated with the Legion of Honor."

"It is he!" said Villefort, turning pale.

"Eh, *pardieu*," said the individual whose description we have twice given, entering the door, "what a great deal of ceremony! Is it the custom in Marseilles for sons to keep their fathers waiting in their anterooms?"

"Father!" cried Villefort, "then I was not deceived; I felt sure it must be you."

"Well, then, if you felt so sure," replied the new-comer, putting his cane in a corner and his hat on a chair, "allow me to say, my dear Gerard, that it was not very filial of you to keep me waiting at the door."

"Leave us, Germain," said Villefort. The servant quitted the apartment with evident signs of astonishment.

Chapter 12. Father and Son.

M. Noirtier—for it was, indeed, he who entered—looked after the servant until the door was closed, and then, fearing, no doubt, that he might be overheard in the ante-chamber, he opened the door again, nor was the precaution useless, as appeared from the rapid retreat of Germain, who proved that he was not exempt from the sin which ruined our first parents. M. Noirtier then took the trouble to close and bolt the ante-chamber door, then that of the bed-chamber, and then extended his hand to Villefort, who had followed all his motions with surprise which he could not conceal.

"Well, now, my dear Gerard," said he to the young man, with a very significant look, "do you know, you seem as if you were not very glad to see me?"

"My dear father," said Villefort, "I am, on the contrary, delighted; but I so little expected your visit, that it has somewhat overcome me."

"But, my dear fellow," replied M. Noirtier, seating himself, "I might say the same thing to you, when you announce to me your wedding for the 28th of February, and on the 3rd of March you turn up here in Paris."

"And if I have come, my dear father," said Gerard, drawing closer to M. Noirtier, "do not complain, for it is for you that I came, and my journey will be your salvation."

"Ah, indeed!" said M. Noirtier, stretching himself out at his ease in the chair. "Really, pray tell me all about it, for it must be interesting."

"Father, you have heard speak of a certain Bonapartist club in the Rue Saint-Jacques?"

"No. 53; yes, I am vice-president."

"Father, your coolness makes me shudder."

"Why, my dear boy, when a man has been proscribed by the mountaineers, has escaped from Paris in a hay-cart, been hunted over the plains of Bordeaux by Robespierre's bloodhounds, he becomes accustomed to most things. But go on, what about the club in the Rue Saint-Jacques?"

"Why, they induced General Quesnel to go there, and General Quesnel, who quitted his own house at nine o'clock in the evening, was found the next day in the Seine."

"And who told you this fine story?"

"The king himself."

"Well, then, in return for your story," continued Noirtier, "I will tell you another."

"My dear father, I think I already know what you are about to tell me."

"Ah, you have heard of the landing of the emperor?"

"Not so loud, father, I entreat of you—for your own sake as well as mine. Yes, I heard this news, and knew it even before you could; for three days ago I posted from Marseilles to Paris with all possible speed, half-desperate at the enforced delay."

"Three days ago? You are crazy. Why, three days ago the emperor had not landed."

"No matter, I was aware of his intention."

"How did you know about it?"

"By a letter addressed to you from the Island of Elba."

"To me?"

"To you; and which I discovered in the pocket-book of the messenger. Had that letter fallen into the hands of another, you, my dear father, would probably ere this have been shot." Villefort's father laughed.

"Come, come," said he, "will the Restoration adopt imperial methods so promptly? Shot, my dear boy? What an idea! Where is the letter you speak of? I know you too well to suppose you would allow such a thing to pass you."

"I burnt it, for fear that even a fragment should remain; for that letter must have led to your condemnation."

"And the destruction of your future prospects," replied Noirtier; "yes, I can easily comprehend that. But I have nothing to fear while I have you to protect me."

"I do better than that, sir—I save you."

"You do? Why, really, the thing becomes more and more dramatic—explain yourself."

"I must refer again to the club in the Rue Saint-Jacques."

"It appears that this club is rather a bore to the police. Why didn't they search more vigilantly? they would have found"—

"They have not found; but they are on the track."

"Yes, that the usual phrase; I am quite familiar with it. When the police is at fault, it declares that it is on the track; and the government patiently awaits the day when it comes to say, with a sneaking air, that the track is lost."

"Yes, but they have found a corpse; the general has been killed, and in all countries they call that a murder."

"A murder do you call it? Why, there is nothing to prove that the general was murdered. People are found every day in the Seine, having thrown themselves in, or having been drowned from not knowing how to swim."

"Father, you know very well that the general was not a man to drown himself in despair, and people do not bathe in the Seine in the month of January. No, no, do not be deceived; this was murder in every sense of the word."

"And who thus designated it?"

"The king himself."

"The king! I thought he was philosopher enough to allow that there was no murder in politics. In politics, my dear fellow, you know, as well as I do, there are no men, but ideas—no feelings, but interests; in politics we do not kill a man, we only remove an obstacle, that is all.

Would you like to know how matters have progressed? Well, I will tell you. It was thought reliance might be placed in General Quesnel; he was recommended to us from the Island of Elba; one of us went to him, and invited him to the Rue Saint-Jacques, where he would find some friends. He came there, and the plan was unfolded to him for leaving Elba, the projected landing, etc. When he had heard and comprehended all to the fullest extent, he replied that he was a royalist. Then all looked at each other,—he was made to take an oath, and did so, but with such an ill grace that it was really tempting Providence to swear him, and yet, in spite of that, the general was allowed to depart free—perfectly free. Yet he did not return home. What could that mean? why, my dear fellow, that on leaving us he lost his way, that's all. A murder? really, Villefort, you surprise me. You, a deputy procureur, to found an accusation on such bad premises! Did I ever say to you, when you were fulfilling your character as a royalist, and cut off the head of one of my party, 'My son, you have committed a murder?' No, I said, 'Very well, sir, you have gained the victory; to-morrow, perchance, it will be our turn.'"

"But, Father, take care; when our turn comes, our revenge will be sweeping."

"I do not understand you."

"You rely on the usurper's return?"

"We do."

"You are mistaken; he will not advance two leagues into the interior of France without being followed, tracked, and caught like a wild beast."

"My dear fellow, the emperor is at this moment on the way to Grenoble; on the 10th or 12th he will be at Lyons, and on the 20th or 25th at Paris."

"The people will rise."

"Yes, to go and meet him."

"He has but a handful of men with him, and armies will be dispatched against him."

"Yes, to escort him into the capital. Really, my dear Gerard, you are but a child; you think yourself well informed because the telegraph has told you, three days after the landing, 'The usurper has landed at Cannes with several men. He is pursued.' But where is he? what is he doing? You do not know at all, and in this way they will chase him to Paris, without drawing a trigger."

"Grenoble and Lyons are faithful cities, and will oppose to him an impassable barrier."

"Grenoble will open her gates to him with enthusiasm—all Lyons will hasten to welcome him. Believe me, we are as well informed as you, and our police are as good as your own. Would you like a proof of it? Well, you wished to conceal your journey from me, and yet I knew of your arrival half an hour after you had passed the barrier. You gave your direction to no one but your postilion, yet I have your address, and in proof I am here the very instant you are going to sit at table. Ring, then, if you please, for a second knife, fork, and plate, and we will dine together."

"Indeed!" replied Villefort, looking at his father with astonishment, "you really do seem very well informed."

"Eh? the thing is simple enough. You who are in power have only the means that money produces—we who are in expectation, have those which devotion prompts."

"Devotion!" said Villefort, with a sneer.

"Yes, devotion; for that is, I believe, the phrase for hopeful ambition."

And Villefort's father extended his hand to the bell-rope, to summon the servant whom his son had not called. Villefort caught his arm.

"Wait, my dear father," said the young man, "one word more."

"Say on."

"However stupid the royalist police may be, they do know one terrible thing."

"What is that?"

"The description of the man who, on the morning of the day when General Quesnel disappeared, presented himself at his house."

"Oh, the admirable police have found that out, have they? And what may be that description?"

"Dark complexion; hair, eyebrows, and whiskers, black; blue frock-coat, buttoned up to the chin; rosette of an officer of the Legion of Honor in his button-hole; a hat with wide brim, and a cane."

"Ah, ha, that's it, is it?" said Noirtier; "and why, then, have they not laid hands on him?"

"Because yesterday, or the day before, they lost sight of him at the corner of the Rue Coq-Heron."

"Didn't I say that your police were good for nothing?"

"Yes; but they may catch him yet."

"True," said Noirtier, looking carelessly around him, "true, if this person were not on his guard, as he is;" and he added with a smile, "He will consequently make a few changes in his personal appearance." At these words he rose, and put off his frock-coat and cravat, went towards a table on which lay his son's toilet articles, lathered his face, took a razor, and, with a firm hand, cut off the compromising whiskers. Villefort watched him with alarm not devoid of admiration.

His whiskers cut off, Noirtier gave another turn to his hair; took, instead of his black cravat, a colored neckerchief which lay at the top of an open portmanteau; put on, in lieu of his blue and high-buttoned frock-coat, a coat of Villefort's of dark brown, and cut away in front; tried on before the glass a narrow-brimmed hat of his son's, which appeared to fit him perfectly, and, leaving his cane in the corner where he had deposited it, he took up a small bamboo switch, cut the air with it once or twice, and walked about with that easy swagger which was one of his principal characteristics.

"Well," he said, turning towards his wondering son, when this disguise was completed, "well, do you think your police will recognize me now?"

"No, Father," stammered Villefort; "at least, I hope not."

"And now, my dear boy," continued Noirtier, "I rely on your prudence to remove all the things which I leave in your care."

"Oh, rely on me," said Villefort.

"Yes, yes; and now I believe you are right, and that you have really saved my life; be assured I will return the favor hereafter." Villefort shook his head.

"You are not convinced yet?"

"I hope at least, that you may be mistaken."

"Shall you see the king again?"

"Perhaps."

"Would you pass in his eyes for a prophet?"

"Prophets of evil are not in favor at the court, Father."

"True, but some day they do them justice; and supposing a second restoration, you would then pass for a great man."

"Well, what should I say to the king?"

"Say this to him: 'Sire, you are deceived as to the feeling in France, as to the opinions of the towns, and the prejudices of the army; he whom in Paris you call the Corsican ogre, who at Nevers is styled the usurper, is already saluted as Bonaparte at Lyons, and emperor at Grenoble. You think he is tracked, pursued, captured; he is advancing as rapidly as his own eagles. The soldiers you believe to be dying with hunger, worn out with fatigue, ready to desert, gather like atoms of snow about the rolling ball as it hastens onward. Sire, go, leave France to its real master, to him who acquired it, not by purchase, but by right of conquest; go, sire, not that you incur any risk, for your adversary is powerful enough to show you mercy, but because it would be humiliating for a grandson of Saint

Louis to owe his life to the man of Arcola, Marengo, Austerlitz.' Tell him this, Gerard; or, rather, tell him nothing. Keep your journey a secret; do not boast of what you have come to Paris to do, or have done; return with all speed; enter Marseilles at night, and your house by the back-door, and there remain, quiet, submissive, secret, and, above all, inoffensive; for this time, I swear to you, we shall act like powerful men who know their enemies. Go, my son—go, my dear Gerard, and by your obedience to my paternal orders, or, if you prefer it, friendly counsels, we will keep you in your place.

This will be," added Noirtier, with a smile, "one means by which you may a second time save me, if the political balance should someday take another turn, and cast you aloft while hurling me down. Adieu, my dear Gerard, and at your next journey alight at my door." Noirtier left the room when he had finished, with the same calmness that had characterized him during the whole of this remarkable and trying conversation. Villefort, pale and agitated, ran to the window, put aside the curtain, and saw him pass, cool and collected, by two or three ill-looking men at the corner of the street, who were there, perhaps, to arrest a man with black whiskers, and a blue frock-coat, and hat with broad brim.

Villefort stood watching, breathless, until his father had disappeared at the Rue Bussy. Then he turned to the various articles he had left behind him, put the black cravat and blue frock-coat at the bottom of the portmanteau, threw the hat into a dark closet, broke the cane into small bits and flung it in the fire, put on his travelling-cap, and calling his valet, checked with a look the thousand questions he was ready to ask, paid his bill, sprang into his carriage, which was ready, learned at Lyons that Bonaparte had entered Grenoble, and in the midst of the tumult which prevailed along the road, at length reached Marseilles, a prey to all the hopes and fears which enter into the heart of man with ambition and its first successes.

Chapter 13. The Hundred Days.

M. Noirtier was a true prophet, and things progressed rapidly, as he had predicted. Every one knows the history of the famous return from Elba, a return which was unprecedented in the past, and will probably remain without a counterpart in the future.

Louis XVIII. made but a faint attempt to parry this unexpected blow; the monarchy he had scarcely reconstructed tottered on its precarious foundation, and at a sign from the emperor the incongruous structure of ancient prejudices and new ideas fell to the ground. Villefort, therefore, gained nothing save the king's gratitude (which was rather likely to injure him at the present time) and the cross of the Legion of Honor, which he had the prudence not to wear, although M. de Blacas had duly forwarded the brevet.

Napoleon would, doubtless, have deprived Villefort of his office had it not been for Noirtier, who was all powerful at court, and thus the Girondin of '93 and the Senator of 1806 protected him who so lately had been his protector. All Villefort's influence barely enabled him to stifle the secret Dantes had so nearly divulged. The king's procureur alone was deprived of his office, being suspected of royalism.

However, scarcely was the imperial power established—that is, scarcely had the emperor re-entered the Tuileries and begun to issue orders from the closet into which we have introduced our readers,—he found on the table there Louis XVIII.'s half-filled snuff-box,—scarcely had this occurred when Marseilles began, in spite of the authorities, to rekindle the flames of civil war, always smoldering in the south, and it required but little to excite the populace to acts of far greater violence than the shouts and insults with which they assailed the royalists whenever they ventured abroad.

Owing to this change, the worthy shipowner became at that moment—we will not say all powerful, because Morrel was a prudent and rather a timid man, so much so, that many of the most zealous partisans of Bonaparte accused him of "moderation"—but sufficiently influential to make a demand in favor of Dantes.

Villefort retained his place, but his marriage was put off until a more favorable opportunity. If the emperor remained on the throne, Gerard required a different alliance to aid his career; if Louis XVIII. returned, the influence of M. de Saint-Meran, like his own, could be vastly increased, and the marriage be still more suitable. The deputy-procureur was, therefore, the first magistrate of Marseilles, when one morning his door opened, and M. Morrel was announced.

Any one else would have hastened to receive him; but Villefort was a man of ability, and he knew this would be a sign of weakness. He made Morrel wait in the ante-chamber, although he had no one with him, for the simple reason that the king's procureur always makes everyone wait, and after passing a quarter of an hour in reading the papers, he ordered M. Morrel to be admitted.

Morrel expected Villefort would be dejected; he found him as he had found him six weeks before, calm, firm, and full of that glacial politeness, that most insurmountable barrier which separates the well-bred from the vulgar man.

He had entered Villefort's office expecting that the magistrate would tremble at the sight of him; on the contrary, he felt a cold shudder all over him when he saw Villefort sitting there with his elbow on his desk, and his head leaning on his hand. He stopped at the door; Villefort gazed at him as if he had some difficulty in recognizing him; then, after a brief interval, during which the honest ship-owner turned his hat in his hands,—

"M. Morrel, I believe?" said Villefort.

"Yes, sir."

"Come nearer," said the magistrate, with a patronizing wave of the hand, "and tell me to what circumstance I owe the honor of this visit."

"Do you not guess, monsieur?" asked Morrel.

"Not in the least; but if I can serve you in any way I shall be delighted."

"Everything depends on you."

"Explain yourself, pray."

"Monsieur," said Morrel, recovering his assurance as he proceeded, "do you recollect that a few days before the landing of his majesty the emperor, I came to intercede for a young man, the mate of my ship, who was accused of being concerned in correspondence with the Island of Elba? What was the other day a crime is to-day a title to favor. You then served Louis XVIII., and you did not show any favor—it was your duty; to-day you serve Napoleon, and you ought to protect him—it is equally your duty; I come, therefore, to ask what has become of him?"

Villefort by a strong effort sought to control himself. "What is his name?" said he. "Tell me his name."

"Edmond Dantes."

Villefort would probably have rather stood opposite the muzzle of a pistol at five-and-twenty paces than have heard this name spoken; but he did not blanch.

"Dantes," repeated he, "Edmond Dantes."

"Yes, monsieur." Villefort opened a large register, then went to a table, from the table turned to his registers, and then, turning to Morrel,—

"Are you quite sure you are not mistaken, monsieur?" said he, in the most natural tone in the world.

Had Morrel been a more quick-sighted man, or better versed in these matters, he would have been surprised at the king's procureur answering him on such a subject, instead of referring him to the governors of the prison or the prefect of the department. But Morrel, disappointed in his expectations of exciting fear, was conscious only of the other's condescension. Villefort had calculated rightly.

"No," said Morrel; "I am not mistaken. I have known him for ten years, the last four of which he was in my service. Do not you recollect, I came about six weeks ago to plead for clemency, as I come to-day to plead for justice. You received me very coldly. Oh, the royalists were very severe with the Bonapartists in those days."

"Monsieur," returned Villefort, "I was then a royalist, because I believed the Bourbons not only the heirs to the throne, but the chosen of the nation. The miraculous return of Napoleon has conquered me, the legitimate monarch is he who is loved by his people."

"That's right!" cried Morrel. "I like to hear you speak thus, and I augur well for Edmond from it."

"Wait a moment," said Villefort, turning over the leaves of a register; "I have it—a sailor, who was about to marry a young Catalan girl. I recollect now; it was a very serious charge."

"How so?"

"You know that when he left here he was taken to the Palais de Justice."

"Well?"

"I made my report to the authorities at Paris, and a week after he was carried off."

"Carried off!" said Morrel. "What can they have done with him?"

"Oh, he has been taken to Fenestrelles, to Pignerol, or to the Sainte-Marguerite islands. Some fine morning he will return to take command of your vessel."

"Come when he will, it shall be kept for him. But how is it he is not already returned? It seems to me the first care of government should be to set at liberty those who have suffered for their adherence to it."

"Do not be too hasty, M. Morrel," replied Villefort. "The order of imprisonment came from high authority, and the order for his liberation must proceed from the same source; and, as Napoleon has scarcely been reinstated a fortnight, the letters have not yet been forwarded."

"But," said Morrel, "is there no way of expediting all these formalities—of releasing him from arrest?"

"There has been no arrest."

"How?"

"It is sometimes essential to government to cause a man's disappearance without leaving any traces, so that no written forms or documents may defeat their wishes."

"It might be so under the Bourbons, but at present"—

"It has always been so, my dear Morrel, since the reign of Louis XIV. The emperor is more strict in prison discipline than even Louis himself, and the number of prisoners whose names are not on the register is incalculable." Had Morrel even any suspicions, so much kindness would have dispelled them.

"Well, M. de Villefort, how would you advise me to act?" asked he.

"Petition the minister."

"Oh, I know what that is; the minister receives two hundred petitions every day, and does not read three."

"That is true; but he will read a petition countersigned and presented by me."

"And will you undertake to deliver it?"

"With the greatest pleasure. Dantes was then guilty, and now he is innocent, and it is as much my duty to free him as it was to condemn him." Villefort thus forestalled any danger of an inquiry, which, however improbable it might be, if it did take place would leave him defenceless.

"But how shall I address the minister?"

"Sit down there," said Villefort, giving up his place to Morrel, "and write what I dictate."

"Will you be so good?"

"Certainly. But lose no time; we have lost too much already."

"That is true. Only think what the poor fellow may even now be suffering." Villefort shuddered at the suggestion; but he had gone too far to draw back. Dantes must be crushed to gratify Villefort's ambition.

Villefort dictated a petition, in which, from an excellent intention, no doubt, Dantes' patriotic services were exaggerated, and he was made out one of the most active agents of Napoleon's return. It was evident that at the sight of this document the minister would instantly release him. The petition finished, Villefort read it aloud.

"That will do," said he; "leave the rest to me."

"Will the petition go soon?"

"To-day."

"Countersigned by you?"

"The best thing I can do will be to certify the truth of the contents of your petition." And, sitting down, Villefort wrote the certificate at the bottom.

"What more is to be done?"

"I will do whatever is necessary." This assurance delighted Morrel, who took leave of Villefort, and hastened to announce to old Dantes that he would soon see his son.

As for Villefort, instead of sending to Paris, he carefully preserved the petition that so fearfully compromised Dantes, in the hopes of an event that seemed not unlikely,—that is, a second restoration. Dantes remained a prisoner, and heard not the noise of the fall of Louis XVIII.'s throne, or the still more tragic destruction of the empire.

Twice during the Hundred Days had Morrel renewed his demand, and twice had Villefort soothed him with promises.

At last there was Waterloo, and Morrel came no more; he had done all that was in his power, and any fresh attempt would only compromise himself uselessly.

Louis XVIII. remounted the throne; Villefort, to whom Marseilles had become filled with remorseful memories, sought and obtained the situation of king's procureur at Toulouse, and a fortnight afterwards he married Mademoiselle de Saint-Meran, whose father now stood higher at court than ever.

And so Dantes, after the Hundred Days and after Waterloo, remained in his dungeon, forgotten of earth and heaven. Danglars comprehended the full extent of the wretched fate that overwhelmed Dantes; and, when Napoleon returned to France, he, after the manner of mediocre minds, termed the coincidence, "a decree of Providence." But when Napoleon returned to Paris, Danglars' heart failed him, and he lived in constant fear of Dantes' return on a mission of vengeance. He therefore informed M. Morrel of his wish to quit the sea, and obtained a recommendation from him to a Spanish merchant, into whose service he entered at the end of March, that is, ten or twelve days after Napoleon's return. He then left for Madrid, and was no more heard of.

Fernand understood nothing except that Dantes was absent. What had become of him he cared not to inquire. Only, during the respite the absence of his rival afforded him, he reflected, partly on the means of deceiving Mercedes as to the cause of his absence, partly on plans of emigration and abduction, as from time to time he sat sad and motionless on the summit of Cape Pharo, at the spot from whence Marseilles and the Catalans are visible, watching for the apparition of a young and handsome man, who was for him also the messenger of vengeance. Fernand's mind was made up; he would shoot Dantes, and then kill himself. But Fernand was mistaken; a man of his disposition never kills himself, for he constantly hopes.

During this time the empire made its last conscription, and every man in France capable of bearing arms rushed to obey the summons of the emperor. Fernand departed with the rest, bearing with him the terrible thought that while he was away, his rival would perhaps return and marry Mercedes. Had Fernand really meant to kill himself, he would have done so when he parted from Mercedes. His devotion, and the compassion he showed for her misfortunes, produced the effect they always produce on noble minds—Mercedes had always had a sincere regard for Fernand, and this was now strengthened by gratitude.

"My brother," said she as she placed his knapsack on his shoulders, "be careful of yourself, for if you are killed, I shall be alone in the world." These words carried a ray of hope into Fernand's heart. Should Dantes not return, Mercedes might one day be his.

Mercedes was left alone face to face with the vast plain that had never seemed so barren, and the sea that had never seemed so vast. Bathed in tears she wandered about the Catalan village. Sometimes she stood mute and motionless as a statue, looking towards Marseilles, at other times gazing on the sea, and debating as to whether it were not better to cast herself into the abyss of the ocean, and thus end her woes. It was not want of courage that prevented her putting this resolution into execution; but her religious feelings came to her aid and saved her. Caderousse was, like Fernand, enrolled in the army, but, being married and eight years older, he was merely sent to the frontier. Old Dantes, who was only sustained by hope, lost all hope at Napoleon's downfall. Five months after he had been separated from his son, and almost at the hour of his arrest, he breathed his last in Mercedes' arms. M. Morrel paid the expenses of his funeral, and a few small debts the poor old man had contracted.

There was more than benevolence in this action; there was courage; the south was aflame, and to assist, even on his death-bed, the father of so dangerous a Bonapartist as Dantes, was stigmatized as a crime.

Chapter 14. The Two Prisoners.

A year after Louis XVIII.'s restoration, a visit was made by the inspector-general of prisons. Dantes in his cell heard the noise of preparation,—sounds that at the depth where he lay would have been inaudible to any but the ear of a prisoner, who could hear the splash of the drop of water that every hour fell from the roof of his dungeon. He guessed something uncommon was passing among the living; but he had so long ceased to have any intercourse with the world, that he looked upon himself as dead.

The inspector visited, one after another, the cells and dungeons of several of the prisoners, whose good behavior or stupidity recommended them to the clemency of the government. He inquired how they were fed, and if they had any request to make. The universal response was, that the fare was detestable, and that they wanted to be set free.

The inspector asked if they had anything else to ask for. They shook their heads. What could they desire beyond their liberty? The inspector turned smilingly to the governor.

"I do not know what reason government can assign for these useless visits; when you see one prisoner, you see all,—always the same thing,—ill fed and innocent. Are there any others?"

"Yes; the dangerous and mad prisoners are in the dungeons."

"Let us visit them," said the inspector with an air of fatigue. "We must play the farce to the end. Let us see the dungeons."

"Let us first send for two soldiers," said the governor. "The prisoners sometimes, through mere uneasiness of life, and in order to be sentenced to death, commit acts of useless violence, and you might fall a victim."

"Take all needful precautions," replied the inspector.

Two soldiers were accordingly sent for, and the inspector descended a stairway, so foul, so humid, so dark, as to be loathsome to sight, smell, and respiration.

"Oh," cried the inspector, "who can live here?"

"A most dangerous conspirator, a man we are ordered to keep the most strict watch over, as he is daring and resolute."

"He is alone?"

"Certainly."

"How long has he been there?"

"Nearly a year."

"Was he placed here when he first arrived?"

"No; not until he attempted to kill the turnkey, who took his food to him."

"To kill the turnkey?"

"Yes, the very one who is lighting us. Is it not true, Antoine?" asked the governor.

"True enough; he wanted to kill me!" returned the turnkey.

"He must be mad," said the inspector.

"He is worse than that,—he is a devil!" returned the turnkey.

"Shall I complain of him?" demanded the inspector.

"Oh, no; it is useless. Besides, he is almost mad now, and in another year he will be quite so."

"So much the better for him,—he will suffer less," said the inspector. He was, as this remark shows, a man full of philanthropy, and in every way fit for his office.

"You are right, sir," replied the governor; "and this remark proves that you have deeply considered the subject. Now we have in a dungeon about twenty feet distant, and to which you descend by another stair, an abbe, formerly leader of a party in Italy, who has been here since 1811, and in 1813 he went mad, and the change is astonishing. He used to weep, he now laughs; he grew thin, he now grows fat. You had better see him, for his madness is amusing."

"I will see them both," returned the inspector; "I must conscientiously perform my duty." This was the inspector's first visit; he wished to display his authority.

"Let us visit this one first," added he.

"By all means," replied the governor, and he signed to the turnkey to open the door. At the sound of the key turning in the lock, and the creaking of the hinges, Dantes, who was crouched in a corner of the dungeon, whence he could see the ray of light that came through a narrow iron grating above, raised his head. Seeing a stranger, escorted by two turnkeys holding torches and accompanied by two soldiers, and to whom the governor spoke bareheaded, Dantes, who guessed the truth, and that the moment to address himself to the superior authorities was come, sprang forward with clasped hands.

The soldiers interposed their bayonets, for they thought that he was about to attack the inspector, and the latter recoiled two or three steps. Dantes saw that he was looked upon as dangerous. Then, infusing all the humility he possessed into his eyes and voice, he addressed the inspector, and sought to inspire him with pity.

The inspector listened attentively; then, turning to the governor, observed, "He will become religious—he is already more gentle; he is afraid, and retreated before the bayonets—madmen are not afraid of anything; I made some curious observations on this at Charenton." Then, turning to the prisoner, "What is it you want?" said he.

"I want to know what crime I have committed—to be tried; and if I am guilty, to be shot; if innocent, to be set at liberty."

"Are you well fed?" said the inspector.

"I believe so; I don't know; it's of no consequence. What matters really, not only to me, but to officers of justice and the king, is that an innocent man should languish in prison, the victim of an infamous denunciation, to die here cursing his executioners."

"You are very humble to-day," remarked the governor; "you are not so always; the other day, for instance, when you tried to kill the turnkey."

"It is true, sir, and I beg his pardon, for he has always been very good to me, but I was mad."

"And you are not so any longer?"

"No; captivity has subdued me—I have been here so long."

"So long?—when were you arrested, then?" asked the inspector.

"The 28th of February, 1815, at half-past two in the afternoon."

"To-day is the 30th of July, 1816,—why it is but seventeen months."

"Only seventeen months," replied Dantes. "Oh, you do not know what is seventeen months in prison!—seventeen ages rather, especially to a man who, like me, had arrived at the summit of his ambition—to a man, who, like me, was on the point of marrying a woman he adored, who saw an honorable career opened before him, and who loses all in an instant—who sees his prospects destroyed, and is ignorant of the fate of his affianced wife, and whether his aged father be still living! Seventeen months' captivity to a sailor accustomed to the boundless ocean, is a worse punishment than human crime ever merited. Have pity on me, then, and ask for me, not intelligence, but a trial; not pardon, but a verdict—a trial, sir, I ask only for a trial; that, surely, cannot be denied to one who is accused!"

"We shall see," said the inspector; then, turning to the governor, "On my word, the poor devil touches me. You must show me the proofs against him."

"Certainly; but you will find terrible charges."

"Monsieur," continued Dantes, "I know it is not in your power to release me; but you can plead for me—you can have me tried— and that is all I ask. Let me know my crime, and the reason why I was condemned. Uncertainty is worse than all."

"Go on with the lights," said the inspector.

"Monsieur," cried Dantes, "I can tell by your voice you are touched with pity; tell me at least to hope."

"I cannot tell you that," replied the inspector; "I can only promise to examine into your case."

"Oh, I am free—then I am saved!"

"Who arrested you?"

"M. Villefort. See him, and hear what he says."

"M. Villefort is no longer at Marseilles; he is now at Toulouse."

"I am no longer surprised at my detention," murmured Dantes, "since my only protector is removed."

"Had M. de Villefort any cause of personal dislike to you?"

"None; on the contrary, he was very kind to me."

"I can, then, rely on the notes he has left concerning you?"

"Entirely."

"That is well; wait patiently, then." Dantes fell on his knees, and prayed earnestly. The door closed; but this time a fresh inmate was left with Dantes—hope.

"Will you see the register at once," asked the governor, "or proceed to the other cell?"

"Let us visit them all," said the inspector. "If I once went up those stairs, I should never have the courage to come down again."

"Ah, this one is not like the other, and his madness is less affecting than this one's display of reason."

"What is his folly?"

"He fancies he possesses an immense treasure. The first year he offered government a million francs for his release; the second, two; the third, three; and so on progressively. He is now in his fifth year of captivity; he will ask to speak to you in private, and offer you five millions."

"How curious!—what is his name?"

"The Abbe Faria."

"No. 27," said the inspector.

"It is here; unlock the door, Antoine." The turnkey obeyed, and the inspector gazed curiously into the chamber of the "mad abbe."

In the centre of the cell, in a circle traced with a fragment of plaster detached from the wall, sat a man whose tattered garments scarcely covered him. He was drawing in this circle geometrical lines, and seemed as much absorbed in his problem as Archimedes was when the soldier of Marcellus slew him.

He did not move at the sound of the door, and continued his calculations until the flash of the torches lighted up with an unwonted glare the somber walls of his cell; then, raising his head, he perceived with astonishment the number of persons present. He hastily seized the coverlet of his bed, and wrapped it round him.

"What is it you want?" said the inspector.

"I, monsieur," replied the abbe with an air of surprise—"I want nothing."

"You do not understand," continued the inspector; "I am sent here by government to visit the prison, and hear the requests of the prisoners."

"Oh, that is different," cried the abbe; "and we shall understand each other, I hope."

"There, now," whispered the governor, "it is just as I told you."

"Monsieur," continued the prisoner, "I am the Abbe Faria, born at Rome. I was for twenty years Cardinal Spada's secretary; I was arrested, why, I know not, toward the beginning of the year 1811; since then I have demanded my liberty from the Italian and French government."

"Why from the French government?"

"Because I was arrested at Piombino, and I presume that, like Milan and Florence, Piombino has become the capital of some French department."

"Ah," said the inspector, "you have not the latest news from Italy?"

"My information dates from the day on which I was arrested," returned the Abbe Faria; "and as the emperor had created the kingdom of Rome for his infant son, I presume that he has realized the dream of Machiavelli and Caesar Borgia, which was to make Italy a united kingdom."

"Monsieur," returned the inspector, "providence has changed this gigantic plan you advocate so warmly."

"It is the only means of rendering Italy strong, happy, and independent."

"Very possibly; only I am not come to discuss politics, but to inquire if you have anything to ask or to complain of."

"The food is the same as in other prisons,—that is, very bad; the lodging is very unhealthful, but, on the whole, passable for a dungeon; but it is not that which I wish to speak of, but a secret I have to reveal of the greatest importance."

"We are coming to the point," whispered the governor.

"It is for that reason I am delighted to see you," continued the abbe, "although you have disturbed me in a most important calculation, which, if it succeeded, would possibly change Newton's system. Could you allow me a few words in private?"

"What did I tell you?" said the governor.

"You knew him," returned the inspector with a smile.

"What you ask is impossible, monsieur," continued he, addressing Faria.

"But," said the abbe, "I would speak to you of a large sum, amounting to five millions."

"The very sum you named," whispered the inspector in his turn.

"However," continued Faria, seeing that the inspector was about to depart, "it is not absolutely necessary for us to be alone; the governor can be present."

"Unfortunately," said the governor, "I know beforehand what you are about to say; it concerns your treasures, does it not?" Faria fixed his eyes on him with an expression that would have convinced anyone else of his sanity.

"Of course," said he; "of what else should I speak?"

"Mr. Inspector," continued the governor, "I can tell you the story as well as he, for it has been dinned in my ears for the last four or five years."

"That proves," returned the abbe, "that you are like those of Holy Writ, who having ears hear not, and having eyes see not."

"My dear sir, the government is rich and does not want your treasures," replied the inspector; "keep them until you are liberated." The abbe's eyes glistened; he seized the inspector's hand.

"But what if I am not liberated," cried he, "and am detained here until my death? This treasure will be lost. Had not government better profit by it? I will offer six millions, and I will content myself with the rest, if they will only give me my liberty."

"On my word," said the inspector in a low tone, "had I not been told beforehand that this man was mad, I should believe what he says."

"I am not mad," replied Faria, with that acuteness of hearing peculiar to prisoners. "The treasure I speak of really exists, and I offer to sign an agreement with you, in which I promise to lead you to the spot where you shall dig; and if I deceive you, bring me here again,—I ask no more."

The governor laughed. "Is the spot far from here?"

"A hundred leagues."

"It is not ill-planned," said the governor. "If all the prisoners took it into their heads to travel a hundred leagues, and their guardians consented to accompany them, they would have a capital chance of escaping."

"The scheme is well known," said the inspector; "and the abbe's plan has not even the merit of originality."

Then turning to Faria—"I inquired if you are well fed?" said he.

"Swear to me," replied Faria, "to free me if what I tell you prove true, and I will stay here while you go to the spot."

"Are you well fed?" repeated the inspector.

"Monsieur, you run no risk, for, as I told you, I will stay here; so there is no chance of my escaping."

"You do not reply to my question," replied the inspector impatiently.

"Nor you to mine," cried the abbe. "You will not accept my gold; I will keep it for myself. You refuse me my liberty; God will give it me." And the abbe, casting away his coverlet, resumed his place, and continued his calculations.

"What is he doing there?" said the inspector.

"Counting his treasures," replied the governor.

Faria replied to this sarcasm with a glance of profound contempt. They went out. The turnkey closed the door behind them.

"He was wealthy once, perhaps?" said the inspector.

"Or dreamed he was, and awoke mad."

"After all," said the inspector, "if he had been rich, he would not have been here." So the matter ended for the Abbe Faria. He remained in his cell, and this visit only increased the belief in his insanity.

Caligula or Nero, those treasure-seekers, those desirers of the impossible, would have accorded to the poor wretch, in exchange for his wealth, the liberty he so earnestly prayed for. But the kings of modern times, restrained by the limits of mere probability, have neither courage nor desire. They fear the ear that hears their orders, and the eye that scrutinizes their actions. Formerly they believed themselves sprung from Jupiter, and shielded by their birth; but nowadays they are not inviolable.

It has always been against the policy of despotic governments to suffer the victims of their persecutions to reappear. As the Inquisition rarely allowed its victims to be seen with their limbs distorted and their flesh lacerated by torture, so madness is always concealed in its cell, from whence, should it depart, it is conveyed to some gloomy hospital, where the doctor has no thought for man or mind in the mutilated being the jailer delivers to him. The very madness of the Abbe Faria, gone mad in prison, condemned him to perpetual captivity.

The inspector kept his word with Dantes; he examined the register, and found the following note concerning him:—

Edmond Dantes:

Violent Bonapartist; took an active part in the return from Elba.
The greatest watchfulness and care to be exercised.

This note was in a different hand from the rest, which showed that it had been added since his confinement. The inspector could not contend against this accusation; he simply wrote,—"Nothing to be done."

This visit had infused new vigor into Dantes; he had, till then, forgotten the date; but now, with a fragment of plaster, he wrote the date, 30th July, 1816, and made a mark every day, in order not to lose his reckoning again. Days and weeks passed away, then months—Dantes still waited; he at first expected to be freed in a fortnight. This fortnight expired, he decided that the inspector would do nothing until his return to Paris, and that he would not reach there until his circuit was finished, he therefore fixed three months; three months passed away, then six more. Finally ten months and a half had gone by and no favorable change had taken place, and Dantes began to fancy the inspector's visit but a dream, an illusion of the brain.

At the expiration of a year the governor was transferred; he had obtained charge of the fortress at Ham. He took with him several of his subordinates, and amongst them Dantes' jailer. A new governor arrived; it would have been too tedious to acquire the names of the prisoners; he learned their numbers instead. This horrible place contained fifty cells; their inhabitants were designated by the numbers of their cell, and the unhappy young man was no longer called Edmond Dantes—he was now number 34.

Chapter 15. Number 34 and Number 27.

Dantes passed through all the stages of torture natural to prisoners in suspense. He was sustained at first by that pride of conscious innocence which is the sequence to hope; then he began to doubt his own innocence, which justified in some measure the governor's belief in his mental alienation; and then, relaxing his sentiment of pride, he addressed his supplications, not to God, but to man. God is always the last resource. Unfortunates, who ought to begin with God, do not have any hope in him till they have exhausted all other means of deliverance.

Dantes asked to be removed from his present dungeon into another; for a change, however disadvantageous, was still a change, and would afford him some amusement. He entreated to be allowed to walk about, to have fresh air, books, and writing materials. His requests were not granted, but he went on asking all the same. He accustomed himself to speaking to the new jailer, although the latter was, if possible, more taciturn than the old one; but still, to speak to a man, even though mute, was something. Dantes spoke for the sake of hearing his own voice; he had tried to speak when alone, but the sound of his voice terrified him. Often, before his captivity, Dantes' mind had revolted at the idea of assemblages of prisoners, made up of thieves, vagabonds, and murderers. He now wished to be amongst them, in order to see some other face besides that of his jailer; he sighed for the galleys, with the infamous costume, the chain, and the brand on the shoulder. The galley-slaves breathed the fresh air of heaven, and saw each other. They were very happy. He besought the jailer one day to let him have a companion, were it even the mad abbe.

The jailer, though rough and hardened by the constant sight of so much suffering, was yet a man. At the bottom of his heart he had often had a feeling of pity for this unhappy young man who suffered so; and he laid the request of number 34 before the governor; but the latter sapiently imagined that Dantes wished to conspire or attempt an escape, and refused his request. Dantes had exhausted all human resources, and he then turned to God.

All the pious ideas that had been so long forgotten, returned; he recollected the prayers his mother had taught him, and discovered a new meaning in every word; for in prosperity prayers seem but a mere medley of words, until misfortune comes and the unhappy sufferer first understands the meaning of the sublime language in which he invokes the pity of heaven! He prayed, and prayed aloud, no longer terrified at the sound of his own voice, for he fell into a sort of ecstasy. He laid every action of his life before the Almighty, proposed tasks to accomplish, and at the end of every prayer introduced the entreaty oftener addressed to man than to God: "Forgive us our trespasses as we forgive them that trespass against us." Yet in spite of his earnest prayers, Dantes remained a prisoner.

Then gloom settled heavily upon him. Dantes was a man of great simplicity of thought, and without education; he could not, therefore in the solitude of his dungeon, traverse in mental vision the history of the ages, bring to life the nations that had perished, and rebuild the ancient cities so vast and stupendous in the light of the imagination, and that pass before the eye glowing with celestial colors in Martin's Babylonian pictures. He could not do this, he whose past life was so short, whose present so melancholy, and his future so doubtful. Nineteen years of light to reflect upon in eternal darkness! No distraction could come to his aid; his energetic spirit, that would have exalted in thus revisiting the past, was imprisoned like an eagle in a cage. He clung to one idea—that of his happiness, destroyed, without apparent cause, by an unheard-of fatality; he considered and reconsidered this idea, devoured it (so to speak), as the implacable Ugolino devours the skull of Archbishop Roger in the Inferno of Dante.

Rage supplanted religious fervor. Dantes uttered blasphemies that made his jailer recoil with horror, dashed himself furiously against the walls of his prison, wreaked his anger upon everything, and chiefly upon himself, so that the least thing,—a grain of sand, a straw, or a breath of air that annoyed him, led to paroxysms of fury. Then the letter that Villefort had showed to him recurred to his mind, and every line gleamed forth in fiery letters on the wall like the *mene tekel upharsin* of Belshazzar. He told himself that it was the enmity of man, and not the vengeance of heaven, that had thus plunged him into the deepest misery. He consigned his unknown persecutors to the most horrible tortures he could imagine, and found them all insufficient, because after torture came death, and after death, if not repose, at least the boon of unconsciousness.

By dint of constantly dwelling on the idea that tranquility was death, and if punishment were the end in view other tortures than death must be invented, he began to reflect on suicide. Unhappy he, who, on the brink of misfortune, broods over ideas like these!

Before him is a dead sea that stretches in azure calm before the eye; but he who unwarily ventures within its embrace finds himself struggling with a monster that would drag him down to perdition. Once thus ensnared, unless the protecting hand of God snatch him thence, all is over, and his struggles but tend to hasten his destruction. This state of mental anguish is, however, less terrible than the sufferings that precede or the punishment that possibly will follow. There is a sort of consolation at the contemplation of the yawning abyss, at the bottom of which lie darkness and obscurity.

Edmond found some solace in these ideas. All his sorrows, all his sufferings, with their train of gloomy specters, fled from his cell when the angel of death seemed about to enter. Dantes reviewed his past life with composure, and, looking forward with terror to his future existence, chose that middle line that seemed to afford him a refuge.

"Sometimes," said he, "in my voyages, when I was a man and commanded other men, I have seen the heavens overcast, the sea rage and foam, the storm arise, and, like a monstrous bird, beating the two horizons with its wings. Then I felt that my vessel was a vain refuge, that trembled and shook before the tempest. Soon the fury of the waves and the sight of the sharp rocks announced the approach of death, and death then terrified me, and I used all my skill and intelligence as a man and a sailor to struggle against the wrath of God. But I did so because I was happy, because I had not courted death, because to be cast upon a bed of rocks and seaweed seemed terrible, because I was unwilling that I, a creature made for the service of God, should serve for food to the gulls and ravens. But now it is different; I have lost all that bound me to life, death smiles and invites me to repose; I die after my own manner, I die exhausted and broken-spirited, as I fall asleep when I have paced three thousand times round my cell."

No sooner had this idea taken possession of him than he became more composed, arranged his couch to the best of his power, ate little and slept less, and found existence almost supportable, because he felt that he could throw it off at pleasure, like a worn-out garment. Two methods of self-destruction were at his disposal. He could hang himself with his handkerchief to the window bars, or refuse food and die of starvation. But the first was repugnant to him. Dantes had always entertained the greatest horror of pirates, who are hung up to the yard-arm; he would not die by what seemed an infamous death. He resolved to adopt the second, and began that day to carry out his resolve. Nearly four years had passed away; at the end of the second he had ceased to mark the lapse of time.

Dantes said, "I wish to die," and had chosen the manner of his death, and fearful of changing his mind, he had taken an oath to die. "When my morning and evening meals are brought," thought he, "I will cast them out of the window, and they will think that I have eaten them."

He kept his word; twice a day he cast out, through the barred aperture, the provisions his jailer brought him—at first gaily, then with deliberation, and at last with regret. Nothing but the recollection of his oath gave him strength to proceed. Hunger made viands once repugnant, now acceptable; he held the plate in his hand for an hour at a time, and gazed thoughtfully at the morsel of bad meat, of tainted fish, of black and moldy bread. It was the last yearning for life contending with the resolution of despair; then his dungeon seemed less somber, his prospects less desperate. He was still young—he was only four or five and twenty—he had nearly fifty years to live. What unforeseen events might not open his prison door, and restore him to liberty? Then he raised to his lips the repast that, like a voluntary Tantalus, he refused himself; but he thought of his oath, and he would not break it. He persisted until, at last, he had not sufficient strength to rise and cast his supper out of the loophole. The next morning he could not see or hear; the jailer feared he was dangerously ill. Edmond hoped he was dying.

Thus the day passed away. Edmond felt a sort of stupor creeping over him which brought with it a feeling almost of content; the gnawing pain at his stomach had ceased; his thirst had abated; when he closed his eyes he saw myriads of lights dancing before them like the will-o'-the-wisps that play about the marshes. It was the twilight of that mysterious country called Death!

Just in that moment, the face of Mercedes appeared above his and when he turned to touch her, somehow, miraculously, she was there. If this was a dream, Edmond didn't want it to end. It seemed Mercedes would usher him to death's embrace.

"Edmond, my love, you must not give up."

"I have nothing left, I will never leave this place, at least this way I have a choice."

"Then choose to live."

"Why should I?"

"Because I love you and need you to return to me."

"I do not believe I shall ever return. The next time I leave this place will be for my grave."

"You are wrong, Edmond, you will leave this place and you will exact your vengeance."

Edmond did not know what was reality or his mind playing a trick in order to buy time. He was a sailor, not a medical man, and had no knowledge of how his body might work in situations such as these. If the mind had some sort of protection against its own workings in order to dissuade a man from thoughts of causing his own death, or just allowing it.

Edmond stroked a hand down Mercedes' skin, it felt like sunlight, and days spent on deck of the *Pharaon,* she felt like home, like France.

Perhaps Mercedes was an angel sent to take him to heaven because Edmond could recall no place more beautiful then Mercedes' arms.

"Am I dead?"

"Not yet, my love." She moved so she lay on top of him. It was odd, the slight weight of her body on his. He immediately recalled his state of filth and dishevel and sought to push her away. She could not see him like this.

"You must leave; you cannot view me thus."

In an instant they were the lovers in Mercedes' house in the Catalans. The sun streamed through the curtains casting dust mote shadows on the floor. Both Edmond and Mercedes looked just as they did that day, that last day they made love. He recalled the taste of salt on her skin from the clean sweat of working around her home. The scent of her hair and sheets as he took her in his arms. All these fragments of memories making up the person of Mercedes came together at once, right here in shadow or imagination.

This was a gift, from heaven or hell, he did not know but he would not cast her aside. He drew her down to him like a parched man seeking water. Her lips tasted of cool rain and he knew he had lost his heart to her all over again. The knot of hair at the nape of her neck was in disarray and Edmond loosened it allowing the mass to fall into his grasp. Spun silk, wild flowers, and ocean spray is exactly what it smelled like, just as he recalled the last time he had the pleasure of that scent.

"Make love to me, Edmond, please."

He did not need instruction, simply pulled their clothing aside in haste, and pressing her down flat on the bed, but he didn't enter her, he wanted to taste her first, carry the exquisite taste of her on his tongue. She was ready for him, wet and waiting. Just as he recalled, she felt like heaven. He eased his tongue into her body, lapping gently, just the way she liked. Mercedes enjoyed a slow evolution to climax and Edmond was happy to oblige her. Once his manhood strained against his pants almost painfully he finished, planting a kiss on the bone protruding from her hip. He pulled himself up and pressed inside her, his ministrations easing the way considerably.

The crumpled clothing hastily cast aside crushed between them as he pressed his hips forward. There was nothing in the world that could stop it. He gripped the straw mattress, driving into Mercedes more fully and she took him.

"Is this a dream," he asked her through the haze of love and lust.

"Of course, my love. Do you wish to wake?"

"No. Never."

"Then show me."

He did. He kissed her lips one last time and began to move in her faster, harder, and with more alacrity then he thought he could muster in his weakened stated. He would push her over the edge before he reached his own completion. This memory, this dream, would be all he had of her for only God knew how long, he wanted to imprint every detail in his memory. If Mercedes was the angel of death, he followed willingly.

He pressed on, the pair merged together, sweat beading on their brows. Mercedes started to pant, drawing in great gasps of air as she climbed the final peak. She gripped Edmond's half open shirt as she plummeted off the other side into an abyss. He followed soon after, holding himself aloft but still completely immersed. It took some time before Edmond could speak and he spent that time analyzing each fleck and shade of Mercedes' skin so she couldn't slip away again.

"If I am dead then I should have embraced it long ago."

"You are not dead." Mercedes stroked his cheek.

"A dream then, one I will cherish for as long as I live."

"It's not over yet." Mercedes moved her leg causing a clenching sensation around her sex. He dropped his head at the onslaught of pleasure against his sensitive flesh.

"I'll take as long as I have." He moved his own hips in response causing them both to gasp aloud.

She only smiled this time. They remained fused at the hips, lying in each other's arms. No words came to either of their minds and each, dream or not, enjoyed the shared time. The sunlight slowly dimmed as Edmond simply held his bride. The night slowly creeping through the window. Just as fast as she appeared, she was gone. Mercedes was gone and Edmond felt nothing again, nothing at all except an acute longing for death, even stronger than before.

Suddenly, about nine o'clock in the evening, Edmond heard a hollow sound in the wall against which he was lying. So many loathsome animals inhabited the prison, that their noise did not, in general, awake him; but whether abstinence had quickened his faculties, or whether the noise was really louder than usual, Edmond raised his head and listened. It was a continual scratching, as if made by a huge claw, a powerful tooth, or some iron instrument attacking the stones.

Although weakened, the young man's brain instantly responded to the idea that haunts all prisoners—liberty! It seemed to him that heaven had at length taken pity on him, and had sent this noise to warn him on the very brink of the abyss. Perhaps one of those beloved ones he had so often thought of was thinking of him, and striving to diminish the distance that separated them.

No, no, doubtless he was deceived, and it was but one of those dreams that forerun death!

Edmond still heard the sound. It lasted nearly three hours; he then heard a noise of something falling, and all was silent.

Some hours afterwards it began again, nearer and more distinct. Edmond was intensely interested. Suddenly the jailer entered.

For a week since he had resolved to die, and during the four days that he had been carrying out his purpose, Edmond had not spoken to the attendant, had not answered him when he inquired what was the matter with him, and turned his face to the wall when he looked too curiously at him; but now the jailer might hear the noise and put an end to it, and so destroy a ray of something like hope that soothed his last moments.

The jailer brought him his breakfast. Dantes raised himself up and began to talk about everything; about the bad quality of the food, about the coldness of his dungeon, grumbling and complaining, in order to have an excuse for speaking louder, and wearying the patience of his jailer, who out of kindness of heart had brought broth and white bread for his prisoner.

Fortunately, he fancied that Dantes was delirious; and placing the food on the rickety table, he withdrew. Edmond listened, and the sound became more and more distinct.

"There can be no doubt about it," thought he; "it is some prisoner who is striving to obtain his freedom. Oh, if I were only there to help him!" Suddenly another idea took possession of his mind, so used to misfortune, that it was scarcely capable of hope—the idea that the noise was made by workmen the governor had ordered to repair the neighboring dungeon.

It was easy to ascertain this; but how could he risk the question? It was easy to call his jailer's attention to the noise, and watch his countenance as he listened; but might he not by this means destroy hopes far more important than the short-lived satisfaction of his own curiosity? Unfortunately, Edmond's brain was still so feeble that he could not bend his thoughts to anything in particular.

He saw but one means of restoring lucidity and clearness to his judgment. He turned his eyes towards the soup which the jailer had brought, rose, staggered towards it, raised the vessel to his lips, and drank off the contents with a feeling of indescribable pleasure. He had often heard that shipwrecked persons had died through having eagerly devoured too much food. Edmond replaced on the table the bread he was about to devour, and returned to his couch—he did not wish to die. He soon felt that his ideas became again collected—he could think, and strengthen his thoughts by reasoning. Then he said to himself, "I must put this to the test, but without compromising anybody. If it is a workman, I need but knock against the wall, and he will cease to work, in order to find out who is knocking, and why he does so; but as his occupation is sanctioned by the governor, he will soon resume it. If, on the contrary, it is a prisoner, the noise I make will alarm him, he will cease, and not begin again until he thinks every one is asleep."

Edmond rose again, but this time his legs did not tremble, and his sight was clear; he went to a corner of his dungeon, detached a stone, and with it knocked against the wall where the sound came. He struck thrice. At the first blow the sound ceased, as if by magic.

Edmond listened intently; an hour passed, two hours passed, and no sound was heard from the wall—all was silent there.

Full of hope, Edmond swallowed a few mouthfuls of bread and water, and, thanks to the vigor of his constitution, found himself well-nigh recovered.

The day passed away in utter silence—night came without recurrence of the noise.

"It is a prisoner," said Edmond joyfully. The night passed in perfect silence. Edmond did not close his eyes.

In the morning the jailer brought him fresh provisions—he had already devoured those of the previous day; he ate these listening anxiously for the sound, walking round and round his cell, shaking the iron bars of the loophole, restoring vigor and agility to his limbs by exercise, and so preparing himself for his future destiny. At intervals he listened to learn if the noise had not begun again, and grew impatient at the prudence of the prisoner, who did not guess he had been disturbed by a captive as anxious for liberty as himself.

Three days passed—seventy-two long tedious hours which he counted off by minutes!

At length one evening, as the jailer was visiting him for the last time that night, Dantes, with his ear for the hundredth time at the wall, fancied he heard an almost imperceptible movement among the stones. He moved away, walked up and down his cell to collect his thoughts, and then went back and listened.

The matter was no longer doubtful. Something was at work on the other side of the wall; the prisoner had discovered the danger, and had substituted a lever for a chisel.

Encouraged by this discovery, Edmond determined to assist the indefatigable laborer. He began by moving his bed, and looked around for anything with which he could pierce the wall, penetrate the moist cement, and displace a stone.

He saw nothing, he had no knife or sharp instrument, the window grating was of iron, but he had too often assured himself of its solidity. All his furniture consisted of a bed, a chair, a table, a pail, and a jug. The bed had iron clamps, but they were screwed to the wood, and it would have required a screw-driver to take them off. The table and chair had nothing, the pail had once possessed a handle, but that had been removed.

Dantes had but one resource, which was to break the jug, and with one of the sharp fragments attack the wall. He let the jug fall on the floor, and it broke in pieces.

Dantes concealed two or three of the sharpest fragments in his bed, leaving the rest on the floor. The breaking of his jug was too natural an accident to excite suspicion. Edmond had all the night to work in, but in the darkness he could not do much, and he soon felt that he was working against something very hard; he pushed back his bed, and waited for day.

All night he heard the subterranean workman, who continued to mine his way. Day came, the jailer entered. Dantes told him that the jug had fallen from his hands while he was drinking, and the jailer went grumblingly to fetch another, without giving himself the trouble to remove the fragments of the broken one. He returned speedily, advised the prisoner to be more careful, and departed.

Dantes heard joyfully the key grate in the lock; he listened until the sound of steps died away, and then, hastily displacing his bed, saw by the faint light that penetrated into his cell, that he had labored uselessly the previous evening in attacking the stone instead of removing the plaster that surrounded it.

The damp had rendered it friable, and Dantes was able to break it off—in small morsels, it is true, but at the end of half an hour he had scraped off a handful; a mathematician might have calculated that in two years, supposing that the rock was not encountered, a passage twenty feet long and two feet broad, might be formed.

The prisoner reproached himself with not having thus employed the hours he had passed in vain hopes, prayer, and despondency. During the six years that he had been imprisoned, what might he not have accomplished?

In three days he had succeeded, with the utmost precaution, in removing the cement, and exposing the stone-work. The wall was built of rough stones, among which, to give strength to the structure, blocks of hewn stone were at intervals imbedded. It was one of these he had uncovered, and which he must remove from its socket.

Dantes strove to do this with his nails, but they were too weak. The fragments of the jug broke, and after an hour of useless toil, he paused.

Was he to be thus stopped at the beginning, and was he to wait inactive until his fellow workman had completed his task? Suddenly an idea occurred to him—he smiled, and the perspiration dried on his forehead.

The jailer always brought Dantes' soup in an iron saucepan; this saucepan contained soup for both prisoners, for Dantes had noticed that it was either quite full, or half empty, according as the turnkey gave it to him or to his companion first.

The handle of this saucepan was of iron; Dantes would have given ten years of his life in exchange for it.

The jailer was accustomed to pour the contents of the saucepan into Dantes' plate, and Dantes, after eating his soup with a wooden spoon, washed the plate, which thus served for every day. Now when evening came Dantes put his plate on the ground near the door; the jailer, as he entered, stepped on it and broke it.

This time he could not blame Dantes. He was wrong to leave it there, but the jailer was wrong not to have looked before him.

The jailer, therefore, only grumbled. Then he looked about for something to pour the soup into; Dantes' entire dinner service consisted of one plate—there was no alternative.

"Leave the saucepan," said Dantes; "you can take it away when you bring me my breakfast." This advice was to the jailer's taste, as it spared him the necessity of making another trip. He left the saucepan.

Dantes was beside himself with joy. He rapidly devoured his food, and after waiting an hour, lest the jailer should change his mind and return, he removed his bed, took the handle of the saucepan, inserted the point between the hewn stone and rough stones of the wall, and employed it as a lever. A slight oscillation showed Dantes that all went well. At the end of an hour the stone was extricated from the wall, leaving a cavity a foot and a half in diameter.

Dantes carefully collected the plaster, carried it into the corner of his cell, and covered it with earth. Then, wishing to make the best use of his time while he had the means of labor, he continued to work without ceasing. At the dawn of day he replaced the stone, pushed his bed against the wall, and lay down. The breakfast consisted of a piece of bread; the jailer entered and placed the bread on the table.

"Well, don't you intend to bring me another plate?" said Dantes.

"No," replied the turnkey; "you destroy everything. First you break your jug, then you make me break your plate; if all the prisoners followed your example, the government would be ruined. I shall leave you the saucepan, and pour your soup into that. So for the future I hope you will not be so destructive."

Dantes raised his eyes to heaven and clasped his hands beneath the coverlet. He felt more gratitude for the possession of this piece of iron than he had ever felt for anything. He had noticed, however, that the prisoner on the other side had ceased to labor; no matter, this was a greater reason for proceeding—if his neighbor would not come to him, he would go to his neighbor. All day he toiled on untiringly, and by the evening he had succeeded in extracting ten handfuls of plaster and fragments of stone. When the hour for his jailer's visit arrived, Dantes straightened the handle of the saucepan as well as he could, and placed it in its accustomed place. The turnkey poured his ration of soup into it, together with the fish—for thrice a week the prisoners were deprived of meat. This would have been a method of reckoning time, had not Dantes long ceased to do so. Having poured out the soup, the turnkey retired. Dantes wished to ascertain whether his neighbor had really ceased to work. He listened—all was silent, as it had been for the last three days. Dantes sighed; it was evident that his neighbor distrusted him. However, he toiled on all the night without being discouraged; but after two or three hours he encountered an obstacle. The iron made no impression, but met with a smooth surface; Dantes touched it, and found that it was a beam. This beam crossed, or rather blocked up, the hole Dantes had made; it was necessary, therefore, to dig above or under it. The unhappy young man had not thought of this. "O my God, my God!" murmured he, "I have so earnestly prayed to you, that I hoped my prayers had been heard. After having deprived me of my liberty, after having deprived me of death, after having recalled me to existence, my God, have pity on me, and do not let me die in despair!"

"Who talks of God and despair at the same time?" said a voice that seemed to come from beneath the earth, and, deadened by the distance, sounded hollow and sepulchral in the young man's ears. Edmond's hair stood on end, and he rose to his knees.

"Ah," said he, "I hear a human voice." Edmond had not heard any one speak save his to a prisoner—he is a living door, a barrier of flesh and blood adding strength to restraints of oak and iron.

"In the name of heaven," cried Dantes, "speak again, though the sound of your voice terrifies me. Who are you?"

"Who are you?" said the voice.

"An unhappy prisoner," replied Dantes, who made no hesitation in answering.

"Of what country?"

"A Frenchman."

"Your name?"

"Edmond Dantes."

"Your profession?"

"A sailor."

"How long have you been here?"

"Since the 28th of February, 1815."

"Your crime?"

"I am innocent."

"But of what are you accused?"

"Of having conspired to aid the emperor's return."

"What! For the emperor's return?—the emperor is no longer on the throne, then?"

"He abdicated at Fontainebleau in 1814, and was sent to the Island of Elba. But how long have you been here that you are ignorant of all this?"

"Since 1811."

Dantes shuddered; this man had been four years longer than himself in prison.

"Do not dig anymore," said the voice; "only tell me how high up is your excavation?"

"On a level with the floor."

"How is it concealed?"

"Behind my bed."

"Has your bed been moved since you have been a prisoner?"

"No."

"What does your chamber open on?"

"A corridor."

"And the corridor?"

"On a court."

"Alas!" murmured the voice.

"Oh, what is the matter?" cried Dantes.

"I have made a mistake owing to an error in my plans. I took the wrong angle, and have come out fifteen feet from where I intended. I took the wall you are mining for the outer wall of the fortress."

"But then you would be close to the sea?"

"That is what I hoped."

"And supposing you had succeeded?"

"I should have thrown myself into the sea, gained one of the islands near here—the Isle de Daume or the Isle de Tiboulen—and then I should have been safe."

"Could you have swum so far?"

"Heaven would have given me strength; but now all is lost."

"All?"

"Yes; stop up your excavation carefully, do not work anymore, and wait until you hear from me."

"Tell me, at least, who you are?"

"I am—I am No. 27."

"You mistrust me, then," said Dantes. Edmond fancied he heard a bitter laugh resounding from the depths.

"Oh, I am a Christian," cried Dantes, guessing instinctively that this man meant to abandon him. "I swear to you by him who died for us that naught shall induce me to breathe one syllable to my jailers; but I conjure you do not abandon me. If you do, I swear to you, for I have got to the end of my strength, that I will dash my brains out against the wall, and you will have my death to reproach yourself with."

"How old are you? Your voice is that of a young man."

"I do not know my age, for I have not counted the years I have been here. All I do know is, that I was just nineteen when I was arrested, the 28th of February, 1815."

"Not quite twenty-six!" murmured the voice; "at that age he cannot be a traitor."

"Oh, no, no," cried Dantes. "I swear to you again, rather than betray you, I would allow myself to be hacked in pieces!"

"You have done well to speak to me, and ask for my assistance, for I was about to form another plan, and leave you; but your age reassures me. I will not forget you. Wait."

"How long?"

"I must calculate our chances; I will give you the signal."

"But you will not leave me; you will come to me, or you will let me come to you. We will escape, and if we cannot escape we will talk; you of those whom you love, and I of those whom I love. You must love somebody?"

"No, I am alone in the world."

"Then you will love me. If you are young, I will be your comrade; if you are old, I will be your son. I have a father who is seventy if he yet lives; I only love him and a young girl called Mercedes. My father has not yet forgotten me, I am sure, but God alone knows if she loves me still; I shall love you as I loved my father."

"It is well," returned the voice; "to-morrow."

These few words were uttered with an accent that left no doubt of his sincerity; Dantes rose, dispersed the fragments with the same precaution as before, and pushed his bed back against the wall. He then gave himself up to his happiness. He would no longer be alone. He was, perhaps, about to regain his liberty; at the worst, he would have a companion, and captivity that is shared is but half captivity. Plaints made in common are almost prayers, and prayers where two or three are gathered together invoke the mercy of heaven.

All day Dantes walked up and down his cell. He sat down occasionally on his bed, pressing his hand on his heart. At the slightest noise he bounded towards the door. Once or twice the thought crossed his mind that he might be separated from this unknown, whom he loved already; and then his mind was made up—when the jailer moved his bed and stooped to examine the opening, he would kill him with his water jug. He would be condemned to die, but he was about to die of grief and despair when this miraculous noise recalled him to life.

The jailer came in the evening. Dantes was on his bed. It seemed to him that thus he better guarded the unfinished opening. Doubtless there was a strange expression in his eyes, for the jailer said, "Come, are you going mad again?"

Dantes did not answer; he feared that the emotion of his voice would betray him. The jailer went away shaking his head. Night came; Dantes hoped that his neighbor would profit by the silence to address him, but he was mistaken. The next morning, however, just as he removed his bed from the wall, he heard three knocks; he threw himself on his knees.

"Is it you?" said he; "I am here."

"Is your jailer gone?"

"Yes," said Dantes; "he will not return until the evening; so that we have twelve hours before us."

"I can work, then?" said the voice.

"Oh, yes, yes; this instant, I entreat you."

In a moment that part of the floor on which Dantes was resting his two hands, as he knelt with his head in the opening, suddenly gave way; he drew back smartly, while a mass of stones and earth disappeared in a hole that opened beneath the aperture he himself had formed. Then from the bottom of this passage, the depth of which it was impossible to measure, he saw appear, first the head, then the shoulders, and lastly the body of a man, who sprang lightly into his cell.

Chapter 16. A Learned Italian.

Seizing in his arms the friend so long and ardently desired, Dantes almost carried him towards the window, in order to obtain a better view of his features by the aid of the imperfect light that struggled through the grating.

He was a man of small stature, with hair blanched rather by suffering and sorrow than by age. He had a deep-set, penetrating eye, almost buried beneath the thick gray eyebrow, and a long (and still black) beard reaching down to his breast. His thin face, deeply furrowed by care, and the bold outline of his strongly marked features, betokened a man more accustomed to exercise his mental faculties than his physical strength. Large drops of perspiration were now standing on his brow, while the garments that hung about him were so ragged that one could only guess at the pattern upon which they had originally been fashioned.

The stranger might have numbered sixty or sixty-five years; but a certain briskness and appearance of vigor in his movements made it probable that he was aged more from captivity than the course of time. He received the enthusiastic greeting of his young acquaintance with evident pleasure, as though his chilled affections were rekindled and invigorated by his contact with one so warm and ardent. He thanked him with grateful cordiality for his kindly welcome, although he must at that moment have been suffering bitterly to find another dungeon where he had fondly reckoned on discovering a means of regaining his liberty.

"Let us first see," said he, "whether it is possible to remove the traces of my entrance here—our future tranquility depends upon our jailers being entirely ignorant of it." Advancing to the opening, he stooped and raised the stone easily in spite of its weight; then, fitting it into its place, he said,—

"You removed this stone very carelessly; but I suppose you had no tools to aid you."

"Why," exclaimed Dantes, with astonishment, "do you possess any?"

"I made myself some; and with the exception of a file, I have all that are necessary,—a chisel, pincers, and lever."

"Oh, how I should like to see these products of your industry and patience."

"Well, in the first place, here is my chisel." So saying, he displayed a sharp strong blade, with a handle made of beechwood.

"And with what did you contrive to make that?" inquired Dantes.

"With one of the clamps of my bedstead; and this very tool has sufficed me to hollow out the road by which I came hither, a distance of about fifty feet."

"Fifty feet!" responded Dantes, almost terrified.

"Do not speak so loud, young man—don't speak so loud. It frequently occurs in a state prison like this, that persons are stationed outside the doors of the cells purposely to overhear the conversation of the prisoners."

"But they believe I am shut up alone here."

"That makes no difference."

"And you say that you dug your way a distance of fifty feet to get here?"

"I do; that is about the distance that separates your chamber from mine; only, unfortunately, I did not curve aright; for want of the necessary geometrical instruments to calculate my scale of proportion, instead of taking an ellipsis of forty feet, I made it fifty. I expected, as I told you, to reach the outer wall, pierce through it, and throw myself into the sea; I have, however, kept along the corridor on which your chamber opens, instead of going beneath it. My labor is all in vain, for I find that the corridor looks into a courtyard filled with soldiers."

"That's true," said Dantes; "but the corridor you speak of only bounds one side of my cell; there are three others—do you know anything of their situation?"

"This one is built against the solid rock, and it would take ten experienced miners, duly furnished with the requisite tools, as many years to perforate it. This adjoins the lower part of the governor's apartments, and were we to work our way through, we should only get into some lock-up cellars, where we must necessarily be recaptured. The fourth and last side of your cell faces on—faces on—stop a minute, now where does it face?"

The wall of which he spoke was the one in which was fixed the loophole by which light was admitted to the chamber. This loophole, which gradually diminished in size as it approached the outside, to an opening through which a child could not have passed, was, for better security, furnished with three iron bars, so as to quiet all apprehensions even in the mind of the most suspicious jailer as to the possibility of a prisoner's escape. As the stranger asked the question, he dragged the table beneath the window.

"Climb up," said he to Dantes. The young man obeyed, mounted on the table, and, divining the wishes of his companion, placed his back securely against the wall and held out both hands. The stranger, whom as yet Dantes knew only by the number of his cell, sprang up with an agility by no means to be expected in a person of his years, and, light and steady on his feet as a cat or a lizard, climbed from the table to the outstretched hands of Dantes, and from them to his shoulders; then, bending double, for the ceiling of the dungeon prevented him from holding himself erect, he managed to slip his head between the upper bars of the window, so as to be able to command a perfect view from top to bottom.

An instant afterwards he hastily drew back his head, saying, "I thought so!" and sliding from the shoulders of Dantes as dexterously as he had ascended, he nimbly leaped from the table to the ground.

"What was it that you thought?" asked the young man anxiously, in his turn descending from the table.

The elder prisoner pondered the matter. "Yes," said he at length, "it is so. This side of your chamber looks out upon a kind of open gallery, where patrols are continually passing, and sentries keep watch day and night."

"Are you quite sure of that?"

"Certain. I saw the soldier's shape and the top of his musket; that made me draw in my head so quickly, for I was fearful he might also see me."

"Well?" inquired Dantes.

"You perceive then the utter impossibility of escaping through your dungeon?"

"Then," pursued the young man eagerly—

"Then," answered the elder prisoner, "the will of God be done!" and as the old man slowly pronounced those words, an air of profound resignation spread itself over his careworn countenance. Dantes gazed on the man who could thus philosophically resign hopes so long and ardently nourished with an astonishment mingled with admiration.

"Tell me, I entreat of you, who and what you are?" said he at length; "never have I met with so remarkable a person as yourself."

"Willingly," answered the stranger; "if, indeed, you feel any curiosity respecting one, now, alas, powerless to aid you in any way."

"Say not so; you can console and support me by the strength of your own powerful mind. Pray let me know who you really are?"

The stranger smiled a melancholy smile. "Then listen," said he. "I am the Abbe Faria, and have been imprisoned as you know in this Chateau d'If since the year 1811; previously to which I had been confined for three years in the fortress of Fenestrelle. In the year 1811 I was transferred to Piedmont in France. It was at this period I learned that the destiny which seemed subservient to every wish formed by Napoleon, had bestowed on him a son, named king of Rome even in his cradle. I was very far then from expecting the change you have just informed me of; namely, that four years afterwards, this colossus of power would be overthrown. Then who reigns in France at this moment—Napoleon II.?"

"No, Louis XVIII."

"The brother of Louis XVII.! How inscrutable are the ways of providence—for what great and mysterious purpose has it pleased heaven to abase the man once so elevated, and raise up him who was so abased?"

Dantes' whole attention was riveted on a man who could thus forget his own misfortunes while occupying himself with the destinies of others.

"Yes, yes," continued he, "'Twill be the same as it was in England. After Charles I., Cromwell; after Cromwell, Charles II., and then James II., and then some son-in-law or relation, some Prince of Orange, a stadtholder who becomes a king. Then new concessions to the people, then a constitution, then liberty. Ah, my friend!" said the abbe, turning towards Dantes, and surveying him with the kindling gaze of a prophet, "you are young, you will see all this come to pass."

"Probably, if ever I get out of prison!"

"True," replied Faria, "we are prisoners; but I forget this sometimes, and there are even moments when my mental vision transports me beyond these walls, and I fancy myself at liberty."

"But wherefore are you here?"

"Because in 1807 I dreamed of the very plan Napoleon tried to realize in 1811; because, like Machiavelli, I desired to alter the political face of Italy, and instead of allowing it to be split up into a quantity of petty principalities, each held by some weak or tyrannical ruler, I sought to form one large, compact, and powerful empire; and, lastly, because I fancied I had found my Caesar Borgia in a crowned simpleton, who feigned to enter into my views only to betray me. It was the plan of Alexander VI. and Clement VII., but it will never succeed now, for they attempted it fruitlessly, and Napoleon was unable to complete his work. Italy seems fated to misfortune." And the old man bowed his head.

Dantes could not understand a man risking his life for such matters. Napoleon certainly he knew something of, inasmuch as he had seen and spoken with him; but of Clement VII. and Alexander VI. he knew nothing.

"Are you not," he asked, "the priest who here in the Chateau d'If is generally thought to be—ill?"

"Mad, you mean, don't you?"

"I did not like to say so," answered Dantes, smiling.

"Well, then," resumed Faria with a bitter smile, "let me answer your question in full, by acknowledging that I am the poor mad prisoner of the Chateau d'If, for many years permitted to amuse the different visitors with what is said to be my insanity; and, in all probability, I should be promoted to the honor of making sport for the children, if such innocent beings could be found in an abode devoted like this to suffering and despair."

Dantes remained for a short time mute and motionless; at length he said,—"Then you abandon all hope of escape?"

"I perceive its utter impossibility; and I consider it impious to attempt that which the Almighty evidently does not approve."

"Nay, be not discouraged. Would it not be expecting too much to hope to succeed at your first attempt? Why not try to find an opening in another direction from that which has so unfortunately failed?"

"Alas, it shows how little notion you can have of all it has cost me to effect a purpose so unexpectedly frustrated, that you talk of beginning over again. In the first place, I was four years making the tools I possess, and have been two years scraping and digging out earth, hard as granite itself; then what toil and fatigue has it not been to remove huge stones I should once have deemed impossible to loosen. Whole days have I passed in these Titanic efforts, considering my labor well repaid if, by night-time I had contrived to carry away a square inch of this hard-bound cement, changed by ages into a substance unyielding as the stones themselves; then to conceal the mass of earth and rubbish I dug up, I was compelled to break through a staircase, and throw the fruits of my labor into the hollow part of it; but the well is now so completely choked up, that I scarcely think it would be possible to add another handful of dust without leading to discovery. Consider also that I fully believed I had accomplished the end and aim of my undertaking, for which I had so exactly husbanded my strength as to make it just hold out to the termination of my enterprise; and now, at the moment when I reckoned upon success, my hopes are forever dashed from me. No, I repeat again, that nothing shall induce me to renew attempts evidently at variance with the Almighty's pleasure."

Dantes held down his head, that the other might not see how joy at the thought of having a companion outweighed the sympathy he felt for the failure of the abbe's plans.

The abbe sank upon Edmond's bed, while Edmond himself remained standing. Escape had never once occurred to him. There are, indeed, some things which appear so impossible that the mind does not dwell on them for an instant. To undermine the ground for fifty feet—to devote three years to a labor which, if successful, would conduct you to a precipice overhanging the sea—to plunge into the waves from the height of fifty, sixty, perhaps a hundred feet, at the risk of being dashed to pieces against the rocks, should you have been fortunate enough to have escaped the fire of the sentinels; and even, supposing all these perils past, then to have to swim for your life a distance of at least three miles ere you could reach the shore—were difficulties so startling and formidable that Dantes had never even dreamed of such a scheme, resigning himself rather to death. But the sight of an old man clinging to life with so desperate a courage, gave a fresh turn to his ideas, and inspired him with new courage. Another, older and less strong than he, had attempted what he had not had sufficient resolution to undertake, and had failed only because of an error in calculation. This same person, with almost incredible patience and perseverance, had contrived to provide himself with tools requisite for so unparalleled an attempt. Another had done all this; why, then, was it impossible to Dantes? Faria had dug his way through fifty feet, Dantes would dig a hundred; Faria, at the age of fifty, had devoted three years to the task; he, who was but half as old, would sacrifice six; Faria, a priest and savant, had not shrunk from the idea of risking his life by trying to swim a distance of three miles to one of the islands—Daume, Rattonneau, or Lemaire; should a hardy sailer, an experienced diver, like himself, shrink from a similar task; should he, who had so often for mere amusement's sake plunged to the bottom of the sea to fetch up the bright coral branch, hesitate to entertain the same project? He could do it in an hour, and how many times had he, for pure pastime, continued in the water for more than twice as long! At once Dantes resolved to follow the brave example of his energetic companion, and to remember that what has once been done may be done again.

After continuing some time in profound meditation, the young man suddenly exclaimed, "I have found what you were in search of!"

Faria started: "Have you, indeed?" cried he, raising his head with quick anxiety; "pray, let me know what it is you have discovered?"

"The corridor through which you have bored your way from the cell you occupy here, extends in the same direction as the outer gallery, does it not?"

"It does."

"And is not above fifteen feet from it?"

"About that."

"Well, then, I will tell you what we must do. We must pierce through the corridor by forming a side opening about the middle, as it were the top part of a cross. This time you will lay your plans more accurately; we shall get out into the gallery you have described; kill the sentinel who guards it, and make our escape. All we require to insure success is courage, and that you possess, and strength, which I am not deficient in; as for patience, you have abundantly proved yours—you shall now see me prove mine."

"One instant, my dear friend," replied the abbe; "it is clear you do not understand the nature of the courage with which I am endowed, and what use I intend making of my strength. As for patience, I consider that I have abundantly exercised that in beginning every morning the task of the night before, and every night renewing the task of the day. But then, young man (and I pray of you to give me your full attention), then I thought I could not be doing anything displeasing to the Almighty in trying to set an innocent being at liberty—one who had committed no offence, and merited not condemnation."

"And have your notions changed?" asked Dantes with much surprise; "do you think yourself more guilty in making the attempt since you have encountered me?"

"No; neither do I wish to incur guilt. Hitherto I have fancied myself merely waging war against circumstances, not men. I have thought it no sin to bore through a wall, or destroy a staircase; but I cannot so easily persuade myself to pierce a heart or take away a life." A slight movement of surprise escaped Dantes.

"Is it possible," said he, "that where your liberty is at stake you can allow any such scruple to deter you from obtaining it?"

"Tell me," replied Faria, "what has hindered you from knocking down your jailer with a piece of wood torn from your bedstead, dressing yourself in his clothes, and endeavoring to escape?"

"Simply the fact that the idea never occurred to me," answered Dantes.

"Because," said the old man, "the natural repugnance to the commission of such a crime prevented you from thinking of it; and so it ever is because in simple and allowable things our natural instincts keep us from deviating from the strict line of duty. The tiger, whose nature teaches him to delight in shedding blood, needs but the sense of smell to show him when his prey is within his reach, and by following this instinct he is enabled to measure the leap necessary to permit him to spring on his victim; but man, on the contrary, loathes the idea of blood—it is not alone that the laws of social life inspire him with a shrinking dread of taking life; his natural construction and physiological formation"—

Dantes was confused and silent at this explanation of the thoughts which had unconsciously been working in his mind, or rather soul; for there are two distinct sorts of ideas, those that proceed from the head and those that emanate from the heart.

"Since my imprisonment," said Faria, "I have thought over all the most celebrated cases of escape on record. They have rarely been successful. Those that have been crowned with full success have been long meditated upon, and carefully arranged; such, for instance, as the escape of the Duc de Beaufort from the Chateau de Vincennes, that of the Abbe Dubuquoi from For l'Eveque; of Latude from the Bastille. Then there are those for which chance sometimes affords opportunity, and those are the best of all. Let us, therefore, wait patiently for some favorable moment, and when it presents itself, profit by it."

"Ah," said Dantes, "you might well endure the tedious delay; you were constantly employed in the task you set yourself, and when weary with toil, you had your hopes to refresh and encourage you."

"I assure you," replied the old man, "I did not turn to that source for recreation or support."

"What did you do then?"

"I wrote or studied."

"Were you then permitted the use of pens, ink, and paper?"

"Oh, no," answered the abbe; "I had none but what I made for myself."

"You made paper, pens and ink?"

"Yes."

Dantes gazed with admiration, but he had some difficulty in believing. Faria saw this.

"When you pay me a visit in my cell, my young friend," said he, "I will show you an entire work, the fruits of the thoughts and reflections of my whole life; many of them meditated over in the shades of the Colosseum at Rome, at the foot of St. Mark's column at Venice, and on the borders of the Arno at Florence, little imagining at the time that they would be arranged in order within the walls of the Chateau d'If. The work I speak of is called 'A Treatise on the Possibility of a General Monarchy in Italy,' and will make one large quarto volume."

"And on what have you written all this?"

"On two of my shirts. I invented a preparation that makes linen as smooth and as easy to write on as parchment."

"You are, then, a chemist?"

"Somewhat; I know Lavoisier, and was the intimate friend of Cabanis."

"But for such a work you must have needed books—had you any?"

"I had nearly five thousand volumes in my library at Rome; but after reading them over many times, I found out that with one hundred and fifty well-chosen books a man possesses, if not a complete summary of all human knowledge, at least all that a man need really know. I devoted three years of my life to reading and studying these one hundred and fifty volumes, till I knew them nearly by heart; so that since I have been in prison, a very slight effort of memory has enabled me to recall their contents as readily as though the pages were open before me. I could recite you the whole of Thucydides, Xenophon, Plutarch, Titus Livius, Tacitus, Strada, Jornandes, Dante, Montaigne, Shakespeare, Spinoza, Machiavelli, and Bossuet. I name only the most important."

"You are, doubtless, acquainted with a variety of languages, so as to have been able to read all these?"

"Yes, I speak five of the modern tongues—that is to say, German, French, Italian, English, and Spanish; by the aid of ancient Greek I learned modern Greek—I don't speak it so well as I could wish, but I am still trying to improve myself."

"Improve yourself!" repeated Dantes; "why, how can you manage to do so?"

"Why, I made a vocabulary of the words I knew; turned, returned, and arranged them, so as to enable me to express my thoughts through their medium. I know nearly one thousand words, which is all that is absolutely necessary, although I believe there are nearly one hundred thousand in the dictionaries. I cannot hope to be very fluent, but I certainly should have no difficulty in explaining my wants and wishes; and that would be quite as much as I should ever require."

Stronger grew the wonder of Dantes, who almost fancied he had to do with one gifted with supernatural powers; still hoping to find some imperfection which might bring him down to a level with human beings, he added, "Then if you were not furnished with pens, how did you manage to write the work you speak of?"

"I made myself some excellent ones, which would be universally preferred to all others if once known. You are aware what huge whitings are served to us on maigre days. Well, I selected the cartilages of the heads of these fishes, and you can scarcely imagine the delight with which I welcomed the arrival of each Wednesday, Friday, and Saturday, as affording me the means of increasing my stock of pens; for I will freely confess that my historical labors have been my greatest solace and relief. While retracing the past, I forget the present; and traversing at will the path of history I cease to remember that I am myself a prisoner."

"But the ink," said Dantes; "of what did you make your ink?"

"There was formerly a fireplace in my dungeon," replied Faria, "but it was closed up long ere I became an occupant of this prison. Still, it must have been many years in use, for it was thickly covered with a coating of soot; this soot I dissolved in a portion of the wine brought to me every Sunday, and I assure you a better ink cannot be desired. For very important notes, for which closer attention is required, I pricked one of my fingers, and wrote with my own blood."

"And when," asked Dantes, "may I see all this?"

"Whenever you please," replied the abbe.

"Oh, then let it be directly!" exclaimed the young man.

"Follow me, then," said the abbe, as he re-entered the subterranean passage, in which he soon disappeared, followed by Dantes.

Chapter 17. The Abbe's Chamber.

After having passed with tolerable ease through the subterranean passage, which, however, did not admit of their holding themselves erect, the two friends reached the further end of the corridor, into which the abbe's cell opened; from that point the passage became much narrower, and barely permitted one to creep through on hands and knees. The floor of the abbe's cell was paved, and it had been by raising one of the stones in the most obscure corner that Faria had to been able to commence the laborious task of which Dantes had witnessed the completion.

As he entered the chamber of his friend, Dantes cast around one eager and searching glance in quest of the expected marvels, but nothing more than common met his view.

"It is well," said the abbe; "we have some hours before us—it is now just a quarter past twelve o'clock." Instinctively Dantes turned round to observe by what watch or clock the abbe had been able to accurately to specify the hour.

"Look at this ray of light which enters by my window," said the abbe, "and then observe the lines traced on the wall. Well, by means of these lines, which are in accordance with the double motion of the earth, and the ellipse it describes round the sun, I am enabled to ascertain the precise hour with more minuteness than if I possessed a watch; for that might be broken or deranged in its movements, while the sun and earth never vary in their appointed paths."

This last explanation was wholly lost upon Dantes, who had always imagined, from seeing the sun rise from behind the mountains and set in the Mediterranean, that it moved, and not the earth. A double movement of the globe he inhabited, and of which he could feel nothing, appeared to him perfectly impossible.

Each word that fell from his companion's lips seemed fraught with the mysteries of science, as worthy of digging out as the gold and diamonds in the mines of Guzerat and Golconda, which he could just recollect having visited during a voyage made in his earliest youth.

"Come," said he to the abbe, "I am anxious to see your treasures."

The abbe smiled, and, proceeding to the disused fireplace, raised, by the help of his chisel, a long stone, which had doubtless been the hearth, beneath which was a cavity of considerable depth, serving as a safe depository of the articles mentioned to Dantes.

"What do you wish to see first?" asked the abbe.

"Oh, your great work on the monarchy of Italy!"

Faria then drew forth from his hiding-place three or four rolls of linen, laid one over the other, like folds of papyrus. These rolls consisted of slips of cloth about four inches wide and eighteen long; they were all carefully numbered and closely covered with writing, so legible that Dantes could easily read it, as well as make out the sense—it being in Italian, a language he, as a Provencal, perfectly understood.

"There," said he, "there is the work complete. I wrote the word finis at the end of the sixty-eighth strip about a week ago. I have torn up two of my shirts, and as many handkerchiefs as I was master of, to complete the precious pages. Should I ever get out of prison and find in all Italy a printer courageous enough to publish what I have composed, my literary reputation is forever secured."

"I see," answered Dantes. "Now let me behold the curious pens with which you have written your work."

"Look!" said Faria, showing to the young man a slender stick about six inches long, and much resembling the size of the handle of a fine painting-brush, to the end of which was tied, by a piece of thread, one of those cartilages of which the abbe had before spoken to Dantes; it was pointed, and divided at the nib like an ordinary pen. Dantes examined it with intense admiration, then looked around to see the instrument with which it had been shaped so correctly into form.

"Ah, yes," said Faria; "the penknife. That's my masterpiece. I made it, as well as this larger knife, out of an old iron candlestick." The penknife was sharp and keen as a razor; as for the other knife, it would serve a double purpose, and with it one could cut and thrust.

Dantes examined the various articles shown to him with the same attention that he had bestowed on the curiosities and strange tools exhibited in the shops at Marseilles as the works of the savages in the South Seas from whence they had been brought by the different trading vessels.

"As for the ink," said Faria, "I told you how I managed to obtain that—and I only just make it from time to time, as I require it."

"One thing still puzzles me," observed Dantes, "and that is how you managed to do all this by daylight?"

"I worked at night also," replied Faria.

"Night!—why, for heaven's sake, are your eyes like cats', that you can see to work in the dark?"

"Indeed they are not; but God has supplied man with the intelligence that enables him to overcome the limitations of natural conditions. I furnished myself with a light."

"You did? Pray tell me how."

"I separated the fat from the meat served to me, melted it, and so made oil—here is my lamp." So saying, the abbe exhibited a sort of torch very similar to those used in public illuminations.

"But light?"

"Here are two flints and a piece of burnt linen."

"And matches?"

"I pretended that I had a disorder of the skin, and asked for a little sulphur, which was readily supplied." Dantes laid the different things he had been looking at on the table, and stood with his head drooping on his breast, as though overwhelmed by the perseverance and strength of Faria's mind.

"You have not seen all yet," continued Faria, "for I did not think it wise to trust all my treasures in the same hiding-place. Let us shut this one up." They put the stone back in its place; the abbe sprinkled a little dust over it to conceal the traces of its having been removed, rubbed his foot well on it to make it assume the same appearance as the other, and then, going towards his bed, he removed it from the spot it stood in. Behind the head of the bed, and concealed by a stone fitting in so closely as to defy all suspicion, was a hollow space, and in this space a ladder of cords between twenty-five and thirty feet in length. Dantes closely and eagerly examined it; he found it firm, solid, and compact enough to bear any weight.

"Who supplied you with the materials for making this wonderful work?"

"I tore up several of my shirts, and ripped out the seams in the sheets of my bed, during my three years' imprisonment at Fenestrelle; and when I was removed to the Chateau d'If, I managed to bring the ravellings with me, so that I have been able to finish my work here."

"And was it not discovered that your sheets were unhemmed?"

"Oh, no, for when I had taken out the thread I required, I hemmed the edges over again."

"With what?"

"With this needle," said the abbe, as, opening his ragged vestments, he showed Dantes a long, sharp fish-bone, with a small perforated eye for the thread, a small portion of which still remained in it. "I once thought," continued Faria, "of removing these iron bars, and letting myself down from the window, which, as you see, is somewhat wider than yours, although I should have enlarged it still more preparatory to my flight; however, I discovered that I should merely have dropped into a sort of inner court, and I therefore renounced the project altogether as too full of risk and danger. Nevertheless, I carefully preserved my ladder against one of those unforeseen opportunities of which I spoke just now, and which sudden chance frequently brings about." While affecting to be deeply engaged in examining the ladder, the mind of Dantes was, in fact, busily occupied by the idea that a person so intelligent, ingenious, and clear-sighted as the abbe might probably be able to solve the dark mystery of his own misfortunes, where he himself could see nothing.

"What are you thinking of?" asked the abbe smilingly, imputing the deep abstraction in which his visitor was plunged to the excess of his awe and wonder.

"I was reflecting, in the first place," replied Dantes, "upon the enormous degree of intelligence and ability you must have employed to reach the high perfection to which you have attained. What would you not have accomplished if you had been free?"

"Possibly nothing at all; the overflow of my brain would probably, in a state of freedom, have evaporated in a thousand follies; misfortune is needed to bring to light the treasures of the human intellect. Compression is needed to explode gunpowder. Captivity has brought my mental faculties to a focus; and you are well aware that from the collision of clouds electricity is produced—from electricity, lightning, from lightning, illumination."

"No," replied Dantes. "I know nothing. Some of your words are to me quite empty of meaning. You must be blessed indeed to possess the knowledge you have."

The abbe smiled. "Well," said he, "but you had another subject for your thoughts; did you not say so just now?"

"I did!"

"You have told me as yet but one of them—let me hear the other."

"It was this,—that while you had related to me all the particulars of your past life, you were perfectly unacquainted with mine."

"Your life, my young friend, has not been of sufficient length to admit of your having passed through any very important events."

"It has been long enough to inflict on me a great and undeserved misfortune. I would fain fix the source of it on man that I may no longer vent reproaches upon heaven."

"Then you profess ignorance of the crime with which you are charged?"

"I do, indeed; and this I swear by the two beings most dear to me upon earth,—my father and Mercedes."

"Come," said the abbe, closing his hiding-place, and pushing the bed back to its original situation, "let me hear your story."

Dantes obeyed, and commenced what he called his history, but which consisted only of the account of a voyage to India, and two or three voyages to the Levant until he arrived at the recital of his last cruise, with the death of Captain Leclere, and the receipt of a packet to be delivered by himself to the grand marshal; his interview with that personage, and his receiving, in place of the packet brought, a letter addressed to a Monsieur Noirtier—his arrival at Marseilles, and interview with his father—his affection for Mercedes, and their nuptial feast—his arrest and subsequent examination, his temporary detention at the Palais de Justice, and his final imprisonment in the Chateau d'If. From this point everything was a blank to Dantes—he knew nothing more, not even the length of time he had been imprisoned.

The abbe remained silent so Edmond allowed his mind to wander and as it usually did his mind brought thoughts of Mercedes. The scent of her skin and her hair so black, like a raven's wing. The few moments the night preceding their betrothal dinner, he spent time imagining the wedding night, the wedding bed to be more precise. The bed he made up perfectly for the pair of them in the house he shared with his father.

Those imaginings, up until now had remained un-recollected, swamped his memory. Oh how he had planned, precisely, how he might romance his bride, have her swooning at his feet. Mercedes was not similar to other women with their delicate sensibilities and faint natures. She had the spark of life, something that reminded him a little of the sea with its gentle rolling waves and magnificent storms.

They had no money; she was to have worn a simple gown with beading at the hem, hand sewn. Great care would have been taken to preserve her clothing as he stripped every inch of it from her flesh. Then once she was spread before him like a feast he would take her as he willed and she would give no objection. Her sweet voice even sounded through his head.

"Edmond, husband, how would you have me?"

"In every way, Mercedes, in all ways."

"Then join me, I wish to look upon you as well."

He used considerable less care in his own disrobement before joining her on the bed.

"There you are." Mercedes tentatively reached out and gripped the neck of Edmond, drawing him to her lips for a kiss. Edmond was the only man Mercedes had ever known but he treated her with respect and care and Edmond could feel the tension humming under her skin as she initiated the contact.

He could never think ill of her. She might climb a top his knees and straddle him like a horse and he still would only love and cherish her. The altered course his mind veered toward brought a new image to mind, one of Mercedes, nude and astride him, her hair streaming behind her in a heavy curtain. It was an erotic thought just at the inception. Edmond could feel the tight grip of her knees surrounding his lower body and it caused a lustful haze unlike any he felt previously.

Even in his musings she still played the innocent.

"Am I doing this correctly, my husband?"

"Say it again." Edmond pleaded.

"Husband."

No more powerful a word had ever reverberated throughout Edmond's brain. The sound of the word "husband" falling from Mercedes lips had his manhood erect and straining against the tattered cloth of his pants. Edmond listened to the whisper of those lips with outward calm and reserve, the abbe none the wiser, but inside his heart, a rapid beating signified his utter ruin at the hand of his beloved.

She undid him completely. In his mind he gripped the milk white flesh of her hips and drew her onto his erect manhood. A soft sigh and a hushed groan were all the sounds the two made. He did not hurry. Mercedes was a woman of exacting patience, and Edmond was content on learning how that exactitude might pay in his favor.

It took only moments for her to gain her bearings and then moments further to choose the correct gait with which to ride him. Edmond took great pleasure as she experimented with the sensations coursing through them both. She tilted forward her hands catching the hard planes of Edmond's chest, sprinkled with sparse hair she spread between her fingers.

Once she found the seat she sought, the wonderful sensations transversed to heavenly. Edmond fixed on her face a searching, penetrating gaze before running his palms up the gentle curve of her waist. Her skin fairly gleamed and Edmond would have had the sensation of idleness with Mercedes doing all the giving of pleasure. It was a fantasy after all, Edmond could do with some pleasure in any form, fantasy or fiction.

Mercedes increased the pressure and angle from which she moved and it brought Edmond to the edge of completion in only seconds.

"My love, are you close to your own end?"

A bright pink blush suffused her cheeks and she ducked her head, nodding. Edmond scooped her up from behind her buttocks and quickly flipped them both. Mercedes took his weight from the bottom. He felt a sharper edge to his need in this position and he was content to drive himself into Mercedes until he rang every last shout of pleasure she possessed.

"Edmond. Husband." Mercedes shouted fractured syllables of those words as she gripped his arms, tethering herself in reality through her climax. Her tight little muscles squeezing and adding to the pressure already cupping him.

Edmond resumed his pace, letting her ride out the sensations as she neared his own completion. He did not cry out or utter even a whisper as he poured his seed inside of her. It was enough, another memory, another fantasy to add to the collection growing in an ever increasing catalog in his mind. He still held her, in this dream of his, held her flush along his own body, completely wrapped between her appendages. Legs, hands, arms, and toes intertwined so that neither of them could see where one ended and the other began.

"How do the words Madame Dantes sound to you?"

Mercedes smiled up at him.

"Wonderful. Monsieur. Perfect, even."

That final kiss was too much for Edmond. Dragging himself from her lips even in fantasy was too much for him. He was shocked back to the present by the abbe's furious thinking. Something he'd grown accustomed to, the man could not sit still to think, he had to move at least some part to get the maximum effect of his knowledge. A tear escaped the corner of his eye but he ignored it, waiting for the abbe's speech.

His recital finished, the abbe reflected long and earnestly.

"There is," said he, at the end of his meditations, "a clever maxim, which bears upon what I was saying to you some little while ago, and that is, that unless wicked ideas take root in a naturally depraved mind, human nature, in a right and wholesome state, revolts at crime. Still, from an artificial civilization have originated wants, vices, and false tastes, which occasionally become so powerful as to stifle within us all good feelings, and ultimately to lead us into guilt and wickedness. From this view of things, then, comes the axiom that if you visit to discover the author of any bad action, seek first to discover the person to whom the perpetration of that bad action could be in any way advantageous. Now, to apply it in your case,—to whom could your disappearance have been serviceable?"

"To no one, by heaven! I was a very insignificant person."

"Do not speak thus, for your reply evinces neither logic nor philosophy; everything is relative, my dear young friend, from the king who stands in the way of his successor, to the employee who keeps his rival out of a place. Now, in the event of the king's death, his successor inherits a crown,—when the employee dies, the supernumerary steps into his shoes, and receives his salary of twelve thousand livres. Well, these twelve thousand livres are his civil list, and are as essential to him as the twelve millions of a king. Everyone, from the highest to the lowest degree, has his place on the social ladder, and is beset by stormy passions and conflicting interests, as in Descartes' theory of pressure and impulsion. But these forces increase as we go higher, so that we have a spiral which in defiance of reason rests upon the apex and not on the base. Now let us return to your particular world. You say you were on the point of being made captain of the *Pharaon*?"

"Yes."

"And about to become the husband of a young and lovely girl?"

"Yes."

"Now, could anyone have had any interest in preventing the accomplishment of these two things? But let us first settle the question as to its being the interest of any one to hinder you from being captain of the *Pharaon*. What say you?"

"I cannot believe such was the case. I was generally liked on board, and had the sailors possessed the right of selecting a captain themselves, I feel convinced their choice would have fallen on me.

There was only one person among the crew who had any feeling of ill-will towards me. I had quarreled with him some time previously, and had even challenged him to fight me; but he refused."

"Now we are getting on. And what was this man's name?"

"Danglars."

"What rank did he hold on board?"

"He was supercargo."

"And had you been captain, should you have retained him in his employment?"

"Not if the choice had remained with me, for I had frequently observed inaccuracies in his accounts."

"Good again! Now then, tell me, was any person present during your last conversation with Captain Leclere?"

"No; we were quite alone."

"Could your conversation have been overheard by anyone?"

"It might, for the cabin door was open—and—stay; now I recollect,—Danglars himself passed by just as Captain Leclere was giving me the packet for the grand marshal."

"That's better," cried the abbe; "now we are on the right scent. Did you take anybody with you when you put into the port of Elba?"

"Nobody."

"Somebody there received your packet, and gave you a letter in place of it, I think?"

"Yes; the grand marshal did."

"And what did you do with that letter?"

"Put it into my portfolio."

"You had your portfolio with you, then? Now, how could a sailor find room in his pocket for a portfolio large enough to contain an official letter?"

"You are right; it was left on board."

"Then it was not till your return to the ship that you put the letter in the portfolio?"

"No."

"And what did you do with this same letter while returning from Porto-Ferrajo to the vessel?"

"I carried it in my hand."

"So that when you went on board the *Pharaon*, everybody could see that you held a letter in your hand?"

"Yes."

"Danglars, as well as the rest?"

"Danglars, as well as others."

"Now, listen to me, and try to recall every circumstance attending your arrest. Do you recollect the words in which the information against you was formulated?"

"Oh yes, I read it over three times, and the words sank deeply into my memory."

"Repeat it to me."

Dantes paused a moment, then said, "This is it, word for word: 'The king's attorney is informed by a friend to the throne and religion, that one Edmond Dantes, mate on board the *Pharaon*, this day arrived from Smyrna, after having touched at Naples and Porto-Ferrajo, has been entrusted by Murat with a packet for the usurper; again, by the usurper, with a letter for the Bonapartist Club in Paris. This proof of his guilt may be procured by his immediate arrest, as the letter will be found either about his person, at his father's residence, or in his cabin on board the *Pharaon*.'"

The abbe shrugged his shoulders. "The thing is clear as day," said he; "and you must have had a very confiding nature, as well as a good heart, not to have suspected the origin of the whole affair."

"Do you really think so? Ah, that would indeed be infamous."

"How did Danglars usually write?"

"In a handsome, running hand."

"And how was the anonymous letter written?"

"Backhanded."

Again the abbe smiled. "Disguised."

"It was very boldly written, if disguised."

"Stop a bit," said the abbe, taking up what he called his pen, and, after dipping it into the ink, he wrote on a piece of prepared linen, with his left hand, the first two or three words of the accusation. Dantes drew back, and gazed on the abbe with a sensation almost amounting to terror.

"How very astonishing!" cried he at length. "Why your writing exactly resembles that of the accusation."

"Simply because that accusation had been written with the left hand; and I have noticed that"—

"What?"

"That while the writing of different persons done with the right hand varies, that performed with the left hand is invariably uniform."

"You have evidently seen and observed everything."

"Let us proceed."

"Oh, yes, yes!"

"Now as regards the second question."

"I am listening."

"Was there any person whose interest it was to prevent your marriage with Mercedes?"

"Yes; a young man who loved her."

"And his name was"—

"Fernand."

"That is a Spanish name, I think?"

"He was a Catalan."

"You imagine him capable of writing the letter?"

"Oh, no; he would more likely have got rid of me by sticking a knife into me."

"That is in strict accordance with the Spanish character; an assassination they will unhesitatingly commit, but an act of cowardice, never."

"Besides," said Dantes, "the various circumstances mentioned in the letter were wholly unknown to him."

"You had never spoken of them yourself to any one?"

"To no one."

"Not even to your mistress?"

"No, not even to my betrothed."

"Then it is Danglars."

"I feel quite sure of it now."

"Wait a little. Pray, was Danglars acquainted with Fernand?"

"No—yes, he was. Now I recollect"—

"What?"

"To have seen them both sitting at table together under an arbor at Pere Pamphile's the evening before the day fixed for my wedding. They were in earnest conversation. Danglars was joking in a friendly way, but Fernand looked pale and agitated."

"Were they alone?"

"There was a third person with them whom I knew perfectly well, and who had, in all probability made their acquaintance; he was a tailor named Caderousse, but he was very drunk. Stay!—stay!—How strange that it should not have occurred to me before! Now I remember quite well, that on the table round which they were sitting were pens, ink, and paper. Oh, the heartless, treacherous scoundrels!" exclaimed Dantes, pressing his hand to his throbbing brows.

"Is there anything else I can assist you in discovering, besides the villainy of your friends?" inquired the abbe with a laugh.

"Yes, yes," replied Dantes eagerly; "I would beg of you, who see so completely to the depths of things, and to whom the greatest mystery seems but an easy riddle, to explain to me how it was that I underwent no second examination, was never brought to trial, and, above all, was condemned without ever having had sentence passed on me?"

"That is altogether a different and more serious matter," responded the abbe. "The ways of justice are frequently too dark and mysterious to be easily penetrated. All we have hitherto done in the matter has been child's play. If you wish me to enter upon the more difficult part of the business, you must assist me by the most minute information on every point."

"Pray ask me whatever questions you please; for, in good truth, you see more clearly into my life than I do myself."

"In the first place, then, who examined you,—the king's attorney, his deputy, or a magistrate?"

"The deputy."

"Was he young or old?"

"About six or seven and twenty years of age, I should say."

"So," answered the abbe. "Old enough to be ambitions, but too young to be corrupt. And how did he treat you?"

"With more of mildness than severity."

"Did you tell him your whole story?"

"I did."

"And did his conduct change at all in the course of your examination?"

"He did appear much disturbed when he read the letter that had brought me into this scrape. He seemed quite overcome by my misfortune."

"By your misfortune?"

"Yes."

"Then you feel quite sure that it was your misfortune he deplored?"

"He gave me one great proof of his sympathy, at any rate."

"And that?"

"He burnt the sole evidence that could at all have criminated me."

"What? the accusation?"

"No; the letter."

"Are you sure?"

"I saw it done."

"That alters the case. This man might, after all, be a greater scoundrel than you have thought possible."

"Upon my word," said Dantes, "you make me shudder. Is the world filled with tigers and crocodiles?"

"Yes; and remember that two-legged tigers and crocodiles are more dangerous than the others."

"Never mind; let us go on."

"With all my heart! You tell me he burned the letter?"

"He did; saying at the same time, 'You see I thus destroy the only proof existing against you.'"

"This action is somewhat too sublime to be natural."

"You think so?"

"I am sure of it. To whom was this letter addressed?"

"To M. Noirtier, No. 13 Coq-Heron, Paris."

"Now can you conceive of any interest that your heroic deputy could possibly have had in the destruction of that letter?"

"Why, it is not altogether impossible he might have had, for he made me promise several times never to speak of that letter to any one, assuring me he so advised me for my own interest; and, more than this, he insisted on my taking a solemn oath never to utter the name mentioned in the address."

"Noirtier!" repeated the abbe; "Noirtier!—I knew a person of that name at the court of the Queen of Etruria,—a Noirtier, who had been a Girondin during the Revolution! What was your deputy called?"

"De Villefort!" The abbe burst into a fit of laughter, while Dantes gazed on him in utter astonishment.

"What ails you?" said he at length.

"Do you see that ray of sunlight?"

"I do."

"Well, the whole thing is more clear to me than that sunbeam is to you. Poor fellow! poor young man! And you tell me this magistrate expressed great sympathy and commiseration for you?"

"He did."

"And the worthy man destroyed your compromising letter?"

"Yes."

"And then made you swear never to utter the name of Noirtier?"

"Yes."

"Why, you poor short-sighted simpleton, can you not guess who this Noirtier was, whose very name he was so careful to keep concealed? Noirtier was his father."

Had a thunderbolt fallen at the feet of Dantes, or hell opened its yawning gulf before him, he could not have been more completely transfixed with horror than he was at the sound of these unexpected words. Starting up, he clasped his hands around his head as though to prevent his very brain from bursting, and exclaimed, "His father! His father!"

"Yes, his father," replied the abbe; "his right name was Noirtier de Villefort." At this instant a bright light shot through the mind of Dantes, and cleared up all that had been dark and obscure before. The change that had come over Villefort during the examination, the destruction of the letter, the exacted promise, the almost supplicating tones of the magistrate, who seemed rather to implore mercy than to pronounce punishment,—all returned with a stunning force to his memory. He cried out, and staggered against the wall like a drunken man, then he hurried to the opening that led from the abbe's cell to his own, and said, "I must be alone, to think over all this."

When he regained his dungeon, he threw himself on his bed, where the turnkey found him in the evening visit, sitting with fixed gaze and contracted features, dumb and motionless as a statue. During these hours of profound meditation, which to him had seemed only minutes, he had formed a fearful resolution, and bound himself to its fulfillment by a solemn oath.

Dantes was at length roused from his revery by the voice of Faria, who, having also been visited by his jailer, had come to invite his fellow-sufferer to share his supper. The reputation of being out of his mind, though harmlessly and even amusingly so, had procured for the abbe unusual privileges. He was supplied with bread of a finer, whiter quality than the usual prison fare, and even regaled each Sunday with a small quantity of wine. Now this was a Sunday, and the abbe had come to ask his young companion to share the luxuries with him. Dantes followed; his features were no longer contracted, and now wore their usual expression, but there was that in his whole appearance that bespoke one who had come to a fixed and desperate resolve. Faria bent on him his penetrating eye: "I regret now," said he, "having helped you in your late inquiries, or having given you the information I did."

"Why so?" inquired Dantes.

"Because it has instilled a new passion in your heart—that of vengeance."

Dantes smiled. "Let us talk of something else," said he.

Again the abbe looked at him, then mournfully shook his head; but in accordance with Dantes' request, he began to speak of other matters. The elder prisoner was one of those persons whose conversation, like that of all who have experienced many trials, contained many useful and important hints as well as sound information; but it was never egotistical, for the unfortunate man never alluded to his own sorrows. Dantes listened with admiring attention to all he said; some of his remarks corresponded with what he already knew, or applied to the sort of knowledge his nautical life had enabled him to acquire. A part of the good abbe's words, however, were wholly incomprehensible to him; but, like the aurora which guides the navigator in northern latitudes, opened new vistas to the inquiring mind of the listener, and gave fantastic glimpses of new horizons, enabling him justly to estimate the delight an intellectual mind would have in following one so richly gifted as Faria along the heights of truth, where he was so much at home.

"You must teach me a small part of what you know," said Dantes, "if only to prevent your growing weary of me. I can well believe that so learned a person as yourself would prefer absolute solitude to being tormented with the company of one as ignorant and uninformed as myself. If you will only agree to my request, I promise you never to mention another word about escaping."

The abbe smiled. "Alas, my boy," said he, "human knowledge is confined within very narrow limits; and when I have taught you mathematics, physics, history, and the three or four modern languages with which I am acquainted, you will know as much as I do myself. Now, it will scarcely require two years for me to communicate to you the stock of learning I possess."

"Two years!" exclaimed Dantes; "do you really believe I can acquire all these things in so short a time?"

"Not their application, certainly, but their principles you may; to learn is not to know; there are the learners and the learned. Memory makes the one, philosophy the other."

"But cannot one learn philosophy?"

"Philosophy cannot be taught; it is the application of the sciences to truth; it is like the golden cloud in which the Messiah went up into heaven."

"Well, then," said Dantes, "What shall you teach me first? I am in a hurry to begin. I want to learn."

"Everything," said the abbe. And that very evening the prisoners sketched a plan of education, to be entered upon the following day. Dantes possessed a prodigious memory, combined with an astonishing quickness and readiness of conception; the mathematical turn of his mind rendered him apt at all kinds of calculation, while his naturally poetical feelings threw a light and pleasing veil over the dry reality of arithmetical computation, or the rigid severity of geometry. He already knew Italian, and had also picked up a little of the Romaic dialect during voyages to the East; and by the aid of these two languages he easily comprehended the construction of all the others, so that at the end of six months he began to speak Spanish, English, and German. In strict accordance with the promise made to the abbe, Dantes spoke no more of escape. Perhaps the delight his studies afforded him left no room for such thoughts; perhaps the recollection that he had pledged his word (on which his sense of honor was keen) kept him from referring in any way to the possibilities of flight. Days, even months, passed by unheeded in one rapid and instructive course. At the end of a year Dantes was a new man. Dantes observed, however, that Faria, in spite of the relief his society afforded, daily grew sadder; one thought seemed incessantly to harass and distract his mind. Sometimes he would fall into long reveries, sigh heavily and involuntarily, then suddenly rise, and, with folded arms, begin pacing the confined space of his dungeon. One day he stopped all at once, and exclaimed, "Ah, if there were no sentinel!"

"There shall not be one a minute longer than you please," said Dantes, who had followed the working of his thoughts as accurately as though his brain were enclosed in crystal so clear as to display its minutest operations.

"I have already told you," answered the abbe, "that I loathe the idea of shedding blood."

"And yet the murder, if you choose to call it so, would be simply a measure of self-preservation."

"No matter! I could never agree to it."

"Still, you have thought of it?"

"Incessantly, alas!" cried the abbe.

"And you have discovered a means of regaining our freedom, have you not?" asked Dantes eagerly.

"I have; if it were only possible to place a deaf and blind sentinel in the gallery beyond us."

"He shall be both blind and deaf," replied the young man, with an air of determination that made his companion shudder.

"No, no," cried the abbe; "impossible!" Dantes endeavored to renew the subject; the abbe shook his head in token of disapproval, and refused to make any further response. Three months passed away.

"Are you strong?" the abbe asked one day of Dantes. The young man, in reply, took up the chisel, bent it into the form of a horseshoe, and then as readily straightened it.

"And will you engage not to do any harm to the sentry, except as a last resort?"

"I promise on my honor."

"Then," said the abbe, "we may hope to put our design into execution."

"And how long shall we be in accomplishing the necessary work?"

"At least a year."

"And shall we begin at once?"

"At once."

"We have lost a year to no purpose!" cried Dantes.

"Do you consider the last twelve months to have been wasted?" asked the abbe.

"Forgive me!" cried Edmond, blushing deeply.

"Tut, tut!" answered the abbe, "man is but man after all, and you are about the best specimen of the genus I have ever known. Come, let me show you my plan." The abbe then showed Dantes the sketch he had made for their escape. It consisted of a plan of his own cell and that of Dantes, with the passage which united them. In this passage he proposed to drive a level as they do in mines; this level would bring the two prisoners immediately beneath the gallery where the sentry kept watch; once there, a large excavation would be made, and one of the flag-stones with which the gallery was paved be so completely loosened that at the desired moment it would give way beneath the feet of the soldier, who, stunned by his fall, would be immediately bound and gagged by Dantes before he had power to offer any resistance. The prisoners were then to make their way through one of the gallery windows, and to let themselves down from the outer walls by means of the abbe's ladder of cords. Dantes' eyes sparkled with joy, and he rubbed his hands with delight at the idea of a plan so simple, yet apparently so certain to succeed.

That very day the miners began their labors, with a vigor and alacrity proportionate to their long rest from fatigue and their hopes of ultimate success. Nothing interrupted the progress of the work except the necessity that each was under of returning to his cell in anticipation of the turnkey's visits. They had learned to distinguish the almost imperceptible sound of his footsteps as he descended towards their dungeons, and happily, never failed of being prepared for his coming. The fresh earth excavated during their present work, and which would have entirely blocked up the old passage, was thrown, by degrees and with the utmost precaution, out of the window in either Faria's or Dantes' cell, the rubbish being first pulverized so finely that the night wind carried it far away without permitting the smallest trace to remain. More than a year had been consumed in this undertaking, the only tools for which had been a chisel, a knife, and a wooden lever; Faria still continuing to instruct Dantes by conversing with him, sometimes in one language, sometimes in another; at others, relating to him the history of nations and great men who from time to time have risen to fame and trodden the path of glory.

The abbe was a man of the world, and had, moreover, mixed in the first society of the day; he wore an air of melancholy dignity which Dantes, thanks to the imitative powers bestowed on him by nature, casily acquired, as well as that outward polish and politeness he had before been wanting in, and which is seldom possessed except by those who have been placed in constant intercourse with persons of high birth and breeding. At the end of fifteen months the level was finished, and the excavation completed beneath the gallery, and the two workmen could distinctly hear the measured tread of the sentinel as he paced to and fro over their heads.

Compelled, as they were, to await a night sufficiently dark to favor their flight, they were obliged to defer their final attempt till that auspicious moment should arrive; their greatest dread now was lest the stone through which the sentry was doomed to fall should give way before its right time, and this they had in some measure provided against by propping it up with a small beam which they had discovered in the walls through which they had worked their way. Dantes was occupied in arranging this piece of wood when he heard Faria, who had remained in Edmond's cell for the purpose of cutting a peg to secure their rope-ladder, call to him in a tone indicative of great suffering. Dantes hastened to his dungeon, where he found him standing in the middle of the room, pale as death, his forehead streaming with perspiration, and his hands clinched tightly together.

"Gracious heavens!" exclaimed Dantes, "what is the matter? what has happened?"

"Quick! quick!" returned the abbe, "listen to what I have to say." Dantes looked in fear and wonder at the livid countenance of Faria, whose eyes, already dull and sunken, were surrounded by purple circles, while his lips were white as those of a corpse, and his very hair seemed to stand on end.

"Tell me, I beseech you, what ails you?" cried Dantes, letting his chisel fall to the floor.

"Alas," faltered out the abbe, "all is over with me. I am seized with a terrible, perhaps mortal illness; I can feel that the paroxysm is fast approaching. I had a similar attack the year previous to my imprisonment. This malady admits but of one remedy; I will tell you what that is. Go into my cell as quickly as you can; draw out one of the feet that support the bed; you will find it has been hollowed out for the purpose of containing a small phial you will see there half-filled with a red-looking fluid. Bring it to me—or rather—no, no!—I may be found here, therefore help me back to my room while I have the strength to drag myself along. Who knows what may happen, or how long the attack may last?"

In spite of the magnitude of the misfortune which thus suddenly frustrated his hopes, Dantes did not lose his presence of mind, but descended into the passage, dragging his unfortunate companion with him; then, half-carrying, half-supporting him, he managed to reach the abbe's chamber, when he immediately laid the sufferer on his bed.

"Thanks," said the poor abbe, shivering as though his veins were filled with ice. "I am about to be seized with a fit of catalepsy; when it comes to its height I shall probably lie still and motionless as though dead, uttering neither sigh nor groan. On the other hand, the symptoms may be much more violent, and cause me to fall into fearful convulsions, foam at the mouth, and cry out loudly. Take care my cries are not heard, for if they are it is more than probable I should be removed to another part of the prison, and we be separated forever. When I become quite motionless, cold, and rigid as a corpse, then, and not before,—be careful about this,—force open my teeth with the knife, pour from eight to ten drops of the liquor contained in the phial down my throat, and I may perhaps revive."

"Perhaps!" exclaimed Dantes in grief-stricken tones.

"Help! help!" cried the abbe, "I—I—die—I"—

So sudden and violent was the fit that the unfortunate prisoner was unable to complete the sentence; a violent convulsion shook his whole frame, his eyes started from their sockets, his mouth was drawn on one side, his cheeks became purple, he struggled, foamed, dashed himself about, and uttered the most dreadful cries, which, however, Dantes prevented from being heard by covering his head with the blanket. The fit lasted two hours; then, more helpless than an infant, and colder and paler than marble, more crushed and broken than a reed trampled underfoot, he fell back, doubled up in one last convulsion, and became as rigid as a corpse.

Edmond waited till life seemed extinct in the body of his friend, then, taking up the knife, he with difficulty forced open the closely fixed jaws, carefully administered the appointed number of drops, and anxiously awaited the result. An hour passed away and the old man gave no sign of returning animation. Dantes began to fear he had delayed too long ere he administered the remedy, and, thrusting his hands into his hair, continued gazing on the lifeless features of his friend. At length a slight color tinged the livid cheeks, consciousness returned to the dull, open eyeballs, a faint sigh issued from the lips, and the sufferer made a feeble effort to move.

"He is saved! he is saved!" cried Dantes in a paroxysm of delight.

The sick man was not yet able to speak, but he pointed with evident anxiety towards the door. Dantes listened, and plainly distinguished the approaching steps of the jailer. It was therefore near seven o'clock; but Edmond's anxiety had put all thoughts of time out of his head. The young man sprang to the entrance, darted through it, carefully drawing the stone over the opening, and hurried to his cell. He had scarcely done so before the door opened, and the jailer saw the prisoner seated as usual on the side of his bed. Almost before the key had turned in the lock, and before the departing steps of the jailer had died away in the long corridor he had to traverse, Dantes, whose restless anxiety concerning his friend left him no desire to touch the food brought him, hurried back to the abbe's chamber, and raising the stone by pressing his head against it, was soon beside the sick man's couch.

Faria had now fully regained his consciousness, but he still lay helpless and exhausted.

"I did not expect to see you again," said he feebly, to Dantes.

"And why not?" asked the young man. "Did you fancy yourself dying?"

"No, I had no such idea; but, knowing that all was ready for flight, I thought you might have made your escape." The deep glow of indignation suffused the cheeks of Dantes.

"Without you? Did you really think me capable of that?"

"At least," said the abbe, "I now see how wrong such an opinion would have been. Alas, alas! I am fearfully exhausted and debilitated by this attack."

"Be of good cheer," replied Dantes; "your strength will return." And as he spoke he seated himself near the bed beside Faria, and took his hands. The abbe shook his head.

"The last attack I had," said he, "lasted but half an hour, and after it I was hungry, and got up without help; now I can move neither my right arm nor leg, and my head seems uncomfortable, which shows that there has been a suffusion of blood on the brain. The third attack will either carry me off, or leave me paralyzed for life."

"No, no," cried Dantes; "you are mistaken—you will not die! And your third attack (if, indeed, you should have another) will find you at liberty. We shall save you another time, as we have done this, only with a better chance of success, because we shall be able to command every requisite assistance."

"My good Edmond," answered the abbe, "be not deceived. The attack which has just passed away, condemns me forever to the walls of a prison. None can fly from a dungeon who cannot walk."

"Well, we will wait,—a week, a month, two months, if need be,—and meanwhile your strength will return. Everything is in readiness for our flight, and we can select any time we choose. As soon as you feel able to swim we will go."

"I shall never swim again," replied Faria. "This arm is paralyzed; not for a time, but forever. Lift it, and judge if I am mistaken." The young man raised the arm, which fell back by its own weight, perfectly inanimate and helpless. A sigh escaped him.

"You are convinced now, Edmond, are you not?" asked the abbe. "Depend upon it, I know what I say. Since the first attack I experienced of this malady, I have continually reflected on it. Indeed, I expected it, for it is a family inheritance; both my father and grandfather died of it in a third attack. The physician, who prepared for me the remedy I have twice successfully taken, was no other than the celebrated Cabanis, and he predicted a similar end for me."

"The physician may be mistaken!" exclaimed Dantes. "And as for your poor arm, what difference will that make? I can take you on my shoulders, and swim for both of us."

"My son," said the abbe, "you, who are a sailor and a swimmer, must know as well as I do that a man so loaded would sink before he had done fifty strokes. Cease, then, to allow yourself to be duped by vain hopes, that even your own excellent heart refuses to believe in. Here I shall remain till the hour of my deliverance arrives, and that, in all human probability, will be the hour of my death. As for you, who are young and active, delay not on my account, but fly—go—I give you back your promise."

"It is well," said Dantes. "Then I shall also remain." Then, rising and extending his hand with an air of solemnity over the old man's head, he slowly added, "By the blood of Christ I swear never to leave you while you live."

Faria gazed fondly on his noble-minded, single-hearted, high-principled young friend, and read in his countenance ample confirmation of the sincerity of his devotion and the loyalty of his purpose.

"Thanks," murmured the invalid, extending one hand. "I accept. You may one of these days reap the reward of your disinterested devotion. But as I cannot, and you will not, quit this place, it becomes necessary to fill up the excavation beneath the soldier's gallery; he might, by chance, hear the hollow sound of his footsteps, and call the attention of his officer to the circumstance. That would bring about a discovery which would inevitably lead to our being separated. Go, then, and set about this work, in which, unhappily, I can offer you no assistance; keep at it all night, if necessary, and do not return here to-morrow till after the jailer his visited me. I shall have something of the greatest importance to communicate to you."

Dantes took the hand of the abbe in his, and affectionately pressed it. Faria smiled encouragingly on him, and the young man retired to his task, in the spirit of obedience and respect which he had sworn to show towards his aged friend.

Chapter 18. The Treasure.

When Dantes returned next morning to the chamber of his companion in captivity, he found Faria seated and looking composed. In the ray of light which entered by the narrow window of his cell, he held open in his left hand, of which alone, it will be recollected, he retained the use, a sheet of paper, which, from being constantly rolled into a small compass, had the form of a cylinder, and was not easily kept open. He did not speak, but showed the paper to Dantes.

"What is that?" he inquired.

"Look at it," said the abbe with a smile.

"I have looked at it with all possible attention," said Dantes, "and I only see a half-burnt paper, on which are traces of Gothic characters inscribed with a peculiar kind of ink."

"This paper, my friend," said Faria, "I may now avow to you, since I have the proof of your fidelity—this paper is my treasure, of which, from this day forth, one-half belongs to you."

The sweat started forth on Dantes brow. Until this day and for how long a time!—he had refrained from talking of the treasure, which had brought upon the abbe the accusation of madness. With his instinctive delicacy Edmond had preferred avoiding any touch on this painful chord, and Faria had been equally silent. He had taken the silence of the old man for a return to reason; and now these few words uttered by Faria, after so painful a crisis, seemed to indicate a serious relapse into mental alienation.

"Your treasure?" stammered Dantes. Faria smiled.

"Yes," said he. "You have, indeed, a noble nature, Edmond, and I see by your paleness and agitation what is passing in your heart at this moment. No, be assured, I am not mad. This treasure exists, Dantes, and if I have not been allowed to possess it, you will. Yes—you. No one would listen or believe me, because everyone thought me mad; but you, who must know that I am not, listen to me, and believe me so afterwards if you will."

"Alas," murmured Edmond to himself, "this is a terrible relapse! There was only this blow wanting." Then he said aloud, "My dear friend, your attack has, perhaps, fatigued you; had you not better repose awhile? To-morrow, if you will, I will hear your narrative; but to-day I wish to nurse you carefully. Besides," he said, "a treasure is not a thing we need hurry about."

"On the contrary, it is a matter of the utmost importance, Edmond!" replied the old man. "Who knows if to-morrow, or the next day after, the third attack may not come on? and then must not all be over? Yes, indeed, I have often thought with a bitter joy that these riches, which would make the wealth of a dozen families, will be forever lost to those men who persecute me. This idea was one of vengeance to me, and I tasted it slowly in the night of my dungeon and the despair of my captivity. But now I have forgiven the world for the love of you; now that I see you, young and with a promising future,—now that I think of all that may result to you in the good fortune of such a disclosure, I shudder at any delay, and tremble lest I should not assure to one as worthy as yourself the possession of so vast an amount of hidden wealth." Edmond turned away his head with a sigh.

"You persist in your incredulity, Edmond," continued Faria. "My words have not convinced you. I see you require proofs. Well, then, read this paper, which I have never shown to anyone."

"To-morrow, my dear friend," said Edmond, desirous of not yielding to the old man's madness. "I thought it was understood that we should not talk of that until to-morrow."

"Then we will not talk of it until to-morrow; but read this paper to-day."

"I will not irritate him," thought Edmond, and taking the paper, of which half was wanting,—having been burnt, no doubt, by some accident,—he read:

"This treasure, which may amount to two…of Roman crowns in the most distant a…of the second opening wh…declare to belong to him alo…heir. 25th April, 149-"

"Well!" said Faria, when the young man had finished reading it.

"Why," replied Dantes, "I see nothing but broken lines and unconnected words, which are rendered illegible by fire."

"Yes, to you, my friend, who read them for the first time; but not for me, who have grown pale over them by many nights' study, and have reconstructed every phrase, completed every thought."

"And do you believe you have discovered the hidden meaning?"

"I am sure I have, and you shall judge for yourself; but first listen to the history of this paper."

"Silence!" exclaimed Dantes. "Steps approach—I go—adieu."

And Dantes, happy to escape the history and explanation which would be sure to confirm his belief in his friend's mental instability, glided like a snake along the narrow passage; while Faria, restored by his alarm to a certain amount of activity, pushed the stone into place with his foot, and covered it with a mat in order the more effectually to avoid discovery.

It was the governor, who, hearing of Faria's illness from the jailer, had come in person to see him.

Faria sat up to receive him, avoiding all gestures in order that he might conceal from the governor the paralysis that had already half stricken him with death. His fear was lest the governor, touched with pity, might order him to be removed to better quarters, and thus separate him from his young companion. But fortunately this was not the case, and the governor left him, convinced that the poor madman, for whom in his heart he felt a kind of affection, was only troubled with a slight indisposition.

During this time, Edmond, seated on his bed with his head in his hands, tried to collect his scattered thoughts. Faria, since their first acquaintance, had been on all points so rational and logical, so wonderfully sagacious, in fact, that he could not understand how so much wisdom on all points could be allied with madness. Was Faria deceived as to his treasure, or was all the world deceived as to Faria?

Dantes remained in his cell all day, not daring to return to his friend, thinking thus to defer the moment when he should be convinced, once for all, that the abbe was mad—such a conviction would be so terrible!

But, towards the evening after the hour for the customary visit had gone by, Faria, not seeing the young man appear, tried to move and get over the distance which separated them. Edmond shuddered when he heard the painful efforts which the old man made to drag himself along; his leg was inert, and he could no longer make use of one arm. Edmond was obliged to assist him, for otherwise he would not have been able to enter by the small aperture which led to Dantes' chamber.

"Here I am, pursuing you remorselessly," he said with a benignant smile.

"You thought to escape my munificence, but it is in vain. Listen to me."

Edmond saw there was no escape, and placing the old man on his bed, he seated himself on the stool beside him.

"You know," said the abbe, "that I was the secretary and intimate friend of Cardinal Spada, the last of the princes of that name. I owe to this worthy lord all the happiness I ever knew. He was not rich, although the wealth of his family had passed into a proverb, and I heard the phrase very often, 'As rich as a Spada.' But he, like public rumor, lived on this reputation for wealth; his palace was my paradise. I was tutor to his nephews, who are dead; and when he was alone in the world, I tried by absolute devotion to his will, to make up to him all he had done for me during ten years of unremitting kindness. The cardinal's house had no secrets for me. I had often seen my noble patron annotating ancient volumes, and eagerly searching amongst dusty family manuscripts. One day when I was reproaching him for his unavailing searches, and deploring the prostration of mind that followed them, he looked at me, and, smiling bitterly, opened a volume relating to the History of the City of Rome. There, in the twentieth chapter of the Life of Pope Alexander VI., were the following lines, which I can never forget:—

"'The great wars of Romagna had ended; Caesar Borgia, who had completed his conquest, had need of money to purchase all Italy. The pope had also need of money to bring matters to an end with Louis XII. King of France, who was formidable still in spite of his recent reverses; and it was necessary, therefore, to have recourse to some profitable scheme, which was a matter of great difficulty in the impoverished condition of exhausted Italy. His holiness had an idea. He determined to make two cardinals.'

"By choosing two of the greatest personages of Rome, especially rich men—this was the return the Holy Father looked for. In the first place, he could sell the great appointments and splendid offices which the cardinals already held; and then he had the two hats to sell besides. There was a third point in view, which will appear hereafter. The pope and Caesar Borgia first found the two future cardinals; they were Giovanni Rospigliosi, who held four of the highest dignities of the Holy See, and Caesar Spada, one of the noblest and richest of the Roman nobility; both felt the high honor of such a favor from the pope. They were ambitious, and Caesar Borgia soon found purchasers for their appointments. The result was, that Rospigliosi and Spada paid for being cardinals, and eight other persons paid for the offices the cardinals held before their elevation, and thus eight hundred thousand crowns entered into the coffers of the speculators.

"It is time now to proceed to the last part of the speculation. The pope heaped attentions upon Rospigliosi and Spada, conferred upon them the insignia of the cardinalate, and induced them to arrange their affairs and take up their residence at Rome. Then the pope and Caesar Borgia invited the two cardinals to dinner. This was a matter of dispute between the holy father and his son. Caesar thought they could make use of one of the means which he always had ready for his friends, that is to say, in the first place, the famous key which was given to certain persons with the request that they go and open a designated cupboard. This key was furnished with a small iron point,—a negligence on the part of the locksmith. When this was pressed to effect the opening of the cupboard, of which the lock was difficult, the person was pricked by this small point, and died next day. Then there was the ring with the lion's head, which Caesar wore when he wanted to greet his friends with a clasp of the hand. The lion bit the hand thus favored, and at the end of twenty-four hours, the bite was mortal. Caesar proposed to his father, that they should either ask the cardinals to open the cupboard, or shake hands with them; but Alexander VI., replied: 'Now as to the worthy cardinals, Spada and Rospigliosi, let us ask both of them to dinner, something tells me that we shall get that money back. Besides, you forget, Caesar, indigestion declares itself immediately, while a prick or a bite occasions a delay of a day or two.' Caesar gave way before such cogent reasoning, and the cardinals were consequently invited to dinner.

"The table was laid in a vineyard belonging to the pope, near San Pierdarena, a charming retreat which the cardinals knew very well by report. Rospigliosi, quite set up with his new dignities, went with a good appetite and his most ingratiating manner. Spada, a prudent man, and greatly attached to his only nephew, a young captain of the highest promise, took paper and pen, and made his will. He then sent word to his nephew to wait for him near the vineyard; but it appeared the servant did not find him.

"Spada knew what these invitations meant; since Christianity, so eminently civilizing, had made progress in Rome, it was no longer a centurion who came from the tyrant with a message,

'Caesar wills that you die.' but it was a legate a latere, who came with a smile on his lips to say from the pope, 'His holiness requests you to dine with him.'

"Spada set out about two o'clock to San Pierdarena. The pope awaited him. The first sight that attracted the eyes of Spada was that of his nephew, in full costume, and Caesar Borgia paying him most marked attentions. Spada turned pale, as Caesar looked at him with an ironical air, which proved that he had anticipated all, and that the snare was well spread. They began dinner and Spada was only able to inquire of his nephew if he had received his message. The nephew replied no; perfectly comprehending the meaning of the question. It was too late, for he had already drunk a glass of excellent wine, placed for him expressly by the pope's butler. Spada at the same moment saw another bottle approach him, which he was pressed to taste. An hour afterwards a physician declared they were both poisoned through eating mushrooms. Spada died on the threshold of the vineyard; the nephew expired at his own door, making signs which his wife could not comprehend.

"Then Caesar and the pope hastened to lay hands on the heritage, under presence of seeking for the papers of the dead man. But the inheritance consisted in this only, a scrap of paper on which Spada had written:—'I bequeath to my beloved nephew my coffers, my books, and, amongst others, my breviary with the gold corners, which I beg he will preserve in remembrance of his affectionate uncle.'

"The heirs sought everywhere, admired the breviary, laid hands on the furniture, and were greatly astonished that Spada, the rich man, was really the most miserable of uncles—no treasures—unless they were those of science, contained in the library and laboratories. That was all. Caesar and his father searched, examined, scrutinized, but found nothing, or at least very little; not exceeding a few thousand crowns in plate, and about the same in ready money; but the nephew had time to say to his wife before he expired: 'Look well among my uncle's papers; there is a will.'

"They sought even more thoroughly than the august heirs had done, but it was fruitless. There were two palaces and a vineyard behind the Palatine Hill; but in these days landed property had not much value, and the two palaces and the vineyard remained to the family since they were beneath the rapacity of the pope and his son. Months and years rolled on. Alexander VI. died, poisoned,— you know by what mistake. Caesar, poisoned at the same time, escaped by shedding his skin like a snake; but the new skin was spotted by the poison till it looked like a tiger's. Then, compelled to quit Rome, he went and got himself obscurely killed in a night skirmish, scarcely noticed in history. After the pope's death and his son's exile, it was supposed that the Spada family would resume the splendid position they had held before the cardinal's time; but this was not the case. The Spadas remained in doubtful ease, a mystery hung over this dark affair, and the public rumor was, that Caesar, a better politician than his father, had carried off from the pope the fortune of the two cardinals. I say the two, because Cardinal Rospigliosi, who had not taken any precaution, was completely despoiled.

"Up to this point," said Faria, interrupting the thread of his narrative, "this seems to you very meaningless, no doubt, eh?"

"Oh, my friend," cried Dantes, "on the contrary, it seems as if I were reading a most interesting narrative; go on, I beg of you."

"I will."

"The family began to get accustomed to their obscurity. Years rolled on, and amongst the descendants some were soldiers, others diplomatists; some churchmen, some bankers; some grew rich, and some were ruined. I come now to the last of the family, whose secretary I was—the Count of Spada. I had often heard him complain of the disproportion of his rank with his fortune; and I advised him to invest all he had in an annuity. He did so, and thus doubled his income. The celebrated breviary remained in the family, and was in the count's possession. It had been handed down from father to son; for the singular clause of the only will that had been found, had caused it to be regarded as a genuine relic, preserved in the family with superstitious veneration. It was an illuminated book, with beautiful Gothic characters, and so weighty with gold, that a servant always carried it before the cardinal on days of great solemnity.

"At the sight of papers of all sorts,—titles, contracts, parchments, which were kept in the archives of the family, all descending from the poisoned cardinal, I in my turn examined the immense bundles of documents, like twenty servitors, stewards, secretaries before me; but in spite of the most exhaustive researches, I found—nothing. Yet I had read, I had even written a precise history of the Borgia family, for the sole purpose of assuring myself whether any increase of fortune had occurred to them on the death of the Cardinal Caesar Spada; but could only trace the acquisition of the property of the Cardinal Rospigliosi, his companion in misfortune.

"I was then almost assured that the inheritance had neither profited the Borgias nor the family, but had remained unpossessed like the treasures of the Arabian Nights, which slept in the bosom of the earth under the eyes of the genie. I searched, ransacked, counted, calculated a thousand and a thousand times the income and expenditure of the family for three hundred years. It was useless. I remained in my ignorance, and the Count of Spada in his poverty. My patron died. He had reserved from his annuity his family papers, his library, composed of five thousand volumes, and his famous breviary. All these he bequeathed to me, with a thousand Roman crowns, which he had in ready money, on condition that I would have anniversary masses said for the repose of his soul, and that I would draw up a genealogical tree and history of his house. All this I did scrupulously. Be easy, my dear Edmond, we are near the conclusion.

"In 1807, a month before I was arrested, and a fortnight after the death of the Count of Spada, on the 25th of December (you will see presently how the date became fixed in my memory), I was reading, for the thousandth time, the papers I was arranging, for the palace was sold to a stranger, and I was going to leave Rome and settle at Florence, intending to take with me twelve thousand francs I possessed, my library, and the famous breviary, when, tired with my constant labor at the same thing, and overcome by a heavy dinner I had eaten, my head dropped on my hands, and I fell asleep about three o'clock in the afternoon. I awoke as the clock was striking six. I raised my head; I was in utter darkness. I rang for a light, but as no one came, I determined to find one for myself. It was indeed but anticipating the simple manners which I should soon be under the necessity of adopting. I took a wax-candle in one hand, and with the other groped about for a piece of paper (my match-box being empty), with which I proposed to get a light from the small flame still playing on the embers. Fearing, however, to make use of any valuable piece of paper, I hesitated for a moment, then recollected that I had seen in the famous breviary, which was on the table beside me, an old paper quite yellow with age, and which had served as a marker for centuries, kept there by the request of the heirs. I felt for it, found it, twisted it up together, and putting it into the expiring flame, set light to it.

"But beneath my fingers, as if by magic, in proportion as the fire ascended, I saw yellowish characters appear on the paper. I grasped it in my hand, put out the flame as quickly as I could, lighted my taper in the fire itself, and opened the crumpled paper with inexpressible emotion, recognizing, when I had done so, that these characters had been traced in mysterious and sympathetic ink, only appearing when exposed to the fire; nearly one-third of the paper had been consumed by the flame. It was that paper you read this morning; read it again, Dantes, and then I will complete for you the incomplete words and unconnected sense."

Faria, with an air of triumph, offered the paper to Dantes, who this time read the following words, traced with an ink of a reddish color resembling rust:—

"This 25th day of April, 1498, be ...
Alexander VI., and fearing that not ...
he may desire to become my heir, and re ...
and Bentivoglio, who were poisoned, ...
my sole heir, that I have bu ...
and has visited with me, that is, in ...
Island of Monte Cristo, all I poss ...
jewels, diamonds, gems; that I alone ...
may amount to nearly two mil ...
will find on raising the twentieth ro ...
creek to the east in a right line. Two open ...
in these caves; the treasure is in the furthest a ...
which treasure I bequeath and leave en ...
as my sole heir.
25th April, 1498.
Caes ...

"And now," said the abbe, "read this other paper;" and he presented to Dantes a second leaf with fragments of lines written on it, which Edmond read as follows:

"...ing invited to dine by his Holiness
... content with making me pay for my hat,
... serves for me the fate of Cardinals Caprara
... I declare to my nephew, Guido Spada
... ried in a place he knows
... the caves of the small

... essed of ingots, gold, money,

... know of the existence of this treasure, which

... lions of Roman crowns, and which he

... ck from the small

... ings have been made

... ngle in the second;

... tire to him

... ar Spada."

Faria followed him with an excited look, "And now," he said, when he saw that Dantes had read the last line, "put the two fragments together, and judge for yourself." Dantes obeyed, and the conjointed pieces gave the following:—

"This 25th day of April, 1498, be…ing invited to dine by his Holiness

Alexander VI., and fearing that not…content with making me pay

for my

hat, he may desire to become my heir, and re…serves for me the

fate of

Cardinals Caprara and Bentivoglio, who were poisoned…I declare

to my

nephew, Guido Spada, my sole heir, that I have bu…ried in a place

he knows and has visited with me, that is, in…the caves of the

small

Island of Monte Cristo all I poss…ssed of ingots, gold, money,

jewels,

diamonds, gems; that I alone…know of the existence of this

treasure,

which may amount to nearly two mil…lions of Roman crowns, and

which he

will find on raising the twentieth ro…ck from the small creek to the

east in a right line. Two open…ings have been made in these

caves;

the treasure is in the furthest a...ngle in the second; which treasure I

bequeath and leave en...tire to him as my sole heir. 25th April,
1498.

Caes...ar Spada."

"Well, do you comprehend now?" inquired Faria.

"It is the declaration of Cardinal Spada, and the will so long sought for," replied Edmond, still incredulous.

"Yes; a thousand times, yes!"

"And who completed it as it now is?"

"I did. Aided by the remaining fragment, I guessed the rest; measuring the length of the lines by those of the paper, and divining the hidden meaning by means of what was in part revealed, as we are guided in a cavern by the small ray of light above us."

"And what did you do when you arrived at this conclusion?"

"I resolved to set out, and did set out at that very instant, carrying with me the beginning of my great work, the unity of the Italian kingdom; but for some time the imperial police (who at this period, quite contrary to what Napoleon desired so soon as he had a son born to him, wished for a partition of provinces) had their eyes on me; and my hasty departure, the cause of which they were unable to guess, having aroused their suspicions, I was arrested at the very moment I was leaving Piombino.

"Now," continued Faria, addressing Dantes with an almost paternal expression, "now, my dear fellow, you know as much as I do myself. If we ever escape together, half this treasure is yours; if I die here, and you escape alone, the whole belongs to you."

"But," inquired Dantes hesitating, "has this treasure no more legitimate possessor in the world than ourselves?"

"No, no, be easy on that score; the family is extinct. The last Count of Spada, moreover, made me his heir, bequeathing to me this symbolic breviary, he bequeathed to me all it contained; no, no, make your mind satisfied on that point. If we lay hands on this fortune, we may enjoy it without remorse."

"And you say this treasure amounts to"—

"Two millions of Roman crowns; nearly thirteen millions of our money." *

*$2,600,000 in 1894.

"Impossible!" said Dantes, staggered at the enormous amount.

"Impossible? and why?" asked the old man. "The Spada family was one of the oldest and most powerful families of the fifteenth century; and in those times, when other opportunities for investment were wanting, such accumulations of gold and jewels were by no means rare; there are at this day Roman families perishing of hunger, though possessed of nearly a million in diamonds and jewels, handed down by entail, and which they cannot touch." Edmond thought he was in a dream—he wavered between incredulity and joy.

"I have only kept this secret so long from you," continued Faria, "that I might test your character, and then surprise you. Had we escaped before my attack of catalepsy, I should have conducted you to Monte Cristo; now," he added, with a sigh, "it is you who will conduct me thither. Well, Dantes, you do not thank me?"

"This treasure belongs to you, my dear friend," replied Dantes, "and to you only. I have no right to it. I am no relation of yours."

"You are my son, Dantes," exclaimed the old man. "You are the child of my captivity. My profession condemns me to celibacy. God has sent you to me to console, at one and the same time, the man who could not be a father, and the prisoner who could not get free." And Faria extended the arm of which alone the use remained to him to the young man who threw himself upon his neck and wept.

Chapter 19. The Third Attack

Now that this treasure, which had so long been the object of the abbe's meditations, could insure the future happiness of him whom Faria really loved as a son, it had doubled its value in his eyes, and every day he expatiated on the amount, explaining to Dantes all the good which, with thirteen or fourteen millions of francs, a man could do in these days to his friends; and then Dantes' countenance became gloomy, for the oath of vengeance he had taken recurred to his memory, and he reflected how much ill, in these times, a man with thirteen or fourteen millions could do to his enemies.

The abbe did not know the Island of Monte Cristo; but Dantes knew it, and had often passed it, situated twenty-five miles from Pianosa, between Corsica and the Island of Elba, and had once touched there. This island was, always had been, and still is, completely deserted. It is a rock of almost conical form, which looks as though it had been thrust up by volcanic force from the depth to the surface of the ocean. Dantes drew a plan of the island for Faria, and Faria gave Dantes advice as to the means he should employ to recover the treasure. But Dantes was far from being as enthusiastic and confident as the old man. It was past a question now that Faria was not a lunatic, and the way in which he had achieved the discovery, which had given rise to the suspicion of his madness, increased Edmond's admiration of him; but at the same time Dantes could not believe that the deposit, supposing it had ever existed, still existed; and though he considered the treasure as by no means chimerical, he yet believed it was no longer there.

However, as if fate resolved on depriving the prisoners of their last chance, and making them understand that they were condemned to perpetual imprisonment, a new misfortune befell them; the gallery on the sea side, which had long been in ruins, was rebuilt. They had repaired it completely, and stopped up with vast masses of stone the hole Dantes had partly filled in. But for this precaution, which, it will be remembered, the abbe had made to Edmond, the misfortune would have been still greater, for their attempt to escape would have been detected, and they would undoubtedly have been separated. Thus a new, a stronger, and more inexorable barrier was interposed to cut off the realization of their hopes.

"You see," said the young man, with an air of sorrowful resignation, to Faria, "that God deems it right to take from me any claim to merit for what you call my devotion to you. I have promised to remain forever with you, and now I could not break my promise if I would. The treasure will be no more mine than yours, and neither of us will quit this prison. But my real treasure is not that, my dear friend, which awaits me beneath the somber rocks of Monte Cristo, it is your presence, our living together five or six hours a day, in spite of our jailers; it is the rays of intelligence you have elicited from my brain, the languages you have implanted in my memory, and which have taken root there with all their philological ramifications. These different sciences that you have made so easy to me by the depth of the knowledge you possess of them, and the clearness of the principles to which you have reduced them—this is my treasure, my beloved friend, and with this you have made me rich and happy. Believe me, and take comfort, this is better for me than tons of gold and cases of diamonds, even were they not as problematical as the clouds we see in the morning floating over the sea, which we take for terra firma, and which evaporate and vanish as we draw near to them. To have you as long as possible near me, to hear your eloquent speech,—which embellishes my mind, strengthens my soul, and makes my whole frame capable of great and terrible things, if I should ever be free,—so fills my whole existence, that the despair to which I was just on the point of yielding when I knew you, has no longer any hold over me; and this—this is my fortune—not chimerical, but actual. I owe you my real good, my present happiness; and all the sovereigns of the earth, even Caesar Borgia himself, could not deprive me of this."

Thus, if not actually happy, yet the days these two unfortunates passed together went quickly. Faria, who for so long a time had kept silence as to the treasure, now perpetually talked of it. As he had prophesied would be the case, he remained paralyzed in the right arm and the left leg, and had given up all hope of ever enjoying it himself. But he was continually thinking over some means of escape for his young companion, and anticipating the pleasure he would enjoy. For fear the letter might be some day lost or stolen, he compelled Dantes to learn it by heart; and Dantes knew it from the first to the last word. Then he destroyed the second portion, assured that if the first were seized, no one would be able to discover its real meaning. Whole hours sometimes passed while Faria was giving instructions to Dantes,—instructions which were to serve him when he was at liberty. Then, once free, from the day and hour and moment when he was so, he could have but one only thought, which was, to gain Monte Cristo by some means, and remain there alone under some pretext which would arouse no suspicions; and once there, to endeavor to find the wonderful caverns, and search in the appointed spot,—the appointed spot, be it remembered, being the farthest angle in the second opening.

In the meanwhile the hours passed, if not rapidly, at least tolerably. Faria, as we have said, without having recovered the use of his hand and foot, had regained all the clearness of his understanding, and had gradually, besides the moral instructions we have detailed, taught his youthful companion the patient and sublime duty of a prisoner, who learns to make something from nothing. They were thus perpetually employed,—Faria, that he might not see himself grow old; Dantes, for fear of recalling the almost extinct past which now only floated in his memory like a distant light wandering in the night. So life went on for them as it does for those who are not victims of misfortune and whose activities glide along mechanically and tranquilly beneath the eye of providence.

But beneath this superficial calm there were in the heart of the young man, and perhaps in that of the old man, many repressed desires, many stifled sighs, which found vent when Faria was left alone, and when Edmond returned to his cell. One night Edmond awoke suddenly, believing that he heard someone calling him. He opened his eyes upon utter darkness. His name, or rather a plaintive voice which essayed to pronounce his name, reached him. He sat up in bed and a cold sweat broke out upon his brow. Undoubtedly the call came from Faria's dungeon.

"Alas," murmured Edmond; "can it be?"

He moved his bed, drew up the stone, rushed into the passage, and reached the opposite extremity; the secret entrance was open. By the light of the wretched and wavering lamp, of which we have spoken, Dantes saw the old man, pale, but yet erect, clinging to the bedstead. His features were writhing with those horrible symptoms which he already knew, and which had so seriously alarmed him when he saw them for the first time.

"Alas, my dear friend," said Faria in a resigned tone, "you understand, do you not, and I need not attempt to explain to you?"

Edmond uttered a cry of agony, and, quite out of his senses, rushed towards the door, exclaiming, "Help, help!" Faria had just sufficient strength to restrain him.

"Silence," he said, "or you are lost. We must now only think of you, my dear friend, and so act as to render your captivity supportable or your flight possible. It would require years to do again what I have done here, and the results would be instantly destroyed if our jailers knew we had communicated with each other. Besides, be assured, my dear Edmond, the dungeon I am about to leave will not long remain empty; some other unfortunate being will soon take my place, and to him you will appear like an angel of salvation. Perhaps he will be young, strong, and enduring, like yourself, and will aid you in your escape, while I have been but a hindrance. You will no longer have half a dead body tied to you as a drag to all your movements. At length providence has done something for you; he restores to you more than he takes away, and it was time I should die."

Edmond could only clasp his hands and exclaim, "Oh, my friend, my friend, speak not thus!" and then resuming all his presence of mind, which had for a moment staggered under this blow, and his strength, which had failed at the words of the old man, he said, "Oh, I have saved you once, and I will save you a second time!" And raising the foot of the bed, he drew out the phial, still a third filled with the red liquor.

"See," he exclaimed, "there remains still some of the magic draught. Quick, quick! tell me what I must do this time; are there any fresh instructions? Speak, my friend; I listen."

"There is not a hope," replied Faria, shaking his head, "but no matter; God wills it that man whom he has created, and in whose heart he has so profoundly rooted the love of life, should do all in his power to preserve that existence, which, however painful it may be, is yet always so dear."

"Oh, yes, yes!" exclaimed Dantes; "and I tell you that I will save you yet."

"Well, then, try. The cold gains upon me. I feel the blood flowing towards my brain. These horrible chills, which make my teeth chatter and seem to dislocate my bones, begin to pervade my whole frame; in five minutes the malady will reach its height, and in a quarter of an hour there will be nothing left of me but a corpse."

"Oh!" exclaimed Dantes, his heart wrung with anguish.

"Do as you did before, only do not wait so long, all the springs of life are now exhausted in me, and death," he continued, looking at his paralyzed arm and leg, "has but half its work to do. If, after having made me swallow twelve drops instead of ten, you see that I do not recover, then pour the rest down my throat. Now lift me on my bed, for I can no longer support myself."

Edmond took the old man in his arms, and laid him on the bed.

"And now, my dear friend," said Faria, "sole consolation of my wretched existence,—you whom heaven gave me somewhat late, but still gave me, a priceless gift, and for which I am most grateful,—at the moment of separating from you forever, I wish you all the happiness and all the prosperity you so well deserve. My son, I bless thee!" The young man cast himself on his knees, leaning his head against the old man's bed.

"Listen, now, to what I say in this my dying moment. The treasure of the Spadas exists. God grants me the boon of vision unrestricted by time or space. I see it in the depths of the inner cavern. My eyes pierce the inmost recesses of the earth, and are dazzled at the sight of so much riches. If you do escape, remember that the poor abbe, whom all the world called mad, was not so. Hasten to Monte Cristo—avail yourself of the fortune—for you have indeed suffered long enough." A violent convulsion attacked the old man. Dantes raised his head and saw Faria's eyes injected with blood. It seemed as if a flow of blood had ascended from the chest to the head.

"Adieu, adieu!" murmured the old man, clasping Edmond's hand convulsively—"adieu!"

"Oh, no,—no, not yet," he cried; "do not forsake me! Oh, succor him! Help—help—help!"

"Hush—hush!" murmured the dying man, "that they may not separate us if you save me!"

"You are right. Oh, yes, yes; be assured I shall save you! Besides, although you suffer much, you do not seem to be in such agony as you were before."

"Do not mistake. I suffer less because there is in me less strength to endure. At your age we have faith in life; it is the privilege of youth to believe and hope, but old men see death more clearly. Oh, 'tis here—'tis here—'tis over—my sight is gone—my senses fail! Your hand, Dantes! Adieu—adieu!" And raising himself by a final effort, in which he summoned all his faculties, he said,— "Monte Cristo, forget not Monte Cristo!" And he fell back on the bed. The crisis was terrible, and a rigid form with twisted limbs, swollen eyelids, and lips flecked with bloody foam, lay on the bed of torture, in place of the intellectual being who so lately rested there.

Dantes took the lamp, placed it on a projecting stone above the bed, whence its tremulous light fell with strange and fantastic ray on the distorted countenance and motionless, stiffened body. With steady gaze he awaited confidently the moment for administering the restorative.

When he believed that the right moment had arrived, he took the knife, pried open the teeth, which offered less resistance than before, counted one after the other twelve drops, and watched; the phial contained, perhaps, twice as much more. He waited ten minutes, a quarter of an hour, half an hour,—no change took place. Trembling, his hair erect, his brow bathed with perspiration, he counted the seconds by the beating of his heart. Then he thought it was time to make the last trial, and he put the phial to the purple lips of Faria, and without having occasion to force open his jaws, which had remained extended, he poured the whole of the liquid down his throat.

The draught produced a galvanic effect, a violent trembling pervaded the old man's limbs, his eyes opened until it was fearful to gaze upon them, he heaved a sigh which resembled a shriek, and then his convulsed body returned gradually to its former immobility, the eyes remaining open.

Half an hour, an hour, an hour and a half elapsed, and during this period of anguish, Edmond leaned over his friend, his hand applied to his heart, and felt the body gradually grow cold, and the heart's pulsation become more and more deep and dull, until at length it stopped; the last movement of the heart ceased, the face became livid, the eyes remained open, but the eyeballs were glazed. It was six o'clock in the morning, the dawn was just breaking, and its feeble ray came into the dungeon, and paled the ineffectual light of the lamp. Strange shadows passed over the countenance of the dead man, and at times gave it the appearance of life. While the struggle between day and night lasted, Dantes still doubted; but as soon as the daylight gained the pre-eminence, he saw that he was alone with a corpse. Then an invincible and extreme terror seized upon him, and he dared not again press the hand that hung out of bed, he dared no longer to gaze on those fixed and vacant eyes, which he tried many times to close, but in vain—they opened again as soon as shut. He extinguished the lamp, carefully concealed it, and then went away, closing as well as he could the entrance to the secret passage by the large stone as he descended.

It was time, for the jailer was coming. On this occasion he began his rounds at Dantes' cell, and on leaving him he went on to Faria's dungeon, taking thither breakfast and some linen. Nothing betokened that the man knew anything of what had occurred. He went on his way.

Dantes was then seized with an indescribable desire to know what was going on in the dungeon of his unfortunate friend. He therefore returned by the subterraneous gallery, and arrived in time to hear the exclamations of the turnkey, who called out for help. Other turnkeys came, and then was heard the regular tramp of soldiers. Last of all came the governor.

Edmond heard the creaking of the bed as they moved the corpse, heard the voice of the governor, who asked them to throw water on the dead man's face; and seeing that, in spite of this application, the prisoner did not recover, they sent for the doctor. The governor then went out, and words of pity fell on Dantes' listening ears, mingled with brutal laughter.

"Well, well," said one, "the madman has gone to look after his treasure. Good journey to him!"

"With all his millions, he will not have enough to pay for his shroud!" said another.

"Oh," added a third voice, "the shrouds of the Chateau d'If are not dear!"

"Perhaps," said one of the previous speakers, "as he was a churchman, they may go to some expense in his behalf."

"They may give him the honors of the sack."

Edmond did not lose a word, but comprehended very little of what was said. The voices soon ceased, and it seemed to him as if everyone had left the cell. Still he dared not to enter, as they might have left some turnkey to watch the dead. He remained, therefore, mute and motionless, hardly venturing to breathe. At the end of an hour, he heard a faint noise, which increased. It was the governor who returned, followed by the doctor and other attendants. There was a moment's silence;—it was evident that the doctor was examining the dead body. The inquiries soon commenced.

The doctor analyzed the symptoms of the malady to which the prisoner had succumbed, and declared that he was dead. Questions and answers followed in a nonchalant manner that made Dantes indignant, for he felt that all the world should have for the poor abbe a love and respect equal to his own.

"I am very sorry for what you tell me," said the governor, replying to the assurance of the doctor, "that the old man is really dead; for he was a quiet, inoffensive prisoner, happy in his folly, and required no watching."

"Ah," added the turnkey, "there was no occasion for watching him: he would have stayed here fifty years, I'll answer for it, without any attempt to escape."

"Still," said the governor, "I believe it will be requisite, notwithstanding your certainty, and not that I doubt your science, but in discharge of my official duty, that we should be perfectly assured that the prisoner is dead." There was a moment of complete silence, during which Dantes, still listening, knew that the doctor was examining the corpse a second time.

"You may make your mind easy," said the doctor; "he is dead. I will answer for that."

"You know, sir," said the governor, persisting, "that we are not content in such cases as this with such a simple examination. In spite of all appearances, be so kind, therefore, as to finish your duty by fulfilling the formalities described by law."

"Let the irons be heated," said the doctor; "but really it is a useless precaution." This order to heat the irons made Dantes shudder. He heard hasty steps, the creaking of a door, people going and coming, and some minutes afterwards a turnkey entered, saying,—

"Here is the brazier, lighted." There was a moment's silence, and then was heard the crackling of burning flesh, of which the peculiar and nauseous smell penetrated even behind the wall where Dantes was listening in horror. The perspiration poured forth upon the young man's brow, and he felt as if he should faint.

"You see, sir, he is really dead," said the doctor; "this burn in the heel is decisive. The poor fool is cured of his folly, and delivered from his captivity."

"Wasn't his name Faria?" inquired one of the officers who accompanied the governor.

"Yes, sir; and, as he said, it was an ancient name. He was, too, very learned, and rational enough on all points which did not relate to his treasure; but on that, indeed, he was intractable."

"It is the sort of malady which we call monomania," said the doctor.

"You had never anything to complain of?" said the governor to the jailer who had charge of the abbe.

"Never, sir," replied the jailer, "never; on the contrary, he sometimes amused me very much by telling me stories. One day, too, when my wife was ill, he gave me a prescription which cured her."

"Ah, ah!" said the doctor, "I did not know that I had a rival; but I hope, governor, that you will show him all proper respect."

"Yes, yes, make your mind easy, he shall be decently interred in the newest sack we can find. Will that satisfy you?"

"Must this last formality take place in your presence, sir?" inquired a turnkey.

"Certainly. But make haste—I cannot stay here all day." Other footsteps, going and coming, were now heard, and a moment afterwards the noise of rustling canvas reached Dantes' ears, the bed creaked, and the heavy footfall of a man who lifts a weight sounded on the floor; then the bed again creaked under the weight deposited upon it.

"This evening," said the governor.

"Will there be any mass?" asked one of the attendants.

"That is impossible," replied the governor. "The chaplain of the chateau came to me yesterday to beg for leave of absence, in order to take a trip to Hyeres for a week. I told him I would attend to the prisoners in his absence. If the poor abbe had not been in such a hurry, he might have had his requiem."

"Pooh, pooh;" said the doctor, with the impiety usual in persons of his profession; "he is a churchman. God will respect his profession, and not give the devil the wicked delight of sending him a priest." A shout of laughter followed this brutal jest. Meanwhile the operation of putting the body in the sack was going on.

"This evening," said the governor, when the task was ended.

"At what hour?" inquired a turn key.

"Why, about ten or eleven o'clock."

"Shall we watch by the corpse?"

"Of what use would it be? Shut the dungeon as if he were alive—that is all." Then the steps retreated, and the voices died away in the distance; the noise of the door, with its creaking hinges and bolts ceased, and a silence more sombre than that of solitude ensued,—the silence of death, which was all-pervasive, and struck its icy chill to the very soul of Dantes. Then he raised the flag-stone cautiously with his head, and looked carefully around the chamber. It was empty, and Dantes emerged from the tunnel.

Chapter 20. The Cemetery of the Chateau D'If.

On the bed, at full length, and faintly illuminated by the pale light that came from the window, lay a sack of canvas, and under its rude folds was stretched a long and stiffened form; it was Faria's last winding-sheet,—a winding-sheet which, as the turnkey said, cost so little. Everything was in readiness. A barrier had been placed between Dantes and his old friend. No longer could Edmond look into those wide-open eyes which had seemed to be penetrating the mysteries of death; no longer could he clasp the hand which had done so much to make his existence blessed. Faria, the beneficent and cheerful companion, with whom he was accustomed to live so intimately, no longer breathed. He seated himself on the edge of that terrible bed, and fell into melancholy and gloomy reverie.

Alone—he was alone again—again condemned to silence—again face to face with nothingness! Alone!—never again to see the face, never again to hear the voice of the only human being who united him to earth! Was not Faria's fate the better, after all—to solve the problem of life at its source, even at the risk of horrible suffering? The idea of suicide, which his friend had driven away and kept away by his cheerful presence, now hovered like a phantom over the abbe's dead body.

"If I could die," he said, "I should go where he goes, and should assuredly find him again. But how to die? It is very easy," he went on with a smile; "I will remain here, rush on the first person that opens the door, strangle him, and then they will guillotine me." But excessive grief is like a storm at sea, where the frail bark is tossed from the depths to the top of the wave. Dantes recoiled from the idea of so infamous a death, and passed suddenly from despair to an ardent desire for life and liberty.

"Die? oh, no," he exclaimed—"not die now, after having lived and suffered so long and so much! Die? yes, had I died years ago; but now to die would be, indeed, to give way to the sarcasm of destiny. No, I want to live; I shall struggle to the very last; I will yet win back the happiness of which I have been deprived. Before I die I must not forget that I have my executioners to punish, and perhaps, too, who knows, some friends to reward. Yet they will forget me here, and I shall die in my dungeon like Faria." As he said this, he became silent and gazed straight before him like one overwhelmed with a strange and amazing thought. Suddenly he arose, lifted his hand to his brow as if his brain were giddy, paced twice or thrice round the dungeon, and then paused abruptly by the bed.

Mercedes again took the forefront of his thoughts. If she had waited for him they could easily run away and start a life somewhere else, somewhere away from France, most especially with the treasure. They could live like royalty in a distant land and forget either of them had to endure the torturous time apart. For the first time doubt crept into Edmond's mind. What if she had not waited, what if she moved on with her life, had children, a husband that was not him? Had he not been locked away for at least ten years, maybe more? There was a difficulty in keeping track as the days began to blur together.

Where doubt sought to sow seeds of discord love ripped it up by the roots. He thought of the kiss Mercedes and he shared in her house at the Catalans. It was a kiss of love, not of duty, and love remained hard as stone.

Before he could stop it, another fantasy spread before him, not one of lust or rutting, one of love and devotion. A fantasy of gently kisses and caresses on a beach surrounded by moonlight. This particular beach had changed over the years Edmond and Mercedes had been acquainted, but it always held a few constants. The sand was snow white but dotted with small shells from sea creatures. It also somehow contained a rather large collection of smooth glass beneath its surface. Legend of the place spoke of a ship wreck full of wine so delicious it turned the sea sweet for an entire day, and that the glass still washed up to the beach. Edmond could feel the speckle of sand sticking to his legs and the sharp bite of shells into his arms as they cradled Mercedes in an effort to keep her clean and unmarred. She would never allow herself to be held aloft, however. She was a lady but she most certainly did not mind the dirt and dust of sand or the thrill of hunting sea glass beneath it.

Edmond would lay Mercedes in the sand and bring her body to life with every pass of his hand or lips. Each kiss a representation of the love he bore her. He would kiss her gently and slow as well as passionately and with a purpose. The taste of her lips in the sunshine and the bright red hue from his own lips ravaging hers were the predominate thoughts in his mind. A sight he had previously seen, a sight he had affected himself.

"If I left you and then returned, my love, would you wait for me?" Edmond asked the fantasy of Mercedes, intent on her reply.

"I would always wait for you, Edmond. Would you wait for me?"

It was not even a question. Edmond would wait for her his entire life if need be.

"Yes, my love, I would wait for you until the end of time itself."

"What brings this morbid conversation to your lips?" She asked, a consternated frown creasing her forehead. "Do you doubt my affection for you?"

"Of course not, it is nothing at all." Edmond lied in an attempt to save the purity of the dream, the integrity of the additional memory for his collection, to keep him sane.

Edmond truly loved her sweet nature. The enduring way she could make a disgruntled old man smile or the time she could take picking wild flowers for her modest house. On that same thread Mercedes was passionate, the spark given to her by her Catalan blood.

In the rare moments Mercedes initiated an intimate encounter, Edmond always had cause to sear that memory in his mind for future purpose. Just after Edmond asked Mercedes to be his bride, she took him to their special beach at sunset. They lay in the sand, the waves crashing on the shore below their feet. That was the first night Mercedes allowed Edmond below her skirts. She was modest but as soon as his fingers, deft from tying knots aboard the *Pharaon*, showed her what pleasure he could create for her she opened to him, like the first flower in winter.

Not long after the first time he brought Mercedes to completion, she asked him to allow her to reciprocate. Edmond had his doubts but Mercedes could be stubborn as an ox and ensured she always received exactly what she sought out to achieve. Back at the beach he instructed her on how to touch his manhood, hold it, and stroke it for maximum effect. She was a quick study and the first time he spilled his seed into her palm she knew the power she possessed over him.

The small caresses and petting they participated in with each other was just a precursor to the amazing moment they shared in her bed the first time they made love. Nothing could upend the sensation of her warm, wet, flesh squeezing him, especially as they waited so long to take their lovemaking that far. Each sound Mercedes would try to hold inside was captured forever in the memory of Edmond. His passion for ensuring her pleasure only grew from that first touch of his sun bronzed fingers on her pale bare skin.

Another memory of Mercedes Edmond held in great esteem was the first time she whispered her love for him. They were children by the world's standard but it did not make the heart-clenching sensation any less real.

Mercedes would wait for him, he had no doubt, there was no other alternative, they loved one another since they were children and a life without her would be no life worth living. Once his vengeance was exacted, Mercedes would become his bride but he had to escape the Chateau d'If before he could bring all those wishes to pass.

"Just God!" he muttered, "whence comes this thought? Is it from thee? Since none but the dead pass freely from this dungeon, let me take the place of the dead!" Without giving himself time to reconsider his decision, and, indeed, that he might not allow his thoughts to be distracted from his desperate resolution, he bent over the appalling shroud, opened it with the knife which Faria had made, drew the corpse from the sack, and bore it along the tunnel to his own chamber, laid it on his couch, tied around its head the rag he wore at night around his own, covered it with his counterpane, once again kissed the ice-cold brow, and tried vainly to close the resisting eyes, which glared horribly, turned the head towards the wall, so that the jailer might, when he brought the evening meal, believe that he was asleep, as was his frequent custom; entered the tunnel again, drew the bed against the wall, returned to the other cell, took from the hiding-place the needle and thread, flung off his rags, that they might feel only naked flesh beneath the coarse canvas, and getting inside the sack, placed himself in the posture in which the dead body had been laid, and sewed up the mouth of the sack from the inside.

He would have been discovered by the beating of his heart, if by any mischance the jailers had entered at that moment. Dantes might have waited until the evening visit was over, but he was afraid that the governor would change his mind, and order the dead body to be removed earlier. In that case his last hope would have been destroyed. Now his plans were fully made, and this is what he intended to do. If while he was being carried out the grave-diggers should discover that they were bearing a live instead of a dead body, Dantes did not intend to give them time to recognize him, but with a sudden cut of the knife, he meant to open the sack from top to bottom, and, profiting by their alarm, escape; if they tried to catch him, he would use his knife to better purpose.

If they took him to the cemetery and laid him in a grave, he would allow himself to be covered with earth, and then, as it was night, the grave-diggers could scarcely have turned their backs before he would have worked his way through the yielding soil and escaped. He hoped that the weight of earth would not be so great that he could not overcome it. If he was detected in this and the earth proved too heavy, he would be stifled, and then—so much the better, all would be over. Dantes had not eaten since the preceding evening, but he had not thought of hunger, nor did he think of it now. His situation was too precarious to allow him even time to reflect on any thought but one.

The first risk that Dantes ran was, that the jailer, when he brought him his supper at seven o'clock, might perceive the change that had been made; fortunately, twenty times at least, from misanthropy or fatigue, Dantes had received his jailer in bed, and then the man placed his bread and soup on the table, and went away without saying a word. This time the jailer might not be as silent as usual, but speak to Dantes, and seeing that he received no reply, go to the bed, and thus discover all.

When seven o'clock came, Dantes' agony really began. His hand placed upon his heart was unable to redress its throbbings, while, with the other he wiped the perspiration from his temples. From time to time chills ran through his whole body, and clutched his heart in a grasp of ice. Then he thought he was going to die. Yet the hours passed on without any unusual disturbance, and Dantes knew that he had escaped the first peril. It was a good augury. At length, about the hour the governor had appointed, footsteps were heard on the stairs. Edmond felt that the moment had arrived, summoned up all his courage, held his breath, and would have been happy if at the same time he could have repressed the throbbing of his veins. The footsteps—they were double—paused at the door—and Dantes guessed that the two grave-diggers had come to seek him—this idea was soon converted into certainty, when he heard the noise they made in putting down the hand-bier. The door opened, and a dim light reached Dantes' eyes through the coarse sack that covered him; he saw two shadows approach his bed, a third remaining at the door with a torch in its hand. The two men, approaching the ends of the bed, took the sack by its extremities.

"He's heavy though for an old and thin man," said one, as he raised the head.

"They say every year adds half a pound to the weight of the bones," said another, lifting the feet.

"Have you tied the knot?" inquired the first speaker.

"What would be the use of carrying so much more weight?" was the reply, "I can do that when we get there."

"Yes, you're right," replied the companion.

"What's the knot for?" thought Dantes. They deposited the supposed corpse on the bier. Edmond stiffened himself in order to play the part of a dead man, and then the party, lighted by the man with the torch, who went first, ascended the stairs. Suddenly he felt the fresh and sharp night air, and Dantes knew that the mistral was blowing. It was a sensation in which pleasure and pain were strangely mingled. The bearers went on for twenty paces, then stopped, putting the bier down on the ground. One of them went away, and Dantes heard his shoes striking on the pavement.

"Where am I?" he asked himself.

"Really, he is by no means a light load!" said the other bearer, sitting on the edge of the hand-barrow. Dantes' first impulse was to escape, but fortunately he did not attempt it.

"Give us a light," said the other bearer, "or I shall never find what I am looking for." The man with the torch complied, although not asked in the most polite terms.

"What can he be looking for?" thought Edmond. "The spade, perhaps." An exclamation of satisfaction indicated that the grave-digger had found the object of his search. "Here it is at last," he said, "not without some trouble though."

"Yes," was the answer, "but it has lost nothing by waiting."

As he said this, the man came towards Edmond, who heard a heavy metallic substance laid down beside him, and at the same moment a cord was fastened round his feet with sudden and painful violence.

"Well, have you tied the knot?" inquired the grave-digger, who was looking on.

"Yes, and pretty tight too, I can tell you," was the answer.

"Move on, then." And the bier was lifted once more, and they proceeded.

They advanced fifty paces farther, and then stopped to open a door, then went forward again. The noise of the waves dashing against the rocks on which the chateau is built, reached Dantes' ear distinctly as they went forward.

"Bad weather!" observed one of the bearers; "not a pleasant night for a dip in the sea."

"Why, yes, the abbe runs a chance of being wet," said the other; and then there was a burst of brutal laughter. Dantes did not comprehend the jest, but his hair stood erect on his head.

"Well, here we are at last," said one of them. "A little farther—a little farther," said the other. "You know very well that the last was stopped on his way, dashed on the rocks, and the governor told us next day that we were careless fellows."

They ascended five or six more steps, and then Dantes felt that they took him, one by the head and the other by the heels, and swung him to and fro. "One!" said the grave-diggers, "two! three!" And at the same instant Dantes felt himself flung into the air like a wounded bird, falling, falling, with a rapidity that made his blood curdle. Although drawn downwards by the heavy weight which hastened his rapid descent, it seemed to him as if the fall lasted for a century.

At last, with a horrible splash, he darted like an arrow into the ice-cold water, and as he did so he uttered a shrill cry, stifled in a moment by his immersion beneath the waves.

Dantes had been flung into the sea, and was dragged into its depths by a thirty-six pound shot tied to his feet. The sea is the cemetery of the Chateau d'If.

Chapter 21. The Island of Tiboulen.

Dantes, although stunned and almost suffocated, had sufficient presence of mind to hold his breath, and as his right hand (prepared as he was for every chance) held his knife open, he rapidly ripped up the sack, extricated his arm, and then his body; but in spite of all his efforts to free himself from the shot, he felt it dragging him down still lower. He then bent his body, and by a desperate effort severed the cord that bound his legs, at the moment when it seemed as if he were actually strangled. With a mighty leap he rose to the surface of the sea, while the shot dragged down to the depths the sack that had so nearly become his shroud.

Dantes waited only to get breath, and then dived, in order to avoid being seen. When he arose a second time, he was fifty paces from where he had first sunk. He saw overhead a black and tempestuous sky, across which the wind was driving clouds that occasionally suffered a twinkling star to appear; before him was the vast expanse of waters, sombre and terrible, whose waves foamed and roared as if before the approach of a storm. Behind him, blacker than the sea, blacker than the sky, rose phantom-like the vast stone structure, whose projecting crags seemed like arms extended to seize their prey, and on the highest rock was a torch lighting two figures. He fancied that these two forms were looking at the sea; doubtless these strange grave-diggers had heard his cry. Dantes dived again, and remained a long time beneath the water. This was an easy feat to him, for he usually attracted a crowd of spectators in the bay before the lighthouse at Marseilles when he swam there, and was unanimously declared to be the best swimmer in the port. When he came up again the light had disappeared.

He must now get his bearings. Ratonneau and Pomegue are the nearest islands of all those that surround the Chateau d'If, but Ratonneau and Pomegue are inhabited, as is also the islet of Daume. Tiboulen and Lemaire were therefore the safest for Dantes' venture. The islands of Tiboulen and Lemaire are a league from the Chateau d'If; Dantes, nevertheless, determined to make for them. But how could he find his way in the darkness of the night? At this moment he saw the light of Planier, gleaming in front of him like a star. By leaving this light on the right, he kept the Island of Tiboulen a little on the left; by turning to the left, therefore, he would find it. But, as we have said, it was at least a league from the Chateau d'If to this island. Often in prison Faria had said to him, when he saw him idle and inactive,

"Dantes, you must not give way to this listlessness; you will be drowned if you seek to escape, and your strength has not been properly exercised and prepared for exertion." These words rang in Dantes' ears, even beneath the waves; he hastened to cleave his way through them to see if he had not lost his strength. He found with pleasure that his captivity had taken away nothing of his power, and that he was still master of that element on whose bosom he had so often sported as a boy.

Fear, that relentless pursuer, clogged Dantes' efforts. He listened for any sound that might be audible, and every time that he rose to the top of a wave he scanned the horizon, and strove to penetrate the darkness. He fancied that every wave behind him was a pursuing boat, and he redoubled his exertions, increasing rapidly his distance from the chateau, but exhausting his strength. He swam on still, and already the terrible chateau had disappeared in the darkness. He could not see it, but he felt its presence. An hour passed, during which Dantes, excited by the feeling of freedom, continued to cleave the waves. "Let us see," said he, "I have swum above an hour, but as the wind is against me, that has retarded my speed; however, if I am not mistaken, I must be close to Tiboulen. But what if I were mistaken?" A shudder passed over him. He sought to tread water, in order to rest himself; but the sea was too violent, and he felt that he could not make use of this means of recuperation.

"Well," said he, "I will swim on until I am worn out, or the cramp seizes me, and then I shall sink;" and he struck out with the energy of despair.

Suddenly the sky seemed to him to become still darker and more dense, and heavy clouds seemed to sweep down towards him; at the same time he felt a sharp pain in his knee. He fancied for a moment that he had been shot, and listened for the report; but he heard nothing. Then he put out his hand, and encountered an obstacle and with another stroke knew that he had gained the shore.

Before him rose a grotesque mass of rocks, that resembled nothing so much as a vast fire petrified at the moment of its most fervent combustion. It was the Island of Tiboulen. Dantes rose, advanced a few steps, and, with a fervent prayer of gratitude, stretched himself on the granite, which seemed to him softer than down. Then, in spite of the wind and rain, he fell into the deep, sweet sleep of utter exhaustion. At the expiration of an hour Edmond was awakened by the roar of thunder. The tempest was let loose and beating the atmosphere with its mighty wings; from time to time a flash of lightning stretched across the heavens like a fiery serpent, lighting up the clouds that rolled on in vast chaotic waves.

Dantes had not been deceived—he had reached the first of the two islands, which was, in fact, Tiboulen. He knew that it was barren and without shelter; but when the sea became more calm, he resolved to plunge into its waves again, and swim to Lemaire, equally arid, but larger, and consequently better adapted for concealment.

An overhanging rock offered him a temporary shelter, and scarcely had he availed himself of it when the tempest burst forth in all its fury. Edmond felt the trembling of the rock beneath which he lay; the waves, dashing themselves against it, wetted him with their spray. He was safely sheltered, and yet he felt dizzy in the midst of the warring of the elements and the dazzling brightness of the lightning. It seemed to him that the island trembled to its base, and that it would, like a vessel at anchor, break moorings, and bear him off into the centre of the storm. He then recollected that he had not eaten or drunk for four-and-twenty hours. He extended his hands, and drank greedily of the rainwater that had lodged in a hollow of the rock.

As he rose, a flash of lightning, that seemed to rive the remotest heights of heaven, illumined the darkness. By its light, between the Island of Lemaire and Cape Croiselle, a quarter of a league distant, Dantes saw a fishing-boat driven rapidly like a specter before the power of winds and waves. A second after, he saw it again, approaching with frightful rapidity. Dantes cried at the top of his voice to warn them of their danger, but they saw it themselves. Another flash showed him four men clinging to the shattered mast and the rigging, while a fifth clung to the broken rudder.

The men he beheld saw him undoubtedly, for their cries were carried to his ears by the wind. Above the splintered mast a sail rent to tatters was waving; suddenly the ropes that still held it gave way, and it disappeared in the darkness of the night like a vast sea-bird. At the same moment a violent crash was heard, and cries of distress. Dantes from his rocky perch saw the shattered vessel, and among the fragments the floating forms of the hapless sailors. Then all was dark again.

Dantes ran down the rocks at the risk of being himself dashed to pieces; he listened, he groped about, but he heard and saw nothing—the cries had ceased, and the tempest continued to rage. By degrees the wind abated, vast gray clouds rolled towards the west, and the blue firmament appeared studded with bright stars. Soon a red streak became visible in the horizon, the waves whitened; a light played over them, and gilded their foaming crests with gold. It was day.

Dantes stood mute and motionless before this majestic spectacle, as if he now beheld it for the first time; and indeed since his captivity in the Chateau d'If he had forgotten that such scenes were ever to be witnessed. He turned towards the fortress, and looked at both sea and land. The gloomy building rose from the bosom of the ocean with imposing majesty and seemed to dominate the scene. It was about five o'clock. The sea continued to get calmer.

"In two or three hours," thought Dantes, "the turnkey will enter my chamber, find the body of my poor friend, recognize it, seek for me in vain, and give the alarm. Then the tunnel will be discovered; the men who cast me into the sea and who must have heard the cry I uttered, will be questioned. Then boats filled with armed soldiers will pursue the wretched fugitive. The cannon will warn everyone to refuse shelter to a man wandering about naked and famished. The police of Marseilles will be on the alert by land, whilst the governor pursues me by sea. I am cold, I am hungry. I have lost even the knife that saved me. O my God, I have suffered enough surely! Have pity on me, and do for me what I am unable to do for myself."

As Dantes (his eyes turned in the direction of the Chateau d'If) uttered this prayer, he saw off the farther point of the Island of Pomegue a small vessel with lateen sail skimming the sea like a gull in search of prey; and with his sailor's eye he knew it to be a Genoese tartan. She was coming out of Marseilles harbor, and was standing out to sea rapidly, her sharp prow cleaving through the waves. "Oh," cried Edmond, "to think that in half an hour I could join her, did I not fear being questioned, detected, and conveyed back to Marseilles! What can I do? What story can I invent? under pretext of trading along the coast, these men, who are in reality smugglers, will prefer selling me to doing a good action. I must wait. But I cannot—I am starving. In a few hours my strength will be utterly exhausted; besides, perhaps I have not been missed at the fortress. I can pass as one of the sailors wrecked last night. My story will be accepted, for there is no one left to contradict me."

As he spoke, Dantes looked toward the spot where the fishing-vessel had been wrecked, and started. The red cap of one of the sailors hung to a point of the rock and some timbers that had formed part of the vessel's keel, floated at the foot of the crag. In an instant Dantes' plan was formed. He swam to the cap, placed it on his head, seized one of the timbers, and struck out so as to cut across the course the vessel was taking.

"I am saved!" murmured he. And this conviction restored his strength.

He soon saw that the vessel, with the wind dead ahead, was tacking between the Chateau d'If and the tower of Planier. For an instant he feared lest, instead of keeping in shore, she should stand out to sea; but he soon saw that she would pass, like most vessels bound for Italy, between the islands of Jaros and Calaseraigne. However, the vessel and the swimmer insensibly neared one another, and in one of its tacks the tartan bore down within a quarter of a mile of him. He rose on the waves, making signs of distress; but no one on board saw him, and the vessel stood on another tack. Dantes would have shouted, but he knew that the wind would drown his voice.

It was then he rejoiced at his precaution in taking the timber, for without it he would have been unable, perhaps, to reach the vessel—certainly to return to shore, should he be unsuccessful in attracting attention.

Dantes, though almost sure as to what course the vessel would take, had yet watched it anxiously until it tacked and stood towards him. Then he advanced; but before they could meet, the vessel again changed her course. By a violent effort he rose half out of the water, waving his cap, and uttering a loud shout peculiar to sailors. This time he was both seen and heard, and the tartan instantly steered towards him. At the same time, he saw they were about to lower the boat.

An instant after, the boat, rowed by two men, advanced rapidly towards him. Dantes let go of the timber, which he now thought to be useless, and swam vigorously to meet them. But he had reckoned too much upon his strength, and then he realized how serviceable the timber had been to him. His arms became stiff, his legs lost their flexibility, and he was almost breathless.

He shouted again. The two sailors redoubled their efforts, and one of them cried in Italian, "Courage!"

The word reached his ear as a wave which he no longer had the strength to surmount passed over his head. He rose again to the surface, struggled with the last desperate effort of a drowning man, uttered a third cry, and felt himself sinking, as if the fatal cannon shot were again tied to his feet. The water passed over his head, and the sky turned gray. A convulsive movement again brought him to the surface. He felt himself seized by the hair, then he saw and heard nothing. He had fainted.

When he opened his eyes Dantes found himself on the deck of the tartan. His first care was to see what course they were taking. They were rapidly leaving the Chateau d'If behind. Dantes was so exhausted that the exclamation of joy he uttered was mistaken for a sigh.

As we have said, he was lying on the deck. A sailor was rubbing his limbs with a woolen cloth; another, whom he recognized as the one who had cried out "Courage!" held a gourd full of rum to his mouth; while the third, an old sailer, at once the pilot and captain, looked on with that egotistical pity men feel for a misfortune that they have escaped yesterday, and which may overtake them to-morrow.

A few drops of the rum restored suspended animation, while the friction of his limbs restored their elasticity.

"Who are you?" said the pilot in bad French.

"I am," replied Dantes, in bad Italian, "a Maltese sailor. We were coming from Syracuse laden with grain. The storm of last night overtook us at Cape Morgion, and we were wrecked on these rocks."

"Where do you come from?"

"From these rocks that I had the good luck to cling to while our captain and the rest of the crew were all lost. I saw your vessel, and fearful of being left to perish on the desolate island, I swam off on a piece of wreckage to try and intercept your course. You have saved my life, and I thank you," continued Dantes. "I was lost when one of your sailors caught hold of my hair."

"It was I," said a sailor of a frank and manly appearance; "and it was time, for you were sinking."

"Yes," returned Dantes, holding out his hand, "I thank you again."

"I almost hesitated, though," replied the sailor; "you looked more like a brigand than an honest man, with your beard six inches, and your hair a foot long." Dantes recollected that his hair and beard had not been cut all the time he was at the Chateau d'If.

"Yes," said he, "I made a vow, to our Lady of the Grotto not to cut my hair or beard for ten years if I were saved in a moment of danger; but to-day the vow expires."

"Now what are we to do with you?" said the captain.

"Alas, anything you please. My captain is dead; I have barely escaped; but I am a good sailor. Leave me at the first port you make; I shall be sure to find employment."

"Do you know the Mediterranean?"

"I have sailed over it since my childhood."

"You know the best harbors?"

"There are few ports that I could not enter or leave with a bandage over my eyes."

"I say, Captain," said the sailor who had cried "Courage!" to Dantes, "if what he says is true, what hinders his staying with us?"

"If he says true," said the captain doubtingly. "But in his present condition he will promise anything, and take his chance of keeping it afterwards."

"I will do more than I promise," said Dantes.

"We shall see," returned the other, smiling.

"Where are you going?" asked Dantes.

"To Leghorn."

"Then why, instead of tacking so frequently, do you not sail nearer the wind?"

"Because we should run straight on to the Island of Rion."

"You shall pass it by twenty fathoms."

"Take the helm, and let us see what you know." The young man took the helm, felt to see if the vessel answered the rudder promptly and seeing that, without being a first-rate sailor, she yet was tolerably obedient,—

"To the sheets," said he. The four seamen, who composed the crew, obeyed, while the pilot looked on. "Haul taut."—They obeyed.

"Belay." This order was also executed; and the vessel passed, as Dantes had predicted, twenty fathoms to windward.

"Bravo!" said the captain.

"Bravo!" repeated the sailors. And they all looked with astonishment at this man whose eye now disclosed an intelligence and his body a vigor they had not thought him capable of showing.

"You see," said Dantes, quitting the helm, "I shall be of some use to you, at least during the voyage. If you do not want me at Leghorn, you can leave me there, and I will pay you out of the first wages I get, for my food and the clothes you lend me."

"Ah," said the captain, "we can agree very well, if you are reasonable."

"Give me what you give the others, and it will be all right," returned Dantes.

"That's not fair," said the seaman who had saved Dantes; "for you know more than we do."

"What is that to you, Jacopo?" returned the Captain. "Everyone is free to ask what he pleases."

"That's true," replied Jacopo; "I only make a remark."

"Well, you would do much better to find him a jacket and a pair of trousers, if you have them."

"No," said Jacopo; "but I have a shirt and a pair of trousers."

"That is all I want," interrupted Dantes. Jacopo dived into the hold and soon returned with what Edmond wanted.

"Now, then, do you wish for anything else?" said the patron.

"A piece of bread and another glass of the capital rum I tasted, for I have not eaten or drunk for a long time." He had not tasted food for forty hours. A piece of bread was brought, and Jacopo offered him the gourd.

"Larboard your helm," cried the captain to the steersman. Dantes glanced that way as he lifted the gourd to his mouth; then paused with hand in mid-air.

"Hollo! What's the matter at the Chateau d'If?" said the captain.

A small white cloud, which had attracted Dantes' attention, crowned the summit of the bastion of the Chateau d'If. At the same moment the faint report of a gun was heard. The sailors looked at one another.

"What is this?" asked the captain.

"A prisoner has escaped from the Chateau d'If, and they are firing the alarm gun," replied Dantes. The captain glanced at him, but he had lifted the rum to his lips and was drinking it with so much composure, that suspicions, if the captain had any, died away.

"At any rate," murmured he, "if it be, so much the better, for I have made a rare acquisition." Under pretence of being fatigued, Dantes asked to take the helm; the steersman, glad to be relieved, looked at the captain, and the latter by a sign indicated that he might abandon it to his new comrade. Dantes could thus keep his eyes on Marseilles.

"What is the day of the month?" asked he of Jacopo, who sat down beside him.

"The 28th of February."

"In what year?"

"In what year—you ask me in what year?"

"Yes," replied the young man, "I ask you in what year!"

"You have forgotten then?"

"I got such a fright last night," replied Dantes, smiling, "that I have almost lost my memory. I ask you what year is it?"

"The year 1829," returned Jacopo. It was fourteen years day for day since Dantes' arrest. He was nineteen when he entered the Chateau d'If; he was thirty-three when he escaped. A sorrowful smile passed over his face; he asked himself what had become of Mercedes, who must believe him dead. Then his eyes lighted up with hatred as he thought of the three men who had caused him so long and wretched a captivity. He renewed against Danglars, Fernand, and Villefort the oath of implacable vengeance he had made in his dungeon. This oath was no longer a vain menace; for the fastest sailor in the Mediterranean would have been unable to overtake the little tartan, that with every stitch of canvas set was flying before the wind to Leghorn.

Dantes released the helm and moved off to curl up in the corner at the front of the small skiff, with a borrowed jacket, worn but faded at the elbows from sea splash. As always, in quiet moments such as these, Dantes thought of Mercedes. He's imagining his bride in many ways since he became a guest of the Chateau d'If but this one fantasy, the most depraved of all his mind could muster, he had saved until he was free to enjoy the memory it might create. The cool fresh air bolstered Dantes' sense of freedom and in that moment he imagined Mercedes in his most erotic fantasy.

When Dantes had travelled East, experimenting with spices and tobacco, he had a fortunate encounter with *les putains*. Dantes did not avail himself of their services but he witnessed such an event as he had never seen before. At first he thought it was the drink simmering his blood to a boil for his debauched thoughts but the reality of the situation became evident rather quickly. This particular fetish was sold as a specialty in that region of the world and Dantes did not need to pay for it when a saucy young wench offered to let him watch for free. She must have taken a fancy to him, *les putains* never did any task for free.

Man and woman engaged in the act of lovemaking like animals. The man mounted his conquest from behind and both the parties were so engrossed in the act they did not see his shock and surprise, nor did they notice his presence. He watched them rut for longer than he should have in good conscience and the image of that position was forever scorched into his mind.

Mercedes was a lady, unlike any he ever had the pleasure of meeting, but she would do this for him if asked and he would prepare her so well she would forget her sensibilities and succumb to the pleasure he might spark in her.

He would remove every stitch of clothing and spread her thighs wide before him. She would remain open and waiting as he lapped at her wet flesh until she climaxed, her knees pressing against his ears. Most of all he wanted to hear those tiny whimpers she squeaked out as she attempted in vain to remain proper and still feel the full measure of the sensation.

Dantes' manhood pressed against his borrowed trousers, he arranged the coat to give himself a modicum of privacy should anyone pass him on deck. He closed his eyes and resumed his musings, his thoughts wandering to how simple it would be to turn her so her breasts pressed into the sheets and her hips created a tantalizing angle with her waist.

Once he held her soft fleshy hips in his palms, Dantes would take her, gently, so she would not feel the need to shy away from his touch. Inserting his turgid member into the waiting sheath she provided would feel like heaven on Earth. Just the image in his mind of having Mercedes in that way, her black hair falling around them in a curtain, awakened something primal and forbidden he didn't know he possessed. He might even play with a few tendrils while he thrust into her, adding to the sensation he sought to build.

His imaginings were interrupted by Jacapo.

"Is it a woman you dream of?

Dantes had not even heard him approach, it was testament to how engrossing his fantasy had become.

"Yes, my betrothed."

Jacapo smiled an odd lopsided thing, a knowing smile.

"Then she waits for you at port?"

"It is my most fervent hope."

"Mine too, then" Jacapo said, evenly.

Jacapo nodded to Dantes, inserted his hands into his pants pocket, and wandered back the way he had evidently came. Dantes watched him depart and only felt comfortable resuming his trail of thoughts once the man was gone permanently. The task of hiding his erect member was an embarrassment; he did not relish the thought of fighting off a robbery while sporting it.

Dantes ensured the coat covered the noticeable bulge at the front of his breeches before closing his eyes. In an instant he was transported back to his Mercedes. His mind opened like a flower bud at the same place he was interrupted. The sensation of driving his manhood into his bride, even imagined, was overwhelming. He had not let his mind wander in this way sometimes. The sweet pressure of Mercedes, warm and wet around him, almost had him spilling his seed, right there, with no stimulation at all.

By the end of their assignation, Dantes was all but certain Mercedes would be grinding back against him, endeavoring to reach her own completion alongside his. He might run a hand down her flat belly and stimulate her even further as her excitement grew.

In his mind they climaxed, reached that high peak, at the exact same moment, sharing in the wave of pleasure that would crush both of them. They rode the wave, each holding themselves against the other as the small ripples of pleasure passed through them unseen. When it was over Dantes could feel the imprint of her body as they aligned back to front, nude, and warm.

Dantes opened his eyes and stared up at the sky the clouds fluffy and white. What is Mercedes decided not to wait? What if she did these depraved things with her husband and it was no longer his place to imagine her as his own?

All the doubts he previously held before leaving the Chateau d'If flooded his mind. She could be deceased or possibly worse still, married to someone else. Dantes could honestly profess he had no thoughts on which would actually be worse. He stopped his mind from wandering too far into dark corners else he might not have the strength to return to the light.

Chapter 22. The Smugglers.

Dantes had not been a day on board before he had a very clear idea of the men with whom his lot had been cast. Without having been in the school of the Abbe Faria, the worthy master of *The Young Amelia* (the name of the Genoese tartan) knew a smattering of all the tongues spoken on the shores of that large lake called the Mediterranean, from the Arabic to the Provencal, and this, while it spared him interpreters, persons always troublesome and frequently indiscreet, gave him great facilities of communication, either with the vessels he met at sea, with the small boats sailing along the coast, or with the people without name, country, or occupation, who are always seen on the quays of seaports, and who live by hidden and mysterious means which we must suppose to be a direct gift of providence, as they have no visible means of support. It is fair to assume that Dantes was on board a smuggler.

At first the captain had received Dantes on board with a certain degree of distrust. He was very well known to the customs officers of the coast; and as there was between these worthies and himself a perpetual battle of wits, he had at first thought that Dantes might be an emissary of these industrious guardians of rights and duties, who perhaps employed this ingenious means of learning some of the secrets of his trade. But the skillful manner in which Dantes had handled the lugger had entirely reassured him; and then, when he saw the light plume of smoke floating above the bastion of the Chateau d'If, and heard the distant report, he was instantly struck with the idea that he had on board his vessel one whose coming and going, like that of kings, was accompanied with salutes of artillery. This made him less uneasy, it must be owned, than if the new-comer had proved to be a customs officer;

but this supposition also disappeared like the first, when he beheld the perfect tranquility of his recruit.

Edmond thus had the advantage of knowing what the owner was, without the owner knowing who he was; and however the old sailor and his crew tried to "pump" him, they extracted nothing more from him; he gave accurate descriptions of Naples and Malta, which he knew as well as Marseilles, and held stoutly to his first story. Thus the Genoese, subtle as he was, was duped by Edmond, in whose favor his mild demeanor, his nautical skill, and his admirable dissimulation, pleaded. Moreover, it is possible that the Genoese was one of those shrewd persons who know nothing but what they should know, and believe nothing but what they should believe.

In this state of mutual understanding, they reached Leghorn. Here Edmond was to undergo another trial; he was to find out whether he could recognize himself, as he had not seen his own face for fourteen years. He had preserved a tolerably good remembrance of what the youth had been, and was now to find out what the man had become. His comrades believed that his vow was fulfilled. As he had twenty times touched at Leghorn, he remembered a barber in St. Ferdinand Street; he went there to have his beard and hair cut. The barber gazed in amazement at this man with the long, thick and black hair and beard, which gave his head the appearance of one of Titian's portraits. At this period it was not the fashion to wear so large a beard and hair so long; now a barber would only be surprised if a man gifted with such advantages should consent voluntarily to deprive himself of them. The Leghorn barber said nothing and went to work.

When the operation was concluded, and Edmond felt that his chin was completely smooth, and his hair reduced to its usual length, he asked for a hand-glass. He was now, as we have said, three-and-thirty years of age, and his fourteen years' imprisonment had produced a great transformation in his appearance. Dantes had entered the Chateau d'If with the round, open, smiling face of a young and happy man, with whom the early paths of life have been smooth, and who anticipates a future corresponding with his past. This was now all changed. The oval face was lengthened, his smiling mouth had assumed the firm and marked lines which betoken resolution; his eyebrows were arched beneath a brow furrowed with thought; his eyes were full of melancholy, and from their depths occasionally sparkled gloomy fires of misanthropy and hatred; his complexion, so long kept from the sun, had now that pale color which produces, when the features are encircled with black hair, the aristocratic beauty of the man of the north; the profound learning he had acquired had besides diffused over his features a refined intellectual expression; and he had also acquired, being naturally of a goodly stature, that vigor which a frame possesses which has so long concentrated all its force within itself.

To the elegance of a nervous and slight form had succeeded the solidity of a rounded and muscular figure. As to his voice, prayers, sobs, and imprecations had changed it so that at times it was of a singularly penetrating sweetness, and at others rough and almost hoarse. Moreover, from being so long in twilight or darkness, his eyes had acquired the faculty of distinguishing objects in the night, common to the hyena and the wolf. Edmond smiled when he beheld himself: it was impossible that his best friend—if, indeed, he had any friend left—could recognize him; he could not recognize himself.

The master of *The Young Amelia*, who was very desirous of retaining amongst his crew a man of Edmond's value, had offered to advance him funds out of his future profits, which Edmond had accepted. His next care on leaving the barber's who had achieved his first metamorphosis was to enter a shop and buy a complete sailor's suit—a garb, as we all know, very simple, and consisting of white trousers, a striped shirt, and a cap. It was in this costume, and bringing back to Jacopo the shirt and trousers he had lent him, that Edmond reappeared before the captain of the lugger, who had made him tell his story over and over again before he could believe him, or recognize in the neat and trim sailor the man with thick and matted beard, hair tangled with seaweed, and body soaking in seabrine, whom he had picked up naked and nearly drowned. Attracted by his prepossessing appearance, he renewed his offers of an engagement to Dantes; but Dantes, who had his own projects, would not agree for a longer time than three months.

The Young Amelia had a very active crew, very obedient to their captain, who lost as little time as possible. He had scarcely been a week at Leghorn before the hold of his vessel was filled with printed muslins, contraband cottons, English powder, and tobacco on which the excise had forgotten to put its mark. The master was to get all this out of Leghorn free of duties, and land it on the shores of Corsica, where certain speculators undertook to forward the cargo to France. They sailed; Edmond was again cleaving the azure sea which had been the first horizon of his youth, and which he had so often dreamed of in prison. He left Gorgone on his right and La Pianosa on his left, and went towards the country of Paoli and Napoleon. The next morning going on deck, as he always did at an early hour, the patron found Dantes leaning against the bulwarks gazing with intense earnestness at a pile of granite rocks, which the rising sun tinged with rosy light. It was the Island of Monte Cristo. *The Young Amelia* left it three-quarters of a league to the larboard, and kept on for Corsica.

Dantes thought, as they passed so closely to the island whose name was so interesting to him, that he had only to leap into the sea and in half an hour be at the promised land. But then what could he do without instruments to discover his treasure, without arms to defend himself? Besides, what would the sailors say? What would the patron think? He must wait.

Fortunately, Dantes had learned how to wait; he had waited fourteen years for his liberty, and now he was free he could wait at least six months or a year for wealth. Would he not have accepted liberty without riches if it had been offered to him? Besides, were not those riches chimerical?—offspring of the brain of the poor Abbe Faria, had they not died with him? It is true, the letter of the Cardinal Spada was singularly circumstantial, and Dantes repeated it to himself, from one end to the other, for he had not forgotten a word.

Evening came, and Edmond saw the island tinged with the shades of twilight, and then disappear in the darkness from all eyes but his own, for he, with vision accustomed to the gloom of a prison, continued to behold it last of all, for he remained alone upon deck. The next morn broke off the coast of Aleria; all day they coasted, and in the evening saw fires lighted on land; the position of these was no doubt a signal for landing, for a ship's lantern was hung up at the mast-head instead of the streamer, and they came to within a gunshot of the shore. Dantes noticed that the captain of *The Young Amelia* had, as he neared the land, mounted two small culverins, which, without making much noise, can throw a four ounce ball a thousand paces or so. But on this occasion the precaution was superfluous, and everything proceeded with the utmost smoothness and politeness. Four shallops came off with very little noise alongside the lugger, which, no doubt, in acknowledgement of the compliment, lowered her own shallop into the sea, and the five boats worked so well that by two o'clock in the morning all the cargo was out of *The Young Amelia* and on terra firma. The same night, such a man of regularity was the patron of *The Young Amelia*, the profits were divided, and each man had a hundred Tuscan livres, or about eighty francs. But the voyage was not ended. They turned the bowsprit towards Sardinia, where they intended to take in a cargo, which was to replace what had been discharged. The second operation was as successful as the first, *The Young Amelia* was in luck. This new cargo was destined for the coast of the Duchy of Lucca, and consisted almost entirely of Havana cigars, sherry, and Malaga wines.

There they had a bit of a skirmish in getting rid of the duties; the excise was, in truth, the everlasting enemy of the patron of *The Young Amelia*. A customs officer was laid low, and two sailors wounded; Dantes was one of the latter, a ball having touched him in the left shoulder. Dantes was almost glad of this affray, and almost pleased at being wounded, for they were rude lessons which taught him with what eye he could view danger, and with what endurance he could bear suffering. He had contemplated danger with a smile, and when wounded had exclaimed with the great philosopher, "Pain, thou art not an evil." He had, moreover, looked upon the customs officer wounded to death, and, whether from heat of blood produced by the encounter, or the chill of human sentiment, this sight had made but slight impression upon him. Dantes was on the way he desired to follow, and was moving towards the end he wished to achieve; his heart was in a fair way of petrifying in his bosom. Jacopo, seeing him fall, had believed him killed, and rushing towards him raised him up, and then attended to him with all the kindness of a devoted comrade.

This world was not then so good as Doctor Pangloss believed it, neither was it so wicked as Dantes thought it, since this man, who had nothing to expect from his comrade but the inheritance of his share of the prize-money, manifested so much sorrow when he saw him fall. Fortunately, as we have said, Edmond was only wounded, and with certain herbs gathered at certain seasons, and sold to the smugglers by the old Sardinian women, the wound soon closed. Edmond then resolved to try Jacopo, and offered him in return for his attention a share of his prize-money, but Jacopo refused it indignantly.

As a result of the sympathetic devotion which Jacopo had from the first bestowed on Edmond, the latter was moved to a certain degree of affection. But this sufficed for Jacopo, who instinctively felt that Edmond had a right to superiority of position—a superiority which Edmond had concealed from all others. And from this time the kindness which Edmond showed him was enough for the brave seaman.

Then in the long days on board ship, when the vessel, gliding on with security over the azure sea, required no care but the hand of the helmsman, thanks to the favorable winds that swelled her sails, Edmond, with a chart in his hand, became the instructor of Jacopo, as the poor Abbe Faria had been his tutor. He pointed out to him the bearings of the coast, explained to him the variations of the compass, and taught him to read in that vast book opened over our heads which they call heaven, and where God writes in azure with letters of diamonds. And when Jacopo inquired of him, "What is the use of teaching all these things to a poor sailor like me?" Edmond replied, "Who knows? You may one day be the captain of a vessel. Your fellow-countryman, Bonaparte, became emperor." We had forgotten to say that Jacopo was a Corsican.

Two months and a half elapsed in these trips, and Edmond had become as skillful a coaster as he had been a hardy seaman; he had formed an acquaintance with all the smugglers on the coast, and learned all the Masonic signs by which these half pirates recognize each other. He had passed and re-passed his Island of Monte Cristo twenty times, but not once had he found an opportunity of landing there. He then formed a resolution. As soon as his engagement with the patron of *The Young Amelia* ended, he would hire a small vessel on his own account—for in his several voyages he had amassed a hundred piastres—and under some pretext land at the Island of Monte Cristo. Then he would be free to make his researches, not perhaps entirely at liberty, for he would be doubtless watched by those who accompanied him. But in this world we must risk something. Prison had made Edmond prudent, and he was desirous of running no risk whatever. But in vain did he rack his imagination; fertile as it was, he could not devise any plan for reaching the island without companionship.

Dantes was tossed about on these doubts and wishes, when the patron, who had great confidence in him, and was very desirous of retaining him in his service, took him by the arm one evening and led him to a tavern on the Via del' Oglio, where the leading smugglers of Leghorn used to congregate and discuss affairs connected with their trade. Already Dantes had visited this maritime Bourse two or three times, and seeing all these hardy free-traders, who supplied the whole coast for nearly two hundred leagues in extent, he had asked himself what power might not that man attain who should give the impulse of his will to all these contrary and diverging minds. This time it was a great matter that was under discussion, connected with a vessel laden with Turkey carpets, stuffs of the Levant, and cashmeres. It was necessary to find some neutral ground on which an exchange could be made, and then to try and land these goods on the coast of France. If the venture was successful the profit would be enormous, there would be a gain of fifty or sixty piastres each for the crew. The patron of *The Young Amelia* proposed as a place of landing the Island of Monte Cristo, which being completely deserted, and having neither soldiers nor revenue officers, seemed to have been placed in the midst of the ocean since the time of the heathen Olympus by Mercury, the god of merchants and robbers, classes of mankind which we in modern times have separated if not made distinct, but which antiquity appears to have included in the same category. At the mention of Monte Cristo Dantes started with joy; he rose to conceal his emotion, and took a turn around the smoky tavern, where all the languages of the known world were jumbled in a lingua franca. When he again joined the two persons who had been discussing the matter, it had been decided that they should touch at Monte Cristo and set out on the following night. Edmond, being consulted, was of opinion that the island afforded every possible security and that great enterprises to be well done should be done quickly. Nothing then was altered in the plan, and orders were given to get under way next night, and, wind and weather permitting, to make the neutral island by the following day.

Chapter 23. The Island of Monte Cristo.

Thus, at length, by one of the unexpected strokes of fortune which sometimes befall those who have for a long time been the victims of an evil destiny, Dantes was about to secure the opportunity he wished for, by simple and natural means, and land on the island without incurring any suspicion. One night more and he would be on his way.

The night was one of feverish distraction, and in its progress visions good and evil passed through Dantes' mind. If he closed his eyes, he saw Cardinal Spada's letter written on the wall in characters of flame—if he slept for a moment the wildest dreams haunted his brain. He ascended into grottos paved with emeralds, with panels of rubies, and the roof glowing with diamond stalactites. Pearls fell drop by drop, as subterranean waters filter in their caves. Edmond, amazed, wonderstruck, filled his pockets with the radiant gems and then returned to daylight, when he discovered that his prizes had all changed into common pebbles. He then endeavored to re-enter the marvelous grottos, but they had suddenly receded, and now the path became a labyrinth, and then the entrance vanished, and in vain did he tax his memory for the magic and mysterious word which opened the splendid caverns of Ali Baba to the Arabian fisherman. All was useless; the treasure disappeared, and had again reverted to the genii from whom for a moment he had hoped to carry it off. The day came at length, and was almost as feverish as the night had been, but it brought reason to the aid of imagination, and Dantes was then enabled to arrange a plan which had hitherto been vague and unsettled in his brain. Night came, and with it the preparation for departure, and these preparations served to conceal Dantes' agitation. He had by degrees assumed such authority over his companions that he was almost like a commander on board; and as his orders were always clear, distinct, and easy of execution, his comrades obeyed him with celerity and pleasure.

The old patron did not interfere, for he too had recognized the superiority of Dantes over the crew and himself. He saw in the young man his natural successor, and regretted that he had not a daughter, that he might have bound Edmond to him by a more secure alliance. At seven o'clock in the evening all was ready, and at ten minutes past seven they doubled the lighthouse just as the beacon was kindled. The sea was calm, and, with a fresh breeze from the south-east, they sailed beneath a bright blue sky, in which God also lighted up in turn his beacon lights, each of which is a world. Dantes told them that all hands might turn in, and he would take the helm. When the Maltese (for so they called Dantes) had said this, it was sufficient, and all went to their bunks contentedly. This frequently happened. Dantes, cast from solitude into the world, frequently experienced an imperious desire for solitude; and what solitude is more complete, or more poetical, than that of a ship floating in isolation on the sea during the obscurity of the night, in the silence of immensity, and under the eye of heaven?

Now this solitude was peopled with his thoughts, the night lighted up by his illusions, and the silence animated by his anticipations. When the patron awoke, the vessel was hurrying on with every sail set, and every sail full with the breeze. They were making nearly ten knots an hour. The Island of Monte Cristo loomed large in the horizon. Edmond resigned the lugger to the master's care, and went and lay down in his hammock; but, in spite of a sleepless night, he could not close his eyes for a moment. Two hours afterwards he came on deck, as the boat was about to double the Island of Elba. They were just abreast of Mareciana, and beyond the flat but verdant Island of La Pianosa. The peak of Monte Cristo reddened by the burning sun, was seen against the azure sky. Dantes ordered the helmsman to put down his helm, in order to leave La Pianosa to starboard, as he knew that he should shorten his course by two or three knots. About five o'clock in the evening the island was distinct, and everything on it was plainly perceptible, owing to that clearness of the atmosphere peculiar to the light which the rays of the sun cast at its setting.

Edmond gazed very earnestly at the mass of rocks which gave out all the variety of twilight colors, from the brightest pink to the deepest blue; and from time to time his cheeks flushed, his brow darkened, and a mist passed over his eyes. Never did a gamester, whose whole fortune is staked on one cast of the die, experience the anguish which Edmond felt in hisparoxysms of hope. Night came, and at ten o'clock they anchored. *The Young Amelia* was first at the rendezvous. In spite of his usual command over himself, Dantes could not restrain his impetuosity. He was the first to jump on shore; and had he dared, he would, like Lucius Brutus, have "kissed his mother earth." It was dark, but at eleven o'clock the moon rose in the midst of the ocean, whose every wave she silvered, and then, "ascending high," played in floods of pale light on the rocky hills of this second Pelion.

The island was familiar to the crew of *The Young Amelia*,—it was one of her regular haunts. As to Dantes, he had passed it on his voyage to and from the Levant, but never touched at it. He questioned Jacopo. "Where shall we pass the night?" he inquired.

"Why, on board the tartan," replied the sailor.

"Should we not do better in the grottos?"

"What grottos?"

"Why, the grottos—caves of the island."

"I do not know of any grottos," replied Jacopo. The cold sweat sprang forth on Dantes' brow.

"What, are there no grottos at Monte Cristo?" he asked.

"None."

For a moment Dantes was speechless; then he remembered that these caves might have been filled up by some accident, or even stopped up, for the sake of greater security, by Cardinal Spada. The point was, then, to discover the hidden entrance. It was useless to search at night, and Dantes therefore delayed all investigation until the morning. Besides, a signal made half a league out at sea, and to which *The Young Amelia* replied by a similar signal, indicated that the moment for business had come. The boat that now arrived, assured by the answering signal that all was well, soon came in sight, white and silent as a phantom, and cast anchor within a cable's length of shore.

Then the landing began. Dantes reflected, as he worked, on the shout of joy which, with a single word, he could evoke from all these men, if he gave utterance to the one unchanging thought that pervaded his heart; but, far from disclosing this precious secret, he almost feared that he had already said too much, and by his restlessness and continual questions, his minute observations and evident pre-occupation, aroused suspicions. Fortunately, as regarded this circumstance at least, his painful past gave to his countenance an indelible sadness, and the glimmerings of gayety seen beneath this cloud were indeed but transitory.

No one had the slightest suspicion; and when next day, taking a fowling-piece, powder, and shot, Dantes declared his intention to go and kill some of the wild goats that were seen springing from rock to rock, his wish was construed into a love of sport, or a desire for solitude. However, Jacopo insisted on following him, and Dantes did not oppose this, fearing if he did so that he might incur distrust. Scarcely, however, had they gone a quarter of a league when, having killed a kid, he begged Jacopo to take it to his comrades, and request them to cook it, and when ready to let him know by firing a gun. This and some dried fruits and a flask of Monte Pulciano, was the bill of fare. Dantes went on, looking from time to time behind and around about him. Having reached the summit of a rock, he saw, a thousand feet beneath him, his companions, whom Jacopo had rejoined, and who were all busy preparing the repast which Edmond's skill as a marksman had augmented with a capital dish.

Edmond looked at them for a moment with the sad and gentle smile of a man superior to his fellows. "In two hours' time," said he, "these persons will depart richer by fifty piastres each, to go and risk their lives again by endeavoring to gain fifty more; then they will return with a fortune of six hundred francs, and waste this treasure in some city with the pride of sultans and the insolence of nabobs. At this moment hope makes me despise their riches, which seem to me contemptible. Yet perchance to-morrow deception will so act on me, that I shall, on compulsion, consider such a contemptible possession as the utmost happiness. Oh, no!" exclaimed Edmond, "that will not be. The wise, unerring Faria could not be mistaken in this one thing. Besides, it were better to die than to continue to lead this low and wretched life." Thus Dantes, who but three months before had no desire but liberty had now not liberty enough, and panted for wealth. The cause was not in Dantes, but in providence, who, while limiting the power of man, has filled him with boundless desires.

Meanwhile, by a cleft between two walls of rock, following a path worn by a torrent, and which, in all human probability, human foot had never before trod, Dantes approached the spot where he supposed the grottos must have existed. Keeping along the shore, and examining the smallest object with serious attention, he thought he could trace, on certain rocks, marks made by the hand of man. Time, which encrusts all physical substances with its mossy mantle, as it invests all things of the mind with forgetfulness, seemed to have respected these signs, which apparently had been made with some degree of regularity, and probably with a definite purpose. Occasionally the marks were hidden under tufts of myrtle, which spread into large bushes laden with blossoms, or beneath parasitical lichen. So Edmond had to separate the branches or brush away the moss to know where the guide-marks were. The sight of marks renewed Edmond fondest hopes. Might it not have been the cardinal himself who had first traced them, in order that they might serve as a guide for his nephew in the event of a catastrophe, which he could not foresee would have been so complete. This solitary place was precisely suited to the requirements of a man desirous of burying treasure. Only, might not these betraying marks have attracted other eyes than those for whom they were made? and had the dark and wondrous island indeed faithfully guarded its precious secret?

It seemed, however, to Edmond, who was hidden from his comrades by the inequalities of the ground, that at sixty paces from the harbor the marks ceased; nor did they terminate at any grotto. A large round rock, placed solidly on its base, was the only spot to which they seemed to lead. Edmond concluded that perhaps instead of having reached the end of the route he had only explored its beginning, and he therefore turned round and retraced his steps.

Meanwhile his comrades had prepared the repast, had got some water from a spring, spread out the fruit and bread, and cooked the kid. Just at the moment when they were taking the dainty animal from the spit, they saw Edmond springing with the boldness of a chamois from rock to rock, and they fired the signal agreed upon. The sportsman instantly changed his direction, and ran quickly towards them. But even while they watched his daring progress, Edmond's foot slipped, and they saw him stagger on the edge of a rock and disappear. They all rushed towards him, for all loved Edmond in spite of his superiority; yet Jacopo reached him first.

He found Edmond lying prone, bleeding, and almost senseless. He had rolled down a declivity of twelve or fifteen feet. They poured a little rum down his throat, and this remedy which had before been so beneficial to him, produced the same effect as formerly. Edmond opened his eyes, complained of great pain in his knee, a feeling of heaviness in his head, and severe pains in his loins. They wished to carry him to the shore; but when they touched him, although under Jacopo's directions, he declared, with heavy groans, that he could not bear to be moved.

It may be supposed that Dantes did not now think of his dinner, but he insisted that his comrades, who had not his reasons for fasting, should have their meal. As for himself, he declared that he had only need of a little rest, and that when they returned he should be easier. The sailors did not require much urging. They were hungry, and the smell of the roasted kid was very savory, and your tars are not very ceremonious. An hour afterwards they returned. All that Edmond had been able to do was to drag himself about a dozen paces forward to lean against a moss-grown rock.

But, instead of growing easier, Dantes' pains appeared to increase in violence. The old patron, who was obliged to sail in the morning in order to land his cargo on the frontiers of Piedmont and France, between Nice and Frejus, urged Dantes to try and rise. Edmond made great exertions in order to comply; but at each effort he fell back, moaning and turning pale.

"He has broken his ribs," said the commander, in a low voice. "No matter; he is an excellent fellow, and we must not leave him. We will try and carry him on board the tartan." Dantes declared, however, that he would rather die where he was than undergo the agony which the slightest movement cost him. "Well," said the patron, "let what may happen, it shall never be said that we deserted a good comrade like you. We will not go till evening." This very much astonished the sailors, although, not one opposed it. The patron was so strict that this was the first time they had ever seen him give up an enterprise, or even delay in its execution. Dantes would not allow that any such infraction of regular and proper rules should be made in his favor. "No, no," he said to the patron, "I was awkward, and it is just that I pay the penalty of my clumsiness. Leave me a small supply of biscuit, a gun, powder, and balls, to kill the kids or defend myself at need, and a pickaxe, that I may build a shelter if you delay in coming back for me."

"But you'll die of hunger," said the patron.

"I would rather do so," was Edmond reply, "than suffer the inexpressible agonies which the slightest movement causes me." The patron turned towards his vessel, which was rolling on the swell in the little harbor, and, with sails partly set, would be ready for sea when her toilet should be completed.

"What are we to do, Maltese?" asked the captain. "We cannot leave you here so, and yet we cannot stay."

"Go, go!" exclaimed Dantes.

"We shall be absent at least a week," said the patron, "and then we must run out of our course to come here and take you up again."

"Why," said Dantes, "if in two or three days you hail any fishing-boat, desire them to come here to me. I will pay twenty-five piastres for my passage back to Leghorn. If you do not come across one, return for me." The patron shook his head.

"Listen, Captain Baldi; there's one way of settling this," said Jacopo." Do you go, and I will stay and take care of the wounded man."

"And give up your share of the venture," said Edmond, "to remain with me?"

"Yes," said Jacopo, "and without any hesitation."

"You are a good fellow and a kind-hearted messmate," replied Edmond, "and heaven will recompense you for your generous intentions; but I do not wish any one to stay with me. A day or two of rest will set me up, and I hope I shall find among the rocks certain herbs most excellent for bruises."

A peculiar smile passed over Dantes' lips; he squeezed Jacopo's hand warmly, but nothing could shake his determination to remain—and remain alone. The smugglers left with Edmond what he had requested and set sail, but not without turning about several times, and each time making signs of a cordial farewell, to which Edmond replied with his hand only, as if he could not move the rest of his body. Then, when they had disappeared, he said with a smile,—"'Tis strange that it should be among such men that we find proofs of friendship and devotion." Then he dragged himself cautiously to the top of a rock, from which he had a full view of the sea, and thence he saw the tartan complete her preparations for sailing, weigh anchor, and, balancing herself as gracefully as a water-fowl ere it takes to the wing, set sail. At the end of an hour she was completely out of sight; at least, it was impossible for the wounded man to see her any longer from the spot where he was. Then Dantes rose more agile and light than the kid among the myrtles and shrubs of these wild rocks, took his gun in one hand, his pickaxe in the other, and hastened towards the rock on which the marks he had noted terminated. "And now," he exclaimed, remembering the tale of the Arabian fisherman, which Faria had related to him, "now, open sesame!"

Chapter 24. The Secret Cave.

The sun had nearly reached the meridian, and his scorching rays fell full on the rocks, which seemed themselves sensible of the heat. Thousands of grasshoppers, hidden in the bushes, chirped with a monotonous and dull note; the leaves of the myrtle and olive trees waved and rustled in the wind. At every step that Edmond took he disturbed the lizards glittering with the hues of the emerald; afar off he saw the wild goats bounding from crag to crag. In a word, the island was inhabited, yet Edmond felt himself alone, guided by the hand of God. He felt an indescribable sensation somewhat akin to dread—that dread of the daylight which even in the desert makes us fear we are watched and observed. This feeling was so strong that at the moment when Edmond was about to begin his labor, he stopped, laid down his pickaxe, seized his gun, mounted to the summit of the highest rock, and from thence gazed round in every direction.

But it was not upon Corsica, the very houses of which he could distinguish; or on Sardinia; or on the Island of Elba, with its historical associations; or upon the almost imperceptible line that to the experienced eye of a sailor alone revealed the coast of Genoa the proud, and Leghorn the commercial, that he gazed. It was at the brigantine that had left in the morning, and the tartan that had just set sail, that Edmond fixed his eyes. The first was just in the straits of Bonifacio; the other, following an opposite direction, was about to round the Island of Corsica. This sight reassured him. He then looked at the objects near him. He saw that he was on the highest point of the island,—a statue on this vast pedestal of granite, nothing human appearing in sight, while the blue ocean beat against the base of the island, and covered it with a fringe of foam. Then he descended with cautious and slow step, for he dreaded lest an accident similar to that he had so adroitly feigned should happen in reality.

Dantes, as we have said, had traced the marks along the rocks, and he had noticed that they led to a small creek, which was hidden like the bath of some ancient nymph. This creek was sufficiently wide at its mouth, and deep in the centre, to admit of the entrance of a small vessel of the lugger class, which would be perfectly concealed from observation.

Then following the clew that, in the hands of the Abbe Faria, had been so skilfully used to guide him through the Daedalian labyrinth of probabilities, he thought that the Cardinal Spada, anxious not to be watched, had entered the creek, concealed his little barque, followed the line marked by the notches in the rock, and at the end of it had buried his treasure. It was this idea that had brought Dantes back to the circular rock. One thing only perplexed Edmond, and destroyed his theory. How could this rock, which weighed several tons, have been lifted to this spot, without the aid of many men? Suddenly an idea flashed across his mind. Instead of raising it, thought he, they have lowered it. And he sprang from the rock in order to inspect the base on which it had formerly stood. He soon perceived that a slope had been formed, and the rock had slid along this until it stopped at the spot it now occupied. A large stone had served as a wedge; flints and pebbles had been inserted around it, so as to conceal the orifice; this species of masonry had been covered with earth, and grass and weeds had grown there, moss had clung to the stones, myrtle-bushes had taken root, and the old rock seemed fixed to the earth.

Dantes dug away the earth carefully, and detected, or fancied he detected, the ingenious artifice. He attacked this wall, cemented by the hand of time, with his pickaxe. After ten minutes' labor the wall gave way, and a hole large enough to insert the arm was opened. Dantes went and cut the strongest olive-tree he could find, stripped off its branches, inserted it in the hole, and used it as a lever. But the rock was too heavy, and too firmly wedged, to be moved by any one man, were he Hercules himself. Dantes saw that he must attack the wedge. But how? He cast his eyes around, and saw the horn full of powder which his friend Jacopo had left him. He smiled; the infernal invention would serve him for this purpose. With the aid of his pickaxe, Dantes, after the manner of a labor-saving pioneer, dug a mine between the upper rock and the one that supported it, filled it with powder, then made a match by rolling his handkerchief in saltpetre. He lighted it and retired. The explosion soon followed; the upper rock was lifted from its base by the terrific force of the powder; the lower one flew into pieces; thousands of insects escaped from the aperture Dantes had previously formed, and a huge snake, like the guardian demon of the treasure, rolled himself along in darkening coils, and disappeared.

Dantes approached the upper rock, which now, without any support, leaned towards the sea. The intrepid treasure-seeker walked round it, and, selecting the spot from whence it appeared most susceptible to attack, placed his lever in one of the crevices, and strained every nerve to move the mass. The rock, already shaken by the explosion, tottered on its base. Dantes redoubled his efforts; he seemed like one of the ancient Titans, who uprooted the mountains to hurl against the father of the gods. The rock yielded, rolled over, bounded from point to point, and finally disappeared in the ocean.

On the spot it had occupied was a circular space, exposing an iron ring let into a square flag-stone. Dantes uttered a cry of joy and surprise; never had a first attempt been crowned with more perfect success. He would fain have continued, but his knees trembled, and his heart beat so violently, and his sight became so dim, that he was forced to pause. This feeling lasted but for a moment. Edmond inserted his lever in the ring and exerted all his strength; the flag-stone yielded, and disclosed steps that descended until they were lost in the obscurity of asubterraneous grotto. Any one else would have rushed on with a cry of joy. Dantes turned pale, hesitated, and reflected. "Come," said he to himself, "be a man. I am accustomed to adversity. I must not be cast down by the discovery that I have been deceived. What, then, would be the use of all I have suffered? The heart breaks when, after having been elated by flattering hopes, it sees all its illusions destroyed. Faria has dreamed this; the Cardinal Spada buried no treasure here; perhaps he never came here, or if he did, Caesar Borgia, the intrepid adventurer, the stealthy and indefatigable plunderer, has followed him, discovered his traces, pursued them as I have done, raised the stone, and descending before me, has left me nothing." He remained motionless and pensive, his eyes fixed on the gloomy aperture that was open at his feet.

"Now that I expect nothing, now that I no longer entertain the slightest hopes, the end of this adventure becomes simply a matter of curiosity." And he remained again motionless and thoughtful.

"Yes, yes; this is an adventure worthy a place in the varied career of that royal bandit. This fabulous event formed but a link in a long chain of marvels. Yes, Borgia has been here, a torch in one hand, a sword in the other, and within twenty paces, at the foot of this rock, perhaps two guards kept watch on land and sea, while their master descended, as I am about to descend, dispelling the darkness before his awe-inspiring progress.

"But what was the fate of the guards who thus possessed his secret?" asked Dantes of himself.

"The fate," replied he, smiling, "of those who buried Alaric."

"Yet, had he come," thought Dantes, "he would have found the treasure, and Borgia, he who compared Italy to an artichoke, which he could devour leaf by leaf, knew too well the value of time to waste it in replacing this rock. I will go down."

Then he descended a smile on his lips, and murmuring that last word of human philosophy, "Perhaps!" But instead of the darkness, and the thick and mephitic atmosphere he had expected to find, Dantes saw a dim and bluish light, which, as well as the air, entered, not merely by the aperture he had just formed, but by the interstices and crevices of the rock which were visible from without, and through which he could distinguish the blue sky and the waving branches of the evergreen oaks, and the tendrils of the creepers that grew from the rocks. After having stood a few minutes in the cavern, the atmosphere of which was rather warm than damp, Dantes' eye, habituated as it was to darkness, could pierce even to the remotest angles of the cavern, which was of granite that sparkled like diamonds. "Alas," said Edmond, smiling, "these are the treasures the cardinal has left; and the good abbe, seeing in a dream these glittering walls, has indulged in fallacious hopes."

But he called to mind the words of the will, which he knew by heart. "In the farthest angle of the second opening," said the cardinal's will. He had only found the first grotto; he had now to seek the second. Dantes continued his search. He reflected that this second grotto must penetrate deeper into the island; he examined the stones, and sounded one part of the wall where he fancied the opening existed, masked for precaution's sake. The pickaxe struck for a moment with a dull sound that drew out of Dantes' forehead large drops of perspiration. At last it seemed to him that one part of the wall gave forth a more hollow and deeper echo; he eagerly advanced, and with the quickness of perception that no one but a prisoner possesses, saw that there, in all probability, the opening must be.

However, he, like Caesar Borgia, knew the value of time; and, in order to avoid fruitless toil, he sounded all the other walls with his pickaxe, struck the earth with the butt of his gun, and finding nothing that appeared suspicious, returned to that part of the wall whence issued the consoling sound he had before heard. He again struck it, and with greater force. Then a singular thing occurred. As he struck the wall, pieces of stucco similar to that used in the ground work of arabesques broke off, and fell to the ground in flakes, exposing a large white stone. The aperture of the rock had been closed with stones, then this stucco had been applied, and painted to imitate granite. Dantes struck with the sharp end of his pickaxe, which entered someway between the interstices. It was there he must dig. But by some strange play of emotion, in proportion as the proofs that Faria, had not been deceived became stronger, so did his heart give way, and a feeling of discouragement stole over him. This last proof, instead of giving him fresh strength, deprived him of it; the pickaxe descended, or rather fell; he placed it on the ground, passed his hand over his brow, and remounted the stairs, alleging to himself, as an excuse, a desire to be assured that no one was watching him, but in reality because he felt that he was about to faint. The island was deserted, and the sun seemed to cover it with its fiery glance; afar off, a few small fishing boats studded the bosom of the blue ocean.

Dantes had tasted nothing, but he thought not of hunger at such a moment; he hastily swallowed a few drops of rum, and again entered the cavern. The pickaxe that had seemed so heavy, was now like a feather in his grasp; he seized it, and attacked the wall. After several blows he perceived that the stones were not cemented, but had been merely placed one upon the other, and covered with stucco; he inserted the point of his pickaxe, and using the handle as a lever, with joy soon saw the stone turn as if on hinges, and fall at his feet. He had nothing more to do now, but with the iron tooth of the pickaxe to draw the stones towards him one by one. The aperture was already sufficiently large for him to enter, but by waiting, he could still cling to hope, and retard the certainty of deception. At last, after renewed hesitation, Dantes entered the second grotto. The second grotto was lower and more gloomy than the first; the air that could only enter by the newly formed opening had the mephitic smell Dantes was surprised not to find in the outer cavern. He waited in order to allow pure air to displace the foul atmosphere, and then went on. At the left of the opening was a dark and deep angle. But to Dantes' eye there was no darkness. He glanced around this second grotto; it was, like the first, empty.

The treasure, if it existed, was buried in this corner. The time had at length arrived; two feet of earth removed, and Dantes' fate would be decided. He advanced towards the angle, and summoning all his resolution, attacked the ground with the pickaxe. At the fifth or sixth blow the pickaxe struck against an iron substance. Never did funeral knell, never did alarm-bell, produce a greater effect on the hearer. Had Dantes found nothing he could not have become more ghastly pale. He again struck his pickaxe into the earth, and encountered the same resistance, but not the same sound. "It is a casket of wood bound with iron," thought he. At this moment a shadow passed rapidly before the opening; Dantes seized his gun, sprang through the opening, and mounted the stair. A wild goat had passed before the mouth of the cave, and was feeding at a little distance. This would have been a favorable occasion to secure his dinner; but Dantes feared lest the report of his gun should attract attention.

He thought a moment, cut a branch of a resinous tree, lighted it at the fire at which the smugglers had prepared their breakfast, and descended with this torch. He wished to see everything. He approached the hole he had dug, and now, with the aid of the torch, saw that his pickaxe had in reality struck against iron and wood. He planted his torch in the ground and resumed his labor. In an instant a space three feet long by two feet broad was cleared, and Dantes could see an oaken coffer, bound with cut steel; in the middle of the lid he saw engraved on a silver plate, which was still untarnished, the arms of the Spada family—viz., a sword, pale, on an oval shield, like all the Italian armorial bearings, and surmounted by a cardinal's hat; Dantes easily recognized them, Faria had so often drawn them for him. There was no longer any doubt: the treasure was there—no one would have been at such pains to conceal an empty casket. In an instant he had cleared every obstacle away, and he saw successively the lock, placed between two padlocks, and the two handles at each end, all carved as things were carved at that epoch, when art rendered the commonest metals precious. Dantes seized the handles, and strove to lift the coffer; it was impossible. He sought to open it; lock and padlock were fastened; these faithful guardians seemed unwilling to surrender their trust. Dantes inserted the sharp end of the pickaxe between the coffer and the lid, and pressing with all his force on the handle, burst open the fastenings. The hinges yielded in their turn and fell, still holding in their grasp fragments of the wood, and the chest was open.

Edmond was seized with vertigo; he cocked his gun and laid it beside him. He then closed his eyes as children do in order that they may see in the resplendent night of their own imagination more stars than are visible in the firmament; then he re-opened them, and stood motionless with amazement. Three compartments divided the coffer. In the first, blazed piles of golden coin; in the second, were ranged bars of unpolished gold, which possessed nothing attractive save their value; in the third, Edmond grasped handfuls of diamonds, pearls, and rubies, which, as they fell on one another, sounded like hail against glass. After having touched, felt, examined these treasures, Edmond rushed through the caverns like a man seized with frenzy; he leaped on a rock, from whence he could behold the sea. He was alone—alone with these countless, these unheard-of treasures! was he awake, or was it but a dream?

He would fain have gazed upon his gold, and yet he had not strength enough; for an instant he leaned his head in his hands as if to prevent his senses from leaving him, and then rushed madly about the rocks of Monte Cristo, terrifying the wild goats and scaring the sea-fowls with his wild cries and gestures; then he returned, and, still unable to believe the evidence of his senses, rushed into the grotto, and found himself before this mine of gold and jewels. This time he fell on his knees, and, clasping his hands convulsively, uttered a prayer intelligible to God alone. He soon became calmer and more happy, for only now did he begin to realize his felicity. He then set himself to work to count his fortune. There were a thousand ingots of gold, each weighing from two to three pounds; then he piled up twenty-five thousand crowns, each worth about eighty francs of our money, and bearing the effigies of Alexander VI. and his predecessors; and he saw that the complement was not half empty. And he measured ten double handfuls of pearls, diamonds, and other gems, many of which, mounted by the most famous workmen, were valuable beyond their intrinsic worth. Dantes saw the light gradually disappear, and cavern, left it, his gun in his hand. A piece of biscuit and a small quantity of rum formed his supper, and he snatched a few hours' sleep, lying over the mouth of the cave.

It was a night of joy and terror, such as this man of stupendous emotions had already experienced twice or thrice in his lifetime.

Chapter 25. The Unknown.

Day, for which Dantes had so eagerly and impatiently waited with open eyes, again dawned. With the first light Dantes resumed his search. Again he climbed the rocky height he had ascended the previous evening, and strained his view to catch every peculiarity of the landscape; but it wore the same wild, barren aspect when seen by the rays of the morning sun which it had done when surveyed by the fading glimmer of eve. Descending into the grotto, he lifted the stone, filled his pockets with gems, put the box together as well and securely as he could, sprinkled fresh sand over the spot from which it had been taken, and then carefully trod down the earth to give it everywhere a uniform appearance; then, quitting the grotto, he replaced the stone, heaping on it broken masses of rocks and rough fragments of crumbling granite, filling the interstices with earth, into which he deftly inserted rapidly growing plants, such as the wild myrtle and flowering thorn, then carefully watering these new plantations, he scrupulously effaced every trace of footsteps, leaving the approach to the cavern as savage-looking and untrodden as he had found it. This done, he impatiently awaited the return of his companions. To wait at Monte Cristo for the purpose of watching like a dragon over the almost incalculable riches that had thus fallen into his possession satisfied not the cravings of his heart, which yearned to return to dwell among mankind, and to assume the rank, power, and influence which are always accorded to wealth—that first and greatest of all the forces within the grasp of man.

On the sixth day, the smugglers returned. From a distance Dantes recognized the rig and handling of *The Young Amelia*, and dragging himself with affected difficulty towards the landing-place, he met his companions with an assurance that, although considerably better than when they quitted him, he still suffered acutely from his late accident. He then inquired how they had fared in their trip. To this question the smugglers replied that, although successful in landing their cargo in safety, they had scarcely done so when they received intelligence that a guard-ship had just quitted the port of Toulon and was crowding all sail towards them. This obliged them to make all the speed they could to evade the enemy, when they could but lament the absence of Dantes, whose superior skill in the management of a vessel would have availed them so materially. In fact, the pursuing vessel had almost overtaken them when, fortunately, night came on, and enabled them to double the Cape of Corsica, and so elude all further pursuit. Upon the whole, however, the trip had been sufficiently successful to satisfy all concerned; while the crew, and particularly Jacopo, expressed great regrets that Dantes had not been an equal sharer with themselves in the profits, which amounted to no less a sum than fifty piastres each.

Edmond preserved the most admirable self-command, not suffering the faintest indication of a smile to escape him at the enumeration of all the benefits he would have reaped had he been able to quit the island; but as *The Young Amelia* had merely come to Monte Cristo to fetch him away, he embarked that same evening, and proceeded with the captain to Leghorn. Arrived at Leghorn, he repaired to the house of a Jew, a dealer in precious stones, to whom he disposed of four of his smallest diamonds for five thousand francs each. Dantes half feared that such valuable jewels in the hands of a poor sailor like himself might excite suspicion; but the cunning purchaser asked no troublesome questions concerning a bargain by which he gained a round profit of at least eighty per cent.

The following day Dantes presented Jacopo with an entirely new vessel, accompanying the gift by a donation of one hundred piastres, that he might provide himself with a suitable crew and other requisites for his outfit, upon condition that he would go at once to Marseilles for the purpose of inquiring after an old man named Louis Dantes, residing in the Allees de Meillan, and also a young woman called Mercedes, an inhabitant of the Catalan village. Jacopo could scarcely believe his senses at receiving this magnificent present, which Dantes hastened to account for by saying that he had merely been a sailor from whim and a desire to spite his family, who did not allow him as much money as he liked to spend; but that on his arrival at Leghorn he had come into possession of a large fortune, left him by an uncle, whose sole heir he was. The superior education of Dantes gave an air of such extreme probability to this statement that it never once occurred to Jacopo to doubt its accuracy. The term for which Edmond had engaged to serve on board *The Young Amelia* having expired, Dantes took leave of the captain, who at first tried all his powers of persuasion to induce him to remain as one of the crew, but having been told the history of the legacy, he ceased to importune him further. The following morning Jacopo set sail for Marseilles, with directions from Dantes to join him at the Island of Monte Cristo.

Having seen Jacopo fairly out of the harbor, Dantes proceeded to make his final adieus on board *The Young Amelia*, distributing so liberal a gratuity among her crew as to secure for him the good wishes of all, and expressions of cordial interest in all that concerned him. To the captain he promised to write when he had made up his mind as to his future plans. Then Dantes departed for Genoa. At the moment of his arrival a small yacht was under trial in the bay; this yacht had been built by order of an Englishman, who, having heard that the Genoese excelled all other builders along the shores of the Mediterranean in the construction of fast-sailing vessels, was desirous of possessing a specimen of their skill; the price agreed upon between the Englishman and the Genoese builder was forty thousand francs. Dantes, struck with the beauty and capability of the little vessel, applied to its owner to transfer it to him, offering sixty thousand francs, upon condition that he should be allowed to take immediate possession. The proposal was too advantageous to be refused, the more so as the person for whom the yacht was intended had gone upon a tour through Switzerland, and was not expected back in less than three weeks or a month, by which time the builder reckoned upon being able to complete another. A bargain was therefore struck. Dantes led the owner of the yacht to the dwelling of a Jew; retired with the latter for a few minutes to a small back parlor, and upon their return the Jew counted out to the shipbuilder the sum of sixty thousand francs in bright gold pieces.

The delighted builder then offered his services in providing a suitable crew for the little vessel, but this Dantes declined with many thanks, saying he was accustomed to cruise about quite alone, and his principal pleasure consisted in managing his yacht himself; the only thing the builder could oblige him in would be to contrive a sort of secret closet in the cabin at his bed's head, the closet to contain three divisions, so constructed as to be concealed from all but himself. The builder cheerfully undertook the commission, and promised to have these secret places completed by the next day, Dantes furnishing the dimensions and plan in accordance with which they were to be constructed.

The following day Dantes sailed with his yacht from Genoa, under the inspection of an immense crowd drawn together by curiosity to see the rich Spanish nobleman who preferred managing his own yacht. But their wonder was soon changed to admiration at seeing the perfect skill with which Dantes handled the helm. The boat, indeed, seemed to be animated with almost human intelligence, so promptly did it obey the slightest touch; and Dantes required but a short trial of his beautiful craft to acknowledge that the Genoese had not without reason attained their high reputation in the art of shipbuilding. The spectators followed the little vessel with their eyes as long as it remained visible; they then turned their conjectures upon her probable destination. Some insisted she was making for Corsica, others the Island of Elba; bets were offered to any amount that she was bound for Spain; while Africa was positively reported by many persons as her intended course; but no one thought of Monte Cristo. Yet thither it was that Dantes guided his vessel, and at Monte Cristo he arrived at the close of the second day; his boat had proved herself a first-class sailer, and had come the distance from Genoa in thirty-five hours. Dantes had carefully noted the general appearance of the shore, and, instead of landing at the usual place, he dropped anchor in the little creek. The island was utterly deserted, and bore no evidence of having been visited since he went away; his treasure was just as he had left it. Early on the following morning he commenced the removal of his riches and ere nightfall the whole of his immense wealth was safely deposited in the compartments of the secret locker.

A week passed by. Dantes employed it in manoeuvring his yacht round the island, studying it as a skillful horseman would the animal he destined for some important service, till at the end of that time he was perfectly conversant with its good and bad qualities. The former Dantes proposed to augment, the latter to remedy.

Upon the eighth day he discerned a small vessel under full sail approaching Monte Cristo. As it drew near, he recognized it as the boat he had given to Jacopo. He immediately signalled it. His signal was returned, and in two hours afterwards the new-comer lay at anchor beside the yacht. A mournful answer awaited each of Edmond's eager inquiries as to the information Jacopo had obtained. Old Dantes was dead, and Mercedes had disappeared. Dantes listened to these melancholy tidings with outward calmness; but, leaping lightly ashore, he signified his desire to be quite alone. In a couple of hours he returned. Two of the men from Jacopo's boat came on board the yacht to assist in navigating it, and he gave orders that she should be steered direct to Marseilles. For his father's death he was in some manner prepared; but he knew not how to account for the mysterious disappearance of Mercedes.

Without divulging his secret, Dantes could not give sufficiently clear instructions to an agent. There were, besides, other particulars he was desirous of ascertaining, and those were of a nature he alone could investigate in a manner satisfactory to himself. His looking-glass had assured him, during his stay at Leghorn, that he ran no risk of recognition; moreover, he had now the means of adopting any disguise he thought proper. One fine morning, then, his yacht, followed by the little fishing-boat, boldly entered the port of Marseilles, and anchored exactly opposite the spot from whence, on the never-to-be-forgotten night of his departure for the Chateau d'If, he had been put on board the boat destined to convey him thither. Still Dantes could not view without a shudder the approach of a gendarme who accompanied the officers deputed to demand his bill of health ere the yacht was permitted to hold communication with the shore; but with that perfect self-possession he had acquired during his acquaintance with Faria, Dantes coolly presented an English passport he had obtained from Leghorn, and as this gave him a standing which a French passport would not have afforded, he was informed that there existed no obstacle to his immediate debarkation.

The first person to attract the attention of Dantes, as he landed on the Canebiere, was one of the crew belonging to the *Pharaon*. Edmond welcomed the meeting with this fellow—who had been one of his own sailors—as a sure means of testing the extent of the change which time had worked in his own appearance. Going straight towards him, he propounded a variety of questions on different subjects, carefully watching the man's countenance as he did so; but not a word or look implied that he had the slightest idea of ever having seen before the person with whom he was then conversing. Giving the sailor a piece of money in return for his civility, Dantes proceeded onwards; but ere he had gone many steps he heard the man loudly calling him to stop. Dantes instantly turned to meet him. "I beg your pardon, sir," said the honest fellow, in almost breathless haste, "but I believe you made a mistake; you intended to give me a two-franc piece, and see, you gave me a double Napoleon."

"Thank you, my good friend. I see that I have made a trifling mistake, as you say; but by way of rewarding your honesty I give you another double Napoleon, that you may drink to my health, and be able to ask your messmates to join you."

So extreme was the surprise of the sailor, that he was unable even to thank Edmond, whose receding figure he continued to gaze after in speechless astonishment. "Some nabob from India," was his comment.

Dantes, meanwhile, went on his way. Each step he trod oppressed his heart with fresh emotion; his first and most indelible recollections were there; not a tree, not a street, that he passed but seemed filled with dear and cherished memories. And thus he proceeded onwards till he arrived at the end of the Rue de Noailles, from whence a full view of the Allees de Meillan was obtained. At this spot, so pregnant with fond and filial remembrances, his heart beat almost to bursting, his knees tottered under him, a mist floated over his sight, and had he not clung for support to one of the trees, he would inevitably have fallen to the ground and been crushed beneath the many vehicles continually passing there. Recovering himself, however, he wiped the perspiration from his brows, and stopped not again till he found himself at the door of the house in which his father had lived.

The nasturtiums and other plants, which his father had delighted to train before his window, had all disappeared from the upper part of the house. Leaning against the tree, he gazed thoughtfully for a time at the upper stories of the shabby little house. Then he advanced to the door, and asked whether there were any rooms to be let. Though answered in the negative, he begged so earnestly to be permitted to visit those on the fifth floor, that, in despite of the oft-repeated assurance of the concierge that they were occupied, Dantes succeeded in inducing the man to go up to the tenants, and ask permission for a gentleman to be allowed to look at them.

The tenants of the humble lodging were a young couple who had been scarcely married a week; and seeing them, Dantes sighed heavily. Nothing in the two small chambers forming the apartments remained as it had been in the time of the elder Dantes; the very paper was different, while the articles of antiquated furniture with which the rooms had been filled in Edmond's time had all disappeared; the four walls alone remained as he had left them. The bed belonging to the present occupants was placed as the former owner of the chamber had been accustomed to have his; and, in spite of his efforts to prevent it, the eyes of Edmond were suffused in tears as he reflected that on that spot the old man had breathed his last, vainly calling for his son. The young couple gazed with astonishment at the sight of their visitor's emotion, and wondered to see the large tears silently chasing each other down his otherwise stern and immovable features; but they felt the sacredness of his grief, and kindly refrained from questioning him as to its cause, while, with instinctive delicacy, they left him to indulge his sorrow alone. When he withdrew from the scene of his painful recollections, they both accompanied him downstairs, reiterating their hope that he would come again whenever he pleased, and assuring him that their poor dwelling would ever be open to him. As Edmond passed the door on the fourth floor, he paused to inquire whether Caderousse the tailor still dwelt there; but he received, for reply, that the person in question had got into difficulties, and at the present time kept a small inn on the route from Bellegarde to Beaucaire.

Having obtained the address of the person to whom the house in the Allees de Meillan belonged, Dantes next proceeded thither, and, under the name of Lord Wilmore (the name and title inscribed on his passport), purchased the small dwelling for the sum of twenty-five thousand francs, at least ten thousand more than it was worth; but had its owner asked half a million, it would unhesitatingly have been given. The very same day the occupants of the apartments on the fifth floor of the house, now become the property of Dantes, were duly informed by the notary who had arranged the necessary transfer of deeds, etc., that the new landlord gave them their choice of any of the rooms in the house, without the least augmentation of rent, upon condition of their living instant possession of the two small chambers they at present inhabited.

This strange event aroused great wonder and curiosity in the neighborhood of the Allees de Meillan, and a multitude of theories were afloat, none of which was anywhere near the truth. But what raised public astonishment to a climax, and set all conjecture at defiance, was the knowledge that the same stranger who had in the morning visited the Allees de Meillan had been seen in the evening walking in the little village of the Catalans, and afterwards observed to enter a poor fisherman's hut, and to pass more than an hour in inquiring after persons who had either been dead or gone away for more than fifteen or sixteen years. But on the following day the family from whom all these particulars had been asked received a handsome present, consisting of an entirely new fishing-boat, with two seines and a tender. The delighted recipients of these munificent gifts would gladly have poured out their thanks to their generous benefactor, but they had seen him, upon quitting the hut, merely give some orders to a sailor, and then springing lightly on horseback, leave Marseilles by the Porte d'Aix.

Chapter 26. The Pont du Gard Inn.

Such of my readers as have made a pedestrian excursion to the south of France may perchance have noticed, about midway between the town of Beaucaire and the village of Bellegarde,—a little nearer to the former than to the latter,—a small roadside inn, from the front of which hung, creaking and flapping in the wind, a sheet of tin covered with a grotesque representation of the Pont du Gard. This modern place of entertainment stood on the left-hand side of the post road, and backed upon the Rhone. It also boasted of what in Languedoc is styled a garden, consisting of a small plot of ground, on the side opposite to the main entrance reserved for the reception of guests. A few dingy olives and stunted fig-trees struggled hard for existence, but their withered dusty foliage abundantly proved how unequal was the conflict. Between these sickly shrubs grew a scanty supply of garlic, tomatoes, and eschalots; while, lone and solitary, like a forgotten sentinel, a tall pine raised its melancholy head in one of the corners of this unattractive spot, and displayed its flexible stem and fan-shaped summit dried and cracked by the fierce heat of the sub-tropical sun.

In the surrounding plain, which more resembled a dusty lake than solid ground, were scattered a few miserable stalks of wheat, the effect, no doubt, of a curious desire on the part of the agriculturists of the country to see whether such a thing as the raising of grain in those parched regions was practicable. Each stalk served as a perch for a grasshopper, which regaled the passers by through this Egyptian scene with its strident, monotonous note.

For about seven or eight years the little tavern had been kept by a man and his wife, with two servants,—a chambermaid named Trinette, and a hostler called Pecaud. This small staff was quite equal to all the requirements, for a canal between Beaucaire and Aiguemortes had revolutionized transportation by substituting boats for the cart and the stagecoach. And, as though to add to the daily misery which this prosperous canal inflicted on the unfortunate inn-keeper, whose utter ruin it was fast accomplishing, it was situated between the Rhone from which it had its source and the post-road it had depleted, not a hundred steps from the inn, of which we have given a brief but faithful description.

The inn-keeper himself was a man of from forty to fifty-five years of age, tall, strong, and bony, a perfect specimen of the natives of those southern latitudes; he had dark, sparkling, and deep-set eyes, hooked nose, and teeth white as those of a carnivorous animal; his hair, like his beard, which he wore under his chin, was thick and curly, and in spite of his age but slightly interspersed with a few silvery threads. His naturally dark complexion had assumed a still further shade of brown from the habit the unfortunate man had acquired of stationing himself from morning till eve at the threshold of his door, on the lookout for guests who seldom came, yet there he stood, day after day, exposed to the meridional rays of a burning sun, with no other protection for his head than a red handkerchief twisted around it, after the manner of the Spanish muleteers. This man was our old acquaintance, Gaspard Caderousse. His wife, on the contrary, whose maiden name had been Madeleine Radelle, was pale, meagre, and sickly-looking. Born in the neighborhood of Arles, she had shared in the beauty for which its women are proverbial; but that beauty had gradually withered beneath the devastating influence of the slow fever so prevalent among dwellers by the ponds of Aiguemortes and the marshes of Camargue. She remained nearly always in her second-floor chamber, shivering in her chair, or stretched languid and feeble on her bed, while her husband kept his daily watch at the door—a duty he performed with so much the greater willingness, as it saved him the necessity of listening to the endless plaints and murmurs of his helpmate, who never saw him without breaking out into bitter invectives against fate; to all of which her husband would calmly return an unvarying reply, in these philosophic words:—

"Hush, La Carconte. It is God's pleasure that things should be so."

The sobriquet of La Carconte had been bestowed on Madeleine Radelle from the fact that she had been born in a village, so called, situated between Salon and Lambesc; and as a custom existed among the inhabitants of that part of France where Caderousse lived of styling every person by some particular and distinctive appellation, her husband had bestowed on her the name of La Carconte in place of her sweet and euphonious name of Madeleine, which, in all probability, his rude gutteral language would not have enabled him to pronounce. Still, let it not be supposed that amid this affected resignation to the will of Providence, the unfortunate inn-keeper did not writhe under the double misery of seeing the hateful canal carry off his customers and his profits, and the daily infliction of his peevish partner's murmurs and lamentations.

Like other dwellers in the south, he was a man of sober habits and moderate desires, but fond of external show, vain, and addicted to display. During the days of his prosperity, not a festivity took place without himself and wife being among the spectators. He dressed in the picturesque costume worn upon grand occasions by the inhabitants of the south of France, bearing equal resemblance to the style adopted both by the Catalans and Andalusians; while La Carconte displayed the charming fashion prevalent among the women of Arles, a mode of attire borrowed equally from Greece and Arabia. But, by degrees, watch-chains, necklaces, parti-colored scarfs, embroidered bodices, velvet vests, elegantly worked stockings, striped gaiters, and silver buckles for the shoes, all disappeared; and Gaspard Caderousse, unable to appear abroad in his pristine splendor, had given up any further participation in the pomps and vanities, both for himself and wife, although a bitter feeling of envious discontent filled his mind as the sound of mirth and merry music from the joyous revellers reached even the miserable hostelry to which he still clung, more for the shelter than the profit it afforded.

Caderousse, then, was, as usual, at his place of observation before the door, his eyes glancing listlessly from a piece of closely shaven grass—on which some fowls were industriously, though fruitlessly, endeavoring to turn up some grain or insect suited to their palate—to the deserted road, which led away to the north and south, when he was aroused by the shrill voice of his wife, and grumbling to himself as he went, he mounted to her chamber, first taking care, however, to set the entrance door wide open, as an invitation to any chance traveller who might be passing.

At the moment Caderousse quitted his sentry-like watch before the door, the road on which he so eagerly strained his sight was void and lonely as a desert at mid-day. There it lay stretching out into one interminable line of dust and sand, with its sides bordered by tall, meagre trees, altogether presenting so uninviting an appearance, that no one in his senses could have imagined that any traveller, at liberty to regulate his hours for journeying, would choose to expose himself in such a formidable Sahara. Nevertheless, had Caderousse but retained his post a few minutes longer, he might have caught a dim outline of something approaching from the direction of Bellegarde; as the moving object drew nearer, he would easily have perceived that it consisted of a man and horse, between whom the kindest and most amiable understanding appeared to exist. The horse was of Hungarian breed, and ambled along at an easy pace. His rider was a priest, dressed in black, and wearing a three-cornered hat; and, spite of the ardent rays of a noonday sun, the pair came on with a fair degree of rapidity.

Having arrived before the Pont du Gard, the horse stopped, but whether for his own pleasure or that of his rider would have been difficult to say. However that might have been, the priest, dismounting, led his steed by the bridle in search of some place to which he could secure him. Availing himself of a handle that projected from a half-fallen door, he tied the animal safely and having drawn a red cotton handkerchief, from his pocket, wiped away the perspiration that streamed from his brow, then, advancing to the door, struck thrice with the end of his iron-shod stick. At this unusual sound, a huge black dog came rushing to meet the daring assailant of his ordinarily tranquil abode, snarling and displaying his sharp white teeth with a determined hostility that abundantly proved how little he was accustomed to society. At that moment a heavy footstep was heard descending the wooden staircase that led from the upper floor, and, with many bows and courteous smiles, mine host of the Pont du Gard besought his guest to enter.

"You are welcome, sir, most welcome!" repeated the astonished Caderousse. "Now, then, Margotin," cried he, speaking to the dog, "will you be quiet? Pray don't heed him, sir!—he only barks, he never bites. I make no doubt a glass of good wine would be acceptable this dreadfully hot day." Then perceiving for the first time the garb of the traveler he had to entertain, Caderousse hastily exclaimed: "A thousand pardons! I really did not observe whom I had the honor to receive under my poor roof. What would the abbe please to have? What refreshment can I offer? All I have is at his service."

The priest gazed on the person addressing him with a long and searching gaze—there even seemed a disposition on his part to court a similar scrutiny on the part of the inn-keeper; then, observing in the countenance of the latter no other expression than extreme surprise at his own want of attention to an inquiry so courteously worded, he deemed it as well to terminate this dumb show, and therefore said, speaking with a strong Italian accent, "You are, I presume, M. Caderousse?"

"Yes, sir," answered the host, even more surprised at the question than he had been by the silence which had preceded it; "I am Gaspard Caderousse, at your service."

"Gaspard Caderousse," rejoined the priest. "Yes,—Christian and surname are the same. You formerly lived, I believe in the Allees de Meillan, on the fourth floor?"

"I did."

"And you followed the business of a tailor?"

"True, I was a tailor, till the trade fell off. It is so hot at Marseilles, that really I believe that the respectable inhabitants will in time go without any clothing whatever. But talking of heat, is there nothing I can offer you by way of refreshment?"

"Yes; let me have a bottle of your best wine, and then, with your permission, we will resume our conversation from where we left off."

"As you please, sir," said Caderousse, who, anxious not to lose the present opportunity of finding a customer for one of the few bottles of Cahors still remaining in his possession, hastily raised a trap-door in the floor of the apartment they were in, which served both as parlor and kitchen. Upon issuing forth from his subterranean retreat at the expiration of five minutes, he found the abbe seated upon a wooden stool, leaning his elbow on a table, while Margotin, whose animosity seemed appeased by the unusual command of the traveller for refreshments, had crept up to him, and had established himself very comfortably between his knees, his long, skinny neck resting on his lap, while his dim eye was fixed earnestly on the traveller's face.

"Are you quite alone?" inquired the guest, as Caderousse placed before him the bottle of wine and a glass.

"Quite, quite alone," replied the man—"or, at least, practically so, for my poor wife, who is the only person in the house besides myself, is laid up with illness, and unable to render me the least assistance, poor thing!"

"You are married, then?" said the priest, with a show of interest, glancing round as he spoke at the scanty furnishings of the apartment.

"Ah, sir," said Caderousse with a sigh, "it is easy to perceive I am not a rich man; but in this world a man does not thrive the better for being honest." The abbe fixed on him a searching, penetrating glance.

"Yes, honest—I can certainly say that much for myself," continued the inn-keeper, fairly sustaining the scrutiny of the abbe's gaze; "I can boast with truth of being an honest man; and," continued he significantly, with a hand on his breast and shaking his head, "that is more than every one can say nowadays."

"So much the better for you, if what you assert be true," said the abbe; "for I am firmly persuaded that, sooner or later, the good will be rewarded, and the wicked punished."

"Such words as those belong to your profession," answered Caderousse, "and you do well to repeat them; but," added he, with a bitter expression of countenance, "one is free to believe them or not, as one pleases."

"You are wrong to speak thus," said the abbe; "and perhaps I may, in my own person, be able to prove to you how completely you are in error."

"What mean you?" inquired Caderousse with a look of surprise.

"In the first place, I must be satisfied that you are the person I am in search of."

"What proofs do you require?"

"Did you, in the year 1814 or 1815, know anything of a young sailor named Dantes?"

"Dantes? Did I know poor dear Edmond? Why, Edmond Dantes and myself were intimate friends!" exclaimed Caderousse, whose countenance flushed darkly as he caught the penetrating gaze of the abbe fixed on him, while the clear, calm eye of the questioner seemed to dilate with feverish scrutiny.

"You remind me," said the priest, "that the young man concerning whom I asked you was said to bear the name of Edmond."

"Said to bear the name!" repeated Caderousse, becoming excited and eager. "Why, he was so called as truly as I myself bore the appellation of Gaspard Caderousse; but tell me, I pray, what has become of poor Edmond? Did you know him? Is he alive and at liberty? Is he prosperous and happy?"

"He died a more wretched, hopeless, heart-broken prisoner than the felons who pay the penalty of their crimes at the galleys of Toulon."

A deadly pallor followed the flush on the countenance of Caderousse, who turned away, and the priest saw him wiping the tears from his eyes with the corner of the red handkerchief twisted round his head.

"Poor fellow, poor fellow!" murmured Caderousse. "Well, there, sir, is another proof that good people are never rewarded on this earth, and that none but the wicked prosper. Ah," continued Caderousse, speaking in the highly colored language of the south, "the world grows worse and worse. Why does not God, if he really hates the wicked, as he is said to do, send down brimstone and fire, and consume them altogether?"

"You speak as though you had loved this young Dantes," observed the abbe, without taking any notice of his companion's vehemence.

"And so I did," replied Caderousse; "though once, I confess, I envied him his good fortune. But I swear to you, sir, I swear to you, by everything a man holds dear, I have, since then, deeply and sincerely lamented his unhappy fate." There was a brief silence, during which the fixed, searching eye of the abbe was employed in scrutinizing the agitated features of the inn-keeper.

"You knew the poor lad, then?" continued Caderousse.

"I was called to see him on his dying bed, that I might administer to him the consolations of religion."

"And of what did he die?" asked Caderousse in a choking voice.

"Of what, think you, do young and strong men die in prison, when they have scarcely numbered their thirtieth year, unless it be of imprisonment?" Caderousse wiped away the large beads of perspiration that gathered on his brow.

"But the strangest part of the story is," resumed the abbe, "that Dantes, even in his dying moments, swore by his crucified Redeemer, that he was utterly ignorant of the cause of his detention."

"And so he was," murmured Caderousse. "How should he have been otherwise? Ah, sir, the poor fellow told you the truth."

"And for that reason, he besought me to try and clear up a mystery he had never been able to penetrate, and to clear his memory should any foul spot or stain have fallen on it."

And here the look of the abbe, becoming more and more fixed, seemed to rest with ill-concealed satisfaction on the gloomy depression which was rapidly spreading over the countenance of Caderousse.

"A rich Englishman," continued the abbe, "who had been his companion in misfortune, but had been released from prison during the second restoration, was possessed of a diamond of immense value; this jewel he bestowed on Dantes upon himself quitting the prison, as a mark of his gratitude for the kindness and brotherly care with which Dantes had nursed him in a severe illness he underwent during his confinement. Instead of employing this diamond in attempting to bribe his jailers, who might only have taken it and then betrayed him to the governor, Dantes carefully preserved it, that in the event of his getting out of prison he might have wherewithal to live, for the sale of such a diamond would have quite sufficed to make his fortune."

"Then, I suppose," asked Caderousse, with eager, glowing looks, "that it was a stone of immense value?"

"Why, everything is relative," answered the abbe. "To one in Edmond's position the diamond certainly was of great value. It was estimated at fifty thousand francs."

"Bless me!" exclaimed Caderousse, "fifty thousand francs! Surely the diamond was as large as a nut to be worth all that."

"No," replied the abbe, "it was not of such a size as that; but you shall judge for yourself. I have it with me."

The sharp gaze of Caderousse was instantly directed towards the priest's garments, as though hoping to discover the location of the treasure. Calmly drawing forth from his pocket a small box covered with black shagreen, the abbe opened it, and displayed to the dazzled eyes of Caderousse the sparkling jewel it contained, set in a ring of admirable workmanship. "And that diamond," cried Caderousse, almost breathless with eager admiration, "you say, is worth fifty thousand francs?"

"It is, without the setting, which is also valuable," replied the abbe, as he closed the box, and returned it to his pocket, while its brilliant hues seemed still to dance before the eyes of the fascinated inn-keeper.

"But how comes the diamond in your possession, sir? Did Edmond make you his heir?"

"No, merely his testamentary executor. 'I once possessed four dear and faithful friends, besides the maiden to whom I was betrothed' he said; 'and I feel convinced they have all unfeignedly grieved over my loss. The name of one of the four friends is Caderousse.'" The inn-keeper shivered.

"'Another of the number,'" continued the abbe, without seeming to notice the emotion of Caderousse, "'is called Danglars; and the third, in spite of being my rival, entertained a very sincere affection for me.'" A fiendish smile played over the features of Caderousse, who was about to break in upon the abbe's speech, when the latter, waving his hand, said, "Allow me to finish first, and then if you have any observations to make, you can do so afterwards. 'The third of my friends, although my rival, was much attached to me,—his name was Fernand; that of my betrothed was'—Stay, stay," continued the abbe, "I have forgotten what he called her."

"Mercedes," said Caderousse eagerly.

"True," said the abbe, with a stifled sigh, "Mercedes it was."

"Go on," urged Caderousse.

"Bring me a carafe of water," said the abbe.

Caderousse quickly performed the stranger's bidding; and after pouring some into a glass, and slowly swallowing its contents, the abbe, resuming his usual placidity of manner, said, as he placed his empty glass on the table,—"Where did we leave off?"

"The name of Edmond's betrothed was Mercedes."

"To be sure. 'You will go to Marseilles,' said Dantes,—for you understand, I repeat his words just as he uttered them. Do you understand?"

"Perfectly."

"'You will sell this diamond; you will divide the money into five equal parts, and give an equal portion to these good friends, the only persons who have loved me upon earth.'"

"But why into five parts?" asked Caderousse; "you only mentioned four persons."

"Because the fifth is dead, as I hear. The fifth sharer in Edmond's bequest, was his own father."

"Too true, too true!" ejaculated Caderousse, almost suffocated by the contending passions which assailed him, "the poor old man did die."

"I learned so much at Marseilles," replied the abbe, making a strong effort to appear indifferent; "but from the length of time that has elapsed since the death of the elder Dantes, I was unable to obtain any particulars of his end. Can you enlighten me on that point?"

"I do not know who could if I could not," said Caderousse. "Why, I lived almost on the same floor with the poor old man. Ah, yes, about a year after the disappearance of his son the poor old man died."

"Of what did he die?"

"Why, the doctors called his complaint gastro-enteritis, I believe; his acquaintances say he died of grief; but I, who saw him in his dying moments, I say he died of"—Caderousse paused.

"Of what?" asked the priest, anxiously and eagerly.

"Why, of downright starvation."

"Starvation!" exclaimed the abbe, springing from his seat. "Why, the vilest animals are not suffered to die by such a death as that. The very dogs that wander houseless and homeless in the streets find some pitying hand to cast them a mouthful of bread; and that a man, a Christian, should be allowed to perish of hunger in the midst of other men who call themselves Christians, is too horrible for belief. Oh, it is impossible—utterly impossible!"

"What I have said, I have said," answered Caderousse.

"And you are a fool for having said anything about it," said a voice from the top of the stairs. "Why should you meddle with what does not concern you?"

The two men turned quickly, and saw the sickly countenance of La Carconte peering between the baluster rails; attracted by the sound of voices, she had feebly dragged herself down the stairs, and, seated on the lower step, head on knees, she had listened to the foregoing conversation. "Mind your own business, wife," replied Caderousse sharply. "This gentleman asks me for information, which common politeness will not permit me to refuse."

"Politeness, you simpleton!" retorted La Carconte. "What have you to do with politeness, I should like to know? Better study a little common prudence. How do you know the motives that person may have for trying to extract all he can from you?"

"I pledge you my word, madam," said the abbe, "that my intentions are good; and that your husband can incur no risk, provided he answers me candidly."

"Ah, that's all very fine," retorted the woman. "Nothing is easier than to begin with fair promises and assurances of nothing to fear; but when poor, silly folks, like my husband there, have been persuaded to tell all they know, the promises and assurances of safety are quickly forgotten; and at some moment when nobody is expecting it, behold trouble and misery, and all sorts of persecutions, are heaped on the unfortunate wretches, who cannot even see whence all their afflictions come."

"Nay, nay, my good woman, make yourself perfectly easy, I beg of you. Whatever evils may befall you, they will not be occasioned by my instrumentality, that I solemnly promise you."

La Carconte muttered a few inarticulate words, then let her head again drop upon her knees, and went into a fit of ague, leaving the two speakers to resume the conversation, but remaining so as to be able to hear every word they uttered. Again the abbe had been obliged to swallow a draught of water to calm the emotions that threatened to overpower him. When he had sufficiently recovered himself, he said, "It appears, then, that the miserable old man you were telling me of was forsaken by every one. Surely, had not such been the case, he would not have perished by so dreadful a death."

"Why, he was not altogether forsaken," continued Caderousse, "for Mercedes the Catalan and Monsieur Morrel were very kind to him; but somehow the poor old man had contracted a profound hatred for Fernand—the very person," added Caderousse with a bitter smile, "that you named just now as being one of Dantes' faithful and attached friends."

"And was he not so?" asked the abbe.

"Gaspard, Gaspard!" murmured the woman, from her seat on the stairs, "mind what you are saying!" Caderousse made no reply to these words, though evidently irritated and annoyed by the interruption, but, addressing the abbe, said, "Can a man be faithful to another whose wife he covets and desires for himself? But Dantes was so honorable and true in his own nature, that he believed everybody's professions of friendship. Poor Edmond, he was cruelly deceived; but it was fortunate that he never knew, or he might have found it more difficult, when on his deathbed, to pardon his enemies. And, whatever people may say," continued Caderousse, in his native language, which was not altogether devoid of rude poetry, "I cannot help being more frightened at the idea of the malediction of the dead than the hatred of the living."

"Imbecile!" exclaimed La Carconte.

"Do you, then, know in what manner Fernand injured Dantes?" inquired the abbe of Caderousse.

"Do I? No one better."

"Speak out then, say what it was!"

"Gaspard!" cried La Carconte, "do as you will; you are master— but if you take my advice you'll hold your tongue."

"Well, wife," replied Caderousse, "I don't know but what you're right!"

"So you will say nothing?" asked the abbe.

"Why, what good would it do?" asked Caderousse. "If the poor lad were living, and came to me and begged that I would candidly tell which were his true and which his false friends, why, perhaps, I should not hesitate. But you tell me he is no more, and therefore can have nothing to do with hatred or revenge, so let all such feeling be buried with him."

"You prefer, then," said the abbe, "that I should bestow on men you say are false and treacherous, the reward intended for faithful friendship?"

"That is true enough," returned Caderousse. "You say truly, the gift of poor Edmond was not meant for such traitors as Fernand and Danglars; besides, what would it be to them? no more than a drop of water in the ocean."

"Remember," chimed in La Carconte, "those two could crush you at a single blow!"

"How so?" inquired the abbe. "Are these persons, then, so rich and powerful?"

"Do you not know their history?"

"I do not. Pray relate it to me!" Caderousse seemed to reflect for a few moments, then said, "No, truly, it would take up too much time."

"Well, my good friend," returned the abbe, in a tone that indicated utter indifference on his part, "you are at liberty, either to speak or be silent, just as you please; for my own part, I respect your scruples and admire your sentiments; so let the matter end. I shall do my duty as conscientiously as I can, and fulfill my promise to the dying man. My first business will be to dispose of this diamond." So saying, the abbe again drew the small box from his pocket, opened it, and contrived to hold it in such a light, that a bright flash of brilliant hues passed before the dazzled gaze of Caderousse.

"Wife, wife!" cried he in a hoarse voice, "come here!"

"Diamond!" exclaimed La Carconte, rising and descending to the chamber with a tolerably firm step; "what diamond are you talking about?"

"Why, did you not hear all we said?" inquired Caderousse. "It is a beautiful diamond left by poor Edmond Dantes, to be sold, and the money divided between his father, Mercedes, his betrothed bride, Fernand, Danglars, and myself. The jewel is worth at least fifty thousand francs."

"Oh, what a magnificent jewel!" cried the astonished woman.

"The fifth part of the profits from this stone belongs to us then, does it not?" asked Caderousse.

"It does," replied the abbe; "with the addition of an equal division of that part intended for the elder Dantes, which I believe myself at liberty to divide equally with the four survivors."

"And why among us four?" inquired Caderousse.

"As being the friends Edmond esteemed most faithful and devoted to him."

"I don't call those friends who betray and ruin you," murmured the wife in her turn, in a low, muttering voice.

"Of course not!" rejoined Caderousse quickly; "no more do I, and that was what I was observing to this gentleman just now. I said I looked upon it as a sacrilegious profanation to reward treachery, perhaps crime."

"Remember," answered the abbe calmly, as he replaced the jewel and its case in the pocket of his cassock, "it is your fault, not mine, that I do so. You will have the goodness to furnish me with the address of both Fernand and Danglars, in order that I may execute Edmond's last wishes." The agitation of Caderousse became extreme, and large drops of perspiration rolled from his heated brow. As he saw the abbe rise from his seat and go towards the door, as though to ascertain if his horse were sufficiently refreshed to continue his journey, Caderousse and his wife exchanged looks of deep meaning.

"There, you see, wife," said the former, "this splendid diamond might all be ours, if we chose!"

"Do you believe it?"

"Why, surely a man of his holy profession would not deceive us!"

"Well," replied La Carconte, "do as you like. For my part, I wash my hands of the affair." So saying, she once more climbed the staircase leading to her chamber, her body convulsed with chills, and her teeth rattling in her head, in spite of the intense heat of the weather. Arrived at the top stair, she turned round, and called out, in a warning tone, to her husband, "Gaspard, consider well what you are about to do!"

"I have both reflected and decided," answered he. La Carconte then entered her chamber, the flooring of which creaked beneath her heavy, uncertain tread, as she proceeded towards her armchair, into which she fell as though exhausted.

"Well," asked the abbe, as he returned to the apartment below, "what have you made up your mind to do?"

"To tell you all I know," was the reply.

"I certainly think you act wisely in so doing," said the priest. "Not because I have the least desire to learn anything you may please to conceal from me, but simply that if, through your assistance, I could distribute the legacy according to the wishes of the testator, why, so much the better, that is all."

"I hope it may be so," replied Caderousse, his face flushed with cupidity.

"I am all attention," said the abbe.

"Stop a minute," answered Caderousse; "we might be interrupted in the most interesting part of my story, which would be a pity; and it is as well that your visit hither should be made known only to ourselves." With these words he went stealthily to the door, which he closed, and, by way of still greater precaution, bolted and barred it, as he was accustomed to do at night. During this time the abbe had chosen his place for listening at his ease. He removed his seat into a corner of the room, where he himself would be in deep shadow, while the light would be fully thrown on the narrator; then, with head bent down and hands clasped, or rather clinched together, he prepared to give his whole attention to Caderousse, who seated himself on the little stool, exactly opposite to him.

"Remember, this is no affair of mine," said the trembling voice of La Carconte, as though through the flooring of her chamber she viewed the scene that was enacting below.

"Enough, enough!" replied Caderousse; "say no more about it; I will take all the consequences upon myself." And he began his story.

A Sneak Peek from Crimson Romance
(From *Emma: The Wild and Wanton Edition* by Micah Persell and Jane Austen)

Emma Woodhouse, handsome, clever, and rich, with a comfortable home and happy disposition, seemed to unite some of the best blessings of existence; and had lived nearly twenty-one years in the world with very little to distress or vex her.

She was the youngest of the two daughters of a most affectionate, indulgent father; and had, in consequence of her sister's marriage, been mistress of his house from a very early period. Her mother had died too long ago for her to have more than an indistinct remembrance of her caresses; and her place had been supplied by an excellent woman as governess, who had fallen little short of a mother in affection.

Sixteen years had Miss Taylor been in Mr. Woodhouse's family, less as a governess than a friend, very fond of both daughters, but particularly of Emma. Between *them* it was more the intimacy of sisters. Even before Miss Taylor had ceased to hold the nominal office of governess, the mildness of her temper had hardly allowed her to impose any restraint; and the shadow of authority being now long passed away, they had been living together as friend and friend very mutually attached, and Emma doing just what she liked; highly esteeming Miss Taylor's judgment, but directed chiefly by her own.

The real evils, indeed, of Emma's situation were the power of having rather too much her own way, and a disposition to think a little too well of herself; these were the disadvantages which threatened alloy to her many enjoyments. The danger, however, was at present so unperceived, that they did not by any means rank as misfortunes with her.

Sorrow came—a gentle sorrow—but not at all in the shape of any disagreeable consciousness—Miss Taylor married.

It was only natural after four years of increasing affection between Miss Taylor and Mr. Weston. Miss Taylor, in her duties as governess, made daily trips to Fords to retrieve the various odds and ends deemed necessary for a fulfilling life. She was certain to meet with everyone in Highbury, and relished these trips because of that. While on one of these trips when Emma was accompanying her, an onset of a sudden rain-storm caused them to turn home before their errand was completed. It was in Broadway Lane that Emma noticed Mr. Weston hurrying toward them—only *two* borrowed umbrellas in his possession.

He quickly handed one umbrella to Emma. The other he opened, and without warning, scooped Miss Taylor into his side. Together, they made their way back to Hartfield, Emma walking behind them and observing with glee that Mr. Weston's arm remained about Miss Taylor for the entire trip.

It was the moment inspiration struck. Emma would make a match of them! She had always fancied herself good at judging the human heart. The plan was quite simple to execute. A suggestion that Mr. Weston accompany them home was expeditiously undertaken by the gentleman, and Emma was delighted to see he continued the duty in Emma's absence in the following months. It was not just Emma's imagination that had her noticing Mr. Weston holding Miss Taylor's hand extraordinarily close in their daily walk from Fords, or the conversations growing increasingly lingering in the garden.

The couple's friendship blossomed, and Emma had stumbled upon them in the garden a few short months ago. Mr. Weston and Miss Taylor had been sitting on a bench beneath a willow tree. Emma watched in congratulatory wonder as Mr. Weston pulled Miss Taylor toward him. He wove his fingers into her hair, whispered something to her Emma could not hear, and then pressed his lips to hers.

Emma had gasped in delight and ducked back into the house to give them the privacy Mr. Weston would need to make his declaration. And make a declaration he had. Within moments, he had secured Miss Taylor's hand as the future Mrs. Weston.

It was then that he had pulled Miss Taylor back into the shelter of the willow, overcome with his good fortune in his future wife. He meant only to kiss her some more, out of the view of Hartfield, but the afternoon sun was dappling her skin so prettily. His soft, close-mouthed kisses quickly morphed into something more passionate, more desperate. It had been several long years since the death of his wife, and he could suddenly stand to be apart from his betrothed no longer.

He began small enough, with a simple pass of his tongue along her bottom lip, but when she gasped in surprise, he could not stop himself from sweeping his tongue into her mouth. And when she moaned against him as he teased her with soft sweeps of his tongue, he could not stop himself from trailing his fingers down from where they nestled in her hair. They fluttered over her throat, her collarbone. Her body seemed to anticipate where they were headed, for she arched her back. He quickly closed the final inches and spread his palm over her warm, firm breast.

She pulled from the kiss with a shocked gasp. "Mr. Weston!" she exclaimed breathlessly.

Chagrined, Mr. Weston looked down at the ground, and readying an apology, began to remove his hand. But her own hand stayed him. It flew to cover his and pressed it more firmly into her flesh.

The gasp this time was his. Without his permission, his fingers flexed, squeezing her wonderful flesh. As his eyes were riveted to her bosom, her free hand wound into his hair and pulled him back into a kiss that was much more wild than their previous kisses had been.

She sucked his tongue into her mouth and mimicked the rhythm he had taught her. Mr. Weston was soon carried away. His hands started to wander even more, both of them squeezing her breasts, and then moving around her ribcage, down her back, and to her curved bottom where he grabbed two handfuls and pulled her hips tightly against his.

His arousal pressed fully against her, and rather than the trepidation he had expected, Miss Taylor moaned around his tongue and writhed against him, causing all further thought to flee. Like a man possessed, he began to pull her skirt up by big handfuls, never breaking their kiss. She sensed his direction and began to help him, holding the skirt for him once it reached the top of her thighs.

Then, his fingers found her drawers, wove inside, and caressed the curls masking her core. Her body jerked. Her hips canted forward. She deepened the kiss.

Mr. Weston felt himself the most blessed of men. She was so responsive; not the least shy. And as his fingers parted her flesh and stroked her intimately, he discovered just how responsive she was. She was *soaking* for him.

Mr. Weston groaned as a fine tremor set into his limbs, and he begged for control. He stroked her bundle of nerves back and forth, and she began to move her hips in time with him. And then suddenly, her hands left his hair and arrived at the fall of his breeches.

With a shuddering breath, Mr. Weston pulled from the kiss. "My darling, you mustn't. I do not know how much more I can take and remain a gentleman." Truly, he could probably not be called a gentleman *now*, what with his fingers stroking inside his future wife's drawers.

Her hands did not desist. "I have been dreaming of touching you for years," she whispered breathlessly. "I am to be your wife."

Her fingers stroked his rigid shaft lightly, wrenching a groan from his chest. "Yes, you are."

"Then love me now. Do not make me wait any more."

He had barely needed convincing before, ready to give in with the light stroke of her fingers, but hearing her breathless plea—

Mr. Weston broke. His lips crashed back to hers. His arms surrounded her in a rough embrace. He lowered her to the ground and settled on top of her, allowing his hips to sink between her thighs.

If he thought she was beautiful before, nothing compared to the sight that met him when he pulled from their kiss. Her beautiful chestnut hair spread around her in a halo, the sun shining through the locks and setting them afire. Her brown eyes sparkled beneath her nearly closed lids. Her lips were wet and plumped from his kisses. She licked them as her hands returned to the front of his breeches. Her first sign of nervousness manifested itself with fingers that could not work the buttons.

Mr. Weston laid a hand over hers to discover that they were shaking badly. "Oh, my love, we can stop now," he said with a gentle smile.

"No!" she said loudly with a blush. "No," she said again softer with an embarrassed smile. "Only help me with the buttons?"

He looked at her closely for several seconds, and when her eyes flashed and she bit into her bottom lip while moving her hips against his impatiently, he determined she was in earnest. His smile grew slightly as he began to unbutton himself. Her fingers eagerly sought the skin he was revealing, and when her fingertips brushed against him skin-to-skin for the first time, Mr. Weston discovered himself questioning his mortality. She tugged his shaft free, and he quickly wrapped his fingers around hers and shewed her how to touch him. She quickly picked up on the rhythm that had his eyes rolling back in his head, and he caught himself with braced arms as he fell forward to kiss her once again.

Before he knew it, she was placing the head of his shaft at her entrance and tilting her hips wantonly. With a groan, he followed her urging and entered her slowly until he was stopped by her maidenhead.

He sucked in a breath, pulling back to look into her eyes. She was virgin. Oh, he had hoped, but had not expected. "Oh, my darling," he breathed before surging forward and claiming her as his for all eternity.

She did not cry out as he feared she would do, but she did stiffen and bury her face in his throat. He shushed her gently and kissed her hair. "I love you so," he whispered. And then he began to move. Slowly at first, but once she had gotten over the pain, she began to meet his thrusts vigorously. And her soft moans were driving him to heights of passion he had never before experienced. His thrusts grew more desperate, and it was by pure luck that she reached her peak before he did. She grabbed two fistfuls of his jacket, threw her head back, and cried out his name. His *given* name.

It sent him over the precipice. He ground against her as he poured himself into her, pressing an open-mouthed kiss to the hallow of her throat.

He held her afterwards for as long as he could. It was Emma's voice calling for her friend from the garden that got them to move. They rushed to their feet in a hurry, and Mr. Weston helped her straighten her dress. Then, with a passionate kiss, he allowed her to leave the shelter of the willow tree and seek out Emma's call.

He had to remain propped against the tree's trunk for some time to come before he could tear himself away from the home of his beloved.

It was with trembling legs that Miss Taylor returned to the house some hour after leaving it to tell the Woodhouses her happy news of impending matrimony.

Emma had greeted her with a warm embrace and a teasing smile as she pulled a leaf from Miss Taylor's hair. Emma's heart was filled with happiness and self-adulation over a match well-made, and she could never imagine being happier than she was in that moment, celebrating her good fortune and the good fortune of her dear friend.

It was Miss Taylor's loss which first brought grief. It was on the wedding-day of this beloved friend that Emma first sat in mournful thought of any continuance. The wedding over, and the bride-people gone, her father and herself were left to dine together, with no prospect of a third to cheer a long evening. Her father composed himself to sleep after dinner, as usual, and she had then only to sit and think of what she had lost.

The event had every promise of happiness for her friend. Mr. Weston was a man of unexceptionable character, easy fortune, suitable age, and pleasant manners; and there was some satisfaction in considering with what self-denying, generous friendship she had always wished and promoted the match; but it was a black morning's work for her. The want of Miss Taylor would be felt every hour of every day. She recalled her past kindness—the kindness, the affection of sixteen years—how she had taught and how she had played with her from five years old—how she had devoted all her powers to attach and amuse her in health—and how nursed her through the various illnesses of childhood. A large debt of gratitude was owing here; but the intercourse of the last seven years, the equal footing and perfect unreserve which had soon followed Isabella's marriage, on their being left to each other, was yet a dearer, tenderer recollection. She had been a friend and companion such as few possessed: intelligent, well-informed, useful, gentle, knowing all the ways of the family, interested in all its concerns, and peculiarly interested in herself, in every pleasure, every scheme of hers—one to whom she could speak every thought as it arose, and who had such an affection for her as could never find fault.

How was she to bear the change? It was true that her friend was going only half a mile from them; but Emma was aware that great must be the difference between a Mrs. Weston, only half a mile from them, and a Miss Taylor in the house; and with all her advantages, natural and domestic, she was now in great danger of suffering from intellectual solitude. She dearly loved her father, but he was no companion for her. He could not meet her in conversation, rational or playful.

The evil of the actual disparity in their ages (and Mr. Woodhouse had not married early) was much increased by his constitution and habits; for having been a valetudinarian all his life, without activity of mind or body, he was a much older man in ways than in years; and though everywhere beloved for the friendliness of his heart and his amiable temper, his talents could not have recommended him at any time.

Her sister, though comparatively but little removed by matrimony, being settled in London, only sixteen miles off, was much beyond her daily reach; and many a long October and November evening must be struggled through at Hartfield, before Christmas brought the next visit from Isabella and her husband, and their little children, to fill the house, and give her pleasant society again.

Highbury, the large and populous village, almost amounting to a town, to which Hartfield, in spite of its separate lawn, and shrubberies, and name, did really belong, afforded her no equals. The Woodhouses were first in consequence there. All looked up to them. She had many acquaintance in the place, for her father was universally civil, but not one among them who could be accepted in lieu of Miss Taylor for even half a day. It was a melancholy change; and Emma could not but sigh over it, and wish for impossible things, till her father awoke, and made it necessary to be cheerful. His spirits required support. He was a nervous man, easily depressed; fond of every body that he was used to, and hating to part with them; hating change of every kind. Matrimony, as the origin of change, was always disagreeable; and he was by no means yet reconciled to his own daughter's marrying, nor could ever speak of her but with compassion, though it had been entirely a match of affection, when he was now obliged to part with Miss Taylor too; and from his habits of gentle selfishness, and of being never able to suppose that other people could feel differently from himself, he was very much disposed to think Miss Taylor had done as sad a thing for herself as for them, and would have been a great deal happier if she had spent all the rest of her life at Hartfield. Emma smiled and chatted as cheerfully as she could, to keep him from such thoughts; but when tea came, it was impossible for him not to say exactly as he had said at dinner,

"Poor Miss Taylor! I wish she were here again. What a pity it is that Mr. Weston ever thought of her!"

"I cannot agree with you, papa; you know I cannot. Mr. Weston is such a good-humoured, pleasant, excellent man, that he thoroughly deserves a good wife; and you would not have had Miss Taylor live with us forever, and bear all my odd humours, when she might have a house of her own?"

"A house of her own! But where is the advantage of a house of her own? This is three times as large. And you have never any odd humours, my dear."

"How often we shall be going to see them, and they coming to see us! We shall be always meeting! *We* must begin; we must go and pay our wedding visit very soon."

"My dear, how am I to get so far? Randalls is such a distance. I could not walk half so far."

"No, papa, nobody thought of your walking. We must go in the carriage, to be sure."

"The carriage! But James will not like to put the horses to for such a little way; and where are the poor horses to be while we are paying our visit?"

"They are to be put into Mr. Weston's stable, papa. You know we have settled all that already. We talked it all over with Mr. Weston last night. And as for James, you may be very sure he will always like going to Randalls, because of his daughter's being housemaid there. I only doubt whether he will ever take us anywhere else. That was your doing, papa. You got Hannah that good place. Nobody thought of Hannah till you mentioned her—James is so obliged to you!"

"I am very glad I did think of her. It was very lucky, for I would not have had poor James think himself slighted upon any account; and I am sure she will make a very good servant: she is a civil, pretty-spoken girl; I have a great opinion of her. Whenever I see her, she always curtseys and asks me how I do, in a very pretty manner; and when you have had her here to do needlework, I observe she always turns the lock of the door the right way and never bangs it. I am sure she will be an excellent servant; and it will be a great comfort to poor Miss Taylor to have somebody about her that she is used to see. Whenever James goes over to see his daughter, you know, she will be hearing of us. He will be able to tell her how we all are."

Emma spared no exertions to maintain this happier flow of ideas, and hoped, by the help of backgammon, to get her father tolerably through the evening, and be attacked by no regrets but her own. The backgammon-table was placed; but a visitor immediately afterwards walked in and made it unnecessary.

Mr. Knightley—a sensible man about seven or eight-and-thirty with thick brown hair that sometimes fell over his forehead, warm brown eyes framed by long lashes, and an active gentleman's build from his personal inclination to ride his horse everywhere— was not only a very old and intimate friend of the family, but particularly connected with it, as the elder brother of Isabella's husband. He lived about a mile from Highbury, was a frequent visitor, and always welcome, and at this time more welcome than usual, as coming directly from their mutual connexions in London. He had returned to a late dinner, after some days' absence, and now walked up to Hartfield to say that all were well in Brunswick Square. It was a happy circumstance, and animated Mr. Woodhouse for some time. Mr. Knightley had a cheerful manner, which always did him good; and his many inquiries after "poor Isabella" and her children were answered most satisfactorily. When this was over, Mr. Woodhouse gratefully observed, "It is very kind of you, Mr. Knightley, to come out at this late hour to call upon us. I am afraid you must have had a shocking walk."

"Not at all, sir," he said with a wink in Emma's direction "It is a beautiful moonlight night; and so mild that I must draw back from your great fire."

Emma frowned. So mild? She herself was feeling rather heated. A flare of heat had shot up her spine oddly enough at the same moment as that wink of Mr. Knightley's. She fanned her neck with one hand as her father quickly settled into his favorite topic of weather and all of the consummate ways it could affect one's health.

"But you must have found it very damp and dirty. I wish you may not catch cold."

"Dirty, sir! Look at my shoes. Not a speck on them."

"Well! that is quite surprising, for we have had a vast deal of rain here. It rained dreadfully hard for half an hour while we were at breakfast. I wanted them to put off the wedding."

"By the bye—I have not wished you joy." His lips twitched with suppressed humour. "Being pretty well aware of what sort of joy you must both be feeling, I have been in no hurry with my congratulations; but I hope it all went off tolerably well. How did you all behave? Who cried most?"

"Ah! poor Miss Taylor! 'Tis a sad business."

"Poor Mr. and Miss Woodhouse, if you please; but I cannot possibly say 'poor Miss Taylor.' I have a great regard for you and Emma; but when it comes to the question of dependence or independence! At any rate, it must be better to have only one to please than two."

"Especially when *one* of those two is such a fanciful, troublesome creature!" said Emma playfully, leaning forward to tease Mr. Knightley with a coquettish smile. "That is what you have in your head, I know—and what you would certainly say if my father were not by."

Mr. Knightley's brows rose at her final words, and Emma could almost swear that his gaze shifted as he looked at her; became more heated somehow. And then that gaze dipped to her lips, leaving Emma quite breathless. Why did she have a feeling that if her father were indeed not near, she would not have gotten away with such close proximity without some sort of consequence? And why did she have the feeling that she would not have minded at all the consequence Mr. Knightley's sudden sharp gaze seemed to promise? Oh heavens, this close, he smelled far too good to ignore. She leaned in even further, then jumped back in alarm as her father resumed the conversation, jerking her from her foolish reverie.

"I believe it is very true, my dear, indeed," said Mr. Woodhouse, with a sigh. "I am afraid I am sometimes very fanciful and troublesome."

"My dearest papa! You do not think I could mean *you*, or suppose Mr. Knightley to mean *you*. What a horrible idea! Oh no! I meant only myself. Mr. Knightley loves to find fault with me, you know—in a joke—it is all a joke. We always say what we like to one another."

Mr. Knightley, in fact, was one of the few people who could see faults in Emma Woodhouse, and the only one who ever told her of them: and though this was not particularly agreeable to Emma herself, she knew it would be so much less so to her father, that she would not have him really suspect such a circumstance as her not being thought perfect by every body. Besides, when one was as perfect as Mr. Knightley, correction was tolerable.

"Emma knows I never flatter her," said Mr. Knightley, a warm glow in his eyes as he looked at her softened the words, "but I meant no reflection on any body. Miss Taylor has been used to have two persons to please; she will now have but one. The chances are that she must be a gainer."

"Well," said Emma, willing to let it pass—"you want to hear about the wedding; and I shall be happy to tell you, for we all behaved charmingly. Every body was punctual, every body in their best looks: not a tear, and hardly a long face to be seen. Oh no; we all felt that we were going to be only half a mile apart, and were sure of meeting every day."

"Dear Emma bears every thing so well," said her father. "But, Mr. Knightley, she is really very sorry to lose poor Miss Taylor, and I am sure she *will* miss her more than she thinks for."

Emma turned away her head, divided between tears and smiles. She jumped when she felt a warm hand cover hers. Her eyes flew back to see Mr. Knightley gifting her with a soft, knowing smile. He squeezed her hand gently, and a corresponding throb lit through her abdomen and shot down to the secret place between her legs. "It is impossible that Emma should not miss such a companion," said Mr. Knightley, his deep, soft voice rumbling through her and setting off more alarming sensations. "We should not like her so well as we do, sir," he squeezed her hand once more, "if we could suppose it; but she knows how much the marriage is to Miss Taylor's advantage; she knows how very acceptable it must be, at Miss Taylor's time of life, to be settled in a home of her own, and how important to her to be secure of a comfortable provision, and therefore cannot allow herself to feel so much pain as pleasure. Every friend of Miss Taylor must be glad to have her so happily married."

She felt the mild rebuke in his words, but the comfort of his hand overshadowed all. She gave him as cheerful a smile as she could manage. "And you have forgotten one matter of joy to me," said Emma, "and a very considerable one—that I made the match myself. I made the match, you know, four years ago; and to have it take place, and be proved in the right, when so many people said Mr. Weston would never marry again, may comfort me for any thing."

Mr. Knightley shook his head at her, gave a great sigh, and withdrew his hand. Emma was just feeling a curious loss from the missing warmth of the gesture and almost sought out his hand again to keep the warm, liquid feeling rolling through her belly and even further down when her father fondly replied, "Ah! my dear, I wish you would not make matches and foretell things, for whatever you say always comes to pass. Pray do not make any more matches."

"I promise you to make none for myself, papa; but I must, indeed, for other people. It is the greatest amusement in the world! And after such success, you know! Every body said that Mr. Weston would never marry again. Oh dear, no! Mr. Weston, who had been a widower so long, and who seemed so perfectly comfortable without a wife, so constantly occupied either in his business in town or among his friends here, always acceptable wherever he went, always cheerful—Mr. Weston need not spend a single evening in the year alone if he did not like it. Oh no! Mr. Weston certainly would never marry again. Some people even talked of a promise to his wife on her deathbed, and others of the son and the uncle not letting him. All manner of solemn nonsense was talked on the subject, but I believed none of it.

"Ever since the day—about four years ago—that Miss Taylor and I met with him in Broadway Lane, when, because it began to drizzle, he darted away with so much gallantry, and borrowed two umbrellas for us from Farmer Mitchell's, I made up my mind on the subject. I planned the match from that hour; and when such success has blessed me in this instance, dear papa, you cannot think that I shall leave off match-making."

"I do not understand what you mean by 'success,'" said Mr. Knightley, his lips quirked. "Success supposes endeavour. Your time has been properly and delicately spent, if you have been endeavouring for the last four years to bring about this marriage. A worthy employment for a young lady's mind! But if, which I rather imagine, your making the match, as you call it, means only your planning it, your saying to yourself one idle day, 'I think it would be a very good thing for Miss Taylor if Mr. Weston were to marry her,' and saying it again to yourself every now and then afterwards, why do you talk of success? Where is your merit? What are you proud of? You made a lucky guess; and *that* is all that can be said."

Emma leaned back and crossed her arms beneath her bosom. "And have you never known the pleasure and triumph of a lucky guess? I pity you. I thought you cleverer—for, depend upon it a lucky guess is never merely luck. There is always some talent in it. And as to my poor word 'success,' which you quarrel with, I do not know that I am so entirely without any claim to it. You have drawn two pretty pictures; but I think there may be a third—a something between the do-nothing and the do-all. If I had not promoted Mr. Weston's visits here, and given many little encouragements, and smoothed many little matters, it might not have come to any thing after all. I think you must know Hartfield enough to comprehend that."

"A straightforward, open-hearted man like Weston, and a rational, unaffected woman like Miss Taylor, may be safely left to manage their own concerns. You are more likely to have done harm to yourself, than good to them, by interference." His brows drew together in the typical concerned expression he donned when lecturing Emma. It cast his eyes in a shadow that did not diminish the glow that sprang from their warm depth. Emma looked away, disconcerted.

"Emma never thinks of herself, if she can do good to others," rejoined Mr. Woodhouse, understanding but in part. "But, my dear, pray do not make any more matches; they are silly things, and break up one's family circle grievously."

Emma uncrossed her arms and sat up straight, excitement tinting her tone. "Only one more, papa; only for Mr. Elton. Poor Mr. Elton! You like Mr. Elton, papa—I must look about for a wife for him. There is nobody in Highbury who deserves him—and he has been here a whole year, and has fitted up his house so comfortably, that it would be a shame to have him single any longer—and I thought when he was joining their hands to-day, he looked so very much as if he would like to have the same kind office done for him! I think very well of Mr. Elton, and this is the only way I have of doing him a service."

"Mr. Elton is a very pretty young man, to be sure, and a very good young man, and I have a great regard for him. But if you want to shew him any attention, my dear, ask him to come and dine with us some day. That will be a much better thing. I dare say Mr. Knightley will be so kind as to meet him."

"With a great deal of pleasure, sir, at any time," said Mr. Knightley, laughing, his eyes crinkling at the corner, his teeth flashing white, "and I agree with you entirely, that it will be a much better thing. Invite him to dinner, Emma, and help him to the best of the fish and the chicken, but leave him to chuse his own wife. Depend upon it, a man of six or seven-and-twenty can take care of himself."

Mr. Knightley left the Woodhouses at his first opportunity after dinner. He breathed an uneasy sigh as he mounted his horse and kneed him into a canter toward Donwell Abbey. His mind was a flurry of activity that spurred his body into a flurry of activity as well.

What, exactly, had Emma been about this evening? Smiling and leaning close and crossing her arms beneath her bosom. Had she taken complete leave of her senses?

His mind automatically countered, defending her. No, she had behaved in much the same way as she usually did. It had been *Mr. Knightley's* reaction that had differed from the routine.

Mr. Knightley groaned as he admitted he had to come to terms with the fact that Emma Woodhouse, his sister-in-law's younger sister, was no longer a child.

"Devil take it," he muttered as he realized it was much, much worse than that. No, he could take Emma growing up. What he could not take, evidently, was her turning into a beautiful woman.

He should not have touched her; of that he was certain. What kind of fool's errand had driven him to take her hand? Her slim fingers beneath his hand had almost been his undoing, but that had only been because of what came just prior.

If her mother had still been living, she would have told Emma that leaning far over when talking to a gentleman was a bad idea. Mr. Knightley had to confess that he had very little idea of what had been said between them while she had leaned close and smiled so prettily at him. No, his attention had been focused a bit below her mouth.

He had first noticed the enticing way her pulse fluttered at the base of her throat. The errant thought that he would like to place his mouth over it had stricken him like a blow. He had moved his eyes away, mortified that he had let his thoughts turn in such a direction, when he had encountered her breasts.

Atop his horse, Mr. Knightley sucked in a breath and closed his eyes. The vision of her beautiful bosom was still emblazoned across the backs of his eyelids. So full. So tempting. Mr. Knightley's breath shuddered out of his chest.

His eyes sprang open with dread. Like a man facing the gallows, Mr. Knightley slowly directed his line of sight to his hips. He cursed at the inarguable evidence of where his thoughts had led him. His arousal pressed against the front of his breeches so fully, Mr. Knightley was obscenely unfit for polite company. He thanked heaven that his body had waited until he had been away from Emma and—he suppressed a shiver of mortification—*Mr. Woodhouse* before betraying him in such a manner.

Mr. Knightley shifted in the saddle trying to find a comfortable position to accommodate his current predicament, but after several moments, he gave up the endeavor as hopeless.

He readjusted his thighs' grip on his mount and clicked his tongue twice while flicking the reins. The stallion immediately broke into a gallop, eager to work off the powerful energy of his impeccable bloodlines. Mr. Knightley leaned into the wind, hoping the elements would slap some sense into his traitorous body.